I0676308

THE FALCONER'S LOST BARON

A SWEET REGENCY ROMANCE OF FALCONS,
FORGIVENESS, AND THE COURAGE TO HEAL

DOUBLE-DILEMMA ROANCE
BOOK FOUR

SUSANNE DUNLAP

The Falconer's Lost Baron

First Paperback Print Edition: 2025

Published by Comfortable Prose Publishing

Cover design by 100Covers

eBook: 979-8-9926490-6-2; Paperback: 979-8-9926490-7-9

A NOTE FROM THE AUTHOR

Thank you for choosing to read *The Falconer's Lost Baron!* I hope you enjoy getting to know Antonella, Belinda, Malcolm, and Hector. This is the fourth book in my series of Double-Dilemma romances, where two couples have intertwined destinies and go through trials so they end up where they ought to be. Although this books stands alone, you'll recognize some characters who reappear in other books in the series.

Reviews are important to authors. If you like *The Falconer's Lost Baron,* I would be immensely grateful if you took the time to review it on Goodreads and Amazon.

Want to stay informed of upcoming books in the series? Enjoy exclusive content? And get behind-the-scenes peeks of what it's like to be an author?

Sign up for my newsletter!

You'll get a free novella just to start, and be the first to hear about any forthcoming books and events.

Thank you again for taking your valuable time to read my book. 🤍

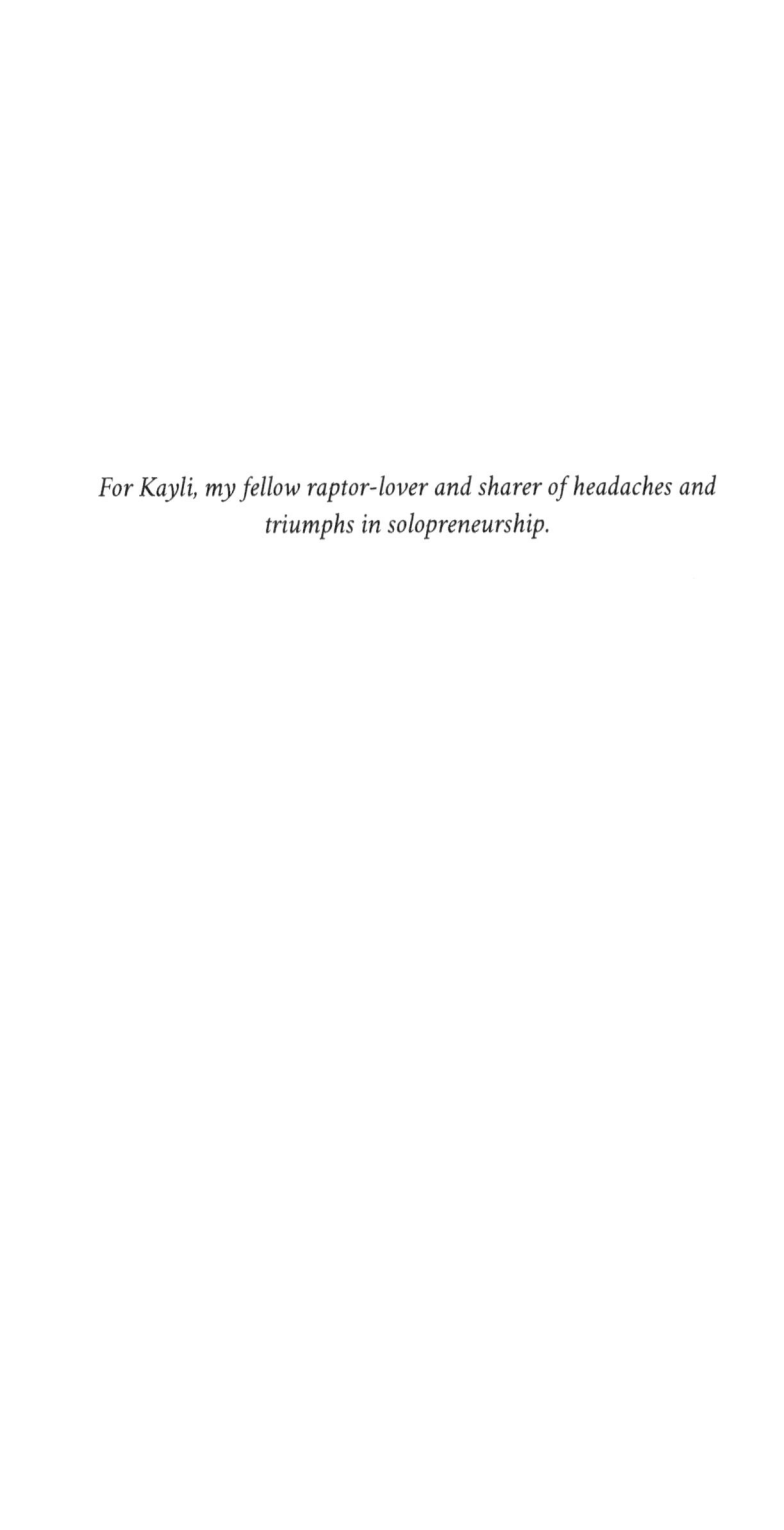

For Kayli, my fellow raptor-lover and sharer of headaches and triumphs in solopreneurship.

CHAPTER 1

"Tomorrow we go to London!" Lady Belinda Ambleton squealed and twirled around in her twin sister Lady Antonella's bed chamber.

Antonella sat quietly in the chair by the hearth, wrapped in her shawl with her slippered toes as close as she dared to the feeble flames. Amblemere Court was a rambling, drafty pile of a mansion on the north shore of Cornwall with a wing that dated from Tudor times. It lacked modern comforts but was steeped in history. Antonella sometimes joked that the ghosts curled up next to them in bed for warmth. "I only wonder what will become of the goldcrests while I'm gone," she said, stifling a yawn.

"You and your birds. Of course they'll just go on as usual. In any case, it's winter. What are they doing now? All that nesting and breeding happens in the spring." Belinda paused in her dancing and patted her sister affectionately on the head. "Don't pretend you aren't excited to be visiting Harry and Olivia. The baby is due soon, I think. Wouldn't it be wonderful to be there when it comes?"

Antonella smiled. "Yes, it would be lovely. Of course, no

one will be really happy unless it's a boy. Girls are of no use to anyone." Her accompanying wry smile only made Belinda frown.

"Whatever you say, you're not going to spoil my good mood. At last! We shall have such fun."

The twins had turned eighteen the day before, and Belinda was more than ready to dip her toes into London society. It was only the end of the Little Season. But their mama, the dowager marchioness of Lewiston, had planned it thus so they could test the waters a little before their big come-out in the spring. Belinda paused again in her flitting about the room. "I think you'll find it so exciting once you're there. There are plays and concerts, even if the opera isn't performed at this time of year. You enjoy the theatre, you know you do. And you're a better dancer than I am—you're as light on your feet as if you were a little bird yourself."

Belinda flopped down on the floor next to Antonella's chair, breathing hard from her exertions, and laid her head on her sister's knee. They were not identical—far from it. While Belinda was all golden, blue-eyed, statuesque beauty, Antonella's small, delicate frame hid wiry strength, and her wide, deep brown eyes and hair as black as a raven's wing reflected the ancient Cornish stock of the family. Their differences transcended mere looks, though. Antonella's keen intellect and passion for the outdoors awed and mystified Belinda, who was happier with the ladylike pursuits befitting her station. These divergent interests did nothing to hinder their close relationship, however. After all, what would it serve for them to be mirror images of each other, Belinda often thought. They reveled in their differences and delighted in surprising people with their twinship.

Antonella gently moved Belinda's head from her lap, stood, and stretched. "Tell me honestly, Bee," she said, grabbing hold of her sister's hand and pulling her to a stand again. "Aren't you the least bit afraid of it all? Of showing yourself to the *ton,* having them pass judgment on you?"

Belinda was about to start twirling again, but she stayed still and cocked her head on one side. "I suppose I'm nervous. But Mama and Miss Wilkins have prepared us for this."

Antonella laughed drily. "Yes, we are well able to curtsy and say polite nothings. Pity we won't be required to recite a Latin verse. That at least would give some indication that we've had a decent education. At least we won't have to be presented to the queen."

"Oh but we will still go to a drawing room! Mama says it's likely to be Princess Mary who receives us."

Antonella raised an eyebrow. "We'll only go if Mama can persuade Harry to give her the money for court dresses."

"Don't spoil my mood!" Belinda said, pushing out her lower lip in mock petulance. She couldn't keep the pretense up for long, though, and grasped both Antonella's hands. "There's only one thing I'm really afraid of, Ant."

"What's that?" Antonella returned her squeeze reassuringly.

"What happens when we're both married? Will we end by living far away from each other?" Belinda could not imagine life without Antonella's acerbic, sometimes biting, always lively presence. No one, she thought, could hold a candle to Ant's wisdom and intelligence. Not just her book knowledge, but her deep understanding of birds and wild creatures and everything about the surrounding countryside. What if Antonella had to go somewhere else? Somewhere far from the sea, or where there weren't glorious woods to explore, where she hadn't counted nests year upon year or healed wounded birds in her makeshift infirmary? Some of those rescued may well have gone on to breed and populate the woods around Amblemere with their children and grandchildren, and all because of Antonella.

A shadow passed across Antonella's normally cheerful expression. "I don't know, Bee," she said. "I suppose we may end up at opposite ends of the country. But if you fall in love, it won't matter! You won't think of me anymore."

"Nonsense! I will always think of you. You are the other half of my soul."

Antonella grinned. "That's what you're supposed to think about the man you marry!"

Belinda laughed and commenced twirling again until Falk, their abigail, opened the door and said without ceremony, "Her ladyship wants to see you both." Falk was well used to the sisters' antics and didn't bat an eye.

"What, now?" Antonella said. "It's after eleven. Can't it wait until morning?"

Falk pursed her lips and lifted her eyebrows in the haughty way only abigails seemed capable of and said, "Lady Lewiston says it cannot wait a moment longer."

She nodded and left. Belinda and Antonella turned questioning eyes to each other. "I suppose we'd better go," Belinda said, and threaded her arm through her sister's to head to their mother's private parlor.

CHAPTER 2

*T*he girls were still full of giggling enthusiasm when they skipped into Lady Lewiston's apartment. She was not alone. Their governess, Miss Wilkins, stood a little behind her. Although the sisters had been released from the schoolroom a year ago, Miss Wilkins was so much a part of the family that the dowager asked her to stay on to help run the household, especially since Belinda and Antonella would be launched into society that year.

Antonella looked a question at Miss Wilkins, but the governess gave a minute shake of her head. Clearly she didn't know what Lady Lewiston was going to say any more than they did.

She then turned her attention to her mother. Widowhood had not dimmed Lady Lewiston's handsome grandeur. She was a diamond of the first water when she made her come-out twenty-seven years earlier. The story of her presentation at court, where Queen Charlotte had pronounced her *sharming* in her German accent, was a favorite of Antonella and Belinda's childhood.

"Please—Belinda, Antonella. Sit down." Lady Lewiston

nodded toward the small settee near the hearth but remained standing herself, twisting her hands together, while Miss Wilkins discreetly moved farther away.

Antonella—who had assumed when Falk came to fetch them that perhaps her mother had thought of some piece of advice she wanted to impart to them before their departure for London the next day—revised her initial conjecture. *Mama looks as though she is about to dose us with caster oil,* she thought.

The dowager paced slowly across the room and took a few deep breaths before finally facing them. She cleared her throat and said, "What I have to say may come as a shock to you both, but I find I … It's time that I … It can no longer be allowed to stand."

A trickle of dread made its way down Antonella's spine. This was something serious indeed. What could it be? She'd never seen her mama so discomposed. Lady Lewiston normally faced everything with unflappable calm. So why this? Antonella wanted to leap up and say, *tell us now! Don't keep us waiting!* But etiquette and respect demanded that she remain quiet, her hands folded in her lap. She could feel Belinda tensing, straightening up next to her. She too was alert for something important.

After another deep breath, the dowager said, "You may perhaps have heard of the dreadful scandal of last season. Lord Cranborne. A love child he tried to pass off as legitimate."

The news of the foolish baron trying to secure a lofty match for a daughter his mistress bore to him—without revealing her parentage to the hapless suitor—had recently been the talk of the *ton*. So much so that it even reached the ears of the Ambletons all the way in Cornwall. What could their mother possibly want to say that could have anything to do with it?

Lady Lewiston moved toward the pier glass by her dressing room door and looked into it at the girls' reflection. "There is no easy way to say this, and I blame myself for going along with your father's—the marquess's wishes against my better judgment for so many years. But while he lived it was my duty to do as he said, and so now we find ourselves in this unusual predicament."

Antonella's mouth had gone dry. Whatever could be so momentous that her mama was unable to utter the words?

After a moment in which she visibly straightened and erased the hint of a crease in her brow, Lady Lewiston turned and fixed Antonella with an unflinching stare. "Antonella, you are not my daughter."

Antonella blinked. Did she hear correctly? It wasn't possible. No, more than that, it was ridiculous. "What?" she squeaked out in a strangled voice.

"As I said. I am sorry to have to inform you that you are not my daughter." This time the dowager lifted her chin and stood even straighter, repetition somehow giving her words more strength.

It was always cold at Amblemere Court in the wintertime. But in that moment Antonella experienced a chill that penetrated deep into her marrow, from the top of her head down to her toes. She didn't dare even glance at Belinda. If the woman standing before them was in fact not her mother, that meant that Belinda, at the same time, was not her twin sister. Or even her sister at all. Had she been living in a dream that had just become a nightmare? How was this possible?

After a period of silence so full of questions it felt as if the air would burst and a quick, troubled look at Antonella, Belinda said, "Mama, I don't understand. What can you be saying? Surely this is a hoax … No. I don't believe it at all." Belinda clutched Antonella's hand in a fierce grip.

Antonella had no strength to return the pressure and didn't move a muscle. If this was true, it explained the way her mother treated her sometimes. Little things, most only noticeable to her, but Belinda had always found more favor with the dowager than Antonella had. Still, how could it be? Parents sometimes were simply more in sympathy with one child than another. There was nothing strange in that. These thoughts tripped over each other in her mind, but she could not force them into any semblance of coherence.

"We are sisters. I know it." Belinda continued, taking charge, her voice rising.

Antonella could not move. Her throat ached and her chest tightened. If she tried to speak her voice would be no more than a hoarse sob. *Mama wouldn't like that at all* she thought. But not Mama anymore. Never Mama in the first place.

For a full minute there was no other sound than that of a sharp wind whistling down the chimney and scattering sparks from the logs blazing in the hearth. The faded hearthrug showed evidence of such assaults in the tiny black spots that dotted it in an irregular pattern.

It was the first day of December. The start of Advent. A season of beginning, of preparation. Yet instead of the excitement Antonella expected to feel, the anticipation of holiday celebrations and the parties in London, blank confusion overwhelmed her.

And then she realized why her mother—who was not her mother, she had to keep reminding herself—felt constrained to say this now. It wasn't just the recent scandal concerning someone else's subterfuge. She must tell them before the planned departure tomorrow because she, Antonella, would not after all be going to London.

Everything crowded in on her, suffocating her, muddling her mind. She experienced the odd sensation of having all her nimble joints suddenly loosen, her muscles become slack, and tiny white dots swim before her eyes.

"Miss Wilkins, give Antonella the vinaigrette," Lady Lewiston said.

The governess stepped forward.

Antonella looked up in confusion when Miss Wilkins waved the phial of sal volatile beneath her nose. The acrid scent flooded her with awareness in an instant. What had her mother said? That was it. "You are not my mother, then." Antonella's voice barely rose above a whisper. She fixed her glittering, deep brown eyes on the dowager.

Without looking at her, Lady Lewiston said. "No, I am not."

"Then why..." She had so many questions, but that was the only one that she could make her lips form.

She and Belinda didn't look alike, but they *were* alike. They had the same mannerisms, the same laugh, the same way of walking. Of course, Antonella thought, all those attributes could have resulted from familiarity, could have been acquired through the years of their shared lives.

"I've asked Miss Wilkins to be here because she will have to know, and will also have to ensure that the other servants understand the alteration of your position in the household, Antonella," the dowager said.

What did that matter? There were more important things to discuss! "Whose daughter am I then?"

"Your mother is dead," Lady Lewiston said.

"But she existed at one time. Who was she?" She needed answers as surely as she needed to breathe. "And what about my father?"

"Your mother was a distant relation on the Ambleton distaff side, at some remove from the line of succession."

Why would she not say? Did she not know?

"You will still be a respected member of the family, but as

a poor relation, you will not enjoy the same advantages as Lady Belinda. And of course … this also means that you are no longer Lady Antonella, but shall hereafter be known as Miss Ambleton. And there may be other alterations ahead." Lady Lewiston, who had recommenced pacing slowly back and forth in front of them, paused to return Antonella's unwavering gaze but looked away almost immediately.

"What other alterations?" Antonella asked, half afraid that, like Cinderella, she would instantly be relegated to the position of a chambermaid.

"Nothing for the moment. You will have enough to contend with. But I believe my telling you now is best for everyone."

Of course. The dowager must have known all this from the very beginning. It was not news to her. Yet she had said nothing for eighteen years. How it must have grated to have her husband insist on calling this poor relation *Lady* Antonella. Why did he do it? He was gone. He'd left his widow to deliver the difficult news. Her papa—the marquess —always avoided unpleasantness when he could, and everyone forgave him for it, but this was too much.

"Why now?" Belinda, who had gone silent, finally spoke up again, her voice sharp, accusing. "I still don't believe it. But say it's true. Why could we not have continued as we were? Why does it matter? Who but the family would care if we do not?"

The dowager sighed, shrinking just a bit. "Haven't I told you? Consider the Misses Mottram, Lord Cranborne's daughters. On the shelf because of his indiscretion."

"Yes, but why *exactly* now?" Antonella echoed Belinda's question, her voice a shadow of her sister's.

"Your father would have maintained the fiction forever." Lady Lewiston addressed the answer to Belinda, as if she had not heard Antonella. "But to do so would have been illegal—

immoral. Out of respect for him, I continued for these three years since his death to claim you both as my own. But as you are now of an age to think about being married, I thought it unwise to risk having a suitor discover the truth, as in the case of Lord Cranborne, and the exposure and scandal that would likely cause. Your prospects have materially altered, Antonella, but you remain my responsibility."

Her responsibility. Her burden. Was that all she had ever been? "How?" she croaked out from her suddenly raspy throat.

"How what?" the dowager asked.

"How did I come to be here?" Antonella wished she could grow wings and fly away, or simply sink into the floor. She might as well. With every word, the woman she'd spent her entire life believing was her mother was slowly erasing her, as if she were no more than a child's mark on a slate.

"A few days before I was confined with Belinda, your father—I mean, a distant cousin of his—brought you to this house begging that we care for you as if you were our own. You could not be raised in your own family as both your parents had died. You were only days old yourself."

Suddenly seized with intense agitation, Antonella leapt up and turned in a circle, her arms wrapped defensively around herself. "It still makes no sense! Why not just say that for my whole life then? And who was this person who brought me here? What about the midwife? She must have known it if you didn't birth twins. And the doctor! And the vicar!" Having finally spoken, the words poured out of her as from an unstoppered cask tipped on its side.

The dowager put her hands over her ears as if hearing Antonella speak gave her pain. Then she took a deep breath and said, "They were well paid to keep the secret. And the late marquess insisted that you and Lady Belinda be treated as equals."

She wasn't telling them everything, Antonella was certain. Clearly it was all she saw fit to reveal just at that moment, though. And in truth, Antonella wasn't certain she could bear to hear any more. "What ... what do I call you?" Her voice faded to a whisper at the end.

Until this point, Lady Lewiston had maintained a fragile calm, her face under strict control. Antonella watched as the individual she had only ever seen as an unflappable, regal lady who never failed to meet every obstacle or inconvenience with grace and poise crumpled in on herself. Her expressive gray eyes drilled into Antonella's with a searing combination of pain, anger, and helplessness. "You may call me Aunt Caroline."

Belinda leapt to her feet and placed herself like a shield between her mother and her sister. "Surely Ant will still be coming to London with us. She must find a match too!"

"I had a letter from your brother, Belinda. The baby is imminent, and the marchioness is afraid of the disruption extra guests will cause."

Antonella knew this for a fabrication. Harry had written to them full of his wish for their visit. Such an excuse would never have been suggested by Harry. Her mother—Aunt Caroline—wished it so. Which made her wonder: Did Harry know? And if so, how long had he known it?

After that, the dowager walked slowly to the door, her ample yet upright figure steely straight. When she reached it she turned and said in a ragged voice, "I would not have raised you with such high expectations, Antonella, but it was the express wish of your—of the late marquess. It was not until we reached this juncture, your impending launch into society, that I knew I must tell you—and the rest of world—the truth." She nodded to Miss Wilkins and held the door open for all three of them to pass through. "Now I shall retire to bed."

The once-familiar corridor seemed strange and hostile to Antonella as she walked in a daze to her bedchamber farther along the west wing of the house.

Miss Wilkins said, "Antonella—"

"No!" Antonella turned abruptly away from the governess. "Not now. I can't talk about it now."

Belinda followed Antonella into her bedchamber and for a moment, hardly a breath escaped them. Then all in a rush Belinda said, "Oh Ant!" and threw her arms around her.

Antonella patted Belinda on the back before gently pushing her away. Were they in fact only distant relations? It was too much. She needed time to think about this. "No, Bee. Let me be alone. It's time for bed."

Belinda's tears flowed freely down her cheeks, but Antonella's eyes were dry. The news had shocked her too deeply, bypassing the ready relief of tears and going straight to her heart.

After Antonella finally convinced Belinda to go to her own room she paced back and forth late into the night until she was too tired to stand, then sat in the armchair by the hearth, watching the flames gradually die.

Her world had just disintegrated to ashes.

As soon as the team of bays pulled the chaise carrying the dowager and Lady Belinda out of the courtyard and through the entrance arch, Antonella—who had forced herself to maintain a stony indifference all morning—tore off in the direction of the ancient book room. The sting of hot tears behind her eyes threatened to overcome her, but she gulped down her sobs, concentrating on not tripping on the uneven flags of the floors in the oldest wing of the house. She raced through two saloons full of time-darkened, heavy oak furniture and ornate tapestries, through the old dining room with its refectory table and hard wooden benches, to the ancient library, the one that had been largely neglected since the creation of a more modern and congenial book room in the west wing. She turned and slammed the door closed behind her before sinking to the floor and finally letting the pressure in her chest explode in wrenching sobs.

It wasn't that she particularly wanted to go to London. It would have been amusing enough, and she and Belinda would have enjoyed the entertainments, but Antonella vastly preferred this corner of Cornwall and the freedom it gave her to pursue the things that really interested her. But before, when she spent long hours rambling through the woods looking for wounded birds, she'd been secure in the knowledge that she was Lady Antonella Ambleton, twin sister of Lady Belinda, daughter of the Marquess and Marchioness of Lewiston. Not that she ever traded on her rank, or treated servants and peasants in that high-handed way she'd seen some fine ladies do. It was simply who she was. Her identity.

Now, who, indeed, was she? The idea that she'd been brought up to believe a lie twisted something in her stomach, nauseating her and flooding her with shame.

Antonella curled up on the floor in front of the unlit hearth, tears coursing down her cheeks and splotching the sleeves of her drab kerseymere dress. She allowed herself a good half hour of unrelenting sorrow and wretchedness. No one could hear her in the rest of the house, so no one would come running to see what was the matter. The kitchens were four rooms distant, and everything else—aside from some old guest bedchambers on the floor above that were only used in the direst of emergencies—took place in the newer wing on the other side of the courtyard.

She gradually calmed herself, taking raw, hiccupping breaths, and sat up, knees bent, arms wrapped around them.

I must think, I must decide what to do. But what was there to decide? Ladies, even wealthy ladies with handsome dowries and titles, had few choices, if any. They were raised and trained to marry well, become mistresses of their own households, and produce heirs. That was what she and Belinda had been groomed to expect. Now, even that uninteresting future was doubtful. So what then?

Did her change in status mean she was no longer required to behave like a lady? Or would it mean she would have to work even harder to be accepted among people of her previous station? Did she even care?

Antonella's head pounded and her eyes burned. Outside, icy winter rain beat against the mullioned windows as if in sympathy with her mood.

Only one thing stood a chance of taking her mind away from wallowing in self-pity. She rose, shook out her skirts, wrapped her warm shawl about her more securely, and went over to the book stand near the window that looked out on the kitchen garden. On it lay the ancient, well-thumbed Volume III of *De Arte Venandi Cum Avibus*, The Art of Hunting with Birds, by Frederick II Hohenstaufen, Holy Roman Emperor in the Middle Ages. Thanks to Miss Wilkins, she had read all five volumes by the time she was fourteen. Seeing Antonella's passionate interest in all things avian, the governess unearthed the tomes and used them to teach her Latin. This subject was by no means part of the usual ladies' curriculum—modern languages were a more practical acquisition—and Belinda never even attempted it. But Antonella had a knack for languages and a thirst for knowledge that Miss Wilkins fostered at every opportunity. And in truth, Antonella had to confess that her mother—no, Aunt Caroline now—did not concern herself with hers and Belinda's education overmuch, beyond ensuring that they were thoroughly schooled in etiquette and the appropriate ladies' accomplishments. Her hands-off approach—rather than inhibiting their scholarly pursuits—gave them free rein to read or study whatever they wished, to gain arcane knowledge they would likely never need to use. Lady Lewiston herself had been well educated by a dedicated teacher, and often told the girls stories about the literary salons and political lectures she had attended during the London seasons before the demands of motherhood and society claimed most of her time.

Antonella took several deep, calming breaths. She ran her fingers over the time-warped cover of the book then opened it to her favorite section, the pages that dealt with the training of hawks. Hawks and falcons, although related, had some important differences. She had never hunted with either, or been closer to those birds than seeing the sparrow hawks swooping through the trees in the coombe and occasionally getting a glimpse of a merlin in the wild. Few estates still practiced the noble art. Only the wealthiest or the most eccentric of them devoted the time and resources to raising and training birds for hunting. It was a very demanding, time-consuming thing to do.

Yet as chance would have it their neighbor, a baron, possessed a mews—or used to. Harry told her about it before he moved to London. Once, when she was quite young, she had strayed beyond the boundaries of the Amblemere estate and found herself at the edge of an uncultivated field, where she spied two gentlemen standing in the middle of it. One had a large bird perched on his fist, which was covered with a stout glove. As she watched, he lifted his fist toward the sky and the bird took off up into the air, so high that it nearly disappeared, becoming no more than a spec against the bright sky. The other gentleman—who might have been a servant, a groom perhaps—began swinging something around his head and whistling. A few moments later, seemingly out of nowhere, the bird dove out of the sky and grasped the object in its talons, bringing it down to earth.

All these years later, the idea of that moment still enchanted her. One of the moth-eaten tapestries in the largest of the Tudor saloons showed a group of mounted nobles with falcons on their gloves, both men and women. *In those times,* Miss Wilkins had told her during a history lesson, *only royalty were permitted to hunt eagles or gyrfalcons.* Nobles, she said, could hunt peregrines and hawks. Ladies hunted kestrels or merlins. It was a very rigid hierarchy. Yet the birds themselves knew nothing of rank. Their hierarchy was based on strength, speed, ability to survive—not on which bird came from which breeding pair, or whose ancestry could be traced the farthest back.

Antonella drew in a deep, ragged breath. All she had of falconry was that one memory, her imagination, and Frederick II. She dreamed of one day holding a hunting bird on her own gloved fist. It was the nearest thing she could imagine to flying herself. Flying, escaping, removing herself far above the petty concerns of the *ton.*

She smoothed her black curls away from her face and shook the dust off her skirt. The book and the idea of falconry had its usual effect. She regained control of herself and felt ready to face the world. Belinda and the dowager would be away for a few weeks. Perhaps by the time they came back she would have found some peace, some acceptance of her position in the family and her changed expectations for the future. After all, she needn't marry. She could be the poor maiden aunt and take pleasure in Belinda's and Harry's broods. Perhaps that would be better, in fact. She couldn't see herself falling in love with anyone. The young gentlemen of her acquaintance were as silly and vacuous as most of the ladies. She did not think she would have met anyone more interesting in London anyway.

And yet ... Antonella wasn't being honest with herself and she knew it. She was far from ready to accept her new status in the world. It was too big a change. She would not ask it of herself, not right away. She'd done her crying, her moaning and chest-beating. That much was over. After one last long, shuddering breath and a vow never to shed another tear about the business, she stood tall and looked around her.

The light was fading, and with no fire to warm the room or candles to light it, soon she would not be able to read and her teeth would start to chatter in earnest. They wouldn't dress for dinner as it was just the two of them, Miss Wilkins had told her at breakfast that morning, but she would go back to her room and splash some water on her face, try to erase the evidence of tears.

Of course, Wilkie would know she'd been crying no matter what. The governess had an uncanny ability to perceive every nuance of Antonella's moods. She also had the wisdom not to interfere in any obvious way, but ensured that Antonella knew she was there should she ever need her.

Antonella allowed this thought to comfort her as she made her way back to the modern wing of the house and her new life as a poor relation.

CHAPTER 3

$\mathcal{H}$ector Gainesworth tried to persuade Major Malcolm Tennant, Lord Atherleigh, to stay in London after he'd been let out of hospital—where he'd been for months ever since returning from the Peninsula.

"It would do you good. A little society. Plenty of pretty girls around even at this time of year," he'd said over brandy in Tennant House a few weeks earlier.

"Not in my line right now, Hector," Atherleigh said.

"So you'll go to be all alone in the wilds of Cornwall for the winter? How very dreary. Perhaps you have decent neighbors. Isn't one of Lewiston's estates near you?"

Atherleigh sighed. "Yes. But I had it on the authority of my steward that the family is in London for the little season, so they won't trouble me."

Gainesworth shook his head. "I don't think hiding yourself away is the answer to anything. I'm tempted to join you at the manor for the holidays and get you out and about. This wallowing won't do you any good, you know."

Malcolm took this with a pinch of salt. His lively friend would hardly choose to decamp to the country unless it was for a house party where he knew there would be plenty of entertainment. "Surely you've been invited elsewhere by now! In any case, you mustn't concern yourself with me. Best I don't make a spectacle of myself."

"Don't you see? A war wound makes you interesting! You aren't less attractive, you're more so. Who would look at me at a party if there's a genuine hero about?"

Malcolm gave a short, mirthless laugh. "I don't have a fascinating scar on my cheek to raise the sympathy of romantic young ladies. A missing hand is altogether more prosaic—and more disturbing."

"If you're determined to let this injury define your life, there's little I can do to help." Gainesworth downed the remainder of his brandy and stood in preparation to take his leave.

"I know you mean well Hector, but I'd be grateful if you would drop this line of reasoning." Malcolm said, effectively ending the conversation.

He left for Cornwall the very next day.

As the hired post chaise rumbled along the turnpike roads west, Malcolm shuddered, fixing his eyes on his bandaged arm. Three painful surgeries had been necessary following the amputation of his left hand, two while he was still in France, the third and final one in London. The bones of his forearm had been badly broken as well, his wrist crushed.

Malcolm wished he didn't have to think about it. He certainly never wanted to talk about it again, never wanted to face his old friends and neighbors and see the pity in their eyes. The country had been at war. Men were injured in a war. Killed. He'd seen much, much worse on the battlefields of Spain and France. He survived, though. Until Nivelle, he'd had only minor injuries. Everyone told him to be grateful for that, but he couldn't force his mind in that direction.

Thinking of men he knew with far worse injuries, or whose eyes closed for the last time on a foreign battlefield, did not have the effect of inspiring gratitude. Try as he might, his thoughts would swerve back to anger, frustration, and regret.

And now, the war was over. The wounded of all ranks were returning to England, and that hooligan Napoleon was confined to the island of Elba.

It was time for him to pick up the threads of his former life—a daunting task, with the fingers of only one hand at his disposal. He stared ahead through the window of the carriage at the December-brown countryside less than ten miles from Atherleigh Manor and getting closer all the time. The necessity of taking on the mantle of responsibility for the estate his father had left him was ample excuse for his hasty departure from London, if he needed one.

Atherleigh. He wondered if it had changed at all in the four years since he'd been there. At least his father didn't live to see his son maimed for life.

He and his father had the usual rather distant, formal father-son relationship so common among the nobility. The late baron had been content to leave his son to the management of a nurse and then tutors until it was time for him to go to school. Consequently, Malcolm had taken little interest in the management of the home farm and tenantry when his father was alive. The only activity that drew him back to Cornwall despite everything centered in an outbuilding situated on the opposite side of the main house to the stables, near a ruined chapel that was older than the house itself. Both of those structures backed onto a spinney that crossed over from his lands to Lewiston's much larger estate. These environs had been his frequent escape as a boy, where the Indian falconer Rafiq—an import brought over on an East Indiaman through the agency of his uncle—initiated him into the mysteries of hunting with birds.

Falconry had been the principle thread that bound Malcolm and his self-absorbed father together. Left with his three-year-old son after his wife ran away with a French nobleman, the late baron had become little more than a recluse. From this arose a deep aversion to foreigners—and the French in particular.

These dislikes and passions formed the backdrop of Malcolm's young life. Not only would Lord Atherleigh and the honorable Malcolm spend hours training and flying his noble birds under Rafiq's watchful eye, but after Rugby, Malcolm did not go up to Oxford. Instead, on his eighteenth birthday, his father purchased him a Lieutenancy in the Coldstream Guards, exhorting him to kill as many of the French as he could. *And when it's all over, come home and make your birds the finest hunters in Cornwall. Rafiq will show you how.*

A surge of pain shot up Malcolm's left arm from the stump where his hand had been. He'd lost count of the French he had felled in the Pyrenees, so in that he fulfilled his father's wishes. But there would be no falconry for him anymore. He could not wear a glove on his left hand, or hold the jesses between his thumb and forefinger inside it. Even if he learned to perch the bird on his right hand, he still needed the other one to perform the delicate operations of hooding on and off, as well as casting a lure.

"Do you require a composer, My Lord?"

The voice startled him until he remembered that he himself had insisted that his valet, Carter, travel with him in the chaise rather than come separately on the stage coach. "No. The smallest twinge." Carter, aside from being necessary to help with the luggage when they stopped at posting houses for the night during the three-day journey, knew how to help him with anything he was unable to do because of his injury. He had been his batman in the peninsula, and his experience also meant he was more than capable of changing Malcolm's bandages and dressing the wound.

After a moment, the two men relapsed into silence. What use was it wondering how things stood with the hawks and falcons? It would be better, Malcolm thought, for the birds to have been sold or destroyed, not remain to remind him of something he could no longer do, would never be able to do again. He closed his eyes and pretended to go to sleep, not wanting to catch sight of the landmarks that signaled his arrival at the home where he had passed his strange, solitary boyhood.

After instructing Penrose, the old butler, to pay off the post boys and send them back to the nearest inn, Malcolm entered the flagged hall of the manor house with a mixture of sadness and trepidation. The smell—old dust with an undercurrent of mildew—transported him instantly back to vacations from school. Even then, the house had felt isolated and nearly empty. Now, without even the presence of his father, it was desolate. "Good to see you, Penrose. Perhaps you could send to the kitchen to get me a plate of cold meat and cheese for dinner. No need to do anything more."

"Of course, My Lord. Although we had heard you were no longer in hospital and would be joining us, until Mr. Tregellis had his letter from you two days ago we had no way of knowing exactly when you would arrive. So I'm afraid cook has had to make her decisions about provisioning a little by guess."

It was a veiled dig at him for not writing to inform the staff of his imminent arrival, Malcolm knew. "Of course. I'm afraid I was preoccupied with my own concerns." He held up his still-bandaged arm. "Although that's no excuse for a lack of consideration. A tray in the library will do."

After the footman, Jenkins, led Carter up the stairs to take the remainder of the luggage to Atherleigh's room on the first floor, Malcolm crossed the hall to a door toward the back that opened into a handsome library. The collection of volumes was far grander than his family should have had any pretensions to. Old Lord Atherleigh had been no scholar, and Malcolm himself, although he loved to read, had not been disappointed to go into the army instead of to Oxford. The library was the darling of his grandfather, who had become enamored of some of the great libraries on the Continent while he was on his grand tour. Yet even that ancestor, Malcolm suspected, had collected the books more for their rarity than their content. The only well-thumbed volumes in it were the five that comprised *The Art of Hunting with Birds*, by Frederick II. They still lay on the reading stand, one of them open to the page on hunting while mounted on a horse.

He sighed. Of all the reminders to greet him right away. However painful the associations, though, the library was by far the most comfortable room in the manor house. He would have found himself there soon enough. Malcolm sank into the wing chair on one side of the crackling fire, stretched his legs out before him, and stared unseeing into the dancing flames.

A moment later the door opened and Penrose brought in a tray bearing a decanter and glass, which he set down on the small table at his elbow. "It's the Mountain, Sir. Your dinner will be served in half an hour. Do you require anything else?"

"No, thank you," Malcolm said, with a dismissive wave. He reached for the decanter—clever of Penrose to find one of the bottles of superb Malaga he'd sent home from Spain.

He paused, however, before filling the glass. Lying on the tray next to the decanter was a letter, addressed to him. Who in the neighborhood even knew he'd be here at this time? It bore no frank, so it had clearly been hand delivered. He picked it up, idly turning it with the fingers of his right hand, feeling the texture of the paper, noting the wafer of an indiscriminate color that sealed it.

Here was something else he couldn't do one-handed. At least, not in sight of anyone else. More than anything he dreaded the well-meaning *let me help you with that.*

He replaced the letter down on the tray, anchoring one corner with the decanter, then slid his index finger under the wafer to break the seal. It was an awkward business, but he managed to unfold it with one hand.

He poured himself a glass of the Mountain, sipped it, and took a deep, calming breath before reading.

To the most honorable Lord Atherleigh,

I trust this finds you as well as your God sees fit to make you after the grievous trial of your injury.

Sir, it is my duty to report that the goshawk, Chakor, did not return from her last flight. I searched the northern coombe and the spinney by the chapel, where she was last seen stooping. I found no trace of her.

I believe—though this belief weighs upon my heart—that she has returned to the wild, drawn by the call of her kind or perhaps by the spirit that will not be tamed, even by trust and time.

If it pleases you, I would seek a replacement worthy of your mews, and I await your command in this matter. I remain your obedient servant.

Rafiq Khan, falconer in your service

If God was looking for a way to punish Malcolm for choosing to return to Cornwall, such a letter would have been the perfect vehicle. Instead of being allowed to come to terms with the matter that most weighed on his mind and heart, here it was, thrust upon him in a way that could not be ignored as he could the open volumes of the falconry book. He remembered that his father wrote to him about the goshawk, his pride at how Rafiq had captured the eyas and raised it as a hunter evident in every line.

But she was gone. Perhaps it was a sign that the time for hunting with the birds was truly at an end, that his decision concerning the matter had in essence been made for him.

He supposed that tomorrow he would have to visit the mews—something he'd have preferred to postpone for at least a se'nnight.

Penrose entered the library again, this time bringing the tray of cold supper. Malcolm picked at it and sat staring into the fire for he knew not how long before retiring.

That night his dreams took him back to his boyhood, hawking with his father in a golden field, the sky vibrant blue dotted with puffs of cloud.

CHAPTER 4

*L*ady Belinda and her mama arrived in London three days after the dowager's shocking revelation. As Tibbs, the footman, helped Fairing, Lord Lewiston's butler, take their luggage up to the second-floor guest rooms, Lady Lewiston looked over her shoulder at Belinda and said, "I know you think it was unkind not to bring Antonella. But the *ton* must become accustomed to seeing only you in society. They need not know of Antonella's previous pretensions."

Pretensions indeed! How could she have been pretending when she didn't know anything about it? Well, her mother might think that pushing Antonella to the back was the right thing to do, but Belinda did not. Nonetheless, arguing with the dowager would be a sleeveless effort. Nothing could change the fact that it was she alone who would be introduced to society and expected to find a suitable match.

That said, Belinda had had some time—the entire long journey from Cornwall to London—to concoct a plan that she hoped would help make amends for Antonella's sudden loss of rank. If Antonella couldn't come to London to find a husband, she, Belinda, would find one for her. As to exactly how, well, she would figure that out. How difficult could it be? Antonella was lively, pretty, witty, and educated. Belinda sighed. That last attribute might present a bit of a problem, if what her mother told them what the *ton* considered the most desirable qualities in a lady. Education, far from being a requirement, could in some cases be considered a hindrance. Well, perhaps she need not mention that about Antonella.

Belinda's first two days in the capital passed in a bustle of shopping for gowns, hats, and gloves. And then, on the third day, when she should have been attending her first ball at Lady Rockingham's house, Olivia—Marchioness of Lewiston—gave birth to a healthy baby boy.

Of course, Belinda was delighted. Her mother, although glad of the advent of an heir, appeared less so. The birth threw their plans into chaos. All activity in the house turned away from Belinda's social aspirations and focused instead on the infant. Belinda couldn't help feeling that she and her mother were very much in the way.

"If only it were spring! We could stay with your Aunt Amelia. But her London house is quite shut up now. She's in Bedfordshire and will only return to London in March," the dowager said of her sister over breakfast the morning after the birth of James William Harold Ambleton, Earl of Tregarrick.

"Not to worry, Mama. I'm only just eighteen, and we can come back in the spring for Almack's and the opera."

At this last, her mother wrinkled up her aquiline nose. Belinda was the only other member of the Ambleton family who shared her brother and sister-in-law's love of opera—or music in general. She played the pianoforte a great deal better than most come-outs because she actually enjoyed practicing. In her heart she wished she could learn the violin —like Harry—or the cello, but those instruments weren't considered suitable for a gently bred female. The violin had disreputable associations with the devil, the cello forced one to sit with one's legs spread wide apart while playing.

So, when she wasn't practicing the pianoforte in the ball-room that Lewiston had transformed into a magnificent little opera house for his bride—whose powerful voice had caused a scandal when she was a come-out—or writing a long letter to Antonella, Belinda entered into the baby fever with as good grace as she could manage. But in a very short time—thirty-six hours, to be exact—the sound of, "Lord Tregarrick needs changing!" or "Has Lord Tregarrick had his nap?"—all the servants quickly becoming accustomed to using the tiny infant's courtesy title—began to grate on her nerves. Yes, the succession was assured barring any accidents or ill fortune, and this six-pound bundle would be the Earl of Tregarrick until such time as he inherited the marquisate. Which, since Harry had not yet passed his thirtieth birthday, would likely be many years hence.

Altogether, Belinda's time in London had proved a bitter disappointment. She was frustrated on her own behalf, certainly. But having spent the entire carriage journey from Cornwall thinking of ways to find someone to marry Antonella, she was doubly vexed. Neither project had a hope of succeeding—let alone even starting—until she went into society.

It wasn't fair. Antonella should have been with them in London. She'd pretended not to care, to brush it off, to say it didn't matter. But when Belinda took a last look out the back carriage window as they set out for town, Antonella stood alone in the doorway of the Court, all pretense of insouciance gone, her face a picture of desolation. That image haunted Belinda. She knew that, despite Ant's unladylike penchant for rambling around the countryside looking for wounded birds, she *wanted* to make her come-out and be presented at a drawing room. She had been raised to expect it They talked about it as girls, imagining what their gowns would look like and what the queen—or one of her daughters—would say to them. Now it would never be.

Whatever the case now, Belinda had her plan. She would concentrate on finding Antonella a suitor before she even thought about finding a husband for herself.

That task wouldn't be easy. Belinda was a loving, kind sister, but she was also a realist. She knew well enough that her own style of beauty would please in the *ton*, that her ease of manners and many accomplishments would assure that she captured the interest of plenty of eligible *partis* during the season, and therefore she needn't go to any extraordinary efforts to attract a suitable mate.

Finding someone to suit the idiosyncratic Antonella was a taller order—even without the uncertainty surrounding her relationship to the family. But she would try her hardest. She had to. And she would succeed. She may not have Antonella's cleverness, but Belinda had deep resources of determination, which Miss Wilkins sometimes called stubbornness. So be it. She would stubbornly do what she felt was right for the sister she had loved all her life.

AFTER BREAKFAST ON THE THIRD MORNING FOLLOWING THE birth of Lord Tregarrick, Belinda was at a loss as to how she would pass the time for the remaining ten days of their intended stay if she couldn't go to any parties or balls, and thought she might at least find something good to read. She was on her way to peruse the shelves of Harry's well-stocked library, but stopped short at the sound of raised voices coming through the closed door.

"… You could exert some pressure on the marchioness if you chose. Don't you see how difficult this is going to be?"

"Belinda will do well. Her dowry is modest, yes, but she is appealing in so many other ways."

"Ways that no one in the *ton* has yet had the opportunity to glimpse! And Lord Bartleson won't be here until next week. You know he's the best possible prospect for Belinda. He's apparently come to London this year for the express purpose of finding a wife."

"Bartleson!" Harry's voice dripped with skepticism. "You wouldn't. He's a tolerable fellow, but Bee deserves better."

"What is better, I ask you, than an earl with impeccable lineage and a reputation to match? Not to mention his immense fortune. And the more quickly she is settled the better."

After a pause in the conversation, Harry spoke again. "You forgot to mention his entire lack of intelligence and the fact that all he cares about is horse racing. Really, Mama, you're not to push either of my sisters into matches they do not want. I don't understand the hurry!"

"Hah! You well know why I want Belinda safely married to a man of rank. Think of the Cranborne affair. The scandal ruined the whole family. The legitimate daughters are still unbetrothed."

While that fact explained her mother's actions in part, Belinda still didn't understand why the pretense had gone on for so long. Her father, who had apparently instigated the whole thing, had been dead these three years.

The conversation in the library went quiet for a while. All Belinda could hear was the indistinct murmur of her mother's and her brother's voices. Until, that was, the dowager said something that made Harry raise his voice again.

"It's madness Mama! What do you suggest Antonella does

then? The daughter of a nobleman cannot be a governess, and she's too young and pretty to be a lady's companion."

The floor creaked as though her mother were pacing back and forth in front of the fireplace. "If Belinda marries well enough, Antonella could simply go and live with her. I'm not sure she really wants to marry. Her interests are so unusual. Really, Harry, how can you ask it of me! Haven't I done enough?"

"You would consign her to the role of aunt? She is far too intelligent and beautiful for her life to be over before it even begins."

"She might have a remote possibility of finding someone willing to overlook her status and her idiosyncracies if she had a large enough dowry," the dowager said with a note of triumph at having made her point. "Olivia's fortune became yours when you married! Well I know how that system works."

Harry's sigh was loud enough to carry through the closed door. "As I said, I think you would be better served by taking Belinda back to Cornwall soon and waiting until spring to launch her properly. We simply cannot have this disruption now. The birth was difficult, and Olivia is far from her usual sanguine self."

"It would be the work of a few minutes to make the suggestion. I don't see why you are so stubborn about this! Or why you can't simply arrange it all yourself."

"Because I choose not to treat my wife's money as my own. It is to be used in the service of all that is ours: our homes, our children, our lives."

The argument was a familiar one. Belinda was well aware that her mother, having become reconciled to her son marrying the granddaughter of a cit because of her fortune, had been frustrated to learn that Harry had no intention of exercising his authority as head of his family and taking control of his wife's funds—and liberally distributing them to his family, where they were sorely needed. Belinda thought it honorable of Harry. Everyone knew that once married, a woman and all she owned became the property of her husband—unless very specific provisions were made with the full cooperation of the husband.

But what was that they had said about Antonella? Harry had called her the daughter of a nobleman. Had he not been told that she wasn't? Impossible. He must know. Perhaps he meant some other nobleman, the unknown distant relation. Yet her Mama had implied that the connection was not of high rank.

Harry spoke again. "I cannot, I *will* not, raise the matter with Olivia at this juncture. It would be insensitive and imprudent."

"What's the use of marrying a fortune if it doesn't benefit your family!" the dowager said, an edge of tears in her voice. "You have no idea how hard it is, what a responsibility, to settle two such different young ladies."

"Mama, be reasonable. Olivia and I have only been married for a little over a year, and she hardly knows Ant and Bee—"

"Do not, I beg you, be so vulgar as to use those ridiculous names. You know I detest them." She sniffed then continued, "Very well. We shall leave you to deal with your domestic matters. I can see we are not welcome here. But we won't go until Belinda has attended at least one *ton* party. I'm convinced that now, when the competition is less numerous, would be the best time for her to make an indelible impression on a gentleman of good birth and fortune. Bartleson is not here, but I daresay there are other possible candidates."

All was quiet for a moment. And then Harry said, "I shall send word around to the Duchess of Hartland's house to see if she might chaperone Belinda to the Granville's dress party this evening. Olivia and I had an invitation we already declined, so it wouldn't do for you to go in our stead."

Rapid footsteps approached the library door. Belinda hastened across the hall and ducked back into the breakfast parlor. A dress party! Dared she hope? It would be such a shame to leave London without going anywhere. *Oh please, Duchess!* she thought, crossing her fingers and saying a silent and rather irreverent prayer.

After that, Belinda couldn't settle to reading and so spent most of the morning embroidering a cap for the heir. She was about to unpick the work she'd already done, deciding it wasn't neat enough, when the dowager burst in upon her, all smiles, and said, "Belinda, dear! I have wonderful news!"

She looked guiltily at the partially sewn lacy baby cap in her hands. At the rate she was going it would never be finished. "What is it Mama?"

"The duchess of Hartland has agreed to chaperone you to the Granville's dress party tonight." She waved a letter in the air before handing it to Belinda to read. "Hartland is still in Leicestershire, apparently, and she is alone and desirous of some company. Mind you, I don't think she's as careful a chaperone as she ought to be, but you're a sensible girl."

So, Harry had come through. She wanted to thank him, but she wasn't supposed to know it had been his effort that secured the invitation. A party was one thing. But to be chaperoned by Her Grace of Hartland was something else. Belinda was a little in awe of the duchess. She hadn't seen her since Harry and Olivia's wedding the previous summer, and then they'd hardly spoken. At the time, Belinda couldn't take her eyes off her—which was embarrassing, because it should have been the bride that captured all her attention.

But Olivia—who was pretty in a different way and gowned exquisitely—hadn't a hope of being able to compete with the duchess. In point of fact, Adelheid was simply the most beautiful woman Belinda had ever beheld. She had no doubt whatever that all eyes would be on them when they arrived at Lady Granville's together.

"I'll wear the ivory silk," Belinda said, tossing the baby cap aside and pacing around the room. "And my pearls. Do you think that will be enough?" She had hoped for an assembly or ball before facing the more formal dress party, although she would show creditably in her new evening gown, and no one expected come-outs to wear jewels.

THE REST OF THE DAY WAS OCCUPIED WITH PREPARATIONS. Belinda's stomach fluttered and her appetite deserted her. She hoped, for herself, that her dance card would be filled with the names of handsome, eligible gentlemen—she did not agree with her mother that her suitor must be titled and wealthy. He could be titled or not as far as she was concerned, so long as he was respectable. Besides, she resolutely reminded herself that she must for the moment set aside her own ambitions and concentrate on finding someone to suit her extraordinary sister.

And that started her thinking about what kind of a man *would* be suitable. He mustn't be too tall. No bruising riders or Corinthians for her either, or anyone who took pleasure in shooting birds of any kind. Although perhaps she wouldn't mind someone who found sport in chasing after foxes, which often terrorized the bird populations. And it would be no good to suggest any man with dandy tendencies. Although Antonella appreciated a beautiful gown as much as any other girl and often pored over the Mirror of Fashion or the Ladies' Monthly Museum with Belinda, such things did not occupy a very important place in her world.

Of course, this theoretical suitor would also have to want to spend most of the year in the country. Although Belinda wished for her sister's company in town, she knew Antonella well enough to believe that however much the change of scene seemed beguiling, she would soon have tired of the tame and precious entertainments on offer in town. Paying visits, shopping, going for rides or drives in the park—ah, there was that as well. Antonella was terrified of horses.

Added to it all was the fact that she had no real accomplishments, come to think of it. Ant could barely play the pianoforte and had no voice. She could dance well enough, but her needlework was execrable. She lacked the patience for it.

Oh dear, Belinda thought. Had she set herself an impossible task? All she could think of were the qualities of gentlemen who would *not* suit Antonella. She could only come up with a few attributes that might tempt Antonella to even consider marrying. He must be kind. He must love all living creatures. He must not mind having to talk about science and literature rather than gossip about the *ton* or make small talk about the weather. She supposed such men existed. But how would she be able to find one in an environment where none of those qualities were encouraged or even much valued?

There was one other consideration, Belinda thought. He must be handsome. Or at least, attractive. Antonella was not pretty in the same way she was, but she had the kind of presence that drew eyes to her. Her profile was not classically proportioned nor her face a perfect oval. Hers tended rather to be a little square, although still delicate, and her nose was a bit short for the fashion and upward tipped. Her full upper lip made her look as if she was always about to say something, or smile. But somehow Antonella managed to be striking. She could be beautiful at times, when she wore a certain expression. Belinda couldn't define her quality exactly, except to say that it wasn't anything that could be perceived in her looks—although her bright, dark eyes were certainly arresting. It was more something that emanated from within, a warmth that made people trust her.

She had little time to waste thinking on it further, though. The duchess would be coming to fetch her for the short carriage ride to Lady Granville's soon, and her abigail hadn't quite finished dressing her hair.

CHAPTER 5

"Where do you think you're going, Antonella?" Miss Wilkins's voice stopped her halfway down the last flight of stairs to the entrance hall of Amblemere Court about a week after Belinda and the dowager had gone to London.

Antonella found it remarkable that the governess could tell her footsteps apart from Belinda's and always seemed to know where she was going and what she was thinking—as well as anticipating whether she was appropriately dressed. Although no longer under her direct aegis, the habit of control had been hard for the dedicated—and much beloved—governess to break.

"It's not so cold out. I would rather have gone to London, but I refuse to stay trapped inside just because I'm no longer a lady." In truth, she'd been out for hours every day that it wasn't raining almost since watching the carriage drive out of sight.

Miss Wilkins finished her progress down the stairs and rested a cool hand on Antonella's arm. "You will always be a lady in the ways that matter most. Of course, scampering through the woods on your own is not calculated to give anyone the impression that you wish to be thought one!" She held out the warm shawl and merino cloak she had draped over her arm. "You'll need something more substantial than that flimsy tippet you've got on."

"Thank you, Wilkie," Antonella said, reaching out to take the garments and grasping Miss Wilkins's hand briefly.

"Don't stay out more than an hour, my dear," she said. "The sun's not as warm as it looks, and dark draws in early."

"I promise I won't be long," Antonella said. "I just have to go to the woods and see if the goldcrests are finding enough food before the winter." She held up a cloth bag filled with smaller bags of suet. "I'll hang some on low branches, just in case."

Miss Wilkins shook her head and tsked. "You and your birds. But you will come and tell me what you found, I hope?"

Of all the inhabitants of rambling, disorganized Amblemere Court, only Miss Wilkins humored Antonella in her strange obsession with creatures of the air. A different lady in charge of her education might have discouraged her, but Persephone Wilkins encouraged Antonella to study the natural sciences, doing her best to teach her from her own limited store of knowledge. She ordered books from the nearest lending library and dug out long-forgotten illustrated tomes from the Court's extensive collection—in both the book rooms.

A faint smile played on Antonella's lips as she made her way through the garden and out beyond the park, now denuded of green and lying dormant. She hastened down the gravel path to where it became dirt and forked to two different walks: one toward the lake and trout stream, the other into the beech, sycamore, and fir trees of the dense spinney. Once through the spinney the path continued beyond that a mile or two down to the coombe with its stream at the bottom. From there and up the other side of the coombe she could reach the rocky trail that led to the cove. Her different domains. Hers, and the birds'.

Although bird song was not as raucous at that time of year as it was at the height of the spring mating and nesting season, the avian residents of the spinney were nonetheless frantically occupied with the serious business of fattening up to make it through the winter, staking out their nesting territory, and evading the many predators on land and in the air. Antonella paused in the middle of the densest part of the woods and listened. Here, she was safe. The woodland birds and creatures didn't care who she was or to what degree of nobility she was born. To them she was simply a human.

A human, she thought, who must be vaguely familiar to some of them by now. Listening and observing weren't her only occupations on these rambles, or even her chiefest ones. She was not one of those bird enthusiasts who drew watercolor pictures of what she saw and kept a notebook. Her role, Antonella believed, was something far more important. She considered it her duty to comb the woods as often as she could to see where the robins, kestrels, blue tits, and goldcrests nested, following their lives, counting the hatchlings when they appeared in the spring if she could see into the nests, and watching over them all.

Nine times out of ten, as they grew and became fledglings, one would fall out of the nest or be pushed out by its stronger siblings. If she found it before it became prey to a cat or a fox, Antonella would carry it to the abandoned shed all but hidden near the stables that she'd adopted as her bird infirmary. There she would feed it and help it heal in safety until—if it survived—such time as it was strong enough to be let out into the world. She found she could often successfully mend a broken wing or foot—the most common injuries. And usually simply feeding a fledgling well in a situation where it needn't compete with its nest-mates for nourishment was all that was required of her.

Once she had taken the measure of the spinney, she passed through it and followed the path as it dwindled and sloped downward into the wooded coombe—sheltered enough from the relentless sea breezes for larger trees to flourish. She had to slow down and pick her way carefully over twisted roots and fallen branches, every once in a while lifting her eyes to the treetops, looking for the bright spots of gold as the tiny birds busied themselves. They were so much easier to catch sight of at this time of year, without the dense canopy of green to hide them.

Antonella was so focused on the birds in the trees that she found herself almost on top of the hawk before she saw it.

She shrieked before she could stop herself. Perched close to the ground was the largest bird she'd ever seen up close. She knew it for a hawk right away, and not one of the common sparrow hawks that swooped out of the sky and caught the small birds in mid flight. This hawk was at least twice the size of one of those. Antonella quickly took in the powerful, half-clenched talons at the end of the legs and at the opposite extremity the lethally effective curved beak. Those weapons could tear flesh as easily as a sharp kitchen knife.

But what really stopped her in her tracks were the eyes. This creature stared at her out of deep, fire-orange eyes. She froze.

A goshawk.

She'd seen them from a distance on rare occasions before,

watching their swift flight as they hunted through the trees for squirrels and voles, sometimes for unwary small birds as well. But she'd never gazed directly into the eyes of one of these elusive predators. What was it doing there, on the forest floor? Why didn't it fly away?

It took only a moment for her to see that a poacher's net kept the hawk fixed in that unlikely place. A snare meant to lure pheasants and woodcock now held the most powerful bird native to that part of the world captive, incapable of escape.

What can I do? Antonella thought as those uncanny eyes fixed hers in a fierce stare. She couldn't leave it there. For one thing, the image would haunt her. For another, it would surely die, be attacked by a fox or a badger—or worse, simply starve because it couldn't hunt for food.

No, even though this was no delicate bird with a broken wing she could heal in a few weeks and re-release to the wild, it was a bird. And it was in trouble. She reached into her pocket and pulled out the small knife she always carried. Would it be sharp enough to cut the threads of the net? What then?

She took a step closer to the hawk. It struggled and opened its beak and let out a *kek-kek-kek!* Clearly signaling fear and panic. "Easy there, I won't hurt you. I promise," Antonella murmured, and the hawk stilled. Why did she talk to the birds she found? They couldn't understand, so what difference would it make? She supposed it made her feel better, and it didn't do any harm to the birds. "How did you get yourself into such a tangle?" She kept up a low stream of comforting nothings as she inched closer and closer to the hawk. A couple of abrasions on one wing were bleeding slightly. Perhaps that was the worst of any injury. She could see a few broken secondary feathers, but it was hard to tell if anything more serious were amiss. It occurred to Antonella to wonder if the poachers had come to retrieve their booty and abandoned the net when they saw what was in it. In any case, if she had her way, the net wouldn't be used again.

She looked around to see if a passing farmhand or game-keeper could help her, but it was late in the afternoon and the wrong time of year, besides the fact that such persons would have little reason to venture into the wild coombe. She was alone. Or rather, she and the hawk were alone. There was nothing for it but to do what she could to free the bird. She would take great care to stay out of the way of those knife-sharp talons, though.

Starting as far away as she could from the hawk and still reach the net, she went to work with her knife. The netting was course and strong, and it took some effort to cut. The hawk appeared to have injured only the one wing, but she couldn't tell how badly. The legs seemed sound, though. When it shifted its position once, a faint tinkling arose from somewhere amid the rotting leaves on the forest floor. "What is that?" she whispered, and as she crept closer, the hawk fluffed its feathers and took a quick little step.

Ah. The sound came from two tiny bells dangling from the ends of thin leather straps, whose other ends were tied around the hawk's legs just above its talons. Jesses. This wasn't some wild creature in pursuit of prey a little too close to the ground. Someone had spent months—possibly years—training this bird to hunt for the sport of some wealthy landowner. She wasn't sure whether this made everything better or worse. Now, she must not only free it, take it some-where to keep it safe and perhaps heal, but she must try to get it back to its owner.

Who did she know who kept a falconer? The Ambleton family certainly didn't. Could the hawk belong to Lord Atherleigh, a major in the army whose manor marched along their western boundary? The dowager had said something about the major having been injured fighting on the Peninsula. Antonella remembered her early sighting of a tall, dark gentleman in the middle of a field, gauntleted arm outstretched, gazing toward the sky after loosing a falcon to hunt. Was it the young Lord Atherleigh? Or his father, who had died about a year ago?

By the time she'd thought through all this, Antonella was an arm's length away from the ensnared bird's vicious beak. She could have reached out and touched it. But of course, she didn't. Its wing feathers were still caught up in a twisted part of the net. If she got too close, though, either that beak or those talons could rip her arm open.

She took a deep breath. She could move quickly perhaps and avoid a strike if the bird thrashed out. Her heart fluttered against her ribs. "I'm going to try to free you," she said in her most soothing voice as she inched closer. "Please don't hurt me!"

The hawk glared at her and squawked, lifted up one foot and scratched out, but still trapped in the net it couldn't do much of anything except struggle. It seemed to realize that and stilled its restless fretting the nearer she drew to it. Antonella swore she could read comprehension in its fierce orange eye. Of course, that was ridiculous. She said a silent prayer and tried not to think about what might happen as she snip, snip, snipped until she dared to touch the hawk's wing feathers on one side.

She exhaled. "Thank you. Now I just have to do the other side, and I hope you're well enough to fly away, that your wing isn't broken, just twisted around."

With a little more confidence, she kept cutting until the net was in shreds and nothing was holding the hawk in its place anymore. The bird spread its wings wide and Antonella backed away. Its wingspan was nearly as long as her own outstretched arms, and one of the wings didn't entirely straighten at the end.

Something *was* broken. Now what should she do? It would never be able to fly in that condition.

Antonella knew nothing about handling trained hawks. She only knew what she'd read in the Hohenstaufen books, which included nothing about treating injuries.

The hawk stared at her as if waiting for her to do something. "All right. I'll try this, but you have to promise not to go into a distempered freak." Antonella removed her shawl and crept toward the hawk. Once she was near enough, she threw it over its head and quickly stepped in to wrap it around the bird firmly but gently, then lifted. She could feel the hawk twitching and hear its quick breathing, but she had a secure hold—a hold she'd learned when helping the kitchen maid with the hens. This bird was heavier, though. A female, most likely. They were larger and better hunters.

What now? A moment's thought and she realized her only choice was to bring the goshawk to her makeshift bird infirmary. She'd fashioned a few perches in it for smaller birds, but those wouldn't do for a goshawk. What was it the falconry book said? She needed to make a bow perch high enough off the ground so that she wouldn't be looming over the hawk when she approached it. Perhaps the strongest of the small perches would work until she could put something else together.

Antonella took several slow, deep breaths in an attempt to still her racing heart. If she could be calm, the hawk might sense it and settle down. She slowly, carefully climbed up the treacherous path in the coombe and retraced her steps through the spinney. All told it was a little over a mile of hard going back to the shed behind the stables.

By the time she reached her goal, her arms shook with the effort of holding them in one place and a sheen of perspiration damped her face despite the cold weather. She entered the dim hut, righted the hawk, placed it so the talons could grasp the largest perch, then unwrapped her shawl from around it and quickly stepped away. The perch bent a little under the bird's weight, but looked as if it would hold at least temporarily.

How would she keep it from falling or hopping down to the ground? *I must fashion a leash to the end of one of the jesses.* Scanning the hut with its jars of liniments and rags suitable for dealing with much smaller birds, she spied a length of twine. "This will have to do," she murmured, and wished she had a hood to place over the bird's head so it wouldn't see her working. "What I'm doing is so you will be safe," she said, as if explaining her actions might prevent an attack.

To her surprise, the hawk stayed quiet. The dimness of the shed and perhaps the bird's fatigue after struggling against the poachers' net sapped her will to lash out.

"You must be hungry, too," she said. "I'll find something to feed you."

She did her best to secure the tether to one of the jesses and the perch without getting too close and took one last look at the goshawk before leaving and latching the door of the shed behind her. The servants knew not to venture in, having long ago accepted her peculiar obsession with her feathered friends, so she didn't think anyone would discover the goshawk anytime soon.

Her first task after feeding her would be to determine how badly the hawk was injured. Until the bird got more used to her, she wouldn't be able to examine the wing closely. Would she ever be in that position?

What an extraordinary day it had turned out to be. Perhaps she would tell Wilkie about it. But no. She wouldn't say anything to anyone yet. She wanted a day or two to get to know this unlikely visitor and see if she could manage on her own. Antonella was curiously reluctant to discover—or rather, confirm—the goshawk's owner.

What is London compared to this? Antonella thought. She may never have truly belonged in the only family she'd ever known, but she belonged here. Like the goshawk. She was rooted to the land, the woods, the shore. It was her habitat. No one could take that away from her.

CHAPTER 6

*B*elinda was a little in awe of the duchess of Hartland, and so sat in tongue-tied silence in the barouche on the way to the party. The duchess was a widowed Austrian princess before she married the duke around the same time Harry and Olivia wed. Hartland was a good friend of Harry's, and apparently Olivia had been supposed to marry the duke herself. As to how it came about that things ended quite differently, Belinda didn't know. Perhaps she could persuade the duchess to tell her the story, now that she was eighteen.

"Are you nervous, my dear?" her grace of Hartland said as the barouche pulled up to the steps in front of Lady Granville's imposing house in Park Street.

Was she? "I suppose so," she said. "Although I've hardly had time to be."

"I know, my decision to come was rather sudden. Therefore I'm delighted you were not otherwise engaged so that I could have the pleasure of your company. These dress parties can be dull unless the right people are there."

So, the duchess hadn't planned to attend herself until

beseeched by Harry. Belinda had a brief pang of guilt about that, but the idea of what lay ahead soon drove it away.

As she predicted, their arrival caused a bit of a stir. Her grace's glittering beauty, her extraordinary blue-green eyes and luminescent skin, her graceful yet commanding presence, drew all eyes to her and quite put Belinda in the shade. While some girls might have been annoyed by such a circumstance, Belinda was grateful. At the few assemblies and private balls she'd attended the year before in Cornwall, she'd been accustomed to being thought the prettiest girl in the room and being besieged as soon as she walked through the door. She didn't think she actually was so extraordinary, but that her rank conferred an added luster to her in the eyes of the local gentry—a luster that had nothing to do with her actual worthiness. Still, she wasn't certain what to expect in London, and so she wanted a chance to look around her a bit, to be the one observing, unnoticed. Doing so would also give her an opportunity to see if there was anyone who looked promising for Antonella.

For the first few minutes Belinda got her wish. After she and her grace greeted the hostess—who smiled and curtsied in a way that Belinda could only describe as toad-eating— they could hardly take three steps without someone coming up to the duchess to kiss her hand or solicit a dance. Belinda smiled in that bland way she'd been taught by Miss Wilkins, nodded politely and murmured her pleasure at making a vast number of acquaintances, all the while surreptitiously glancing around for potential prospects for her sister.

As she did so, she became distracted by the glittering finery of the guests. The ladies wore full evening gowns with demi trains and lavish lace trimming, and jewel-encrusted tiaras graced the heads of well over half of those present. It was easy for Belinda to spot the few come-outs, those who lived near enough London to easily travel there for the little season, or who—like her—were dipping their toes into a slightly less daunting social scene before facing the terrors of the *haut ton* in the spring. They too wore rich silks and velvets, but their only adornments were modest strings of pearls and flowers and ribbons in their hair—perhaps a few small jewels sparkling in their curls.

Belinda was in the process of deciding which gown of the amazing variety she saw was the prettiest when she caught sight of an elderly lady clad head to toe in the garb of the previous century. Boned panniers stuck out to either side of her from just below her waist and her stiff satin gown was trimmed with quantities of lace. Her powdered hair glistened in the candle glow and her whitened face looked positively spectral. Circles of rouge dotted her cheeks and black moon and star patches peeped at the corners of her mouth. Belinda had never seen anything like it. She pressed her lips together to prevent the impolite laugh that threatened to disrupt the civilized hum of conversation. She had to look away or she feared she would lose control altogether.

That was the moment she saw him.

He stood on the other side of the room from the oddly dressed lady, leaning a shoulder against the wall by the mantelpiece, one foot crossed casually over the other. His elegant but not ostentatious evening clothes—black coat, faun breeches, striped silk stockings, plain white waistcoat, and a neck cloth tied much more simply than the fashion of the time dictated—did not distinguish him in any particular way from the rest of the company. What drew Belinda's eyes to him was that—unlike nearly every other gentleman there —he wasn't gazing adoringly at the duchess by her side and clearly looking for an excuse to find his way to her.

No. Instead, he was looking at her, Belinda, and he raised one eyebrow over eyes that even from a distance Belinda could see were dancing with barely contained mirth. He cocked his head slightly in the direction of the old lady and pressed his lips together, causing a dimple to form in his cheek.

She turned away in confusion. She'd had just enough time to gain a general impression of what he looked like. Tall. Broad shouldered. A head of burnished, gently curling gold hair. Shapely lips that were probably capable of smiling dangerously.

While she was recovering from this disturbing impression, a voice right next to her said, "Lady Belinda, might I have the honor of standing up with you in the next set?"

Belinda glanced at the duchess in confusion, forcing herself to attend to those gathered around them. Had she been introduced to this fellow who stood before her now, with his sandy hair and freckled face, a decided blush in his cheeks?

"Lord Philipston," her grace said and gave Belinda a subtle nudge, "has done you a great honor, Belinda, since he informed me the last time I saw him at a party that he does not generally care to dance."

"Of course, My Lord," Belinda said, her voice higher and more emphatic than she intended. Her tone startled him a little, and she coughed slightly, trying to disguise her discomfiture. *Control yourself, Belinda!* she thought, and put all her effort into not looking over toward the gentleman staring at her.

Lord Philipston soon led her away from the duchess to the ballroom to claim his dance. After that, Belinda found herself standing up for every set with a dizzying parade of gentlemen. She had to consult her dance card every time to remember so many names, and in the sheer joy of moving her feet to the rhythm of the rather excellent ensemble forgot both her project of finding a mate for Antonella—and the gentleman she'd seen across the drawing room.

She forgot until the last dance before supper, that is. It was to be a quadrille. Belinda had actually been hoping for a chance to rest a bit. Her new evening slippers rubbed her heel, and she very much wanted to go to the retiring room and remove them, perhaps bathe her blisters with a little water. But something distracted her—she thought she heard her name called—so her head was turned away from the direction she was walking and she bumped into someone, momentarily losing her balance. Two strong hands gripped her arms and steadied her, and she looked up into a pair of wickedly smiling blue eyes—or were they silver gray? The flickering candlelight made the colors shift and change.

"I-I'm so sorry!" she said, recognizing the gentleman she'd seen earlier across the room, and hoping the heat she felt in her cheeks hadn't stained them deep red.

"Please, the fault is mine," he said in a pleasant voice that matched his looks exactly. In fact, it was precisely the voice she had imagined he would have—that is, if she imagined anything at all about him.

She continued to stare into his eyes. Definitely blue, she thought. At first they seemed a single color, but after a closer look could be seen to consist of slivers of darker blue and silver. Perhaps that was what had made her think they might be gray. She didn't know whether it was the colors themselves or something else that made them appear to sparkle. Belinda thought such a description merely the stuff of romantic novels, but those eyes caught the light in different ways that gave the effect of actually twinkling. *I should say something,* she thought, suddenly aware that she'd been struck utterly dumb.

But he saved her the trouble. "We haven't been introduced. However I think we have a connection that would make it not improper for me to claim the privilege of introducing myself." He held out his hand.

She took it and nodded to him as he executed a perfect bow.

"Hector Gainesworth, your servant. And you are Lady Belinda Ambleton."

How did he know? She couldn't ask, not in so many words. At last she found her voice. "I am pleased to make your acquaintance, Lord Gainesworth, but I'm afraid I am unaware of this connection you speak of."

"Ah, you have elevated my rank! I must in good conscience correct you. I am simply Mr. Gainesworth." He bowed, a comically deprecating expression on his face.

At that point, the duchess walked by and paused. "Ah! I see you have met Hector! I've been wishing to introduce you but you hardly left the dance floor, Belinda dear." She nodded to them both and passed on, having been summoned by a friend on the other side of the room.

So he was known to the duchess. Belinda wasn't sure whether that made her feel more or less comfortable. "The connection?" she asked.

"Well, I must confess it is extremely tenuous. My very good friend is your neighbor in Cornwall. Lord Atherleigh. And I'm a little acquainted with your brother the marquess."

That means he must be too old, Belinda thought, running over in her mind the attributes she'd enumerated for Antonella's mate. Mr. Gainesworth was handsome, so that fit. But he bore too much the air of a man of fashion, looking as though he took great pains over the cut of his coat and the starch of his collar points. Nonetheless, his air of unstudied elegance was very appealing. But how to find out more about him? She didn't want to consider him for Antonella unless she knew he would be a good prospect. Before she could think better of it she blurted out, "Do you shoot?" and immediately regretted it. What an absurd question!

Gainesworth's eyebrows shot up and he stepped slightly

back. "Not generally at dress parties, so you are quite safe. Although I enjoy a day in the coverts as much as the next man."

Belinda bit her lower lip to stop herself from laughing. Of course, it was entirely inappropriate to ask someone such a question in that place at that time and in that way, especially someone she didn't know. Still, if he enjoyed shooting birds, he would not do for Antonella, would he? Well, in for a penny. "You haven't answered me," she said, determinedly maintaining her serious expression, although it wouldn't have taken much to make her dissolve into a fit of giggles.

"I shoot," he said, then lowered his voice and leaned toward her in a conspiratorial manner. "But I never hit anything."

That did it. Belinda let out a little shriek of laughter before she could stifle it, and several of the guests nearby turned toward them. She opened her fan and hid her face behind it, not daring to meet Mr. Gainesworth's eyes.

"Is there anything else you'd like to know about me?" he asked, clearly quizzing her. "Perhaps whether I enjoy fly fishing or course fishing more?"

Tears of suppressed laughter threatened to roll down Belinda's cheeks. What had she started? She cleared her throat and gave a polite cough before saying, "How do you feel about horses?"

This question almost proved too much for Gainesworth, who until then had not succumbed to the mirth that had undone Belinda. With a shaking voice he said, "Um, they are useful beasts. We cannot do without them. And I ride tolerably well and drive a four-in-hand with distinction, I'm told."

She shook her head, biting down on her bottom lip to suppress the laughter that she barely kept in check.

"My answers displease you? Pray, what must I say in

order to secure your hand for the quadrille? I distinguished myself in classics at Oxford." His voice crumpled at the end.

Oh he was unmerciful!

How on earth had she let the conversation go so awry? Belinda could hardly think what to say to this gentleman who entered into the absurdity of her questions with such good grace. And those eyes—no one should have eyes like that. What she wanted to say to him was that her feet hurt and that he might suit Antonella but she couldn't be sure, and she wanted to ask him so many more questions. But she remained silent.

At that moment the orchestra struck up the strains of the quadrille and Gainesworth said, "Is it too bold of me to ask you to stand up with me in this next set? Even if I'm not much of a shot and I like horses?"

"I'm sorry. You surely think me quite the fool," Belinda said, fully aware of the bizarre turn their conversation had taken.

"Not a fool at all," he said. "Just unexpected. Come, we must take our place in the set—unless you're so dissatisfied with what you know of me that you intend to rush away."

At that Belinda flashed him a genuine smile, which brought out the dimples in her cheeks. "I'd be delighted to dance," she said, and let Mr. Gainesworth lead her onto the floor.

Yes, she thought. She could imagine many an entertaining evening if this Mr. Gainesworth were to be her brother-in-law. A man like him must have many friends. Who wouldn't enjoy such witty conversation? Perhaps he and Antonella would have a home somewhere less remote and forbidding than Amblemere, and she could visit them...Why did that thought make her a little sad rather than cheering her?

Once the quadrille finished, Gainesworth claimed the privilege of escorting Belinda into the supper room, as was the usual practice. They hadn't conversed very much during the complicated dance, so Belinda was glad to have a chance to pump him for more information—hopefully without dissolving into laughter. From their light conversation while they stood up, she deduced that he entered into the usual gentlemanly sporting pursuits, but didn't appear to take them too seriously. He even said he preferred long rambles through the woods to pigeon shooting. A Corinthian would rather a ride across country over fences and walls, or perhaps a sparring match with one of his kind. Belinda couldn't imagine Mr. Gainesworth punching anyone.

As he escorted her off the floor to enter the supper room, Gainesworth said, "I intend to spend the holidays with my friend Atherleigh, as I mentioned. You said you were returning to Cornwall when exactly?"

He hadn't mentioned that, and she hadn't said. It was a bit impertinent of him to ask outright. But Belinda couldn't resist the entreaty in Gainesworth's eyes. She shook her head. "I haven't said because I don't know. Probably very soon. I think we are somewhat *de trop* at my brother's house at the moment. And I want to get home to my sister, who couldn't come with us this time."

"Is she much younger, your sister?"

Oh dear. She'd strayed onto treacherous ground here. The last thing she wanted was to have to explain the awkward family situation, that Antonella was the same age as she was, but they weren't twins. So she made something up. "N-no. She's been ill so could not travel. But she is very dear, and much, much cleverer than I am."

"But not as pretty." Gainesworth did not phrase this as a question.

Was that a compliment? Belinda drew herself up and stared at him down her slender, straight nose. "I think she's prettier."

"There's nothing for it then. I shall have to meet her so I can judge for myself."

Yes! Belinda thought. "If you are indeed at Atherleigh during the holidays perhaps we'll see you at our masquerade ball. We always hold one during Advent, usually the week before Christmas." She was aware that she'd probably offered him too much information, and that it might raise expectations in him. On reflection, the thought didn't bother her over much.

At that moment the duchess came to the table. Gainesworth and all the other gentlemen sitting with them rose. "I am terribly sorry to interrupt such lively conversation, but I must claim my young friend. I promised I would not keep her out too late."

Belinda blushed faintly. Now it would be obvious that this was her first *ton* party! She scrambled to think of something to say that might salvage the evening. "Of course, I have an early morning appointment with my groom." She had no such thing, and no idea if that would furnish a decent excuse for leaving a party at what seemed an early hour—not long after midnight—but it was all that came to mind.

"I, too, intend to ride early tomorrow," Gainesworth said. "Perhaps I will see you in the park?"

"Perhaps," Belinda said, smiled, and put her hand out to shake his. No, he wouldn't see her, but she didn't tell him that.

Gainesworth took her hand and bowed over it, squeezing it just the slightest bit as he said, "I don't shoot when I'm in the park either."

Wretch! Belinda thought and pressed her lips together as hard as she could. Gainesworth's eyes shone with amusement.

"I think you have made a conquest in the dashing Mr. Gainesworth," the duchess said once they had settled in her barouche. "He would be a good match. No title, but a decent family on his mother's side. The fortune—which is considerable—came largely from trade, however. But surely that doesn't matter. And he's still in his twenties, although his exact age I do not know."

No! She had it all wrong. Mr. Gainesworth was not her suitor. This was going to be more difficult than she thought. "I don't think so. He was just being polite." Belinda wanted to explain about Antonella to the duchess, but decided against it for the moment. She might think her mad.

"Perhaps," her grace said, a knowing smile on her face. "But what did he mean about not shooting in the park? How absurd!"

Yes, it was, Belinda thought with a smile. She could hardly wait to tell Antonella everything.

CHAPTER 7

*M*alcolm kept the letter from the falconer in his coat pocket, although he wasn't certain why. In any case, he did not go immediately to the mews the next day, using the excuse of other more pressing estate business to attend to. He had to ensure there were adequate household staff to make his solitary existence comfortable. Then there were the books to go over with his steward, Latham, tenants to visit, repairs to be undertaken, and letters to be written.

When he could put it off no longer without offending Rafiq, Malcolm set out on the familiar walk through the garden toward the mews where the hunting birds were kept. It was the last thing he felt like doing just then. He didn't want to hear the crunch of his boots on the gravel, neatly raked into the gently curving paths that led over the rise and down the slope toward the ancient chapel and the mews building joined to it by a fenced-in weathering yard. The sound conjured up a bitter-sweet memory. He associated it with the magical feeling of having a hooded falcon perched on his arm, alert, waiting to be unhooded so she could soar into the air, an arrow of perfect construction for flight, for diving, for seizing prey.

A sigh escaped him as the ruined chapel's square tower came into view, the skeletal remains of a fierce, striving faith. The centuries had taken their toll, and yet the structure that dated back to Norman times endured.

Yes, it all looked exactly the same as he remembered.

Nothing around him had changed, but everything about him had altered beyond recognition. Oh, he looked the same, as far as he could tell. Except that Gainesworth had accused him of being morose and self-pitying, and said that it made his otherwise handsome face appear frightening. Like an angry god of myth. Vulcan, perhaps. Gainesworth's words, not his.

How could he not be morose? He would never again lead the carefree life of the *ton* with time to flirt and dance and drink away the nights. One pursued those activities as a prequel to amorous encounters, which in turn eventually led to finding the perfect wife to assure the continuation of the noble line. But that dream was at an end. No lady in her right mind would want him as a husband in his maimed condition. Now it seemed certain that the barony would pass to that second cousin in the north whom he'd never met.

Malcolm paused at the rise that revealed not just the tower of the chapel, but the entire structure and the mews just beyond it. The weathering yard between the two buildings still held two block perches for the long-winged falcons and one tall bow perch for the restless hawks. Inside the mews building, which had been constructed in the reign of Elizabeth, was space for six hunting birds in partitions far enough apart so their wings wouldn't be damaged when they flapped, and also to prevent aggression. Malcolm couldn't remember a time when all six held falcons or hawks. But there were always at least four birds of different kinds being hunted. Usually two falcons—a peregrine and a merlin, or a rarer lanner or saker falcon, and two hawks—a sparrow hawk and a buzzard, perhaps. Most recently, as Fariq had said, a goshawk. The perches in the yard were at present unoccupied, and from where he stood, Malcolm could not detect a sign of life.

Just as he thought it, a familiar sound issued from the open door of the mews, the eechipping of a peregrine falcon. *Feeding time*, Malcolm thought, and another flood of memories assailed him—Rafiq showing him how to prepare food, teaching him which calls signaled contentment and which alarm, helping him attach jesses to the legs of a merlin—the first falcon he ever hunted.

Malcolm recalled the day Rafiq arrived bearing a Lanner falcon that he'd raised from an eyas, before she could fly. That was long ago. He went away to school soon after and spent less and less time at Atherleigh. Was that falcon still alive? Likely not. Malcolm had never heard of a falcon or hawk living much longer than fifteen years, even when well cared for.

Cared for, yes. But not tamed. That was the devil of it. Those majestic creatures were not pets. They were always a whisper away from being wild again. Perversely, that had been one of the things he'd loved about falconry. To have those delicate, fierce creatures trust him enough to form a partnership whereby the bird kept her essential character— for the best hunters were generally the females—and condescended to be trained for the amusement of the falconers. It would not surprise him if the goshawk—Chakor, the letter called her—simply decided that her contract had come to its end and it was time to take control of her own life again.

The thought brought the hint of an ironic smile to Malcolm's lips. But he'd delayed enough. As he drew closer to the mews the ghost of the fingers that had once been at the end of his arm formed themselves into the shape they would have made inside a gauntlet. *Stop!* he thought, shook his head, and quickened his pace.

"Rafiq?" he called as he strode onto the weathering ground. It was early—not yet eight o'clock—but he would have expected to see at least one hawk outside sitting on a perch, hooded, waiting to hunt.

A moment later the door to the mews opened and a middle-aged man emerged. At first, Malcolm did not recognize him. The Rafiq he remembered had been a young man.

"My Lord," Rafiq said and bowed. "You have grown older and have seen much, Sir," Rafiq said. "Permit me to say how glad I am that you have chosen to return to the home of your ancestors."

"Thank you, Rafiq," Malcolm said, and knowing he would be expected to return the Indian's courtesy continued, "I am glad to see you still in health in mind and body. My father wrote me of how well you have trained and cared for the birds."

Rafiq nodded once, then looked up into his eyes with a direct gaze Malcolm had always found a bit disconcerting. Malcolm soon looked away, pretending to examine the condition of the yard and said, "I received your letter soon after I arrived last evening. I am afraid I know little about the hawks my father kept after I left for the war, or even which ones are still here."

"Oh, yes, sir, you still have a few noble hunters," Rafiq said. "A tiercel peregrine, a merlin, and a sparrow hawk. As my letter gave you to understand, Chakor, the goshawk, has flown away. It is my hope that you will consider replacing her."

For some reason, this suggestion irritated Malcolm. In a harsher voice than he intended, he said, "Why should we replace the goshawk? As you can see, I am incapable of indulging in this sport any longer. You had much better release the native birds to the wild, or perhaps we can find someone to take them off our hands."

Rafiq simply bowed his head, eyes closed, then straightened and said, "Shall you come inside? The mews is ready for your inspection."

Malcolm stood transfixed by the sight of the open door into the mews. It was taller and narrower than one would expect, made that way so handlers would pass sideways through the door when going in or out, always leading with the shoulder away from the arm where the hawk perched so as not to confuse or trouble the bird. He drew in a ragged breath. The ever-present salty, fish-scented Cornish air was overlaid here with a suggestion of something more—raw flesh, acrid bird feces, oiled leather, and a faint musky smell Malcolm associated with feathers. He could almost feel the living weight of a hawk on his forearm.

"My Lord?" Rafiq said, calling Malcolm back to the present.

"Yes, yes I suppose I must. I should." He followed the falconer into the dusky shelter of the mews, his mind and body dreading and craving the sensation at the same time.

IT DIDN'T TAKE LONG FOR ANTONELLA TO DECIDE TO GIVE THE creature who had come to her in such an unexpected way a name. She'd landed on Zephyra because goshawks could fly like the wind. A pity the injured wing prevented her from doing so at that time. Antonella knew little about the details of caring for hawks, but judging by the illustrations in the falconry books, it was apparent that they needed to be in the open air at least some of the time each day. How would she manage that without anyone seeing her? And what about the wing? Did a broken wing cause pain? How was she to keep her healthy? Was she feeding her correctly? She had so many questions.

After a few days, Zephyra seemed to be getting used to her and would allow her to approach her even at the times when she didn't have raw meat to feed her. The ability to touch Zephyra without sending her into a panic made it possible for Antonella to examine her injuries more closely. The broken feathers would soon grow back, but that one wing clearly had more serious damage. It seemed to be on the outer end, near the wingtip, so perhaps a small bone was broken, or a tendon strained. Either way, there was only one method of treatment that Antonella could think of. She would have to bind the injured wing to the hawk's body after ensuring that the bones were properly aligned. At least, that was what she would have done for the small birds. She hoped it would work equally well for Zephyra. In any case, it was unlikely to cause any serious harm. She had some strips of cambric she'd taken from the laundry for that purpose and set to work. She felt the wing tip, locating the slight lump that indicated a bone out of place. It was not completely severed, so she didn't have to do anything much, just ensure that it wouldn't be strained. What to do next though. It would be much easier if she had someone with her to hold Zephyra, or at least a hood to cover her eyes. But neither was possible. Moving slowly and deliberately, she began to wrap the wing to Zephyra's body using a strip of cloth—not too tight, though. Just enough so she wouldn't be able to flap. She left enough extra cloth to tie a knot on the outside, hoping the hawk wouldn't peck it off.

"Please heal!" Antonella said when she finished.

The next day she half expected to find the cambric in shreds beneath Zephyra's perch, but it remained miraculously in place. Zephyra chirruped softly in a sound Antonella had come to understand as a kind of greeting.

"When may I remove the bandage? Hm? Can you tell me?"

Antonella put on the stout gardening glove she'd liberated from the conservatory, placed a scrap of rabbit meat on it and held it out to Zephyra. She snatched it off the glove and made short work it, then now swiveled her head in jerks, as if listening for something.

"You're a clever lady, I think. I know you'd rather be out hunting, and I'm sorry for it, but you can't fly yet." Would she lose her training, not be willing to return when she flew off to hunt if she'd had no practice for a time?

Much as she wished she could keep Zephyra to herself forever, Antonella's practical side told her it would be impossible even if the bird wasn't clearly the property of someone, and that she'd been indulging her own pleasure thus far. That wasn't entirely fair to Zephyra. It was high time to find more experienced help. The kind of help that didn't exist in the grounds of Amblemere Court.

Still unwilling to expose her secret to anyone—even Miss Wilkins—Antonella decided she would steal onto Atherleigh Manor's lands and see if the mews she assumed to be there from everything Harry had told her years ago still stood, and whether it still housed birds or if it had been left to disuse. In any case, if abandoned, it might furnish her with some equipment—perhaps a discarded hood, or maybe a gauntlet left behind. What she really needed, though, was something better than the twine she'd used to tether Zephyra to her makeshift perch.

What, after all, would be the harm in investigating for herself? She could approach the grounds through the coombe and the spinney and claim to have got lost if anyone questioned her. As a member of a marquess's household, no matter her exact relationship, she had no doubt that she would be treated with courtesy.

And so she closed and latched the door to her makeshift mews and set off down the path toward the woods.

CHAPTER 8

*A*ntonella didn't really know what she expected to find when she crossed over onto Atherleigh land. The boundary was not well marked in the dense woods—it would have been ridiculous to expect the game it sheltered to stay on one or the other side of an arbitrary property line. She wasn't even entirely sure exactly where the border lay.

So she moved as quietly as she could and stayed in the shelter of the larger trees whenever possible. After about a quarter of a mile when she was certain she'd left Amblemere's grounds, a crumbling stone structure showed through the trees. Could that be the mews? When she drew a little closer, however, it became clear from the arched windows and the tower that the ancient stone building was a ruined chapel. A newer wooden fence had been built extending out from its north side, and as she approached, Antonella saw that it enclosed an open yard of some sort and was connected to a newer and better-kept building.

Any lingering doubt that this was indeed a mews was put to flight by the sound of a chittering call emanating from a small open window, one of three that pierced the stone wall of the mews building in the direction of the spinney.

A shiver of excitement passed down her spine. She'd never watched trained hawks hunting from close enough to really see how it was done. The one time she remembered seeing a hunt from years ago she'd been far away, across a field. The rest she could only imagine from the illustrations in *The Art of Falconry.*

She ventured still closer to the mews, unafraid of being spotted even if someone were inside the building. The fence was high enough to hide her completely, which meant it was also too high for her to see over. Likely it enclosed the weathering yard, where birds could get some fresh air, be trained, and once trained readied for the hunt. If she stayed near long enough, would the falconer bring out the merlin she had heard? Her pulse quickened at the thought. But what good would that do if she couldn't see over the fence?

Her excitement about having found the mews faded a bit when she thought of Zephyra. It seemed much more than likely that this place was her home, since there were no other neighbors near enough to Amblemere with the means or inclination to keep a falconer. And if she'd found where Zephyra actually belonged, she would have to return her to those who were more capable than she was of caring for her properly. It was only a matter of time until she must find away to bring her back.

First, though, she needed to get a better view of the weathering yard. An ancient oak tree stood at the edge of the spinney. Its lower branches were not far off the ground, and several promising sturdy limbs looked as though they might provide safe perches from which to observe the comings and goings from the mews, if there were to be any.

Antonella gathered her skirts up between her legs and tied them so they wouldn't hamper her climb then started up through the branches. In the summer, she would be all but invisible in such a tree. But so close to the start of winter only a scattering of brown leaves still clung to the branches. She would have to choose her observation point carefully if she was to remain out of view.

Her sturdy half boots slipped on the trunk as she tried to hoist herself up to the lowest branch. That would never do. She knelt down and untied them, placing them next to one of the tree's large roots. *Right, then,* she thought, and used her stockinged feet to grip the rough bark. Once she reached the first limb, her toes helped her balance and cling as she made her way to a perch some dozen feet off the ground.

From there, she could see everything. In fact, ironically, if the trees had been in leaf, she might not have had such a clear view. Of course, that meant she would be easier to see as well. Antonella counted on the fact that the falconer would not expect anyone to be up in the tree and therefore wouldn't look if he happened to come out.

She was right. The fence enclosed a weathering yard with a long wooden perch pierced by iron rings at regular intervals. The hawks would be tethered there when they were brought out for some fresh air. Two hefty wooden block perches, upside-down pyramids partially buried in the ground with tethering rings halfway up their sides, sat at opposite corners of the yard as well.

Come out so I can see! Antonella thought, training her eyes on the door to the mews, willing the falconer to emerge with a bird on his fist—a merlin at the very least. Or perhaps the mews housed a peregrine. Or a gyrfalcon!

"Rafiq!"

The loud voice startled Antonella so that she nearly lost her balance and tumbled out of her perch. A tall, dark-haired gentleman in buckskins and top boots strode down the sloping lawn toward the mews. His right arm swung by his side, but he kept his left arm tucked into his jacket and held close to his body. His movements suggested strength and discipline, with the grace of someone accustomed to moving easily through the world. A scowl gave what would have been a handsome face a fierce, uncompromising expression. This must be Major Lord Atherleigh, Antonella thought.

The baron's barked command brought an extraordinary man out of the mews a few moments later. Antonella had never before seen a person with skin of such a dusty brown hue. But that wasn't his only oddity. His plain white coat buttoned up the front, and he wore baggy pantaloons underneath it and no boots, only leather slippers on his feet. The man—the falconer, Rafiq, she guessed—removed the cloth cap from his head as he made a slow, reverent bow to Atherleigh, his palms pressed prayerfully together, the cap sandwiched between them. His bearing was—if anything—noble.

The two of them spoke for a few moments, too quietly for Antonella to hear what was said. Then Rafiq said something that made Atherleigh frown and turn slightly away, facing more in Antonella's direction. "Why should we replace the goshawk? As you can see, I am incapable of indulging in this sport any longer. You had much better release the birds to the wild, or perhaps we can find someone to take them."

The falconer kept his eyes to the ground for a moment. Then he looked up and said something else to Atherleigh that made him shake his head.

The few words Antonella managed to hear worried her. Did Lord Atherleigh intend to close his mews? Why? And if so, there would be nowhere for her to bring Zephyra. Clearly, this Rafiq had been brought from somewhere far away to care for the hunting birds. He must be very skilled at it.

This knowledge made Antonella feel even more helpless and undecided about Zephyra. She was no longer in any doubt that the goshawk had come from this very mews, which, in addition to boasting an experienced falconer, appeared to be superbly equipped and set up. How could she be so presumptuous as to think that she, who knew nothing at all about falconry beyond what she had read in a book, could possibly be qualified to keep an injured goshawk captive in by far less than ideal conditions? Perhaps she was being cruel.

Antonella continued to watch, waiting for the two men to say something else, but after more conversation she couldn't hear, the falconer gestured to Lord Atherleigh to go inside the building, and they disappeared.

IT WAS THE SMELL THAT FIRST CAUGHT AT MALCOLM'S HEART. That musty odor of feathers and leather. The faintest stench of fresh meat. The distinctive fragrance of the herbs Rafiq used to make his salves and potions—and tea as well. He breathed in and savored it before he even looked around him.

The mews had six main compartments a few feet across immediately inside the door, three on each side. Each compartment had a perch and a small, mesh-covered window opening that could be covered against stormy weather or left wide to allow in fresh air. Only three of the six compartments held birds. The tiercel with his glossy black eyes peered at Malcom from one of the little stalls near the door. After a close examination of this intruder, the bird opened its beak and started up a sharp *kek-kek-kek* sound until Rafiq muttered soothing sounds and swiftly placed a deerskin hood over the bird's head. The sparrow hawk on the other side eyed him, but perhaps his proximity to Rafiq did not alarm her and she made no sound.

And the merlin—she sat in still silence as well, her lower lids blinking up to cover her eyes as if she could not believe what she saw.

"This bird, she knows you," Rafiq said, gesturing toward the merlin.

Yes, he recognized her. She was the last bird he hunted with his father before joining his regiment. "Why are we in here, Rafiq? What have you to show me?" Once again, his words came out sounding angry.

"You see there is no goshawk. But I also wanted to show you something you may not have known, something your father wished more than anything." Rafiq drew him farther into the mews to a larger enclosure separated from the others. Unlike the other empty compartments, this one bore no sign of having ever been occupied. Its block perch was pristine—no scratches from restless talons. The floor was bare, not as if it had recently been cleaned, but as if no sand had ever touched the gleaming wood.

"What is this for?" Atherleigh asked.

"The late Lord Atherleigh's fondest wish was to one day possess a gyrfalcon. I had begun the search for an eyas for his purchase when he died."

"A gyrfalcon? Foolish beyond permission!" he snapped. Yet he and his father had talked of just such a thing at different times in his youth, always as a dream that was unlikely to be fulfilled. Purchasing a gyrfalcon would take more than the estate's annual income, if one could even be found.

"Indeed," Rafiq said. "But since the art has declined in popularity in this country, there have been a few offered for sale at prices I am almost ashamed to mention, as they are insulting to the nobility of those birds."

Did Rafiq assume he would take up his father's obsession and acquire one of those impressive, rare falcons? Then he would have to disabuse him of that notion. "Do not mistake me, Rafiq. I have come not to enlarge the mews, but to discuss dismantling it. You would, of course, receive a handsome pension."

Rafiq turned and, as if he had not heard what Malcolm said, continued. "The goshawk, Chakor, was very dear to him. He treated her with the reverence he would have given a gyrfalcon. That is why I brought her loss to your attention. I felt that, as a dutiful son, and to honor the memory of your father, you would wish to at least replace Chakor."

"No!" It was too much. Malcolm turned on his heel and strode out of the mews before Rafiq could utter another word. Its close atmosphere suddenly felt heavy and he needed to breathe. "We shall talk outside."

Before long Antonella was stiff all over and her backside hurt from sitting on the hard branch of the oak. She wanted to climb down, but was afraid to do it while Lord Atherliegh remained inside the mews. Besides, she hadn't yet caught sight of that merlin whose call she had heard before, or the peregrine that chittered for a short time after Atherleigh had entered the mews. Would Rafiq bring one out to weather, even if he had no intention of hunting?

Pointless to conjecture.

But at that moment, to Antonella's surprise, Atherleigh emerged from the mews with an expression of even greater disapproval, as if what he'd seen within displeased him. Rafiq followed a few moments later with a falcon perched on the gauntlet he wore on his left hand. It was the peregrine, on the small side, so perhaps a male—a tiercel. A perfectly fitted leather hood with a loop on its top covered its head. The bird spread its wings and flapped several times as soon as it was in the open and looked as if it was about to bate. But Rafiq leaned close to the falcon's breast and sprayed a thin stream of water from between his lips, which had the remarkable effect of quieting the bird almost immediately.

Did he intend to fly the peregrine? Antonella yearned to see it! But no. Rafiq took the falcon to one of the block perches, settled it there and clipped the tether to its jesses before gently and smoothly removing the bird's hood.

Antonella's attention had been so focused on the falcon that she hadn't noticed anything else. A movement disturbed her, and she saw Atherleigh put his hand up to cover his eyes and then turn away, but not before she caught an expression of intense pain on his face. Why pain?

A moment later, with a quick nod to Rafiq and not saying another word, Atherleigh marched briskly up the slope in the direction of the manor house. He did not look back.

Antonella had been so rapt in observing what was happening in the weathering yard that she hadn't realized she'd shifted her position in the tree. She'd moved just enough so that anyone who cared to look up in that direction might be able to catch sight of her.

Which was, of course, exactly what happened.

Rafiq stood very still, his eyes trained on her, uncompromising, challenging. Antonella supposed he was waiting for her to come down. What would happen? How could she explain herself? What would he say to her? She was trespassing. This part of the spinney was most definitely on Atherleigh land. But the falconer's expression held more curiosity than anger.

Oh well. She was going to have to ask the question soon anyhow, for the sake of the goshawk. She picked her way down the limbs, retracing her route upward, and dropped the last six feet onto the ground. She put her boots back on and retied the laces. In a moment of indecision, she stood where she was. She could just run away, she thought. But that would be a childish thing to do, and she was no longer that mischievous sprite who could outrun most of the neighbor boys as well as Belinda.

Besides, in the time it had taken her to climb down, Rafiq had opened a section of the wooden fence that separated the weathering yard from the spinney, a gate that she couldn't have seen from her side of the enclosure. He stood unmoving, expectant.

Antonella smoothed down her cloak and patted her hair back into place—it had suffered some dishevelment on her way through the branches—and picked her way toward the open gate and Rafiq. She stopped about a yard away and said, "How do you do. I'm—"

"I know who you are. You are Lady Antonella. Birds interest you?"

She wasn't entirely certain whether the last part of his utterance was a question or a statement.

"Yes," she said, "although it's just Antonella now, or Miss Ambleton."

Rafiq nodded without asking for an explanation, but stepped aside and motioned her to enter the weathering yard.

Her eyes went immediately to the peregrine, and she took a step toward the bird.

"Do not approach. He does not know you."

Of course, this was not a wild bird, but one that had been trained to respond to very particular humans. "He is magnificent," she breathed.

"Why are you here?"

It was not a question Antonella was accustomed to being asked by a servant, and her first instinct was to bristle and snap at him to mind his own business. But then she remembered that she was the interloper here. "I came because I take care of injured birds, and I thought you might be able to give me some advice."

"Advice?"

"I have lately found a bird of a sort I have never tended before, and was hoping you might be able to enlighten me about an aspect of care."

"What sort of bird, and what is its injury?"

"A broken wing, I believe," Antonella said, ignoring the first part of his question.

Rafiq shook his head. "It is important to know which bone is broken. The larger bones are difficult. The smaller can heal. Birds are strong but delicate. You must let nature heal them."

"But on smaller birds I can often help a broken wing mend, even if it's their radius. And I protect them while they are weak so they don't become prey."

At that Rafiq smiled. "It is a circle, My Lady. Some of the small, weak creatures must take their roles as prey for larger birds or other animals so that the cycle may continue. Your foundlings, they will only die when you let them go."

Antonella knew in her heart that this was often true. It didn't stop her doing her best to give them a chance of returning to nest and breed another season. "Still, you must have had hawks, falcons that have become injured. What do you do?"

"We care for them if we can. The smaller wounds need rest and immobility. The larger ones—who can say. The birds mend *insha'Allah*," he said, turning away from her and going over to the peregrine to untwist the tether the bird had managed to tangle. Over his shoulder he said, "Once they are wounded, they become weak with rest. It is a long process to ready them to hunt again."

"But the small birds fly away when I have healed them."

He shrugged. "They are weak. They do not long remain alive after that."

She gulped. She knew it was true, but preferred not to think about it. Still, she needed to get some more practical guidance out of the falconer. "What happens if one of the falcons, or a hawk perhaps, breaks a wing?"

Rafiq pressed his palms together as she'd seen him do when greeting Lord Atherleigh and closed his eyes. "Now, with only myself to care for the birds, if the break is too severe, she is destroyed."

Antonella felt as if someone had just dumped a bucket of icy water over her. She had come here hoping to enlist the falconer—or even Lord Atherleigh—to help her heal Zephyra. But that's not what they would do. They would condemn her to death rather than try to make her whole again. She didn't think Zephyra's break was very bad, but how was she to know?

So it was up to her. She would have to learn what she could about caring for the goshawk, get Rafiq to help her unknowingly. And then, when Zephyra was whole again, bring her back—but only if she was certain they would let her live.

If not, she would cut off her jesses and release her to the wild. She would have been dead to them already anyway.

CHAPTER 9

*A*ntonella had stayed talking to Rafiq for an hour. At first, she felt wary, afraid that he would guess that her questions were not general, but pertained specifically to Zephyra. She told Rafiq that she overheard mention of the goshawk, hoping that would encourage him to talk more about how to care for a hawk that large. Apparently, the name of the missing goshawk was Chakor, which was from the folklore of Rafiq's homeland, the Punjab in India. Chakor was a legendary bird that longed for the moon. That could fit Zephyra as well. But did hawks recognize their names? Dogs and cats did, she knew. Yet birds were somehow different.

As she wandered the long way home, Antonella wondered if she should start calling Zephyra Chakor instead, whether it would possibly make a difference. Other thoughts came and went as she considered all that Rafiq had told her, wondering how she might wheedle more guidance from him without revealing her secret.

A horse whinnied from the other side of a hedge a few yards away that bordered the field. A moment later came a heavy thump and a crash of breaking twigs. "Damn and blast this cursed arm!"

Antonella ran toward the curses, which continued to erupt sporadically, although with less and less heat and anger.

Soon enough their source came into view. A gentleman she recognized as Lord Atherleigh from his coat, buckskin breeches, and the dark hair that curled out from under his hat was on the ground next to a horse, holding its reins. The beast stood docile now, snorting occasionally. "Are you hurt?" Antonella called as she drew cautiously nearer.

She had not seen much of Atherleigh's face from her perch up high in the oak tree, and was therefore unprepared for the piercing, anguished look of his shadowed brown eyes, the sculpted cheekbones and noble nose above a strong but shapely mouth—a mouth that might be able to smile but just then was drawn down in a fierce scowl.

"No!" he barked, then took a breath. "Forgive me. I'm not accustomed to female society. I imagine your delicate sensibilities have been offended by my language."

Although Antonella had never heard a gentleman use the kind of expressions that had issued from Atherleigh's mouth, she'd spent enough time near the farm hands and menials to know what they meant. "I'm sure I don't know what you mean," she said.

This made one corner of Atherleigh's mouth lift in an ironic half smile. "Putting on the airs of a fine lady. Or are you one of the fey who live in the woods? You have the look of the pixie about you." He got to his knees and tried to rise in the slick mud, but did not let go of the reins and kept his other arm tucked inside his coat, which unbalanced him. "You need not trouble yourself over me. I'll get out of this mess by and by."

He continued to struggle and muttered another vile

expletive under his breath. Clearly something prevented him from regaining his footing. Antonella wondered if it was the muddy patch that made him slip. "Sir, Lord Atherleigh I believe, please allow me to help you." She stepped forward, setting aside her usual reticence.

"No!" he said in a voice so gruff that she halted in her tracks.

"But, My Lord..."

He shook his head, then hung it dejectedly. "Hah! Who am I fooling? Only myself. My horse spooked when a rabbit jumped across his path. He shied sideways and it caught me off guard. I have only one hand to use, you see. I'm useless. Which is also why I find myself unable to rise from the ground."

Ah, Antonella thought. The wound. His left hand. That was it. Had it not yet entirely healed? "Do you intend to just stay there all night? If not, I suggest you let me help you, and then you can go on your way. I assure you I am quite human, and stronger than I look."

"Bolder as well, I see," he said, but not in a disapproving way. After a brief, considering gaze, he added, "Better come and see what can be done then."

Antonella closed the distance between them, wondering if his mishap had occurred on Atherleigh or Amblemere land. How silly, she thought, the idea that one could own a piece of the earth and presume to keep others from it. When she made her way to Atherleigh she reached down to take him by the left elbow.

Again he uttered a gruff, "No! If you could take my horse's reins I can manage on my own."

Antonella gulped. A horse. As long as it was far away from her, with Atherleigh between her and it, she was fine. But to hold the reins she would have to be closer. The animal was huge. She pictured herself trampled beneath those hooves. "I-I'd rather not," she squeaked out.

He looked up at her, his eyes penetrating. "Are you afraid? I thought all girls in the country were bruising riders."

"Not this one, My Lord." Antonella backed a little away.

"Well, then, we do have a problem. I was going to ask you to hold the gelding's head while I did my best to scramble up in an altogether ungainly fashion, with no mounting block or groom to help me back into the saddle. You see, it's normally a two-handed operation."

At that, he removed his left arm from where it was hidden inside his coat and held up the bandaged end of a stump. No hand at all. So not an injury that could be healed with time. He was permanently maimed.

The comprehension of this fact deprived Antonella momentarily of the ability to speak. With no left hand it would be nearly impossible for him to hunt his birds. That must have been the reason he told Rafiq that he would be reducing his mews, perhaps closing it altogether.

"Don't stand there like a simpleton," Atherleigh said, his voice dripping with disdain. "If you aren't willing to help me then please leave me to figure it out on my own. Or better still, run and tell my groom where he can find me." His tone of command made it clear he thought she was some trades-man's daughter or other person of low estate. Which, for all she knew, she was.

Nonetheless, she couldn't bring herself to just leave him there, even to go get help. "What's its name?"

"I beg your pardon?" Atherleigh paused, one knee on the ground, the other bent up and serving as a rest for his left elbow.

"The horse."

"Mercury. Although he might once have been so fleet of

foot, he's an old fellow now—twelve years, I think—and as quiet as can be. You needn't worry over him."

That was easy for him to say. "Perhaps his name should be Invidia, then." It was insane that she should be so fearful of horses. Horses were an unavoidable fact of life, especially in the country. Yet for all their ubiquity, nothing else truly frightened her. Antonella believed she could face a badger more easily. Perhaps it was the gross imbalance in size, she thought, between her own small self and that powerful package of muscle and bone. That, and the memory of her first disastrous riding lesson, when she was thrown and broke her arm. *Don't be so foolish!* she admonished herself. *You're not four anymore.* She stood tall and reached her hand out to take the reins from Atherleigh.

"Don't be tentative. But don't grip them hard. He'll sense your fear. He won't hurt you, but he'll be skittish and it will be harder for me to manage to mount again."

Antonella's hands were perspiring inside her gloves, yet the afternoon had turned quite cold. Was it the fear, or something else?

"Not like that. Here." Atherleigh slipped his hand up the reins to where she'd barely touched them and covered them easily with his one hand. "That's it."

Antonella had little experience of men, and certainly had never felt the touch of a strong male hand holding so tightly onto hers. A jolt of something passed up her arms and down into her stomach. The sensation was not unpleasant. In fact, quite the opposite. And Mercury stood blessedly still.

"I'm going to let go now," Atherleigh said, his voice curiously rough.

For a moment, an unaccustomed wave of panic and disappointment washed over Antonella. She swallowed hard.

"You can do it," he said.

With an effort, Antonella smiled, although it wasn't

sincere enough to mask her true sentiments. To her great surprise, Atherleigh smiled back and his eyes lit up in amusement. A moment later, he released her hands.

She wished he hadn't. The warmth of his contact had given her a little courage. Now she had only her own resources to call upon. She put all her effort into trying not to clutch the reins too hard.

Atherleigh pushed himself up with his good hand and stood next to her. He was very tall. She had to crane her neck to look up into his face.

"What I'm now going to do is very ungainly, and Mercury won't like it." He took the reins from her and tossed them back over the horse's head. "I need you to take hold of both reins again, just above the bit."

This was pushing Antonella so far into the realm of her worst fears that she started to tremble. But that was foolish. What did she have to worry about? This man, this soldier, had been terribly wounded in battle, and he wasn't afraid. She had the sense, in fact, that nothing could frighten him. Surely it was not beyond her ability to hold the reins of a calm horse. She stretched out her arm and grasped them as he instructed, standing as far away as possible.

"You know, this fellow likes nothing better than to have his nose rubbed. Do you think you could get closer and do that?"

Antonella shook her head, eyes wide.

"Very well. I'd be grateful if you didn't watch me."

She turned her gaze away, looking toward the spinney, noticing that the light was already fading. It must be near dinner time.

Aside from a few grunts and a sensation that Atherleigh's large presence no longer stood next to her, Antonella had no idea how the baron managed to get up into the saddle without being able to use his left hand. The horse shifted under his weight and she started.

"You can let go now. And I have been very impolite. I was so concerned with my own predicament that I did not ask your name," he said. "Especially rude of me since you know mine."

"Antonella, Sir." Something made her withhold her surname. He needn't know precisely who she was.

"Antonella? Quite a mouthful. Who do you belong to? One of Lewiston's tenants? Someone in town?"

What could she say? She opted for saying nothing, but merely smiled and dipped a small curtsy.

"Very well. I won't tell tales if you're trespassing. What are you doing out here all on your own? It's not safe. There could be gypsies. Unless you..."

"No, I'm not a traveler!" She lifted one eyebrow and stood as tall as she could, unaccountably insulted by his assumption. "And if I am trespassing, so are you."

She expected him to be affronted by her tone, but he let out a short bark of a laugh. "Is this Amblemere land? I suppose it is. You won't tell anyone, I hope?" The gleam in his eye told her that he well knew she wouldn't. With a nod, he said, "Good day, Antonella."

He turned the horse, then clucked and took off at a trot, which became a canter that soon lengthened into a gallop. How did he manage? Wasn't he afraid he'd fall again?

Antonella stood and watched him disappear across the field. He looked solid and confident in the saddle, even with only one hand to hold him there. When he'd gone over the rise and disappeared, she turned and continued toward home.

Something had shifted that day. Her two experiences—at the mews and then coming to Lord Atherleigh's aid—had disturbed her on levels she could hardly imagine. First the strange, foreign falconer with his air of wisdom and willingness to tell her whatever she wanted to know about raptors, except the one thing she really needed to know. And then this magnificent noble soldier. So physically perfect. So flawed. She imagined that his wounds were deeper than those that showed on his body. How could one's heart and soul not suffer damage from the sharp, unremitting horrors of war?

He'd chosen to return to the manor, his manor, rather than remain in London where doubtless he had friends. Was he here alone? Odd that she had no recollection of ever having met or even seen him before. Unless ... Had it been he all those years ago in the field, perhaps with his father? If so, he must have been sent away to school after that. At first, after helping him back onto his horse she wondered whether she'd ever encounter him again.

But by the time she got home, she knew that fate—in the form of a wounded goshawk—had bound them together in some yet-to-be-determined manner, and found that this thought did not dismay her.

CHAPTER 10

*B*elinda hardly had time to revel in the quantities of flowers that had been delivered to Lewiston House before her mother announced with a tremulous voice that they would be returning to Cornwall the very next day.

"So soon!" Belinda exclaimed. Although she knew—after overhearing the argument between her brother and her mother the day before—that their departure was imminent, she didn't think it would be so immediate. Her spirits plummeted. The image she had in her mind of Gainesworth's brilliant eyes with their glint of humor dissolved like morning fog.

"Really, there's not enough company here to do you any good anyway, and we can't entertain with things as they are. At least, my son tells me his wife is not disposed to do so." Her lower lip trembled as she lifted her coffee cup to sip. "Ladies of her station ought to have a wetnurse. Unless things have changed so very much since I was first a mother. I had no choice in the matter."

The peevish note in her mother's voice didn't escape Belinda. Loath as she was to admit it to herself, she found she was more in sympathy with the dowager's sentiments than was quite kind. To be so near to entering society and then dragged away from it was maddening. Earlier that morning she'd spent a pleasant hour rereading all the cards that came with the posies, often not even being able to conjure up an image of their senders. Except for one, of course. The more she thought about Mr. Gainesworth, the more she tried to picture him with Antonella. She had a hard time of it, unable to get past her own involuntary responses to his expressions, his smile, his firm but gentle touch as he led her onto the dance floor. But what did she really know about him? He was amusing, certainly, but he would have to be more than that to be worthy of Antonella. And would he be interested in her, now that she had no title? He had none either. And according to the duchess, his fortune came from trade.

She sighed. It was no use plotting and scheming on her sister's behalf. Neither of them would see Gainesworth again. He would stay in London and she would go away. Buried in Cornwall, how were either of them to find true love? Almost certainly Mr. Gainesworth's mention of Lord Atherleigh had been nothing more than a way of striking up conversation. And back in Cornwall, the few neighborhood families of rank were bereft of sons of the appropriate age to be considered as suitors. The local assemblies attracted a wider selection of guests, but if the summer was anything to judge by, few if any young men could be of the least interest to either herself or Antonella. Ant had danced twice with an officer from Boscastle at one of them, and Belinda thought something might come of it. He was charming and dashing, but he never called.

Perhaps her mother would relent in the spring and allow Antonella to come to London for the season as well. By then, perhaps, Antonella's position as a distant cousin but still a connection to a noble family would be generally accepted, and having had the protection and sponsorship of a marquess to raise her would confer enough consequence on her to render her eligible to someone who really fell in love with her.

It was all so confusing. When Papa was alive, he loved both of them equally, even slightly favoring clever, mercurial Antonella over her. Had their mother really told them the truth? And if so, why had it been concealed for so long? Belinda had doubts about the convenient tale that Antonella was a poor relation, although she couldn't have said exactly why. She and Antonella bore little enough physical resemblance to each other, yet they had a kinship that suggested something closer than cousins. Whatever it was, Mama seemed to think she and her sister had no need—or right—to know more than she had told them.

So, after a week and a single *ton* party, Belinda and her mother—and the postilion, the groom, two maids, and a mountain of baggage—once more jolted over the roads between London and Cornwall in the old traveling carriage. Instead of high anticipation, Belinda's spirits sank to her feet in expectation of a quiet, tedious holiday season at Amblemere that would be depressingly like all the holidays that had gone before.

THE VERY NEXT MORNING AFTER THE GRANVILLE'S DRESS party, Gainesworth sent a letter express to Atherleigh. He would not leave anything to chance. He would visit for as long as it took in Cornwall—a place he'd been to once or twice as a school friend of Atherleigh, but that he'd seen no need ever to visit again—until now. His threat to come down and keep Malcolm company as he wallowed in self-pity had been just that—a threat, which he had had no real intention of carrying out. Atherleigh Manor was in the middle of nowhere, in a place whose inhospitable climate with its constant wind and storms blowing in from the sea made outdoor sport erratic at best. The hunting was mediocre, although the novelty of watching Atherleigh and his father hunt with the falcons had been memorable. Not memorable enough to make him yearn to see it again, however.

Not until he met Lady Belinda Ambleton.

What was he saying? Had he gone mad in a matter of hours? He wasn't quite certain what had come over him. He'd dallied with many come-outs over the course of a half dozen seasons. He knew the game, could flirt with the best of them up to the point just before any serious hopes would be raised, and then find a way to extricate himself without causing any offense. He'd made rather an art of it, he thought with a degree of satisfaction. There was that time with Lady Violet Chase a few seasons ago. She was quite delectable, as he recalled. Those slanting green, feline eyes. Most fortunate that he'd pulled back from the flirtation when he had, though. He might have found himself leg shackled to her and saddled with a house full of her young siblings and a shrewish mother-in-law who saw in him a fortune to be won.

Yes, he'd had several near misses. So why was he now so willing to throw himself headlong into something that might embroil him in serious consequences? He did not know why. He only knew that he was.

Lady Belinda … How to describe her? He'd seen prettier. More classically beautiful, with better figures. But something about Lady Belinda refused to release its hold on him. Her eyes were a clear, innocent blue—at least, that's how they appeared at first. When she spoke in her outrageous manner or found something ridiculous, a sparkle of intelligent wit lit them from within. She was young and truly innocent—

ingenuous, unspoiled—qualities that had previously sent him running the opposite way as soon as he perceived them. But her blushes lacked artifice, and her ready laugh tumbled cheerily and unaffectedly out of her pert, pouty lips when something was actually funny, not as a way to flatter a gentleman who had tried to appear witty. No, Lady Belinda was no scheming come-out to be toyed with just to give her a taste of her own medicine. The idea that she could ever be a schemer seemed preposterous, even on so little acquaintance.

Yet he supposed she could possibly be ambitious for a brilliant match. As the daughter of a marquess, she might look as high as she wanted if that were her motive in taking part in the season. In fact, it could be that her rank would disqualify him, a mere mister. His mother's family dated back to the Conquest, but his father had been what impolite society called a chicken nabob. It had made the family ludicrously wealthy, and his maternal grandfather had been content to overlook the origins of so handsome a fortune in allowing the match. Had his mother been on the catch for a rich husband? He would never know. His parents had seemed extremely fond of each other. Bartholomew Gainesworth grieved deeply when his wife died giving birth to her last child, his sister Lucy. He went to his own death a few years ago. No, theirs was no match of convenience.

What about Lady Belinda? The title was grand, and Harry had done his best to restore the fortune his father gambled away. Although as far as Hector knew the family lived in comfort, no one called them wealthy. Only Lewiston's marriage to the Ambrose heiress placed him on a lofty financial level. No doubt Lady Belinda had a decent portion in her own right, but he had no need to consider such things. The question was, did she?

No. Lady Belinda did not look around her with that

calculating zeal so many ingenues brought with them when they entered society. She seemed open. Vulnerable. And she probably had no idea of his fortune until after she left, when he had no doubt the duchess would tell her all about it. In the hour he'd spent with her at the party, he'd seen no evidence of guile, nor did she throw out intentional lures. In fact, Lady Belinda had said things calculated to put him off from the very first moment they met. He found her funny. Charming. Enchanting. And completely artless.

The one thing that puzzled him, though, was the way she spoke of her sister. Lady Belinda seemed to believe herself in some way the inferior of the two. Perhaps this sister's opinion carried disproportionate weight with her. Sisters could be important. In his experience, they were either fiercely competitive and fighting over suitors like dogs over a juicy bone, or so close one couldn't separate them with a razor. He feared the latter in Lady Belinda's case. He supposed that would be preferable, at least insofar as what it might reveal of her character. In any event, Gainesworth decided he must cultivate the sister if he was to have a hope of fixing his interest with Lady Belinda.

Naturally, he'd sent a posy around to Lewiston House that morning. Not roses—too ostentatious. Michaelmas daisies and ivy. Would she interpret the gesture as he intended? How many other floral tributes would she receive? She certainly hadn't lacked for partners. He considered paying a call, but remembered that the young Lady Lewiston had just been confined and visitors would not be welcome.

He'd also gone riding in the park that morning earlier than was his wont. The effort proved vain, though. Lady Belinda did not appear.

No matter. He had every intention of availing himself of more exclusive access to her in the country. There he was far less likely to be one among many.

Such were the thoughts going through his mind that afternoon at White's, where he stopped in for a drink and a bit of company before meeting friends for dinner and the theatre. Naturally the conversation turned to the previous evening's party. Nearly everyone had been there.

"Terrible squeeze, don't ye think, Gainesworth?" It was Irwin Batchelder, a deplorable whist player who had just sacrificed a high trump card to his opponent's over-trump, much to the consternation of his partner.

"Yes, and I daresay Lady Granville was delighted. Two young misses fainted from the heat—quite an accomplishment at this time of year—and I have it on good authority that over a dozen flounces were stepped on and torn," said Gainesworth drily as he observed the game, which ended predictably with the complete rout of Batchelder and his long-suffering partner.

"You seemed to be quite taken with Lewiston's young sister, Gainesworth," said Lord Devlin, who stood up from the table having won a substantial sum from Batchelder.

Devlin, Gainesworth recalled, had danced twice with Lady Belinda.

"No chance to take it further, though, if the wind lies in that quarter for you," Devlin said. "Dashing off back to Devonshire—no, Cornwall I believe—tomorrow morning, so my man tells me."

Leaving so soon? She didn't say anything to him about it. Perhaps she hadn't known. Good thing he'd sent the letter to Atherleigh already! If he were to make the most of the situation it would only just arrive before he did. "They haven't been here long, I collect. Did we displease her so much?" Gainesworth hoped his jest would encourage Devlin to disclose a little more information.

Predictably, Devlin obliged. "Apparently the marchioness is indisposed following the birth of the heir. Although the dowager was none too pleased and I gather not altogether sympathetic. She's keen to marry her beautiful daughter to a man of rank as well as fortune, and there are few enough of those in the wilds of Cornwall."

Gainesworth said nothing more. He wasn't certain he liked what he'd just learned about the dowager Lady Lewiston. It sounded as if she wouldn't relish a plain mister as a son-in-law.

Are you mad? he thought again. Who said anything about in-laws! He hardly knew Lady Belinda. And perhaps the time in the country would dampen his enthusiasm. His capacity for flirtation was only matched by his capacity for becoming bored.

Somehow, he didn't think that would happen with Lady Belinda, although he was hard put to say exactly why.

No matter. After finishing his Madeira, Gainesworth took his leave to meet a few friends at Limmer's Hotel and try to distract himself away from constant thoughts of the young, captivating Lady Belinda Ambleton.

CHAPTER 11

"*B*ee! You're here!"

Antonella's screech of joy greeted Belinda as they rumbled into the courtyard that separated the two wings of the house—the feature that gave it the name of Amblemere Court. Antonella ran toward the coach almost before it came to a halt, no shawl and hair flying, and waited a few yards away as the postilion drew the horses to a stop. Bee tapped her foot impatiently until the footman opened the carriage door, let down the step, and handed her mother decorously out. Without waiting to be assisted, she jumped down and raced to Ant.

The two of them embraced and uttered shrieks of laughter, hardly hearing Lady Lewiston say, "Control yourselves! You're behaving like wild creatures. I did not raise you in a back slum."

Antonella dutifully closed her mouth, extricated herself from Belinda's embrace, and curtsied. "Hello Aunt Caroline. Did you have a pleasant journey?"

After the briefest nod to Antonella, the dowager said to

Belinda, "Go in and freshen up. Dinner will be in less than an hour.' She swept past them and into the house.

"I want to hear everything!" Antonella said, threading her arm through Belinda's.

Belinda frowned at the retreating figure of her mother. "Honestly."

"Don't give it a moment's thought!" Antonella said. "All I care about is your news."

Belinda shook off her vexation and smiled. "We were only there for a few days, so *everything* isn't very much."

"But I can see something in your expression. Something's happened, hasn't it! Did you fall in love?"

Belinda opened her eyes wide. "No! What makes you say that? Oh never mind now, let's get out of this cold wind and let me show you the fan I bought for you."

They scampered inside and went up to Belinda's room where Falk was already unpacking her trunk. The maid, although not privy to everything that passed between the girls, was trustworthy enough not to warrant shooing from the room. And so Belinda gave her sister as full an account as she thought prudent of what had occurred during their short stay in Lewiston House.

"Did Mama really say those things to Harry?" Antonella asked.

Belinda nodded. "I think she fears we'll both be left on the shelf."

"Well, I don't think she cares much what becomes of me anymore. I daresay she never really did." Antonella said this with a wistful sigh that held no rancor. "In truth, I don't see myself married. Not now. How could I manage it? Who would want me? I wish I could just remain here forever, keep things exactly as they are. I'm contented enough."

Was she truly? Ant appeared to have reconciled herself to

her altered status. It wasn't in her nature to brood—at least not so anyone knew it. But Belinda believed the sister she knew so well was keeping her true feelings buried. Doing so was bred into her. A lady did not display effusive emotions. She wouldn't be able to shrug off eighteen years of training to be a lady in a few short weeks. And Antonella was a lady, whatever the status of her true parents. The unalterable fact of life was that ladies must marry. Contemplating the alternative sent a shiver down Belinda's spine. "What's so wonderful about the way things are that you wouldn't want them to change?"

An expression Belinda recognized came into Antonella's face. She had a secret. Her sidelong glance at Falk made it a certainty, so Belinda said, "Falk, that's enough for now. Would you just lay out my evening dress? Antonella can help me into it. We have so much catching up to do."

The maid curtsied and smiled her understanding. "I've already put something out for you in your room, Miss Antonella," she said, and closed the door softly behind her.

"Now, what is it? What have you been up to?" Belinda dragged her sister to sit in the chair by the fire and knelt down next to her. "Have *you* fallen in love?"

Antonella was momentarily stunned by Belinda's question. *Have you fallen in love?* It was so out of the blue, so completely unexpected. And yet, some part of what she'd been feeling in these past few days—ever since she had her conversation with Rafiq and helped the wounded Lord Atherleigh climb back onto his horse—had been disturbing in ways she could hardly define.

"Of course not!" she said.

But Belinda's piercing blue eyes gazed fixedly into hers. "I see this absence from each other has put more than time between us. You're not telling me something. Something big."

"I might say the same of you!" Antonella always found

that when dealing with Belinda, attack was the best defense. And indeed, a blush raced into her sister's cheeks.

"Now you're teasing me, and I promise you, I haven't fallen in love. But I have met someone interesting. Someone I wish I could introduce to you, because I have a strong feeling you'd like him." Belinda stood and turned around so Antonella could untie the back of her muslin day dress. "But it's no use. We had to come back to Cornwall much too soon."

Poor Belinda, Antonella thought. She was made for a London season, for flitting from rout party to picnic to Almack's assembly—although there were none of those until the spring. She'd clearly had the merest taste and it had whetted her appetite for more. "But surely the masquerade ball will be in a few days! I'm at least glad you've returned because Mama might not have decided to host it if you'd stayed too long in London and only come home right before Christmas. Now it can be at its usual time."

"Yes, choosing our costumes will occupy some of the time while we suffer the dreary weather. But what else is there to do at this time of year?"

"Well ..." It was the moment to decide how much of her adventures with Zephyra to tell Belinda about. Her sister did not share her deep love of birds, but she understood how important they were to her. "I need to show you something. Tomorrow."

"Oh Ant! How can you be so provoking!"

"I won't do it all justice if I just tell you. Be patient. We can go for a walk in the morning and then you'll see, and I'll tell you everything."

Before Belinda could protest any more, a light tap on the door and the familiar, gentle voice of Miss Wilkins said, "May I come in?"

"Of course," Belinda said.

The governess entered and said, "Antonella! You had better change quickly. I've just come from the dowager's room and she said she will want dinner at precisely five o'clock. That only gives you fifteen minutes!"

Antonella twisted her lips and said, "I don't want to change. It's too cold to wear evening dress. And I said I'd help Belinda."

"Your paisley shawl will keep you warm, and I will help Lady Belinda finish." Miss Wilkins took Antonella's elbow and steered her to the door. "You don't want to start out irritating your M—Aunt. She's tired and out of sorts as it is."

ONCE THE DOOR HAD CLOSED BEHIND ANTONELLA, MISS Wilkins fixed Belinda with a long look before strolling to her and helping her step into her silk twill evening dress. "You didn't stay in London very long. Your sister missed you, but I expect you had other matters to attend to."

Even though Miss Wilkins was standing behind her as she pulled the ties at the back of her gown, Belinda could feel her perceptive gaze. "I did go to one *ton* party. A dress party, with the Duchess of Hartland."

"And?"

Belinda whirled around and took hold of Miss Wilkins's shoulders. "I have a plan! I hate what's happened to Ant. I still don't believe it's really true. And so I'm going to do something about it."

Miss Wilkins tucked one of Belinda's stray curls up into her topknot and said, "I think she's deeply disturbed by what's happened. I'm afraid that the masquerade ball next week will be trying for her."

"So it will definitely be then?"

"That's what your Mama wanted to talk to me about. I'm

glad for you, but It will be the first time Antonella has to face the neighborhood as simply Miss Ambleton."

"I know. I keep trying to imagine how I would feel if it were me." She shivered. "I simply can't. I don't have anything else to give my life any meaning, not like Ant has. I'm just a lady. A lady ready to do all the things necessary for those of my ilk. But oh, Wilkie!" She gave the governess a spontaneous embrace.

"It appears to me as if you had more than your sister's happiness in mind while you were in London." Her keen gray eyes twinkled.

What did she see? Belinda wondered. And then she thought perhaps Miss Wilkins was mistaken. "No, I promise! I did have Antonella on my mind the whole time. You see, I want to find her a match. I did meet a person who I thought would be perfect for Antonella, only he is in London, and unless I can persuade Mama to let her make her come-out with me, it will all be to no avail."

Miss Wilkins continued to help Belinda dress, fastening her pearl necklet and tidying her hair so that she was ready to go down for dinner in just a few moments.

Before she left her room, though, Belinda turned her searching eyes to Miss Wilkins. "Ant says she has something to show me. Do you know what it is? Will I like it?"

Miss Wilkins threw her head back and allowed her musical laugh to fill the room. "I think you had better see for yourself. Antonella would not thank me for spoiling her surprise, even if I knew what it was—which I don't."

Belinda affected an air of pique, but she knew it wouldn't fool the governess. "Are you joining us for dinner?" she said.

Looking away from her, Miss Wilkins said, "Not this evening. I'll take my dinner with Mrs. Cobbey. No doubt the three of you will have much to discuss."

When it was just the family, Miss Wilkins often joined

them for dinner—four at table was preferable to three, according to the dowager, who appreciated the governess's acuity and charm. However, in the few short hours since she had set foot in the house again, Belinda sensed a subtle change. She would have been hard pressed to say exactly what that was, but she had no doubt it was somehow related to Antonella's altered position in the family hierarchy— which only made her more determined to see her plan for Antonella through to its end.

"You will join us in the drawing room for tea, though, won't you?"

Miss Wilkins smiled and nodded. "Now go! Or you'll be late."

SEVERAL THINGS HAPPENED IN THE DAYS AFTER MALCOLM HAD his discussion with Rafiq and made his first attempt at riding one-handed. First, he realized that mounting, controlling, and dismounting a horse with the use of only one hand bore a strong resemblance to managing those operations with a falcon perched on his glove. He had had some practice, in other words. If he tricked himself into thinking that instead lacking a hand to take hold of the pommel or the reins the hand that should have been there was occupied with something else, he thought he could learn to feel quite comfortable in the saddle.

Comfortable, yet still bereft.

Also disturbing was the fact that he found himself unaccountably thinking back to the girl who had helped him rise from the muck at that embarrassing juncture. Something about her seemed familiar. She was too young to be someone he had seen her in his youth. But she looked at him as if she knew him more than just by name, as if she had glimpsed something inside him in some strange, other-worldly way. He'd thought at first that she must be a peasant or a servant or a gypsy. But she didn't speak like one, and her manners were too well-bred besides. Not to mention the fact that not many peasant girls knew enough mythology or had enough education to conjure up the name of the Roman equivalent of Nemesis.

A puzzle. Why did he think he need solve it? Surely he would not encounter her again.

He had little time to consider the matter, however. Gainesworth's letter had arrived three days ago, saying he would be in Cornwall in three days. Which meant he would arrive from London that very day on a hired post chaise, and was having his hunters follow him down with his groom and his curricle.

This was a bad sign. It meant he intended to stay for more than a flying visit. Why he couldn't simply retire to his own estate in Somerset was beyond Atherleigh's power to imagine. It was a pleasant enough place with a large park, but he claimed not to have congenial neighbors, only cousins he didn't like, and would rather not have to entertain. At least, that was his excuse for always angling for an invitation to visit somewhere else over Christmas.

Malcolm smiled grimly. The quick-witted, fashionable gentleman wouldn't get much entertainment at Atherleigh Manor. But he supposed it would be no bad thing to have Hector's company. Better than dining alone. And the fellow could be dashed entertaining. No doubt he'd arrive supplied with all the latest gossip of the *ton.* He played a decent game of piquet, and could hold his own at billiards.

What am I thinking? Doing either of those things would be difficult. It seemed every time Malcolm turned his mind to something new, the extent of the change in his everyday existence because of his incapacity cut into him like a saber.

On the morning of Gainesworth's arrival, Atherleigh received an invitation to the annual costume ball at Amblemere Court. Lady Lewiston's scribbled note said that he and any houseguests he might be entertaining for the holidays would be most welcome to attend. Did she know? Unlikely. Malcolm examined the elegant pasteboard card with misgiving. After such a personal entreaty it would be churlish to stay away. Besides, he doubted Hector would allow him to do so. What was he getting himself into now? It appeared certain that Malcolm's quiet, introverted world was in danger of being turned inside out. What made him think so? To start, the fact that he had no clear idea why Hector was coming to visit him. Surely not simply to prevent his descent into complete misanthropy. There had to be a more compelling reason than that, and Malcolm had a strong suspicion his friend would embroil him in some mischief or other.

It was always that way with Hector. He had the best of intentions, sowed chaos and confusion wherever he went, and somehow—with a smile, a tease, a sheepish look managed to smooth everything over and remain beloved of all his friends.

Gainesworth arrived just before dinner, and the business of his arrival, the settling of his valet and unpacking his things, took up all the time until the two men met in the dining room. The meal was as good as Malcolm's plain but masterful country cook could make it, and Gainesworth did Malcolm the courtesy of not noticing that the meat on his host's plate was served already cut into pieces so as to require only the use of a fork. In any case, the presence of footmen serving inhibited any frank conversation.

When dinner ended, after the covers were removed and Penrose left them alone with the port, Atherleigh spoke without preamble. "Cut line, Hector. What made you decide to come to this god-forsaken place? Surely there are plenty of amusements in London even at this time of year, and it cannot be that you had no more congenial invitation for the holidays."

"There are amusements in London, of course. I've been sampling them ever since I left the Melton country and moved back to my lodgings. It was at one of those very amusements—a dress party that should have been a dead bore—that I decided I must come down to Cornwall with all haste." He paused dramatically, sipped his port, and trained his sparkling eyes on Atherleigh.

"Should have been a bore? I deduce that it wasn't."

Gainesworth maintained a pregnant silence, but the corners of his mouth began to lift into a smile.

"Ah, I see. What's her name?" The fellow was too susceptible by half in Atherleigh's view. He had never met anyone readier to strike up a flirtation with a pretty girl. But those sudden enthusiasms never lasted. And as far as he could remember, had never resulted in his putting himself out to the extent of posting off across the country. "More to the point, why are you here if you met her in London?"

Gainesworth put his glass down, rested both his hands on the table, and leaned forward. "Because she's no longer in London. She is now here. By my calculation only a few miles away."

Atherleigh's brow creased in a puzzled frown. "I don't understand. No one's in the vicinity. Or at least…" Then he remembered the invitation to the Lewiston masquerade ball. Ah. Everything began to fall into place.

"I see by your expression that you're starting to guess, so I'll tell you the rest," Gainesworth said. "I've lost my heart. She's an angel. And a devil, I think. Not a devil, exactly, but perhaps a mischievous spirit. And a beauty beyond price, oh yes, that too. So you see, I had to follow her."

This was not the way Gainesworth usually spoke of his flirts, but perhaps he'd become more intense in his passions of late. "I know of only two ladies in the country hereabouts who are of the right age and station to have been at a *ton* party in London. I take it you've fallen for one of Lewiston's sisters? I don't know their names. I don't think I ever saw them, except perhaps when they were very young. In any case, this girl can't be more than eighteen years old, man! Hardly out of the schoolroom."

Gainesworth leaned back again and picked up his glass, cupping it in his two hands and swirling the amber liquid meditatively. "Young. Yes. But she is not shallow, not giddy. Intelligent. Unexpected. That's what I'd call her."

"Is she equally smitten with you on so short an acquaintance? If I'm right, she cannot have been in town more than a couple of weeks at the most."

Gainesworth knit his brows and pursed his lips. "I think so. But she kept mentioning her sister, as if she wanted me to know something about her, or as if anyone who courted Lady Belinda would have to pass under her sister's review. Apparently they're thick as thieves."

"Ah yes, that makes sense. Lady Belinda. And the sister's name? Twins I think."

Gainesworth's eyes opened wide.

Malcolm laughed. "Easy there! From what I've heard they don't look at all alike. Which happens with twins sometimes."

"That fits." Gainesworth nodded and looked into the guttering flame of one of the candles. "Something she said made me think her sister had some disadvantage or other. She said she hadn't come up to town with her and her mother because of an illness. But that had the whiff of a convenient excuse."

Atherleigh refilled his glass and then passed the crystal decanter to his friend. "You'll have an opportunity to see for yourself in a couple of days. I've an invitation to the Lewiston Masquerade Ball on the seventeenth. I had thought to send my regrets."

Gainesworth's eyes brightened immediately. "Yes! She mentioned it when I said I knew you and was planning to visit. I didn't think to bring a domino. Do you have one I could borrow? Or do you think we should wear costumes? I could go as a cavalier, or a pirate. No! You're the pirate! We'll make a hook for your left hand and you can wear an eye patch."

Nothing sounded less amusing to Malcolm. "I have no desire to do anything that calls attention to my injury. A domino will do. That is, if I go at all."

"You wouldn't do that to me! I cannot forgo this chance. We must both attend. It's important! Vital! Besides, it's about time you faced the world. Hiding away isn't going to make your injury any better. You aren't the only wounded warrior to find himself having to manage despite physical difficulties."

"That's easy for you to say, Hector." Why did people who had no idea what it really felt like to be permanently maimed always try to tell him he should be grateful for what he had? One day, perhaps, he might be able to adopt that attitude. But not now.

"Enough of that. The seventeenth is only three days hence. Have you made your visit of ceremony to your neighbors? If they were away I imagine not."

"I had no intention of doing so. Although I suppose they must know I'm here now and it would be uncivil not to."

"Yes, and no doubt they will think you rag mannered if you don't at least leave your card before you turn up with your houseguest in tow at their annual ball."

Malcolm had to admit that Gainesworth was right. His injury could not be an excuse any longer, now that all the surgeries were done and all that was left was to adjust to life with one hand. Half a life, he thought with a rueful smile. And then he laughed aloud. And kept on laughing.

"I say Atherleigh, are you quite on the go?"

The laughter continued to convulse him. He sputtered out, "N-no! N-not drunk." He struggled to gain enough control of himself to tell his friend what had suddenly struck him as wildly funny. Wiping tears from his eyes, he said, "I-I was just thinking about c-courting. And then, w-what would I say if I found someone to m-marry?" The words he tried to utter at that point struck him as so devastatingly hilarious he could barely form them between gasps of hysteria. "I-I-s-say, may I have your ha-ha-hand in marriage?" He held up his bandaged stump and then folded his arms on the table and sank his head on top of them to laugh and laugh until he had no more breath and his sides ached.

He didn't know how long he was like that before a strong hand grasped his shoulder and Hector's familiar voice said, "It's no bad thing to get it all out like that. I'll ring for Carter to take you up to bed."

It wasn't until Malcolm looked up at Gainesworth standing next to him that he realized that at some point he had stopped laughing and had instead begun to sob. All the pent up sorrow and anger, the frustration and self-pity, spilled out of him as though he were an uncorked cask tipped on its side. He didn't remember the last time he'd wept. Not since he was a boy. He was ashamed.

Ashamed, and yet somehow cleansed. "Sorry old chap," he said in a thick voice.

"No need," Hector said as Carter came into the dining room and Malcolm followed him out and up the stairs.

CHAPTER 12

*A*lthough Antonella trusted her sister, her stomach still twisted uncomfortably as she led her on the roundabout path to her bird infirmary. She had already decided that rather than take her inside and possibly upset Zephyra, she would bring the goshawk out. Zephyra needed weathering in any case. Antonella had detected the symptoms of restlessness in her in the past few days—pacing along the perch, making constant little noises. She suspected keeping her shut up was cruel. The small window in the shed let in little sunlight. But what else could she do? Taking her back to Atherleigh was not an option, not yet. Not until her wing had healed enough that Antonella could be certain they would not deem her no longer of use and destroy her.

In her heart she knew that Zephyra would recover. She just needed a little time.

"Wait out here," Antonella said when they reached the hut. Belinda had been inside it before, but she was a little frightened of birds, scared they would fly and get caught in her hair, so she happily remained where she was.

When Antonella emerged with Zephyra perched on her

gloved forearm, Belinda gave a little shriek and backed away. This startled the goshawk into bating—awkward with only one wing flapping. Antonella feared that she would strain the other wing and damage it further if she continued, so she turned to face away from Belinda and spoke soothingly until Zephyra quieted. "I'll turn to you again now," she said to Belinda over her shoulder. "I have hold of the tether, so she won't fly at you. Just stay calm."

Belinda's eyes were wide with fear. "Ant! It will hurt you! You had better just let it fly free."

"*She* cannot fly. Zephyra is a female. She has an injured wing. I found her caught in a poacher's net. And she wasn't wild. Someone has trained her to hunt."

"Someone?" Belinda said, a light of suspicion in her eyes.

Antonella stayed silent for a moment before deciding that she must open the budget with her sister, who would find out anyway. Better from her than anyone else. "She belongs to Lord Atherleigh."

Belinda gaped. "You must take her back to him immediately!"

"I can't. Not yet."

"Why?"

Antonella explained her fear that Zephyra was too badly injured to be of any further use as a hunter, and thus might be left to fly free and die because she couldn't find food, or worse.

"Surely they would not do such a thing," Belinda said. "But how do you know she belongs to Atherleigh?"

Antonella told her an abbreviated version of her adventures on the day she went to spy on the mews. She did not mention climbing the tree, nor did she mention her encounter with Atherleigh himself. As to why exactly, she couldn't say.

"I see your hesitation," Belinda said, always eyeing

Zephyra with caution. "But I still think you must tell him, and soon. They know they're missing a goshawk, and if someone were to see you out here with one..." She glanced around.

"No one ever comes here. My shed is not visible from the paths that lead to the stables and the farm buildings." Yet Belinda had touched upon something that did indeed worry her. Now that she had taken to weathering Zephyra, she was leaving herself wide open to discovery. All it would take would be someone to hear one of the hawk's cries and follow it to explore. It would be very hard to explain the circumstances.

"You know this cannot be a permanent solution," Belinda said, "and the sooner you get it over with, the better. Can you not enlist this falconer, this Rafiq, to help you? Then perhaps Lord Atherleigh need never know what you've done."

How could she explain to Belinda that, in fact, she would far rather it were Atherleigh who came to retrieve Zephyra? If Atherleigh came, his own injury would make it necessary for her to accompany him back to the mews, and she would have a chance of being able to persuade him to allow her to visit the goshawk. Something told her that Atherleigh, when faced with the reality of the wounded bird and with her persuasive arguments, would ensure that Zephyra received every care. Where if Rafiq came, he could simply take Zephyra away—who would no doubt revert to being called Chakor—and she would not know what happened to her because she might never be allowed to see her again.

But was that the only reason she imagined the baron coming to reclaim Zephyra? Surely Rafiq could convey her wishes to Atherleigh and ask if she could visit the mews. In any case, why would her wishes have any effect on Atherleigh's decision regarding Zephyra? Of course they didn't. But she wanted them to.

Antonella decided not to examine this question too closely, so without another word, she took Zephyra back inside the shed. Once the hawk was tethered to her perch, Antonella took a moment to examine the small scrapes and abrasions on the wingtip. They were healing nicely. She gave Zephyra a scrap of meat, and then went back outside to join her sister.

Confronted with Belinda's frowning face and arms crossed belligerently across her chest, Antonella said, "You must leave me to take care of matters in my own way."

"I'm not happy about this. I think you're in deep, and you'll regret your actions. You must do what you think best, of course, because I am not the one to tell you what you should do with a wounded bird."

Antonella pulled one of Belinda's arms free and tucked her hand in her elbow. "That's right."

But Belinda wasn't quite finished. She said, "Mama instructed Miss Wilkins to send Atherleigh an invitation to our ball. If he comes, perhaps you could find a quiet moment to tell him about—what did you call it, her? Zephyra? Which reminds me, does Wilkie know?"

Distracted by what Belinda just told her, Antonella took a moment to answer. Atherleigh? Coming to the masquerade? She couldn't imagine it. He wouldn't be able to dance. That thought twisted her heart and started her thinking of all the things that a man with only one hand could no longer do. Surely there were ways to accommodate such a disability? No wonder the baron had been so vexed about his fall and so cross with her for offering to help.

"Hello, Ant? Where have you gone?" Belinda tweaked her arm. "Answer me. Does Wilkie know?"

"What? No. I haven't told her. Although in that way she has of seeing through me I know she believes I'm hiding something. I suppose I shall have to tell her eventually."

"Let it be soon. Wilkie always knows what's best."

Antonella couldn't argue with that. The governess had been a source of quiet strength and reason ever since she came to them nine years ago.

"Come! Let's go up to the tower and see if we can find some costumes for the ball," Belinda said, reaching for Antonella's hand.

The tower, a favorite place for them to hide and play as children, was a relic of the times when defenses of country estates were still important. It overlooked the entrance to the courtyard, and its narrow windows—originally designed to give archers a sheltered place from which to repel invaders— gave a view out over the gardens and trees to the sea beyond on a clear day. With no fireplace and nothing but a narrow, steep stair to reach it, the tower was now used primarily for storage. This only added to its appeal. Trunks and chests full of old clothes and wall hangings furnished many a costume for amateur theatricals.

It would be a challenge, Antonella could see, to enter into Belinda's excitement about the coming ball without betraying all that was really occupying her. "I have something else to do first," Antonella said. "You go and get started."

"All right, but don't be long!" Belinda hurried toward the warmth of the house.

As soon as Belinda was out of sight, Antonella ran off to see Rafiq again and try to gain more insight into how she might rehabilitate the goshawk. Sooner or later Wilkie would figure out she was doing more than just rambling through the woods looking for wounded birds. For one thing, she wouldn't dare bring any back to the shed with Zephyra in it. Although goshawks preferred small mammals to birds, they were in the nature of a predator to the wrens, sparrows, and goldcrests that were Antonella's usual patients.

As if her thoughts had the power to conjure, as Antonella took the path that led through the sleeping garden to the spinney, she saw the cloaked form of the governess kneeling by one of the rather overgrown flowerbeds. Before she could alter her route, Miss Wilkins looked up and smiled at her.

"Come and help me up off my knees," she said, lifting hands full of trailing roots.

She altered her path to join the governess. "What are you doing? Weeding at this time of year?" Antonella put her hand under Miss Wilkins's elbow and steadied her as she rose to her feet.

"Just tidying up some dead vines that threatened to take over this bed," she said, tossing the vegetation into a basket a few feet away. "It's easier when they're dormant." She smacked her hands together to brush off the dirt. "I'd love to come and see what you've got in your bird shed. Do you have time to take me before I freeze to death?"

Antonella didn't, but she couldn't explain why to Miss Wilkins. "I was on my way to do a sweep of the woods before the light goes," she said. *Those perceptive eyes.* She knows something. Belinda wouldn't have had time to tell her anything after leaving her moments ago, so she must have discovered it before.

"Still, it will only take a moment. And I confess I'm uneasy. You're not usually so secretive about your activities." Miss Wilkins took hold of her hand. "I wish you would trust me."

Trust. Who could she trust? After living a lie all her life, Antonella didn't feel as if she could be open with anyone ever again. Not even Rafiq, and he cared as much for hawks as she did. She gazed off into the distance and dug the toe of her half boot against the nearly frozen ground. "You see," she finally said, "I'm just not certain I can. You knew, didn't you." Antonella lifted her eyes to meet the governess's, which had melted into sadness, telling her the answer before she spoke a word.

"Yes," Miss Wilkins said.

"Then why didn't you tell me!" Antonella's hoarse cry sent a mourning dove flying up from nearby, its trilling coo fading into the stillness. She turned and walked back the way she had come, not waiting for Miss Wilkins to follow. "I guess you might as well see, so you can go and tell my—Aunt Caroline and spoil everything."

"Antonella, wait!" The governess ran to catch up to her. "I couldn't tell you. It wasn't my secret. I swore to keep it."

Antonella kept up a brisk pace, pumping her arms furiously. "Who made you swear? The marquess? Lady Lewiston? Although why she should have I don't know. Surely she would have been delighted for the world to know I was nobody long since so she could put all her energy into launching Belinda. It's what she always wanted." Her words sounded peevish even to her. "I'm sorry. I shouldn't be bitter. It's just that I sensed something, all along."

By the time they arrived back at the hut, Antonella was so winded she had to stop and bend over with her hands on her knees. When Miss Wilkins tried to place her arm around her shoulders she shook her off.

The governess said, "You don't have to tell me—or show me—anything you don't want to. Please believe I only want what's best for you, as I have ever since I arrived here nine years ago." The governess's voice was unusually quiet.

Antonella righted herself and whirled around to see Miss Wilkins blinking fast and taking deep breaths. At this sight, her righteous anger abated. She didn't mean to exercise her frustration on someone who had nothing to do with it and who had always been kindness itself to her. And then she thought, "Do you know who she was? Who they were?"

Miss Wilkins looked down.

She knows! "Tell me! You must."

"I can't. Not now. You must trust me!"

Antonella shook her head. "Trust you?" She didn't bother to repeat her angry words of a few moments ago. Wilkie knew it all. "How do I know I can trust you with this?" She gestured toward the shed. "But I will show you what I have been keeping to myself. And then you can do what you will with that information. I suppose if you say you'll keep the secret you will, as you have kept that other secret for so long." She couldn't keep the angry edge out of her voice.

Without waiting for Miss Wilkins to say anything more, Ant unlocked the shed door and let herself in. Now two other people would know about Zephyra. No doubt Wilkie would say exactly what Bee said and tell her she must take the goshawk back to her rightful owners. How could she? Hadn't she already lost enough? No one could possibly understand what this all meant to her, especially now.

Zephyra made little chirping noises and cocked her head. "I know you were just out, but let's go out once more, for a little while, then I'll bring you back in." She crooned the comforting words as she put on her makeshift gauntlet and undid the tether so the goshawk could hop onto her fist.

Antonella didn't say anything when she stepped out of the shed. She just stood there, a belligerent scowl on her face.

Miss Wilkins opened her eyes wide. "Oh my God! She's beautiful!" She smiled. "How? Where?"

Zephyra flapped her one free wing unhurriedly and it set the bells on her jesses tinkling. The governess gasped. "She's trained. Just like in the books."

Antonella's icy fury began to thaw in the face of the

governess's wonder and delight. "Yes. She belongs to some-one. I found her in a poacher's net, injured."

"Do you know whose she is? Although I think I may be able to guess."

Antonella nodded. Miss Wilkins had read every bit as much of those books as she had, and doubtless had made an educated guess that the size of the bird meant she was female. "Atherleigh."

Miss Wilkins cocked her head on the side, unconsciously mimicking Zephyra's attitude. "Why have you not taken her back there?"

She didn't say, as Belinda had, *you must return her!* So perhaps, Antonella thought, she might trust Wilkie with a little more. "I wasn't sure at first that she actually was Ather-leigh's. And I wanted to treat her injuries."

"But now you're sure, and she's still here."

"There is a good reason. But I have help. In a way." Zephyra gave another flap. "Let me put her back inside and then I'll tell you more."

She would only tell Miss Wilkins enough to let her know she was dealing fairly and safely with the goshawk. And she would have to swear her to utter secrecy. But a tiny bit of the weight Antonella had been carrying in her heart lifted now that she wasn't the only one to know of Zephyra's existence. She might have to enlist Wilkie's help to prevent Belinda from blurting it out by accident, but she felt that she could count on those two people—the two who still loved her no matter what her rank—to let her resolve the problem of Zephyra in her own time.

When she latched the shed door behind her and rejoined the governess, she said, "I have to go somewhere, alone."

After a quick glance at the sky, Miss Wilkins nodded. "Mind you're back in time for dinner."

Antonella sprang forward and gave the governess a quick, rough, kiss on the cheek and then scampered away.

CHAPTER 13

*I*t was hard work persuading Atherleigh to pay a call of ceremony on Lady Lewiston and her daughters two days before the ball. But Gainesworth pointed out that as someone completely unknown to the family, he himself could hardly show up at their ball without at least a brief introduction beforehand.

It took a while for their knock on the ancient door at the back of the rambling mansion's courtyard to gain any response. After a minute or more, an elderly butler opened the door, a look of complete surprise on his face. Gainesworth deduced that callers were not over common at Amblemere Court. With the only near neighbor Atherleigh, it was no wonder.

Once the butler had recovered from his astonishment, he ushered them up a staircase to the left of the door and into an elegant—if a little old-fashioned—drawing room on the first floor and disappeared, presumably to announce their arrival to the ladies of the house.

Somewhat to Gainesworth's chagrin, only the dowager Lady Lewiston came to greet them.

"What a delightful surprise! Lord Atherleigh, we have not seen you in Cornwall for some years. My condolences on the loss of your father. And I hope your injuries have successfully healed."

Atherleigh murmured his thanks. "As to my injuries, I am afraid one of them will never heal." He did not remove his stump from where he had tucked it inside his coat, but simply patted it with his other hand.

She opened her eyes wide and knitted her brow in confusion.

Blast him for being so coy! Gainesworth thought. "What Atherleigh means to say is that he lost his left hand in the battle of Nivelle."

The dowager went pale, and then color flooded her cheeks. Before she could say anything in response to this devastating information, Atherleigh said, "Allow me to introduce my good friend, Mr. Hector Gainesworth. He is staying with me for the holidays."

The momentary discomfiture in Lady Lewiston's eyes was quickly replaced with a measuring look that Gainesworth had seen in those of countless ambitious mothers throughout the years. He was glad he'd taken care to dress in his best country attire. "Your servant, Lady Lewiston." He stepped forward and bowed over her outstretched hand.

She moved to sit on one of the sofas and waved her hand in the general direction of the chairs opposite her. "Won't you be seated? Might I offer you tea? Or would you prefer wine?"

"Please don't trouble yourself," Atherleigh said, much to Hector's annoyance. If they were able to stay the entire polite half hour, which would be helped by the time it would take to be served tea, there was a chance one of the daughters might come in.

But no such luck, as he discovered when the dowager spoke. "You find me at home alone. Lady Belinda has gone out and I do not know when she will return."

What about the sister? "I had the pleasure of meeting your lovely daughter at a party in London last week," Hector said with his most charming smile.

"Did you indeed? I wonder she did not mention it to me. But we were all in a bustle to leave the day immediately after the party, so perhaps it simply went out of her head."

Atherleigh coughed, likely to hide a laugh. Hector shot him a quick, quelling glance.

"And your other daughter, whose name I do not know. Is she away?" Gainesworth was determined to keep the conversation going.

Lady Lewiston stiffened. "I have only the one daughter, Mr. Gainesworth."

He exchanged a bewildered look with Atherleigh. "But I thought—"

"Oh," the dowager said, as if something had just occurred to her. "Perhaps you mean Antonella. She is not my daughter. A charity case, a distant relative, raised in the family. She and Belinda have been raised together and are very fond of one another. This sometimes leads people to assume they are sisters."

He decided not to press the matter any further. Clearly there was some complicated matter at the root of it. It did not surprise him that Lady Belinda might choose to consider a girl well beneath her in rank and consequence to be like a sister. It rather added to her peculiar charms.

"You have chosen an odd time to visit Cornwall, Mr. Gainesworth. Winter is hardly our most welcoming season." She gestured toward a window that revealed a flat gray sky that looked ominously as though it could release a deluge at any moment.

"You underestimate the allure of your annual masquerade ball, Lady Lewiston," Atherleigh said, casting a significant glance at Gainesworth.

"Well, we must do something to offer entertainment at this dreary time of year. And the servants, you know, expect their own Christmas revels. Although we're rather spread about, I believe we can attract enough young people of quality to make for an evening's lively entertainment." She smiled in a way that awakened a sparkle in her eyes reminiscent of the light in Lady Belinda's. "I hope you will both be among their number on the evening after next. This old house may have its inconveniences, but it also has a great hall that makes a wonderful ballroom."

"We wouldn't miss it," Atherleigh said and stood. "We should not trespass on your kindness any longer."

But as he uttered those words, a commotion arose downstairs. The thunder of running feet and the bubbling tinkle of irrepressible laughter burst into the quiet house. An annoyed furrow creased Lady Lewiston's brow. "Forgive the unseemly boisterousness of my daughters," she said.

Light, tripping steps raced up the stairs, passing the closed drawing room door and continuing to the floor above, the sound of the voices swelling and then receding. "What shall you go as?" "We should paint our faces," and other snatches of excited babble fading away as they climbed higher.

She said daughters, Gainesworth thought again, and wondered if Lady Lewiston had noticed the slip. Something odd was going on here.

"I would have Lady Belinda summoned to greet you, but doubtless she is not fit to be seen. Antonella is often a most unfortunate influence on her." Lady Lewiston pressed her lips together in a determined smile and rang the bell. A moment later the butler reappeared and showed them to the door.

With Gainesworth's help, Atherleigh climbed back into his friend's curricle, which had arrived from town the day before.

"Didn't you find it odd? The business about the daughters?" Hector said as he turned the horses in the courtyard and through the arched entrance and then urged them to a trot down the long avenue. Traveling thus between the two houses turned a three-mile walk into an eight-mile drive.

Atherleigh had sunk into a brown study and it took him a moment to register that Gainesworth was speaking to him. "What? Yes, odd." He'd been thinking a mixture of disturbing thoughts. One was that the last thing he felt like doing was going to a ball. But there was no getting out of it now that they'd paid their visit. Was this girl, Lady Belinda, really worth all Hector's effort?

Of more interest to him was the name of the other daughter—or poor relation, as Lady Lewiston called her. Antonella. So the girl who had helped him when he fell from his horse wasn't some parson's daughter, but a member of the Ambleton household. A relative at least, if not a daughter.

"I fancy you could still play billiards in your current state," Gainesworth said after they'd driven on in silence for a while.

"Don't be ridiculous." But Atherleigh was just as glad for the change of subject. He didn't want to engage in futile conjecture about a girl who likely had considered him both impolite and repulsive. Only the thought that he'd likely never see her again had comforted him after that embarrassing episode. Or had it? In any event, now it seemed likely that he would see her again in a couple of days.

"I'm not being ridiculous! It will require some practice,

but I'm certain it's not an impossibility. You'd better find some ways to entertain yourself beyond reading and moping. Let's give it a go after dinner."

Atherleigh said nothing, but knew he would give in to his friend's well-intentioned urging. At least when he made a fool of himself only Gainesworth would be present, unlike the previous time he had tested his one-handed abilities and ended up in the mud.

Perhaps Miss Antonella wouldn't recognize him behind his mask and he wouldn't have to find a way to redeem himself in her eyes. If she did, the least he could do would be to treat her with greater courtesy. And knowing what she did about him, she would understand why he wouldn't ask her—or any lady—to dance.

There was some comfort in that.

"WHO DO YOU THINK IS HERE?" ANTONELLA ASKED BELINDA once they reached Belinda's bedchamber. They had seen the curricle being walked up and down by one of the stable boys.

Belinda shrugged, but the color in her cheeks seemed exceptionally high, more so than would be caused by running in the cold. The rosiness started at her neck and rather than fading as she warmed herself in front of the fire, intensified. When Belinda wouldn't meet her eyes, Antonella knew something had unsettled her. "What is it? What are you not telling me?" she asked.

Belinda grabbed Antonella's hand. "I may know who is here. But I'm not certain."

"How might you know? I saw no crest on the curricle."

Belinda's flush deepened. "I haven't told you everything that happened in London. I met a gentleman at the one party I attended. He was extremely amiable." She turned away, but not before Antonella caught the smile lifting the corners of her mouth.

"Bee! I asked if you were in love. Are you?"

"No! Don't be so silly. I only said he was amiable."

Antonella took Belinda's hand and drew her to sit on the edge of the bed. "So you think this gentleman is here. But how could he be? If you met him in London?"

Belinda would not meet her eyes. "It happened that he mentioned to me that he had an acquaintance in Cornwall. A good friend, actually. And that he intended to spend the holidays with him."

"Who could that be? Only Lord Atherleigh lives quite near enough to make a morning call feasible. Or Sir William Rawlins—"

Belinda said, "Not Sir William. It's Atherleigh."

Atherleigh? Was he in the house as well? Antonella's pulse unaccountably quickened. "Yes of course. Lord Atherleigh has been at the manor for a week. Or so the servants say." Antonella stopped herself from revealing too much about how she would know such a thing. "Who is this gentleman? What's his name? Does he know Mama, or Harry?"

"He's acquainted with Harry but does not know Mama. His name is Mr. Gainesworth."

Antonella waited in silence for Belinda to say more. She had met someone who clearly made an impression on her. Ant had never seen her so discomposed. Clearly she was in love, or at least had developed a tendre, whatever her protestations to the contrary. But if he was just a *mister*, Lady Lewiston would not be pleased.

"He was amiable and amusing. I thought *you* would find him so, at any rate," Belinda said, not doing a very good job of feigning nonchalance.

"I see. He seems to have arrived in Cornwall quite soon after you did. I wonder why?"

Belinda picked up a cushion from the bed and hit Antonella with it. They both broke into giggles. "You mustn't jump to conclusions, Ant! Perhaps you will meet him. I know Mama invited Atherleigh to the ball. He would hardly leave his friend behind."

Atherleigh at the ball. Antonella could not picture it. He belonged outdoors, in the weathering yard or on his horse, wearing buckskins and top boots, not in a fanciful costume. "Perhaps neither of them will come. You know that Lord Atherleigh was badly wounded on the Peninsula."

"But if he's here and entertaining his friend he must be recovered."

Antonella paused before telling Belinda, "He lost his left hand. So they say. It would make it very difficult for him to dance." She hadn't wanted to give away any information that might lead Bee to suspect she'd met him already. Yet somehow she couldn't bear the thought that Bee would think of Atherleigh uncharitably if he chose to stay at home rather than attend the masquerade ball.

Her subterfuge was not entirely successful. "You seem to know a great deal about our neighbor, who has been absent for some years."

Before Belinda could say anything further she stood and raised her finger to her lips, head cocked, on the listen. "I think they're leaving. Come!"

Antonella found herself dragged in Belinda's wake out of the bedchamber, along the corridor, to the top of the stairs. A landing partway down provided a good place to see what was happening on the floor below. Skilling held the door open for the visitors to leave the saloon. They did not look up, but one glance was enough to assure Antonella that the man with the dark hair just putting on the hat and cloak presented to him by the second footman was indeed Atherleigh. The other gentleman—slightly shorter than the baron with a head of glossy golden-blonde curls—nodded in the direction of the open door before taking his own hat and cloak from the same footman. No doubt he was Mr. Gainesworth. The two men descended the stairs in silence.

Just before they turned the corner at the bottom toward the door, the gentleman who must be Mr. Gainesworth clapped Atherleigh on the shoulder and turned a sunny, smiling countenance on his friend, who only frowned in return.

"Isn't he handsome?" Belinda whispered.

"Yes," Antonella answered, not certain whether she meant Mr. Gainesworth or Lord Atherleigh. Whichever it was, her answer would have been the same.

CHAPTER 14

The next day, Belinda and Antonella spent hours in the tower digging through the trunks full of discarded old gowns, bolts of cloth, threadbare wall hangings, and courtly men's clothing for costume material. Neither heard a carriage pulling up nor the front door opening and someone being ushered into the house.

So when Falk poked her head up through the trap door to the stairs and said, "Lady Belinda, your mother wants to see you in the rose saloon," it took them completely by surprise.

"What, now? What can she want?" Belinda stood up and dusted herself off. "She said nothing about expecting any visitors today." She turned to Falk. "Do you know who it is?"

"No Ma'am, but oh My Lady!" Falk said, taking in Belinda's disheveled appearance, "You must change yer dress before you go down. Her Ladyship won't be pleased to see you in so much dust."

With a huff, Belinda said, "She knows we've been up here! How can she expect me to be pristine? If she wants me I shall go down, but I'll only be coming back here to finish what we've started, and I don't want to get another dress dirty."

She gave her hair a quick smooth and Antonella leapt up, licked her thumb, and wiped away a smudge of dirt on her cheek. "Thanks, Ant. Besides, Mama won't want me to keep her waiting."

"Very good My Lady," Falk said, a note of doubt in her voice.

"Does she not want Miss Antonella to come as well?" Belinda asked.

"Lady Lewiston didn't say. She just said you was to come."

"Thank you, Falk."

After the maid had ducked back down from the hatch and descended the steep stairs, Belinda said, "Ant, perhaps you should come anyway."

Antonella waved her hand dismissively. "Probably something to do with what happened in London. I'd rather stay up here. I think I've found my costume!" She held up a man's coat and breeches and pointed to a pile of old turkey feathers, the remnants of a once fine bonnet. "The only difficulty will be the shoes, but I'll find something."

"You wouldn't dare!" Belinda said, dissolving into giggles.

"Why not? Aunt Caroline can hardly be concerned with the figure I will make at the ball."

"Don't be silly, Ant! Mama cares about you, truly. She's just been distracted lately, and she doesn't quite know what to do about ... But if she sees you in breeches, she'll likely make you come upstairs and change." Belinda didn't quite know how to talk to her sister about the increasingly obvious difference in their status in the household, not to mention their prospects. She and Lady Lewiston had left for London so soon after the earth-shattering announcement that she'd had few opportunities to talk to Antonella. It was as if her sister had faded into the background of a watercolor family portrait, as if the artist's brush had held more water than paint.

Ant put her hands on her hips and lifted her chin defiantly. "I'll wear a cloak so it's hard to see my costume."

"Why would you do that? Making Mama angry won't help anything." Belinda knew that look in her sister's eyes. A flash of defiance that masked hurt. "Wouldn't you rather enjoy the ball? If Mama sends you away, what will that achieve?" Besides that, it would ruin all her plans. Although her sister's legs would look very well in the breeches, dressed thus she would hardly encourage Gainesworth to see that she was a true lady.

Antonella sighed and traced a curving pattern on the floor with her toe. "Very well," she said. "But only because you asked. Not because I care what *Aunt Caroline* thinks of me anymore."

Her sarcastic emphasis struck at Belinda's heart, and she reached out to take Antonella's hand. "I must go down."

"Of course," Antonella said and gave her a little push toward the trap door.

Just as she was about to leave, Belinda spotted a bit of rose satin peeking out of one of the trunks and ran to it. It proved to be an old evening cloak. Its fur trimming was dry and crumbling, but the silk was still good. "Look at this! What do you think?" She swept the cloak up and wrapped it around her shoulders.

"More to the point, what will Mr. Gainesworth think," Antonella said, a laugh in her eyes. "You can't fool me, Bee! I know you have some scheme in your head."

"Very funny. I'm sure I don't know what you're talking about!" How could she further an alliance between Gainesworth and Antonella if her sister thought *she* had a tendre for him? "I danced with so many young gentlemen. Mr. Gainesworth was kind, and a friend of Lord Atherleigh. And I don't have time to talk about it, I must go down to Mama or she'll think me rude." She tossed the cloak aside.

"Can you take the fur off for me? You're so much better at that sort of thing."

"Yes, of course."

"You're a darling!" Belinda said before she clambered down the stairs, hoping she had disabused Antonella of the notion that she was dangling after Gainesworth.

She slowed as she reached the final flight to compose herself and straighten the hair that had been disarranged from trying on so many caps and bonnets in the tower. She paused at the saloon door until her breath slowed to normal and listened. Voices. One a man's. Someone was in there with her mother. Could it be Gainesworth again? Her heart did a little flip, and then she glanced down at her skirt, its hem looking as though she'd been using it to sweep the floor. *Oh no!* Her spirits sank. She was as disheveled as a scullery maid who's just laid all the fires. Why hadn't she listened to Falk? *Mama will be so displeased!*

Oh well, she thought. Too late to do anything about it now. If it was Gainesworth with her mother, she would just have to make a joke of it. He was the type not to mind.

The footman stationed outside the door opened it for Belinda and she stepped in as gracefully as she could, a dazzling smile fixed to her face.

"Darling!" Lady Lewiston said, her voice dripping with more than usual warmth. "I'd like to introduce you to Lord Bartleson. He is staying with Sir William Quilley—you know him, an estate some fifteen miles from here. He was recently made a widower, and Lord Bartleson has come down to keep him company during the holidays. They will be attending the ball tomorrow evening."

Not Gainesworth then. Belinda had a hard time keeping the smile pinned to her face. This was the Lord Bartleson she'd overheard her mother mentioning to Harry during their disagreement in London. And she could see in an instant why he told their Mama not to press her into an alliance with him. He must be well over thirty, she thought. Positively ancient! And his cheeks bore snuff stains. His round face was otherwise not unpleasant, and he smiled at her and made a gallant bow, but he was hardly the dashing, amusing husband she imagined for herself.

"Your most obedient, Lady Belinda. Report of your beauty has not exaggerated." He not only bowed over her extended hand, but planted a wet kiss on her knuckles before righting himself and looking her up and down. "Are you fond of gardening, Lady Belinda? I wouldn't have thought this quite the time of year for it." He erupted in a jolly laugh that shook his entire frame and squished his eyes up to slits, giving him a rather porcine look.

Bartleson's frank appraisal unnerved her a little. Yet at the same time there was something artless about Bartleson, and she decided she must not judge him too harshly on first acquaintance. Perhaps he was merely unintelligent. His round, boyish face glowed with nervous perspiration and his lips trembled when he spoke. He had a sort of pathetic charm, but she knew as soon as she saw him that she would never marry him no matter what pressure her mother exerted.

She turned to Lady Lewiston and noted her raised eyebrows and pinched mouth, clear signs of disapproval.

Acting as if she wasn't a mess from digging around in the attic, Belinda floated to the settee where her mother had perched and sat beside her, back straight, hands folded demurely in her lap. "You're correct about the gardening. I am fond of it, but have not been indulging such a pastime at this unfruitful time of year. My sister and I have been going through some things in the attic, deciding what to give to the poor." She didn't want to mention the ball and furnish her mother with any ideas.

"How charitable of you, Lady Belinda. Your Mama has been telling me of your many accomplishments. I hope to have the pleasure of hearing you play and sing while I am in the neighborhood. And your sister—I assume she is equally accomplished? Perhaps I shall also have the honor of making her acquaintance." He glanced questioningly at the dowager.

After a momentary silencing glance at Belinda, Lady Lewiston said, "You must forgive my daughter, My Lord. When she speaks of her sister, she is speaking of a poor relation who has been raised here out of charity since her infancy. They are very close, almost like sisters. Miss Ambleton has not the same abilities and prospects as Lady Belinda."

How dare she! Belinda thought, wishing she could say something cutting to her mother, but resisting the impulse. Their late father would turn in his grave to hear her speaking thus about the girl he was so very fond of. Fond enough of, she thought, to lie to everyone he knew about her parentage.

"My Lord," the dowager said, changing the subject, "It's a little late in the year for hunting. The ground is too frozen for the horses. However, there is tomorrow evening's masquerade ball, as I mentioned in my note to you. I hope we might depend upon your attendance?" Lady Lewiston said.

"With the greatest pleasure!" Bartleson turned hopeful eyes on Belinda. "Might I be so bold as to engage you for the first two sets, Lady Belinda?"

She smiled weakly. "I'd be honored, Sir." *I'd be chagrined,* was what she would rather have said. She counted on standing up with Gainesworth for as many sets as possible. How else was she to start weaving the connection between him and Antonella? "And now, it is time for me to dress for dinner. Which, as you can see, will involve a little more than just a change of clothes." She patted her unruly hair, stood and looked down at her rather shabby old dimity dress that had faded from its original blue to a nondescript gray, giving it a swish to reveal just how dirty it was at the hem.

Enough of a gentleman not to miss his cue, Bartleson stood and said, "Of course. I must take my leave. Until tomorrow evening."

He bowed to both of them and left through the door that Skilling held open for him.

Belinda did not stay for the raking down her mother was certain to give her, but dashed out of the room and raced back up to the attic where she found Antonella still pulling costume bits out of old trunks. "You won't believe it!" she said.

"What? What has Mama—I mean Aunt Caroline—done now?" Antonella asked.

"There was an old man, or middle-aged, I think, sitting in the drawing room. The one I overheard her mentioning to Harry in London! She invited this ancient fellow to the ball, and he's taken my first two dances." There was no sense telling her what Lady Lewiston had said about her. That had made her more furious than anything.

Antonella laughed. "I think you'll survive! Unless he treads on your toes and breaks them, you'll be able to dance with Gainesworth for the rest of the evening, I imagine."

So she hadn't succeeded in turning Ant's thoughts away from that idea after all. "Don't tease me. I assure you I have no such desire. I want *you* to dance with Mr. Gainesworth as well. I think you'll like him." Belinda felt she was more than capable of deterring Bartleson if he should prove persistent. But having to do that at the same time as maneuvering Antonella toward Gainesworth would be tricky.

"If mother has anything to say to it, I'll be lucky to dance with anyone other than the squire's sons." Antonella punctuated her statement by tossing a bedraggled tricorn across the attic.

Belinda feared Ant was right about that. The ruddy-faced boys were down from Oxford. They'd played together as children. Neither of them would ever be a good marriage prospect, even for Antonella in her reduced state. "Well, at least she won't try to foist Bartleson on you. He's an earl, apparently. Mama seems to feel that is terribly important. I don't see why it matters so very much. As long as the family is good, what do I care for a title? After all, as the daughter of a marquess I'd have to marry a duke to elevate myself, and that is impossible." With a pang, Belinda realized what she'd said and quickly changed the subject.

It wasn't until after dinner that night that Belinda realized the full extent of her mother's machinations. Once the covers were removed and they'd gone into the drawing room for tea, Lady Lewiston said to her, "I want you to be kind to Lord Bartleson. He's the most appropriate match for you, and our finances are in too precarious a state for you to drag your heels about marriage. He is a kind man, an earl as I said, and he has a vast fortune. You won't do better. If he offers for you, I insist that you accept him."

Oh, she insisted, did she? Was she, Lady Belinda Ambleton, to bolt herself to someone she could barely stomach, all for the sake of becoming a countess? Besides, surely they weren't so impoverished as all that. Harry might not be willing to increase their portions out of his wife's fortune, but it was he who paid for the running and upkeep of Amblemere and his house. The smaller property in Somerset had been let out ever since their father's death and so was no drain on the family's resources. "I shall marry someone I love," she said. "And I cannot imagine myself ever falling in love with Lord Bartleson."

Lady Lewiston took her time pouring the tea and handing a cup first to Belinda, then to Miss Wilkins, then to

Antonella. Once she had her own cup she focused her piercing gray eyes on Belinda. "Love is not essential in a marriage, but compatibility is. Suitability. As your mama, I am the best judge of what will insure your happiness in the future." Her hand trembled slightly as she lifted her cup to sip at the steaming tea.

"Is that why you married my father?" Belinda said, digging into what she guessed was an open wound. "You did not love him but your mama thought him suitable?"

The dowager's expression hardened, her posture became more rigid. "We are speaking of your marriage, not mine. Not that it is any of your business now, but the marquess and I were very fond of each other."

She didn't say she loved him. Had she been happy? Belinda remembered her papa as relentlessly cheerful and affectionate to Ant and to her. However, she recalled few signs of anything that could be construed as love toward his wife. The marquess and marchioness spent swaths of time apart, in fact: Papa in London engaged in his parliamentary duties while Mama ran the estate in Cornwall. Added to that, every year he would spend time in Somerset to oversee that smaller property's management. She and Antonella had never been there. Her papa never suggested they go along with him

Besides, Belinda burned to inquire of her mother, *who are you scheming for Antonella?* but she knew it would only anger the dowager and not achieve anything.

After that, conversation dwindled. Miss Wilkins was the first to retire, claiming the need to finish writing a letter. The rest of them went up as soon as they'd finished their first cups of tea.

In the privacy of her own bedchamber, Belinda puzzled over why money had suddenly become such an issue with her mother. Although they'd been scraping and being careful ever since father died, Harry's marriage had gone a long way toward helping matters—even if Olivia's purse strings never opened to increase her sisters-in-law's dowries. Lady Lewiston's jointure was not overly generous, but it was enough to provide for the three of them, and although Harry owned Amblemere, he was content to allow the dowager, Antonella, and herself to live there. He could have insisted they move out and live somewhere supported only by the jointure, but he had made no move to do so.

Of course, Belinda realized, if her brother and his wife decided to live in Cornwall and raise their family in the country, that might change. The three of them would have to move. They had no actual right to remain in the house, and the estate boasted no well-appointed dower house. That would mean the dowager might have to live far away from Harry and any grandchildren, perhaps with her sister Amelia in Bath.

Ah, Belinda thought. She wants me to marry well so she can become part of my household. Widowed mothers sometimes did that if circumstances dictated it. Belinda loved her mother—although her recent actions with regard to Antonella had strained those feelings. Even if all were as it had been, such an arrangement would not be ideal.

It was too knotty a problem to think about just then. Long before any such situation would arise was a masked ball and the opportunity to dance with Mr. Gainesworth again—with the intention, of course, of introducing him to Antonella. It would only be right for her to dance with him herself as well, though.

That thought sent her to sleep with a hint of a smile on her face.

∼

MALCOLM HAD PUT OFF THE TASK OF WRITING TO THE DUKE of Northumberland to offer him his birds for several days after he decided it was what he must do. The delay was foolish, he knew. He would never be able to hunt his birds again, and keeping them would be a waste. He might see if Rafiq would like to go with them at least to settle them, if not to remain as a falconer in the duke's service. That assumed, of course, that the duke would welcome three extra birds of no particular distinction or rarity. And why wouldn't he? Malcolm would not ask for any payment for them.

He took out a sheet of crested paper, trimmed his pen, dipped it into the inkwell, and began to write. *Your Grace,* he wrote, and then stopped. If he gave away the birds, it would be the first time in more than seventy years that the building connected to the ancient chapel would be empty. Did that matter? His family had hunted with hawks and falcons for generations. That didn't mean he had to continue the tradition. He had a perfectly reasonable excuse for not doing so, in fact. In his maimed condition he couldn't participate in a hunt. It would be impossible for him to handle the birds.

He continued his letter. *Your mews is well known throughout England as the finest in the land.* So what? His birds—Rafiq's birds, truly, since he had trained them and cared for them for twenty years—would be insignificant in such a place. What was one more tiercel or merlin to a mews that housed more than one gyrfalcon? The duke might laugh at his presumption in thinking he would care in the slightest about yet another hunting mews being shut down.

And then he started thinking again. He had made the decision, but something kept preventing him from putting it into action. Would it really be impossible for him to hunt with the birds? He still had full use of his right hand. Many falconers handled the birds with a glove on the right hand.

Who was he kidding? Hunting birds properly really

required the use of both hands: one gloved to hold the hawk or falcon, the other to cast the lure, or hold the reins of a horse if the hunt was mounted. That at least would be completely impossible.

Madness! Why torture himself with impossibilities. He tried again to continue the letter. *It was my misfortune to have suffered an injury in the recent war that makes it impossible for me to continue hunting with my hawks.* It was a good enough reason to get rid of the birds.

At that moment, something brought the missing goshawk to his mind. Had she really flown away to the wild again? He had a fanciful idea that she had merely decided to spend some time among her kind, flying far away to explore other lands, and that one day she would return and expect to be cared for as before. If Malcom did as he intended, she would only find her former home shut up and Rafiq gone.

This was absurd! He'd put it off long enough. It was the practical step to take. His fortune was not so great that he could indulge the extravagance of supporting a falconer and a mews simply out of sentiment. Trying hard not to think too closely about the remainder of the letter, he dashed it off, signed it with a flourish and scattered sand over the sheet to dry the ink. Since that first day when he'd had to open the letter Rafiq had sent him, Malcolm had practiced manipulating paper and using his stump to hold a sheet in place so he could write. With satisfaction, he managed to fold the letter to Northumberland and seal it with a wafer. He would leave it on the hall table for Jenkins to take to the receiving office the next day.

The next day. The masquerade ball at Amblemere Court. He had Gainesworth to thank for forcing him to go. It was one thing for Hector to tease and bully him into playing billiards or riding his horse. Those were activities he could do in the privacy of his own estate. But to show himself as he now was at a social event that would no doubt be attended by everyone within a few hours' drive of Amblemere—that was too much too soon.

The one part of it all that made him dread the ordeal less was knowing that at least one person there would already be familiar with his limitations. She had seen him at a low point when she found him kneeling in the mud after being thrown from his horse. Miss Ambleton. The daughter who was no longer a daughter, and who was apparently permitted to jaunter about the countryside unchaperoned. He had thought her a peasant then, in her drab wool cloak and rather worn boots. But he had recognized something in her, a spirit that shone out of those glittering dark eyes. He wasn't entirely surprised to discover that far from being a farmer's daughter she was the gently bred dependent in a noble house. He wished he knew the full story there. Then again, it was probably just a private family matter of no import to anyone other than the Ambletons.

The door to the library burst open to admit Gainesworth. "There you are, Mal! Come see what I've unearthed in a wardrobe in one of the disused rooms in this pile of yours." He held up an old doublet and a metal helmet from an ancient suit of armor.

"What in heaven's name," Atherleigh said, shaking his head.

"Costumes, m'boy. It's a masquerade ball tomorrow."

"I have no intention of making a spectacle of myself. You must do as you see fit." He stood, letter in hand.

"A note to your innamorata?" Gainesworth said with a chuckle.

Atherleigh frowned. "Far from it. Just business. I've decided to shut down my mews."

Hector's impish smile faded. "Why would you do that? You love those birds. You love the hunt."

"Past tense, Hector." Atherleigh held up his bandaged stump.

"If I were you I wouldn't be in so much of a hurry to dispose of everything that reminds you of what you think you've lost."

"What I think I've lost? What I *have* lost!"

Gainesworth shook his head. "Stop cosseting yourself and get to work, man! You still have a life to lead, whether you believe it or not."

"I can lead that life without a mews," Atherleigh said, and strode past Gainesworth to put the letter where it would be taken out the next morning.

CHAPTER 15

*I*n the end, Belinda opted for the simple pink satin domino—the cloak altered by Antonella—and a spangled mask that covered just her eyes. Underneath the domino she wore her deeper rose pink muslin evening dress with lace trim.

"You look heavenly," Antonella said. And Belinda did indeed look a picture, with her glorious tumble of blond curls framing her face, her fair skin and wide forget-me-not eyes.

Belinda wrinkled her nose. "I'm not sure what I think about your costume, Ant. Are you certain you want to wear such an outrageous ensemble?"

Antonella stood in front of the mirror and admired her handiwork. After Belinda's sensible reaction to her idea of wearing breeches, she abandoned the idea. Instead, she found a gentleman's short black cape in one of the trunks in the tower to use as the inspiration for her costume. Once the dust was brushed out of it and a small tear mended, it was quite presentable. Under it, she wore a homespun dress similar to one that their tenants' daughters might wear, to which she'd sewn different colored trailing ribbons. The lining of the cape received the same treatment, although to this and to the plain black mask she added some of the rather bedraggled turkey feathers she'd found decorating a straw bonnet that had seen better days.

Belinda continued to stare at her. "What—or who—are you meant to be?"

"I would have thought that was obvious," Antonella said. "I mean to be exactly what I am." She knew her answer would torment Bee, but she didn't feel like explaining herself just then. "What does it matter anyway? Isn't it time for you to join Mama—excuse me, Lady Lewiston—in the receiving line? At least I'm spared that annoyance." Antonella told herself she didn't care about all those rituals of the class she used to belong to, but it stung her more than she was willing to admit that only Belinda would be standing next to the dowager to greet the guests.

"Are you coming down now?" Belinda asked. "Lord Atherleigh will be here soon I believe, and you must tell him about that bird."

Belinda had not let that matter drop after discovering that Antonella was harboring the injured goshawk. They had been arguing about it on and off ever since. "I don't know. It all depends."

"On what?" Belinda said, planting her fists on her hips and poking her chin forward. "You know it's the right thing to do."

Did she? Perhaps it was. So why was she so reluctant to comply? "I may not have an opportunity. I'll hardly tell him such a thing in the hearing of others, and I daresay it will be difficult to find a private moment."

"Very well. But do try. Come!" Belinda skipped over to the door and opened it wide.

"I'll be down soon. You go," Antonella said.

Antonella counted on Belinda's eagerness to go to the ball to gain a little time alone. She waited until she heard Belinda's steps disappearing down the stairs then tiptoed out of her room and along the corridor to the narrow stairs that led up to the tower. From there she would be able to see the carriages arriving, as it was situated next to the arch that led into the courtyard. She wasn't certain exactly why, but she didn't want to face the guests until Atherleigh was there. She guessed that he, too, would be wishing he didn't have to face all his neighbors. Something big had changed about him as well, although it didn't affect his place in society.

It changed him in a much more obvious way, however. How would he bear having to explain over and over that he had lost part of himself in the war? There were bound to be awkward moments for both of them. People who didn't yet know of her diminished status who would call her Lady Antonella. People who had no idea he'd been injured—let alone lost a hand—who might be offended that he wasn't dancing, even though he was an eligible single gentleman of title and fortune.

At least Lord Atherleigh would be thought brave for having fought for king and country. She, on the other hand, would deserve censure for what might be seen as a deliberate subterfuge. What would the dowager say to her friends and neighbors to explain such a sudden reversal? Likely she would blame it on a caprice of her late husband's and thus gain some sympathy for being put in an awkward position. Although when she thought back to the time immediately following the death of the man she still thought of as her papa, she had to admit that the marchioness had appeared lost. She'd shut herself away for days, grieving sincerely, at least at first. Then when Harry came down to take over the estate, to confer with the steward and see how things stood, her grief began to erode into bitterness. It seemed that every day brought with it a new revelation of the late marquess's mismanagement and poor decisions. The dowager's affection hardened into annoyance and blame. The shift was obvious in her attitudes and manners, her sometimes stony expression, her way of speaking to and treating people—including her adored son and his wealthy wife. And he had made her keep the secret of Antonella's origins and treat her as her own daughter. That must have rankled as much as anything she subsequently discovered.

Antonella took up a position at the window that faced the drive and sat on an upturned crate with her elbows resting on the deep stone sill. A moment later, a voice behind her said, "Antonella? What are you doing up here?"

Miss Wilkins. Antonella sighed. So much for having a chance to gather herself before facing the company downstairs. She turned. "I might ask you the same, Wilkie."

The governess walked forward, a lit candle in her hand. "The party is some distance below you."

"I wish it could stay that way."

Miss Wilkins sighed. "And I wish I could tell you it won't be hard. But it will. You have to face it, though. You cannot hide up here in the tower, or escape to the old library or to your bird shed forever."

She was right. Still … "What is it all for? I mean, Belinda will make a brilliant match and bring honor to the Ambleton name. But why can it possibly matter for me now?"

Miss Wilkins gestured at Antonella's bedraggled costume. "I see you've decided to play the part of outcast."

Antonella pushed out her lower lip in what she knew was a very childish pout. "Why would I bother prettying myself up? I won't find a suitor at a ball like this, or anywhere I daresay. And that's fine. I'll just stay here in Cornwall forever. I can be an eccentric spinster and teach my nieces and nephews about the birds and the animals in the woods.

I'll become their favorite aunt." It was a picture she'd been trying to accustom herself to. The truth was, though, that she didn't much take to children. In her experience they were careless and rough, and were as likely to steal the eggs out of nests as do anything that actually helped the birds.

Miss Wilkins placed her candle in an empty holder she picked up off the floor and rested it on the sill before putting her arm around Antonella's shoulder. "I think you deserve all good things. You deserve love just as much as your sister does."

"But she's not my sister!" Antonella didn't mean to snap, but the mixed messages she was getting from Miss Wilkins and the dowager were beginning to make her head spin.

"All the same, you will go to the party and hold your head up. Nothing has changed about you except that you no longer have a title. Anyone worth bothering about won't care. They'll see you as the sweet, lively girl they've always known."

Miss Wilkins meant well, but those arguments had ceased to mean anything to Antonella, and she hardly attended to her. Instead, she kept her eyes fixed on the carriages pulling up and passing under the arch beneath the tower. She recognized most of them thanks to the light of the flambeaux, and mentally counted off the neighbors as they came. Mostly they arrived in closed chaises or landaulets, the weather being so bitter cold. But just then, a handsome curricle drawn by two perfectly matched bays and driven by a young man swept around the curve in the drive leading to the courtyard.

She had only seen the driver once before from a distance, but she easily recognized his passenger. Atherleigh. Something jumped in her stomach.

"Are you all right?" Miss Wilkins asked.

"What? Oh, yes, fine. I think perhaps you're right. It's time

I went down. Better to get it over with. Perhaps I can slip away before the dancing." She hoped Wilkie wouldn't pry into what made her suddenly change her mind—although knowing the governess, she'd figure it out soon enough. In any case, she couldn't have explained it just then. Perhaps it had something to do with Atherleigh's mews, what she assumed was his one-time love of falconry, and her desire to change his mind about closing them. Or it could have been the remembered sensation of his strong hand covering hers on the reins of the horse he had to mount with her help.

Or perhaps it was the hope that he—with his physical handicap—would be kind to her despite her social handicap. Whatever it was, Antonella decided she could delay her entrance to the ball no longer. She tied her decorated mask over her eyes, nodded to Miss Wilkins, and went downstairs.

MALCOLM CHOSE A SIMPLE BLACK DOMINO WITH A BLACK MASK that covered the top half of his face. He refused to don the elaborate costume Hector had suggested. His friend had unearthed a gold brocade coat from the previous century in one of the closets in a disused bedroom, its flaring skirt and deep cuffs absurd by today's measure. Malcolm also dissuaded Hector from making use of that same coat, saying it made him look like a counter-coxcomb. Instead, Hector coaxed a housemaid to sew some rosettes to his satin knee breeches, wrapped a broad scarlet cummerbund around his middle, pinned ersatz orders all over his lapels, and carried a chapeau-bras. His valet, Hinsdale, covered his plain black mask with gold satin fabric he procured from lord-only-knew where and sewed on glass beads to look like jewels. The effect was humorous rather than glamorous, but it suited Gainesworth.

All the way to Amblemere Atherleigh cursed himself for agreeing to go, but Gainesworth would not be gainsaid.

"It's not your execution, Mal!" Hector said, nudging Atherleigh in the ribs as he steered the frisky pair expertly along the winding country road. "Just smile. If you arrive sporting a scowl all the ladies will be afraid of you."

Would they not be afraid of him anyway when they saw his injury? At least the voluminous domino gave him a way to conceal his wounded arm. "What will I do if the hostess tries to present me with a desirable partner for a dance?"

"She knows about your hand. She wouldn't do that."

No, that was certainly true. Then why had he agreed to go to a ball?

He feared he knew why. Her name had been mentioned almost with derision by her ladyship, but it was a name that had stuck in his mind for a week and refused to become dislodged. Antonella. Apparently *not* Lady Antonella, and the dowager's explanation for her existence was obfusc, to say the least. So why had he heard as long as he could remember that Lewison had two sisters? The girl—Antonella—didn't look like Lewiston very much, it was true, although a kind of resemblance existed. It was as if the marquess's mild features had been exaggerated and refined into a female countenance —his warm brown eyes and light brown hair intensified to a shining pair of almost obsidian eyes and hair so dark as to be nearly black. Also the shape of the face, the patrician nose and that full upper... he could detect the Ambleton features there. Would a distant relationship result in these similarities?

They soon arrived at the Court, which had been transformed in two days from a rather shambolic, sparsely populated mansion to a scene of the liveliest sociability. Its windows blazed with candles and a stream of guests poured out of the coaches that circled the courtyard. Some wore dominos, others sported more elaborate costumes. Everyone laughed and generally displayed the freedom of behavior made possible by a simple mask. The weather cooperated— Malcolm could only imagine what a disaster it would be if it rained, or even snowed. But the night was mild for the time of year, the roads relatively dry, and a full moon promised to light the neighbors home.

The two friends greeted Lady Lewiston and Lady Belinda, who stood inside the door in the front entry hall, just past where footmen were taking cloaks to a parlor to the left of the entrance. Gainesworth hadn't described Lady Belinda to him, but with the image of the dark Antonella in his mind, her fair, ingenuous beauty took him by surprise. He watched Hector's reaction to her to see if he could discern whether the lady was simply one more in a long succession of flirts, or whether the fellow had really fallen in love this time.

He had his answer as soon as Gainesworth's eyes met Lady Belinda's. Hector had not lied about his feelings. He'd never seen him look at a woman in just that way before, as if taking his eyes off her would be exquisite torture. Lady Belinda, although making an effort to behave like a demure, well-bred ingenue, lit up when her gaze fell on Gainesworth.

Yes. They were in a case to be heading toward parson's mousetrap.

Atherleigh and Gainesworth followed the guests into a large saloon that had been festooned with an odd combination of fir garlands and arrangements of dried flowers on the tables placed next to chairs and settees. Only a few of the more elderly guests sat. The groupings of ladies and gentlemen formed and reformed as acquaintances greeted one another. Two footmen moved among them with trays of champagne and ratafia. Malcolm recognized all the gentry who lived within easy distance of Amblemere.

This was a trial indeed. He would have to make introductions for Gainesworth. He turned to say something to his friend only to find that he wasn't there. Where had he gone? Malcolm turned in a circle looking for him, but could not see him anywhere.

"Is that Atherleigh behind that mask?" a gruff voice said as he completed his circuit and took a glass from the tray that had materialized at his elbow. He turned and found himself staring into the eyes of Sir Richard Etherington, middle-aged owner of a tidy estate near Bodmin and local magistrate. The baronet hadn't worn a costume, only nodding to the spirit of the occasion with a short evening cloak. Sir Richard put out his hand to shake, but Malcolm's was occupied holding his champagne glass. He moved as if to put it into his left hand and then realized that would be impossible.

"Sir William, delighted to see you," Malcolm said as he looked around for a surface where he could rest his glass and walked a few steps over to a table to place it down.

When he returned, the baronet's sanguine expression had hardened. No doubt he thought he'd been insulted. An explanation would be in order. "I beg your pardon," Atherleigh said. "You must think me unconscionably rude, but you see, I have the use of only one hand, thanks to the gentle ministrations of the French." He did his best to make a joke of it, but the look that passed over the older man's face said everything Malcolm most dreaded. It conveyed embarrassment, confusion, and pity.

"I'd heard you were wounded. So sorry Atherleigh. Do you plan to make your home here in Cornwall?"

The last thing Malcolm wanted was to discuss his future with someone who was only the barest acquaintance. "My plans are not yet fixed," he said, and then "Excuse me, I must find Gainesworth." Without giving Sir Richard the opportunity to respond, he walked away, not caring if he or anyone else in the room thought him uncivil. Where was Hector?

MUSIC FILTERED UP FROM THE GREAT-HALL-TURNED-ballroom, indicating that the dancing had started. From the landing on the double stairway that led to both wings of the mansion one could peer down into the front entrance hall on one side and the great hall on the other. Both views gave a bizarre perspective of heads and hats and costumes. A bird's-eye view, Antonella thought with a laugh. Most people had thrown themselves with abandon into the opportunity for a joyous event at a dismal time of year, and conversations and laughter ebbed and flowed. In the old days at least, there were those who spent weeks planning what they would wear to the Lewiston masquerade.

"Ant!" Belinda's voice sailed up from the bottom of the stairs, and she ran daintily up them and grasped Antonella's hand. "Come with me. There's someone I want you to meet."

Before she could protest, Belinda was dragging Antonella down the stairs not to the great hall, but through the entrance hall and into a small parlor. Among the few guests who had strayed there perhaps looking for a quieter place to talk stood a golden-haired gentleman arrayed in a patched-together costume that made Antonella smile despite herself. It couldn't be identified as anything in particular, but had the effect of making the gentleman—whom she recognized now as Gainesworth—appear rather like a court jester. Belinda pulled her to stand right in front of her opposite the gentleman. "I'd like to introduce Mr. Gainesworth to you. Sir, this is my sister, Antonella. I told you about her in London."

The mask made it a little difficult to see his expression, but Antonella was sure a quick look of surprise and disappointment flitted through the eyes that peeped out of the holes in his mask.

"Your humble servant, My Lady," he said and bowed over her proffered hand.

She was about to correct him, but Belinda trod on her toe. "Ow!"

"I'm sorry! How clumsy of me," Belinda said. Then she turned to Gainesworth. "As I told you in London, my sister is by far the cleverest of the two of us, and I knew she would have the answer to your question about what kinds of birds we have in our spinney and coverts."

What on earth was Belinda saying? "I daresay you're interested in the birds you can shoot. My sister has misled you, I'm afraid. I only know of the songbirds and raptors."

"Truly?" Gainesworth said, his eyes lighting up. "Then I wish you would come with me. I have little interest in such things, but my friend will be most eager to engage you in conversation. And after that, Lady Belinda, I would be honored if you would stand up with me in the next set."

"But don't you wish to become better acquainted with Antonella?" Belinda said.

Why did she say that? It was clear to Antonella that Gainesworth was more interested in Belinda, and all the signs were there in Belinda that—if she didn't already have a tendre for him—she found him quite attractive.

"Of course! But you promised me."

"I'm afraid you'll have to wait." Belinda peered out into the entrance hall and glanced around. "As soon as Lord Bartleson comes I have to stand up with him. So you may as well talk to Antonella. I must go and do the pretty or my Mama will be furious."

Before either of them could protest, Belinda tripped away and vanished into the saloon.

Antonella found herself almost alone with Gainesworth, who was clearly wishing he could have followed her sister. "So you met Belinda in London?" was all she could think of to say.

"Yes. I must say I think Lady Belinda is quite extraordinary."

Antonella smiled. "Yes, she is. She is the kindest person I know. And she's smarter than she appears—I didn't mean that, I only meant that because of her beauty, sometimes people think that's all she has to offer."

Gainesworth smiled. "I was fortunate to discover immediately that she adds wit and intelligence to her other charms. And the two of you are very fond of each other, I see."

"Yes," Antonella said, a wistful note in her voice.

"Might I be so bold as to ask you something that has been perplexing me since the other day, when Atherleigh and I paid our call on Lady Lewiston? Please tell me if I'm being impertinent."

"Ask me what you will. I do not promise I will answer."

He paused, opened his mouth to speak, then closed it again, then opened it again and said, "Lady Belinda refers to you as her sister, but Lady Lewiston told us you were a more distant relation, a cousin, I believe. Yet I'm certain I've heard Lewiston talk of his younger twin sisters."

Oh dear. He had asked a very direct and inconvenient question. Why did he care? She took some time before responding to him. Couples wandered by on their way to a room where light refreshments were being served for those whose exertions on the dance floor made them hungry before the midnight supper. "We were brought up as twins until recently, and are as close as two sisters could ever be. Upon our eighteenth birthday a few weeks ago, our mother —I shouldn't even call her that—Lady Lewiston told us that it had all been a fiction, that I was only a poor relation left with them to be cared for from infancy."

This was all still so new to Antonella that she hadn't even had time to figure out how to explain her situation. And yet here she was, telling of it to a total stranger. Why? He was a stranger, yes, yet there was something about him that invited confidence. Perhaps it was his eyes. Or his voice. She began to understand what Belinda had found so taking in him. "You mustn't judge us too harshly."

"Please don't make yourself uneasy. I shouldn't have asked. Thank you for confiding in me." He sighed and looked off into the middle distance for a moment before returning all his attention to Antonella. "It seems a strange affair. It can't have been easy for you to go from being a marquess's respected daughter to someone whose origins are shrouded in mystery. From *Lady Antonella* to *Miss Ambleton*. I daresay it still seems unreal to you."

Antonella suddenly felt the sting of tears behind her eyes and blinked furiously. He'd pressed on that very sensitive nerve, the one that had made her feel she might not dare attend the masquerade after all. "What a thing to talk about at a ball!" she said, shaking her head and forcing a smile. 'I imagine you'd like to go and dance with my sister. I think I shall go to the retiring room."

"Truly? Won't *you* dance with me? Unless you're already spoken for in the next set. Lady Belinda is standing up with someone else at the moment, I believe."

At this, Antonella opened her cloak wide and spread her arms to reveal the full effect of her rather cheeky costume.

After a confused moment, Gainesworth grinned, and then laughed. "You and your sister are the two most remarkable ladies I have ever met! Shall we? But you must promise not to fly away."

This surprised a laugh from Antonella. She could, in fact,

fly away if it all became too much for her. He put out his arm and she rested her hand lightly upon it. Her mother would be surprised to see her on the arm of any eligible young gentleman, no doubt. But it was a masquerade after all! Besides, hearing the music and seeing all the guests infected her with a lighter mood. She wanted to dance. She was good at it. And Gainesworth made a charming escort.

CHAPTER 16

It's all going just as I planned! Belinda thought when she saw Antonella enter the great hall on Gainesworth's arm. She will dance with him and charm him. Her lively conversation and mischievous nature will appeal to someone like him, someone with so much address and conversation, someone so open and warm.

And he was kind, too. She could tell that just by the way he smiled at Antonella and treated her as if she were still owed all the consideration due to the daughter of a marquess. Her mother had told them at dinner that she'd set Gainesworth and Atherleigh straight about Antonella's relationship to the family, so Belinda knew he wasn't unaware. She worried at first that his having such knowledge would upset her plans, that he would be unwilling to treat Antonella with respect. Clearly she had underestimated him.

Lord Bartleson was her partner for the same set. He turned out to be a much better dancer than she supposed he might be, judging by his awkwardness and portly build. He did pull her a little closer than necessary when the figure of the dance allowed it and held onto her hand as long as he could at other times. His palms also tended to sweat through his gloves. No wonder, Belinda thought. He'd dressed as a cavalier and wore a heavy brocade cape and slashed sleeves and breeches. Rivulets of perspiration trickled down his cheeks from under the mask that covered his eyes and occasionally found their way onto the pink satin of Belinda's domino.

Out of the corner of her eye Belinda watched Antonella and Gainesworth, trying to judge whether they were enjoying each other's company. From the smile on Ant's face, it certainly seemed as if she was. Why was it, then, that every time she and Mr. Gainesworth joined hands for a figure of the dance and took their turn to go down the center of the line Belinda felt a little pang in her middle? Foolish, she thought. It was just that she felt protective of Antonella. This thought, and her determination to keep to her plan, made her turn her most winning smile toward her partner, who after that grasped her hands harder and looked at her with ardor kindling in his eyes. *Oh dear,* Belinda thought. She did not want the earl to be deceived about how she felt.

At last the set ended and Bartleson clamped her hand in the crook of his arm to lead her off the floor. He asked her if she would like a glass of champagne. "Or perhaps you would prefer lemonade?"

"No, thank you," Belinda said wishing she could extricate herself from him and that Mr. Gainesworth would approach her now to claim his two sets.

Unfortunately, after Gainesworth left Antonella on the side of the room he walked away, perhaps to procure a drink for her. Belinda was about to go to Ant, but a gentleman was approaching her, so she stayed where she was and did her best to make small talk with the winded Bartleson.

Dancing with Mr. Gainesworth had lulled Antonella into

a feeling of safety, of believing that her altered status would not be remarked by anyone. When their set ended, he took her off the floor and excused himself to go and procure her a glass of lemonade. At first she stood in a pleasant haze, remembering his kind eyes, the occasional pressure of his hand, and the grin that made him appear mischievous even through the mask.

It wasn't long, though, before a young gentleman approached her and looked her somewhat impudently up and down. She thought there was something familiar about him, but couldn't quite place him.

"It's Lady Antonella I perceive—forgive me, I mean Miss Ambleton. The poor relation. Quite a come-down I imagine. I'm surprised you're here. Not so high and mighty now, are you? Not fit to associate with any of us," he said with a sweeping gesture that encouraged two other young men to join him.

As soon as he spoke, Antonella knew exactly who he was. Will Parkin. She recognized his pale blue eyes, his pinched face and thin-lipped smirk. He'd been a mean little boy, always preying on younger children and making them cry at birthday parties. At one such, Antonella had defended a little girl whose hair he'd been pulling mercilessly by yanking Parkin's hair in turn just as hard. It made him cry. Everyone laughed at him, exhorting him to run to his Mama. He never forgave her for it.

His unpleasant personality did not interfere with inheriting his title, however. Honors never depended on deserts. He was now Lord Melchet. His father, the viscount, died in a riding accident a year earlier.

The other two were his friends, and every bit as unsavory: James Allen, son of a wealthy landowner, and the honorable Simon Jenkins, whose father was a baron. The three of them stood close together and backed her against the wall, forming a barrier between her and any escape route. When they were children, they had been small enough for Antonella to look them in the eye. Now, they towered over her. *Don't panic,* she thought. After all, they were in a ballroom among genteel guests. What could they do to her?

Jenkins took hold of one side of Antonella's cape and held it open, revealing the ribbons and feathers. They all started to laugh. Jenkins said, "I suppose you'll be flying away soon, back to your hovel."

She lifted her chin and glared at each of them in turn. "If you will excuse me, I believe my Aunt Caroline is looking for me." She took a step forward in an attempt to make them part and let her through, but they stood firm.

"Aunt Caroline? Oh, you mean the dowager marchioness, who it turns out is not your mother." It was Allen's turn to taunt her.

Now she was angry. How dare they! She thrust her hand forward and tried to make a space between two of them so she could wriggle through, but Melchet grabbed her wrist, holding it tight and low so no one outside of their group could see he was doing it. "Let me go!" she spit through clenched teeth, aware that she must not make a scene in the middle of the party.

"What can you do about it?" he said. "I'm here to warn you that you ought not try to mix with your betters anymore or we'll make your life very uncomfortable." He squeezed her wrist harder.

"Gentlemen!" The voice cut through the maleficent laughter of the three men.

Belinda!

"Or are you, in fact gentlemen? Kindly leave my sister alone."

"Sister indeed! Surely you don't want to be tainted with her disgrace," Melchet said.

Eyes flashing and quivering with rage, Belinda said, "She is far more noble than you will ever be!"

"Noble?" he said, a sneer making his unpleasant mouth look positively vile beneath his mask, "I was thinking my Mama could use another scullery maid."

Belinda drew her hand back and Antonella reached out to try to prevent her dealing Melchet a humiliating slap.

But she wasn't able to do so. Gainesworth had appeared from behind Belinda and taken hold of her arm, dropping the glass of lemonade he'd fetched for Antonella, which shattered on the floor. In the chaos, all three of Antonella's tormentors scattered as if a sudden violent wind had swept them away. Two footmen rushed over and began sweeping up the glass and mopping the spill, and Antonella fled, not caring where as along as it was away from there.

It took very little time for Atherleigh to become heartily bored of answering well-meaning questions about his injury. He supposed it was good to get it over with, that perhaps his neighbors would then be saved the necessity of calling on him out of courtesy. He initially hoped he'd changed enough that few people would even realize who he was, but doubtless the gossip network of the servants' halls had spread news of his presence at the manor far and wide. On top of the discomfort of having to explain his injury, the press of so many people unnerved him after his months of enforced solitude. He wished he could find Hector and persuade him that it was time to go home. But judging by his friend's reaction to Lady Belinda, Malcolm thought he'd be as likely to agree to that as fly to the moon.

The mask at least gave him the illusion of anonymity, acting as a barrier between himself and the rest of the world.

Those who didn't know him well were easily fooled by it and saved him some effort. It wasn't enough though. He soon found himself desperate to get away, to be alone again. He thought that if he searched he might find an unoccupied corner somewhere. Amblemere Court was a rambling old place that likely had some half-forgotten rooms.

He wandered through saloons and parlors on the first floor, nodding to acquaintances and behaving as if he was looking for someone in particular. When he found no promising hiding places he descended the grand stairs to the ground floor. There he entered the large dining room, where tables were in the process of being overloaded with dishes of food—everything from lobster patties to raised meat pies to jellies. He supposed Gainesworth wouldn't want to leave before supper, and he shuddered. How was he to eat in front of strangers?

Another saloon had been given over to cards and was already populated by a half dozen of the older guests. An unattractive option for him. He could not deal or shuffle, or even hold a hand well. Perhaps he could find the library, lose himself in a book. Likely such a room would be at the back of the house with a view over the gardens. He did his best to appear as though he had a purpose as he continued to thread through the guests and nod to one or two of them. So far all he'd found was a family breakfast parlor, a butler's pantry, and some kind of anteroom that appeared to lead to the kitchen wing.

He'd seen every room in that part of the house except the ballroom. The great hall—the heart of the old part of the mansion—was by far the most crowded place in the house, all the revelers seeking their enjoyment within it. Much as he'd rather avoid it, he could not reach the back of the house without passing by its entrance.

As he approached the open doors that led into the high-ceilinged, timbered hall, a diminutive figure in a black short cape ran out of them as if being chased by someone who meant her harm. For it was most definitely a lady. The cape winged out behind her to reveal a plain gown underneath and—were they feathers?

She fled toward the rear of the house and through a servants' door that likely led to a back stair. So it appeared she knew the house well. It could only be Miss Ambleton, then. Antonella. What happened to upset her? It had nothing to do with him. He chuckled to himself. Why should he care, beyond being mildly curious?

But he was curious. More than curious. She had intrigued him on that day when she helped him get back on his horse. Lady Lewiston's revelation of her status in the household also confused him. He quickened his pace to reach the door she'd gone through telling himself he was simply trying to find that elusive moment of solitude. If he happened to run into Miss Ambleton, perhaps she could lead him somewhere he would not be disturbed.

The door led to a corridor dimly lit by wall sconces, clearly a passage to another part of the house. Like many centuries-old mansions, Amblemere Court had been modified many times. The original apartments were apparently on the other side of the courtyard from the one where the ball was taking place. This passage must lead to chambers considered too cramped or drafty for comfort, Malcolm thought, abandoned in favor of larger and airier modern saloons. The dark wainscoting carved in elegant relief evoked the taste of a time before the revolution. Passing through that place was like stepping into the past.

If only actually going back in time were so easy. Just a few years, perhaps, before the war. Or would he really change anything? He had served his country and become a man.

That was well enough, but surely there could have been easier ways to reach maturity.

Atherleigh became so lost in his own imaginings that at first he didn't notice the sound of quiet sobs emanating from behind a partly open door, beyond which all was dark. He approached it stealthily, listening. It took only a moment for him to realize that Miss Ambleton must be within, and that whatever had happened in the ballroom to send her hurtling out of it had distressed her enough not only to make her leave, but to send her to the solace of weeping in private. Perhaps she wanted to be alone, and if he intruded she would be angry—or embarrassed.

But the suppressed misery of those sobs tore at his heart. They made something inside him vibrate in sympathy. He couldn't just go away.

He cleared his throat. The weeping stopped. "Is there any way I may help you?" Malcolm said into the dark space.

A loud sniff preceded a somewhat watery reply. "N-no. I'm fine. Please just let me alone."

"You don't sound well. Has something happened to distress you?"

"I said I'm fine. This part of the house is private. Please go back and join the other guests."

He said nothing for a while, listening as Miss Ambleton took a deep, shaky breath, clearly trying to regain control of herself. "I would be happy to bring you a glass of water," Malcolm said and slowly opened the door, letting in a slash of light from the hallway, enough to see that the room was little more than a closet. Miss Ambleton sat in its deepest corner, knees bent, face buried in her folded arms.

The oddest thing, though, was that turkey feathers poked out from under her cape here and there, and she hadn't removed the mask that covered her eyes, which was trimmed with more feathers. She looked for all the world like a little brown wren hiding in a hole in a tree.

"What are you doing here anyway," she said, in a voice that was still somewhat ragged.

"I was looking for the book room." Malcolm realized this sounded quite ridiculous. Who looks for a book room at a ball?

She gave a short, bitter laugh. "You must know you wouldn't find it back here. Only the servants use this part of the house anymore."

"So what are you doing here? You're not a servant."

"No? What am I then?"

"If I am not mistaken, you are Miss Ambleton."

"Yes, but *who is Miss Ambleton?* I don't know her. I've never met her before. She appears to be very well educated and polite, pretty behaved, and can do all the things ladies are taught to do. But she is not a lady."

Malcolm pulled one of the candles out of a nearby sconce and stepped a little inside the small room with it. "I see a lady before me—but she is at the moment disguised as a little bird, perhaps a fledgling, fallen from the nest."

Miss Ambleton gasped.

"What did I say?"

"It's nothing. But I think you should leave now." At last she looked up at him. She removed her mask, and her large dark eyes reflected the candle flame and glittered with tears.

Malcolm was seized by an almost overpowering desire to lift Antonella from where she sat and fold her into his arms. But that, too, was ridiculous. He wouldn't be able to do it with the use of only one hand. To try would be to expose his disgusting weakness—of course, she already knew about it. He stepped back a little and pushed the door open wider. "Perhaps you might like to rejoin the party? Or retire for the night? After you have directed me to the book room, that is."

Miss Ambleton slowly unfolded herself from her tightly crouched position. Malcolm instinctively reached his hand out to help her rise before he realized he couldn't. His only good hand was holding a candle. She must have seen something in his face, because she said, "No need to worry about me. I expect you understand what it's like to find your life suddenly altered beyond all recognition."

"I would have thought that in your situation it was external circumstances only that had suffered an alteration, that you are in essence the same as you always were," Malcolm said, with a sudden realization that Hector had said something very similar to him.

Miss Ambleton smoothed down her skirts and squared her shoulders. "Perhaps you are right. Perhaps I never was a lady at all anyway. If you will forgive me, I think I must leave now."

She came toward him and suddenly he had a vision of her out in the open air, afraid of getting too near his horse but valiantly trying to overcome her fear so she could help him, and he smiled.

"My leaving makes you smile?" she said with a wry quirk of one eyebrow.

"No, I'm sorry. I just remembered our first conversation, when I thought you were one of the forest folk, a sprite."

She uttered a short, mirthless laugh. "For all I know, that is precisely what I am."

"If you are, then you are fortunate. You could disappear at will. Cast spells on those who displease you. Fly to the tree-tops and sing with the birds." Where did these absurd flights of fancy come from?

"What I am not is willing to return to my Mama's—I mean, my Aunt Caroline's—holiday masquerade. I won't be missed. But you will. I expect your friend—Mr. Gainesworth —is wondering where you are."

"No doubt," Malcolm said with a sigh. "Do you suppose supper is over yet?"

She said nothing for a long moment, and then, "Does it trouble you very much?"

Antonella had not looked toward his hand, but he knew exactly what she meant. "Yes. I cannot even cut my own meat. I have been reduced to the helpless state of childhood."

She cocked her head on the side, reminding him even more forcibly of a curious little bird. "You did not look like a child when you rode away on your horse," Antonella said.

"No. I expect everything will become easier with practice, too. But there is one thing I will never be able to do, and until I find a way to accept it, I fear I will be no fit company for anyone." Lord he sounded pathetic!

"Is that your way of saying you wouldn't want to see me again?"

Was it? Atherleigh couldn't decide exactly why he had said all that to this young girl he hardly knew. "No. I would very much like to see you again." The words were out of his mouth before he had time to consider them. He saw her stiffen and draw back a little. "That is, if it would please you," he added, awkwardly, like a schoolboy.

"I think you should go back to the party," Antonella said, but in a much softened voice. "I shall retire. Thank you for cheering me up."

"Is that what I did?" He lifted the candle up and turned, looking for a way to put it back into a sconce so he could shake her hand.

But she reached out and took it from him with her left hand and put her right hand out to shake his. Malcolm grasped it, a tiny, delicate, cold hand, and lifted it to his lips. "Goodbye, Miss Ambleton."

"Don't call me that. It's not me," she said, letting him keep her hand in his.

"Then what shall I call you?"

"My name is Antonella. Belinda calls me Ant." She smiled for the first time that evening, and her sad eyes lit with a gleam of humor. "Aunt Caroline hates it and would be furious to know I told you."

"Antonella is certainly a mouthful," he said. A mouthful of a name for so slight a person. "But Ant is far too abbreviated for my taste. Might I call you Nella?"

She inhaled sharply at this.

"What's wrong?"

Her voice came out in a whisper. "My Papa used to call me that."

"I won't then, if you don't like it," Malcolm said.

"No. I do like it, My Lord."

"That *My Lord* won't do at all," Atherleigh said with a smile. "You shall have to call me Malcolm."

Although meant to lighten the tone of their conversation, Miss Ambleton met this request with a long pause. At last she said, "I-I can't. Good night…Sir," and swept a graceful curtsy to Atherleigh before scampering away down the corridor and through another door.

CHAPTER 17

*I*t was hardly the most gallant way of persuading a lady to dance with him, but Gainesworth saw in an instant that if a terrible scene were to be averted, he must act quickly.

"Let go of me!" Lady Belinda hissed at him as he drew her forcibly from the small knot of louts who had gathered around Miss Ambleton.

"I shall, at the end of this waltz," he murmured, drawing her into his arms for that still somewhat daring dance. He was frankly surprised that the dowager had allowed it to be played. Perhaps she considered it part of the greater license permitted at a masquerade.

Lady Belinda was stiff in his arms, not at all like the soft, amenable girl he'd danced with in London. She had spoken of her sister at that time, but only now did he see how fiercely she cared for her. Yet Lady Lewiston told them quite clearly the other day that Antonella Ambleton was not her daughter—and not Lady Belinda's sister. Although he didn't know the incumbent marquess well, he was positive he had heard him talk about his *two* sisters making their come-outs in the next season.

"Look at me," he said to his reluctant partner. He raised his mask to his forehead so she could see full into his eyes. "Let it go, for now."

Somewhat to his surprise, she obeyed his command and trained her beautiful, searching eyes on his. When he first met her at the Granvilles', they'd been bright and full of wonder—and quite seriously dazzling. Now, shadows dimmed their brightness and they appeared a shade darker than he remembered. He desperately wanted to kiss them back to the joyful irreverence of their first meeting. What exactly had happened in this supposedly happy *ton* family to cut up Lady Belinda's peace like that?

"I have an enormous favor to ask of you, Mr. Gainesworth," she said after what seemed a long silence—a silence filled with the strains of the waltz, the rhythm of shoes tapping on the polished wood floor, and the undulating murmur of other couples chatting.

He wanted to say, *I will gladly do anything for you,* because he felt it. This loving, amusing, beautiful young woman had somehow broken the insouciant shell he surrounded himself with. Not only that, but she had pierced straight through the veneer of sophistication and ennui immediately beneath it that shielded him from the strategically aimed arrows hurled by matchmaking mamas. The wonder of it was that she hadn't really tried. "You have only to say what it is you want," he replied, and slightly pressed the small of her back.

She drew in a quick breath and widened her eyes. "I'm afraid you don't understand. I mean, you've mistaken me."

Before that moment, she had gradually relaxed and given in to the movement of the dance, but suddenly she went as rigid as a tree trunk. "Have I offended you in some way, Lady Belinda?" Gainesworth said.

She shook her head. "Oh dear, I don't know what to say. How to say it, I mean."

"I find that direct and honest usually answers the need."

Lady Belinda bit her lower lip. A surge of desire went through his body. He pictured what it would be like to kiss that lovely mouth. He was so lost in this pleasant vision that he almost missed her words.

"Would you be so kind as to court Antonella? I think you would deal famously together. I want her to be happy."

What? Had he heard her correctly?

He was so surprised by this unexpected request that he opened his mouth to speak, but nothing came out. He couldn't give her an answer. He certainly didn't want to give her the answer she clearly hoped for. Did she not understand that he was very decidedly courting *her*? That he had come to visit his friend in this inhospitable part of Cornwall for no other purpose?

Apparently not.

Noticing his lack of response, Lady Belinda said in a rush, "You don't have to answer right now! Of course you must get to know Antonella better. But you see, it's all so very unfair. She can't have a season, and how else will she find a husband?"

Now Lady Belinda's eyes brimmed with tears and she blinked fast to stop them falling. Hector wanted to halt right there in the middle of the waltz, take her somewhere to sit, and give her his handkerchief so she could dry her eyes. But they were locked in the demands of the dance and to interrupt it would call attention to them in a most unfortunate way.

"Lady Belinda, I—"

"No!" she said. "It was unfair of me to ask you that in public like this. It was just seeing Antonella, and the way those..."

He watched in slight amusement as she sought some way to describe the three ungentlemanly characters.

"...those miscreants attacked her." She gave her head a quick shake.

"I would have employed a more colorful term to describe them," Hector said, suppressing a smile.

"Yes! You see? I need to make her safe, to protect her. We've been everything to each other for our entire lives. If we weren't truly twins, I don't know how we managed to form such a close bond."

The music came to its closing cadence and they stepped apart from each other and bowed. He took Lady Belinda's hand and led her off the floor. A gentleman Gainesworth didn't know caught sight of her and was making a beeline in their direction. Swiftly, before the gentleman could claim her for the next dance, Hector pulled Belinda out of the ball-room, down the hallway, and into a saloon.

It was the rose saloon, the one in which Lady Lewiston had greeted them on their courtesy visit, and in which she had told them the true situation with regard to her daughter and Miss Ambleton. For that evening the space had been transformed from coolly formal but slightly threadbare to unexpectedly cheery and comfortable. A large, rectangular room with windows on two sides, it was now skillfully subdivided into small conversation areas by means of tables and chairs grouped strategically to accommodate a few people, far enough apart for independent conversation. Fresh greens festooned the fireplace and the windows, giving off a pleasant, woodsy scent.

After a quick survey of the room, Hector spotted a small table with two chairs next to it that was tucked a little into a corner, away from the others, and steered Lady Belinda over to it. As soon as they sat down, a footman arrived with a tray of glasses of champagne. He took two of them and gave one to Belinda, ignoring her refusal.

"Now, My Lady, it's time you told me exactly what is going on here. I have no quarrel with you for wishing to find a suitable match for the girl you grew up believing to be your twin sister. But the human heart is impossible to command. Tell me what makes you think you have the right to determine Miss Ambleton's future." Gainesworth congratulated himself on avoiding a direct answer to Lady Belinda's request while at the same time turning the question away from himself.

Lady Belinda sipped her champagne. And then, instead of putting the glass daintily down on the table, tipped it up and drank several big gulps.

"Most unusual lady I have ever met," Gainesworth said, a broad grin lighting his face.

"I know that was unladylike. Ever since Mama's *conversation* with us I've felt sorely tempted to misbehave, to show her that if Antonella is not a lady, then neither am I." She hugged herself tightly and leaned away from him as though fearing an attack.

He reached across, pulled one of her gloved hands free, and placed it on the table, covering it with his own. "You have nothing to fear from me. Won't you tell me the whole?" Of course, he had no right to inquire. He might, if they were actually betrothed. But according to Lady Belinda they weren't even courting. Hector was also aware that he was treating her more like one of his own younger sisters than like someone with whom he was trying to fix his interest. Surely more than simple modesty and reticence lay between him and his goal of winning Lady Belinda Ambleton, however.

And so, Belinda recounted the entire scene in her mother's apartment. It had occurred only days before he and Lady Belinda met at the dress party. No wonder she was in such a fret.

"I understand you feel very sorry for her, but such a situation is not wholly unusual in families."

"No, you don't understand. I am quite certain my mother is not being truthful. I believe that Antonella is probably not my twin—we look so unalike, after all—but how she explained what happened … it made no sense! What would have prevented my parents from allowing it to be known right from the beginning that we had a poor cousin whom they had taken in out of charity?"

He had to admit, she had a point. He thought for a moment, then said, "Would it help you to be in full possession of the facts about your sister's—Miss Ambleton's—birth?"

"It would not change the way things are," Lady Belinda said, "but I hate being lied to. Mama thinks we're still children who don't know anything and don't deserve to understand adult matters. So yes, I suppose it would."

She removed her mask and tossed it onto the table between them, revealing not just her eyes but her long, curling lashes and arched eyebrows. That such a beautiful creature could also possess such a true heart, could be so open and warm, took Hector's breath away. He gave himself a mental shake and refocused on the matter at hand. "Supposing, then, that instead of courting Miss Ambleton, I put my efforts into uncovering the truth of her origins. Surely having certain knowledge of her parentage would be essential in any case."

Belinda instantly looked up, mingled hope and dismay in her eyes. "But how could you? Why would you? You don't know us."

"The *ton* is a very small place. Few secrets can be buried among its ranks forever. Between Atherleigh and myself, we are probably acquainted with or connected to every family of noble or gentle birth in the country."

She shook her head. "I can't ask it of you."

He smiled. "And yet you can ask me to try to fix my interest with Miss Ambleton, not knowing anything for certain about her birth." He immediately regretted his words.

"Of course, how stupid of me," she said, turning away from him.

At that moment, Atherleigh himself strode into the saloon and scanned it, a look of relief crossing his face as soon as he saw Hector and Lady Belinda.

After nodding a greeting to Lady Belinda Atherleigh said, "Supper will begin soon, and I cannot stay for it. I see you've already revealed your identities to each other so there's no need to remain for the unmasking at midnight."

Gainesworth drilled an annoyed look into his friend's eyes. More than anything he wanted to continue speaking with Lady Belinda. Atherleigh had interrupted at a most inopportune moment. He'd had no chance to assure Lady Belinda that, if his heart were engaged with Miss Ambleton, her obscure birth would not weigh with him. But Malcolm was his host, he was recovering from a devastating injury, and he'd only come to the ball at his behest. So he would have to leave Lady Belinda with an unfavorable opinion of himself.

Belinda had recovered her composure and turned a smiling countenance to Atherleigh before rising, forcing Gainesworth to do the same. "I can well imagine you'd prefer to avoid eating supper in company, Lord Atherleigh," she said. "My mother and I are grateful that you came at all." She stood. "I do have one question for you however, My Lord."

"I will answer it if I am able," Atherleigh said.

"If you were in love with a lady, would her birth, her connections, be of any consequence to you?"

Gainesworth saw her challenging look with dismay and willed his friend to give her the answer she wanted.

Atherleigh took some time before speaking. "I am afraid that in our circles, birth and connections are important. Especially when there are titles to inherit. Mind you, sometimes fortune makes up for lack of gentle birth."

"So you would spurn someone, even if you truly loved her, if she was not your equal in rank or consequence?" Lady Belinda seemed not to have heard anything but the beginning of what Atherleigh had said.

"To what purpose do your questions tend, My Lady?" Atherleigh asked.

Belinda turned her seething gaze toward Gainesworth. "I see that you and your friend agree on this matter."

"Lady Belinda, a hypothetical is not a useful measure of what an individual will do in a specific situation. I daresay all would depend on the female in question, who might have qualities that eclipse any irregularities in her birth or heritage," said Hector, desperately trying to salvage them both in her regard.

The fury in her eyes subsided. "Of course," she said. "Forgive me for being so provocative."

She certainly was provocative, but not in the sense she meant.

"Before we go, I must give you a message from Miss Ambleton, My Lady," Atherleigh said. "She asked me to tell you that she has gone up to bed and will not return to the party."

"When did you see her?" Lady Belinda whirled to face Atherleigh.

"I left her a few minutes ago. She was on her way to a back stair, I believe," Atherleigh said.

"Please excuse me, My Lord, Mr. Gainesworth," Belinda said. "I must find my sister."

Atherleigh exchanged a puzzled look with Hector. Resigned to the fact that he would have to forgo the pleasure of supping with Lady Belinda, Gainesworth nodded to his friend and they set about preparing to leave.

CHAPTER 18

$\mathcal{L}$ady Belinda was in a stew of conflicting emotions when she awoke the morning after the masquerade ball—at a much later hour than she was accustomed to rising. The first image that leapt into her mind was Antonella's horrid treatment by the local boys—she would not dignify them by calling them men, even though they were all at Oxford and likely at least nineteen or twenty years old. What had Antonella ever done to them—aside from beating them at their own games and outwitting them every time they tried to get the better of her?

She'd gone up to find Antonella in her bedroom when Atherleigh and Gainesworth left. But when she tapped on her door, Antonella said she was tired and wanted to go to sleep, that Belinda should leave her alone. She was inclined to ignore the request and just walk in. But the thought of her mother's wrath if she discovered that both of them had fled from the party long before it ended persuaded her this would not be the right thing to do.

So she returned to the ball and danced every set. She had already taken her mask off when she was talking with

Gainesworth, so didn't participate in the raucous unmasking, the artificial surprise of discovering that the person you were flirting with was actually your fiancé.

Bartleson then led her in to supper, much to her chagrin. Overall, the evening felt flat and pointless without Antonella there. Or had it been that? Was Antonella all that was missing? Belinda had an inkling she wasn't.

She closed her eyes and imagined the entire evening. It really began for her the moment Mr. Gainesworth and Atherleigh arrived. It only became real at the moment Gainesworth's gentle hand pressed the small of her back and effortlessly led her around the dance floor in the waltz.

A moment before that, Gainesworth had prevented her from making a scene over those horrid fellows' treatment of Antonella, dragging her away from what threatened to be a highly embarrassing episode. At first, her anger overpowered any other feelings she might have had. But as they danced, something else happened. Her resistance faltered and she couldn't hold onto her fury. She melted, becoming a part of the dance and a part of him. So why had she asked him to court Antonella?

Furthermore, Gainesworth raised a point Belinda had not thought of herself. Who was *she* to choose for Antonella? Did she truly know what her sister wanted?

That was ridiculous. How could Antonella *not* like Gainesworth? He had so many fine qualities—his laughing eyes, his brilliant smile, his courtesy and address, and of course, his acute sense of the ridiculous. More than that, his kindness. He considered what other people thought and felt. All these were attributes Belinda was sure Antonella would not only appreciate, but demand in a husband.

But how could she know for sure? Perhaps she merely attributed her own desires to Antonella. Until this year, all their talk of suitors had been fanciful. They made outrageous plans and concocted the most princely beaus who would ride in on white chargers and carry them away to a castle.

Now the time for fancy was done. They were no longer in the schoolroom. Settling their futures as wives and mothers was now her mother's most important consideration. At least, for her if not for Antonella.

There was the rub. The dowager's revelation of Antonella's unworthy origins had cut deeply. For Antonella, the dream didn't just end, it no doubt acquired a nightmarish quality.

If Gainesworth was unwilling to court Antonella, what then? Would he simply go away? Disappear from their lives altogether?

That would be worse than anything.

Belinda caught herself up short. Why should it matter to her what became of him? Unless … It couldn't be. That would be foolish. The idea that she herself might feel more than a friendship for Gainesworth was preposterous. It wasn't that. She only looked forward to the possibility of seeing him, that was all. Never mind the fact that her heartbeat quickened at the sound of his name. She liked him, as she hoped she would like anyone who married Antonella.

After a moment she realized that she wasn't being honest with herself. *Yes,* she thought, *I like him very much.*

She pressed her hands to her cheeks, feeling the heat of what she well knew was a rosy blush. The image of Gainesworth's handsome face and elegant form was all it took to provoke such a reaction in her. She could not deny it. She was falling in love.

Was he falling in love as well?

Belinda threw the covers off and leapt out of bed. She must go and talk to Antonella. Gainesworth and his rather horrid friend, Lord Atherleigh, had left around midnight—early even by country standards. She knew she should feel sorry for the baron because of his unfortunate injury, but he had such a sullen air and voiced her worst fears about Antonella's prospects in her current status. He was not the kind of man she would choose for her dear sister. Yet the one she did choose wouldn't do either. He wouldn't do for Antonella, but perhaps he would do for her. So what if he was only a mister? Her Grace of Hartland had said he was wealthy. Surely his lack of a title wouldn't be unacceptable to her mother.

Then again, her mother had her eye on an earl for her. A chubby, sweaty earl who was too old and had roving hands.

Before she could erase that image from her mind and don her dressing gown a light tap on the door announced Falk, who entered bearing a tray of chocolate and bread and butter. "They's some posies been delivered, though not like them that come in London. Mostly evergreens and ivy."

Belinda thought with a sigh of that small mountain of flowers that greeted her the morning after Lady Granville's dress party. Yet she recalled none of the names of any of her partners. Except one of course. Gainesworth.

There he was again. Had it been merely a coincidence that Lord Atherleigh was his good friend? He made it seem as if he'd already planned to visit the baron for the holidays before meeting her. Still, it was odd for someone like him to go to such a quiet, out of the way place at this time of year. Surely a gentleman with Gainesworth's lively personality was in great demand at house parties. The heat rose into her cheeks again. Had he done it for her?

Falk laid out a pale green kerseymere dress with long sleeves and cut high to the throat. When Belinda wrinkled her nose at it, she said, "It's bitter cold today. Ye'll want a shawl indoors too. Not one o' them flimsy sarsenets. A good wool paisley."

Belinda stepped to the window, pulled the drape aside,

and looked out. Brilliant sunshine made the frost that covered every hard surface in the garden sparkle like diamonds. She shivered, only partly at the thought of the cold. The weather—and her emotions—had changed overnight.

After she dressed and gulped down the chocolate, she headed in the direction of Antonella's room.

Falk stopped her. "Miss Antonella's gone out."

"Gone out? So early? Where?"

Falk shrugged and said, "No one ever knows where Miss Antonella goes. Likely off to look for birds and bring 'em into her shed to keep them warm in this chill."

It was a possibility, Belinda had to admit. If that were the case, Antonella could be anywhere. There would be no point in looking for her.

With a sigh, she turned her steps to the grand stair and went down to the breakfast room.

All the meager little bouquets were ranged along the sideboard together with their cards. Such a paltry showing compared to London, Belinda thought. She took each card up in a desultory fashion as she drank her coffee. None from Gainesworth. Her heart sank. What she'd said to him must have frightened him away. That was the only explanation. She would have to resign herself to his indifference—toward Antonella, and toward her.

While she was lost in thought, Skilling entered with a folded letter on a silver salver. "For you, My Lady," he said with a bow. Belinda didn't wait to see him leave before opening the note, elegantly written on heavy paper.

Dear Lady Belinda,

We spoke last night of solving a mystery that surrounds Miss Ambleton. In order to commence this project, I will need more information from you. It were best if we could meet and discuss it, as we have no way of knowing how sensitive the secret might be, and wouldn't want to act in a way that would cause someone to hinder our inquiries.

Atherleigh plans a card party the night after next. He will invite some of his neighbors, including you and Miss Ambleton. Of course, your mother will want to chaperone, but I think we may find a quiet moment to discuss our plans.

Perhaps you could do a little investigating of your own before then, see if you can find any papers that pertain to Miss Ambleton's arrival at Amblemere Court.

I wanted to send you a floral tribute, but Atherleigh's succession houses are in a sad state of neglect, and nothing more than weeds thrive there at present. I will atone for this lapse when next we meet in London.

Yours Etc.,

Hector Gainesworth

Belinda's spirits underwent an instant transformation from discouragement and lassitude to nervous excitement. His name was Hector. A noble name! A hero's name! And he wasn't angry. He hadn't forgotten. And she would see him again in two days. Perhaps, after all, he did have a *tendre* for her. She would find out soon. If that were the case it was perfectly acceptable to her. Belinda hadn't said anything to Antonella explicitly about her plan to make a match for her with Gainesworth, so it wouldn't be as if she were stealing away her sister's beau.

She did have a pang of conscience, however, at not keeping to her resolve to find someone for Antonella before she thought about her own future. Perhaps she and Gainesworth would discover something that would help raise Antonella at least part of the way up to her previous rank. A distant cousin was likely at least respectable, if not wealthy.

When the time for nuncheon passed and Antonella still

wasn't back, Belinda began to worry in earnest. It had been a distressing evening for Ant. She might well have gone off for a very long ramble through the woods, perhaps even down to the cove. But it was extremely cold and unlike her to stay out so long in such weather.

It occurred to Belinda that she might be keeping company with that hawk she was harboring in her shed. Belinda shivered. She didn't like birds the way Antonella did. They moved so fast and flew at one. She would wait a bit longer.

Yet with each passing hour, Belinda grew more uneasy. What if Ant had met with an accident? Or decided to run away? No, that would be foolish, and Ant was not foolish. She only had her small allowance, even if she rarely spent it and had amassed a tidy sum, which she hid away under a loose board in the floor of her bedroom. Or would she take such a drastic step?

With this thought, Belinda raced up to Antonella's bedroom and looked in. There was no sign that she'd fled. Everything was where it should be. She sighed with relief. Whatever was troubling her, she wouldn't leave that hawk to starve.

Finally, when the early twilight started to descend and there was still no sign of Antonella, Belinda donned her warmest cloak, wrapped a woolen muffler around her neck, and pulled on her fur-lined gloves. She would have to brave the weather and the bird. If Antonella wasn't there, she couldn't think what she would do next.

CHAPTER 19

$\mathcal{B}$y the time Belinda had found her the night of the masquerade, Antonella had prepared for bed and refused to return to the ball. Nothing Bee could say would persuade her, and eventually she gave up.

The next morning after a restless night, before anyone but the servants were up, Antonella dressed in her drab dimity gown, warm cloak, and paisley shawl and crept down to the kitchens.

"Miss Antonella! Shouldn't you still be abed countin' up yer beaus from last night and waitin' fer posies?" said the cook, Mrs. Mudge, already dusted in flour up to her elbows and with a sheen of perspiration on her forehead.

Antonella wanted to laugh in her face, but of course the old woman meant well and could have no idea of the previous evening's events. But Jenkins, the footman who had swept up the broken glass after Mr. Gainesworth's intervention, gave a discreet cough before taking up the teapot and heading toward the servants' hall. No doubt Mrs. Mudge would soon be apprised of Antonella's humiliation. More than anything Antonella dreaded the pitying looks. But it couldn't be helped. "Are there some scraps of rabbit, perhaps, or a raw chicken gizzard that I might take out to give my birds?"

"Yer birds never want sich a queer diet, not if they've any sense in 'em," Mrs. Mudge said, a puzzled frown on her face.

Of course the cook was imagining the usual robins and sparrows she rescued. Before when she'd looked for food for Zephyra, Antonella had simply taken what she required from the larder, unnoticed in the bustle of the kitchen. "I've got a kestrel to feed," she said, hoping that would suffice to explain it.

Mrs. Mudge shrugged. "I only just started a pail for the pigs and there's some bits in it." She gave Antonella a small chipped bowl and a large spoon. "Mind ye don't mucky up yer gloves."

Antonella thanked her, scooped out some scraps of meat from the pig bucket, and went out through the kitchen door that led to the poultry yard.

The cold wind made her eyes sting and her lungs hurt when she breathed deeply. *Good,* she thought. It felt cleansing. What were rude boys—yes, they were only boys despite their effort to appear manly—compared to the forces of nature? *I mustn't care,* she exhorted herself as she hurried across the frozen ground to her bird shed. Caring wouldn't make it any better.

When the shed came in view her heartbeat slowed and a feeling of calm overspread her. No one could take away her joy in tending to Zephyra. Zephyra did not care who she was, or what her condition.

She opened the shed door and went inside. It was a little warmer, but the cold wind whistled through the gaps between the wooden slats of the flimsy walls and rattled the small window in its frame. Zephyra, who normally greeted her with hungry chirps, sat silent on her perch. Antonella's heart sank. Something was wrong.

"What is it, noble Zephyra?" she murmured, approaching the goshawk slowly and reaching out her gloved hand to stroke the bird's breast. With the ball the night before, Antonella hadn't been able to sneak out in the early evening to give Zephyra her treat and clean the mutes from beneath the perch. There was no mistaking that they smelled a bit foul that day, and for all she knew, they could have been that way since last night.

Perhaps she was imagining it. Her senses were sharpened, her nerves frayed. Surely all was well here. "I have something special for you!" Antonella said, pulling on the heavy gardening glove and then placing a choice bit of meat on the side of her fist. She held it out to Zephyra, who eyed it with her cocked head but did not take it. This behavior was so out of keeping with what Antonella had come to expect from the goshawk that her vague unease rose to panic. "Are you ill?" She gently touched the wounded wing. "The abrasions have healed. I see no infection."

But what did she know, after all? She'd been treating Zephyra mostly by guess and extrapolating from the scraps of information she'd gathered from Rafiq the couple of days she visited him in the mews. Could Zephyra be ill? How? Why? What if she died while in her keeping?

No, she wouldn't let that happen. It was foolish of her to believe she could take care of the goshawk—heal her—all on her own and then bring her back to Atherleigh's mews, triumphant. For that was what she had been imagining: arriving with the majestic bird perched on her makeshift gauntlet looking fierce and whole.

Atherleigh would thank her, and, when she told him the whole story, be astounded that she could have done it alone.

Antonella shook her head. Hubris. Pure hubris. She'd

clung to her trust in a gift she believed she had, an affinity for the delicate creatures who took to the air. She assumed she would be able to face any challenge. Her initial uncertainty had been replaced with growing confidence as Zephyra healed and became accustomed to her. In only a few days she had conceived the plan of rehabilitating the goshawk and until now the possibility of its happy conclusion seemed well within reach.

Foolish, foolish girl. She would have to set aside her pride and her worry that Rafiq would not do all he could to save Zephyra if he found her in her wounded state. He had intimated that he was constrained by being the only falconer, the only person in charge of the mews and all the birds, and so would not have time to devote to a seriously injured hawk.

But she would not let him shirk his duty to Zephyra. Chakor, he called her. She would insist he did his best, no matter what Atherleigh planned for his hunting birds now.

There was no time to think. Antonella knew what she must do. She left the scraps where Zephyra could reach them if her appetite returned and turned away from the goshawk, blinking back stupid tears. Stupid, because they would not make any difference.

She hardly noticed her surroundings, not even listening for the birds or watching for flashes of colorful feathers high in the branches, only focusing on reaching Atherleigh's mews as quickly as she could.

It was early yet, but servants would surely be at their work by that time. And Rafiq, for all his specialized knowledge and training, was a servant. No doubt Atherleigh and Gainesworth would still be asleep after a night spent dancing and flirting. At least, Gainesworth would have entertained himself thus. Atherleigh, on the other hand, had looked as unhappy to be there as she was, and he didn't—couldn't—dance.

Was he really trying to find the library when he came upon her hiding away in the old butler's pantry? He'd asked her to call him Malcolm. Her heart did an uncomfortable little flip as she recalled the look in his eyes.

By then she found herself next to the oak tree she'd climbed a few days before. She still couldn't see where the gate was in the wooden fence that enclosed the weathering yard. She would have to attract Rafiq's attention to gain entrance, and so she once more took off her boots and set about climbing up into the tree. It was much colder that day than it had been, a bitter east wind having roared in overnight. She left her shawl at the base of the tree so it wouldn't get caught on the twigs as she climbed. Without it, the wind seemed to find every gap between her buttons and the uncovered place around her neck, and fanned her cloak out away from her. Her gloves, too, were inadequate to shield her hands from the cold, rough bark. What was more, the dew had left a nearly imperceptible icy sheen on the surface, and just as she gained a high enough perch to see into the weathering ground and call out "Rafiq!" her grip faltered.

Down she went, flailing, trying to grasp branches on the way, hearing the rip when one of her sleeves caught on a jutting sliver of wood, until the ground came up to meet her, knocking the breath out of her lungs, and she hit her head on the rock that had served as her means of reaching the lowest branch.

The world swam wildly around in front of her eyes and she closed them, sinking gratefully into oblivion.

≈

Antonella became aware first of the smell of burning lamp oil, then of the musky odor she associated with birds' nests. When she opened her eyes, they refused to focus on anything. The world spun around and her stomach lurched.

"I can't … I must … "

She'd hardly got the words out of her mouth when a firm hand turned her head to the side and held a metal bowl in position so she could cast up her accounts into it. That made her feel a little better, but her eyes still could not make sense of the world. Where was she? And how did she get there?

"It is best that you close your eyes for the moment, but do not fall asleep," said a smooth voice with a faint foreign accent. "You are safe. I shall summon his lordship directly."

His lordship? Now thoroughly confused, Antonella opened her eyes and willed her surroundings into focus. She was in a small room with walls of rough wood and one square window. A modest hearth in the corner crackled comfortably with a fire that somehow managed to heat the space. The chimney didn't smoke, she observed with a faint smile. There wasn't a chimney in the Court that didn't smoke if the wind was in an unfavorable quarter. But that wasn't the only reason she was warm. Someone had spread a heavy, woolen blanket over her and pulled it up to her chin. She eased her arms out from beneath it and laid them on top. "Rafiq," she whispered, not really calling him, just letting the pieces fall into place in her mind.

"Yes, My Lady?"

She turned her head to the side again to see the falconer seated on a low stool next to her, a worried crease in his brow. "I'm so sorry," Antonella said as the events of the morning unthreaded in her mind, from her fall from the oak tree, to her dash though the coombe, to finding Zephyra unwell and off her feed and being in a panic about what she should do.

At that, she sat bolt upright, and immediately the world began to spin again. Rafiq's gentle hands pushed her back down.

"You don't understand!" she said. "You must help me! I've done a terrible thing." Her foolhardiness in thinking she could mend Zephyra on her own made her stomach clench. She was little better than a thief, and if something weren't done soon, she might also be a murderer.

Rafiq rose and retrieved a copper cup from a small table nearby. "Drink this," he said, and held it to her lips.

"What is it?"

"It will not harm you." He pressed the cup to her bottom lip and tilted it until she was forced to drink or spill the warm liquid all down her front.

It was sweet and spiced with something she didn't recognize, other than a faint suggestion of cinnamon. Both the taste and the effect of the concoction soothed her a little. But it did nothing to relieve her agitation of mind. "Listen to me, Rafiq, I need your help."

"It can wait until I bring My Lord to you."

"No it cannot! He mustn't know. At least, not yet. But I have to trust someone. Can I trust you, Rafiq?"

He cocked his head on the side and put his palms together as she had seen him do on that day when she first saw Atherleigh. "I am at your service, My Lady."

That brought even more memories flooding into her mind. "Not *My Lady,* Rafiq. Not anymore." Tears overflowed her eyes and dripped down the sides of her face and onto her earlobes. She wiped them away.

"I do not pretend to fully comprehend the strange customs of the English, although I have lived among you, in a way, for more then twenty years. I fail to understand how you can now be something other than you have been all your life. You have not married, which is the only state that would possibly alter your title. Your caste is fixed."

Antonella shook her head and pushed herself up slowly by leaning on her elbows. When Rafiq tried to press her down again, she waved him away, smiling as she did so, not wanting to seem ungrateful. "It's too long a tale to tell right now when I have something much more urgent that I wish you would attend to."

Rafiq nodded and folded his hands in his lap.

Now upright, Antonella took a moment to ensure that her head was in order, then gingerly swung her legs over the side of the narrow bed she was lying on, exposing her unshod feet below the blanket. "Oh my God!" she shrieked. Her stockings were in shreds and shallow cuts latticed her calves, some of them still oozing.

Rafiq reached behind him to a bowl and took a cloth from it, wringing it out before gently mopping the cuts.

Antonella started to weep again. How would she be able to lead him back to her bird shed to see Zephyra? "It's impossible. Why did I do it?" she said in watery gasps.

"Do what, My Lady?"

She could see he would not alter his manner of addressing her, and simply accepted it. "The goshawk. I found her in a poacher's net. She has an injured wing." Antonella had to pause as her throat tightened and she was afraid of bringing on a renewed flood of tears.

When she felt she had sufficient control of her emotions, she continued. "You see, I heal injured birds. I have a shed for that purpose. I thought I could heal Zephyra ..."

Rafiq put one finger to his lips before saying, "My Lord's goshawk was Chakor, not Zephyra."

"Yes, I know that now, but I didn't know until that day, the first day I came here and you were so kind to me. That doesn't matter. This morning ..." Again she had to pause as she recalled Zephyra's sad state and her refusal of the meat scraps. "This morning—you see, we had become friends. She allowed me to bind her wing to her body—with the greatest care I assure you—and to dress her abrasions. And she greeted me whenever I came into the shed. I had just started taking her outside a little because I could tell she didn't like being shut up in that dark place all the time."

"You did well, My Lady," Rafiq said in his most soothing voice.

"Well that's just it, you see. This morning she would not eat and her mutes smelled foul. Her cuts had healed and were not septic. I used the ointment I have often used on the wrens and goldcrests I rescue."

Rafiq held up one of his tawny hands to stop her. "What, if you will forgive me My Lady, did you intend to do with this goshawk? And what makes you believe she is the missing Chakor?"

"She had on jesses and bells. And she jumped to the glove quite willingly once she ceased being afraid of me. As to my intentions … I'm not sure I know. But when you said you couldn't help wounded birds because it was only you here, I was afraid that if I brought her to you she would be left to die."

Rafiq said nothing, only drilling his gaze into hers until she had to look down.

"Of course, I don't believe you would ever do such a thing. Not now. And I may have made things much worse for Zephyra—I mean, Chakor."

They sat in mutual silence for a while. Antonella's brain whirred trying to figure out how she could get Zephyra to this mews without anyone knowing. "I think I must lead you to the goshawk," she finally said.

"It would be unwise for you to walk over such rough ground with your disordered wits, My Lady."

"Unwise, but necessary I think. No one will let you in, or treat you as anything other than a trespasser if you go alone —even if I could explain to you where to look. They're used to my oddities, and I daresay would not question me bringing someone like you to my bird infirmary."

"Would they also not be surprised to see me take away a goshawk? And how would I transport her here? It is a long way to walk." Rafiq raised these objections dispassionately.

Antonella could not think of any way to answer them that would serve. "There is another possibility, if you would be willing. You would have to keep a secret from Lord Atherleigh." She knew she was asking a lot. For a dependent to do something his employer did not authorize with regard to that employer's property could result in dismissal. On the other hand, Antonella was tolerably certain that few accomplished falconers existed in England now. And perhaps by the time Lord Atherleigh discovered what Rafiq was doing, all would be well, and Zephyra would once more be installed —as Chakor—in the luxurious mews that belonged to Atherleigh Manor.

She took a deep breath and laid her plan before the falconer, praying that he cared enough for Zephyra's well-being to take the risk Antonella proposed.

When she had finished telling him her plan, he said, "There is, if you would forgive me My Lady, the question of how to return you to your home now and explain your injuries."

Yes, Antonella thought. How would she do that? "I think in a little while I shall be well enough to walk back through the woods. And I can simply say I fell. I think they would believe me."

"But his lordship would be most displeased to send you home without an escort."

She grasped his wrist. "You must not tell him I was here!"

The idea of Atherleigh finding her in her disheveled state or knowing how foolish she had been filled her with dismay. "Please! All will be well I promise. Nothing can be gained by bringing Lord Atherleigh into the matter as yet. With your help, it will soon enough be time to tell him everything."

Reluctantly Rafiq agreed. He explained that he could not go with her himself without arousing Lord Atherleigh's suspicion. He never left the environs of the mews.

"Never?" Antonella asked.

"Almost never. All I need is here. And the birds, they cannot be left alone."

She sat in pensive silence for a while. "You must tell me what I should do for Zephyra—Chakor. You know, perhaps, what is wrong with her. I see it in your face."

He nodded once in confirmation. "I shall make a medicine for her. It may work, or it may not. But I shall make this medicine, and you will allow me to inform Lord Atherleigh that you are here so that you may be conveyed home in safety."

She had no choice but to accept his decree.

CHAPTER 20

*M*alcolm stopped in mid shot, his mouth agape. Had he heard Gainesworth right? "You have arranged a card party, instructed my servants to prepare for it, here? In my house? And who, might I ask, do you plan to invite to this event?" He strode up and down next to the billiard table in his shirtsleeves, cue in his hand. It was too cold and the ground too hard for riding, so billiards seemed the next best occupation for a winter afternoon.

"If I left everything to you we'd never get anywhere. I mentioned it to a few people before we left the ball. Besides, look how far you've come already." Gainesworth pointed his cue in the direction of Atherleigh's bandaged stump. "All it took was a little ingenuity and effort. You've made several very good shots. You'll be beating me again before long. Admit it. Everyone knows about your hand. What's the point of hiding away?"

Malcolm stopped and glared at his friend. "You talk about getting somewhere. What do you mean? I collect all this is not solely for my benefit. You clearly have a *tendre* for Lady

Belinda. She's very pretty I'll own, but she's hardly out of the schoolroom for heaven's sake!"

Gainesworth grinned sheepishly. "You must admit, she is delightful. And not just to look at. She has a tender heart."

"Very well, I suppose she's a cut above your usual flirts. But arranging a card party just so you can see her again! How can I play cards with only one hand? I'll look ridiculous."

"Tell me," Gainesworth said, fixing his friend with a penetrating stare, "did Miss Ambleton object to your injury? You said she asked you about it in that *very private* conversation you had with her. Unchaperoned. And you told me she's seen you struggling to adjust to it on your own when you fell off your horse. Also unchaperoned."

Atherleigh's color rose. Gainesworth had a way of finding just that little point of weakness and exposing it. He could not answer. So instead, he took his place at the table for his shot. It was pathetic. Before, when he was whole, he would have made it easily. Now he'd set up a winning run for Hector.

Gainesworth was right, though. Atherleigh had had two extraordinary encounters with Miss Ambleton. In her own way, she was just as broken as he was. Why that should arouse his interest in her he couldn't say. She wasn't a beauty. But those deep eyes, so brown as to be almost black—when she focused them on him he felt exposed, unable to hide any part of himself.

"Don't you see that you have to accept who you are now? I mean, you are who you always were, and that happens to be a strong, intelligent gentleman. Quite handsome, so I'm told by my sisters. A catch, in fact. Losing your left hand in a battle for king and country does not diminish *you*."

Malcolm hated it when Hector was right. He let the conversation lapse.

After another half-hour's play in which Gainesworth won

every game, Atherleigh said, "And you say it's not humiliating! What am I into you for, Hector?"

Gainesworth laughed. "Not more than a plum! But you'll win it back. You probably think I was trying to cheat you. I didn't pull back, I don't deny it." Gainesworth slid his arms into the coat he'd removed for the games. "I'm not going to baby you. You'll soon be putting us all to shame. I'd like to see that day and lay a wager against someone who believes they'll be able to walk to an easy victory over you."

This provoked a rare laugh from Atherleigh. "How is it you always manage to turn things to good account?"

They racked their cues. "Fancy a game of Piquet?" Gainesworth asked. "You may as well practice before the party."

The last thing Malcolm felt like was embarking on yet another activity that would force him to struggle to master something with one hand that he used to manage with two. Not that Hector wasn't right in pushing him to come out of the sullens and make an effort. But if he were to do that, *he* wanted to be the one to choose the challenge. "No. If it's all the same to you, I have some estate business to attend to. I'll see you again at dinner."

"Very well. I'll write the invitations for the card party and have Penrose see that they're delivered."

He surely must be joking. Atherleigh hoped so, anyway. "So you intend to see it through. How will you know who to invite? And had you planned to inform Mrs. Tilly and Mrs. Cobbey of this event? Or will you leave it to me to inform my own cook and housekeeper?"

Gainesworth tapped the side of his nose and pursed his lips. "I have my ways."

It wasn't an answer. Of course, Atherleigh thought as he put on his greatcoat, he has only to ask Penrose. The butler, a high stickler, had been itching to entertain the neighborhood ever since his master returned. He dropped hints every chance he got about the duties of the baron, the credit of his family and so on. He would no doubt make sure the rest of the staff were prepared and provisions got in.

Gainesworth had a way of filling a space wherever he went. He was a benevolent spirit, but there was so much of him—not physically, but psychically—that at times Atherleigh felt a bit stifled, as he did that afternoon. He stepped out into the bracing cold without a clear idea of where he would go. He just needed to be alone for a while. So much had happened since Hector's arrival. Most of it in the nature of things he hadn't planned to face for a long time yet. But Gainesworth was right. Playing the curmudgeonly hermit wouldn't fadge. He must face his responsibilities and conquer his weaknesses.

Why did that thought conjure up the image of Miss Ambleton huddled in a dark corner, her face streaked with tears? Perhaps he envied her the ability to express the despair she felt about her situation in a way that he could not—at least, not since that ridiculous episode on Hector's first night there. Tears were womanish. Allowing anyone to guess one's feelings would lay one bare, make one vulnerable. Tongues could be like swords and stab deep, perhaps deeper than steel. Miss Ambleton had been wounded in that way, he had no doubt. The change in her status would have undone all her upbringing, spoiled her expectations. For a gently bred lady accustomed to being treated like the daughter of a marquess, it would be devastating. The *ton* were unlikely to turn a benevolent eye upon her sad plight. Breeding was everything. Even more than fortune.

While his mind ranged through these thoughts, Atherleigh had allowed his feet to direct him idly through his grounds on that icy afternoon. He had no idea how much time had passed, but when he looked up and cleared his vision of the phantoms that plagued him, he found himself on the rise above the ruined chapel and the mews.

At that time of day, there should have been at least one bird on a perch in the weathering yard. The cold did not affect those predatory creatures. So why weren't they there, and where was Rafiq?

Atherleigh's aimless ramble became purposeful as he strode down the hill to the mews.

"Rafiq!" he called.

No answer. The dignified falconer did not emerge from the mews building. Something seemed wrong. A tense stillness hung over the structure. He entered the yard and listened. Hearing nothing, he opened the narrow door into the mews and called into it, "Rafiq, are you there?"

A moment later, he thought he heard voices. More than one. How could that be? None of the other servants ever trespassed on Rafiq's domain. He stepped inside and closed the door behind him to keep out the cold. As he did so Rafiq emerged from around the corner beyond the stalls where the birds were kept. That place was Rafiq's private sanctuary. Although he could have insisted, Atherleigh never crossed its threshold.

"My Lord," Rafiq said, with a courtly bow.

"Why isn't the peregrine out in the yard? And I thought I heard voices."

"I plan to put Altair and Kezar on the perches in the yard. The sparrow hawk, Branwen, was out this morning."

There was something remote about the way Rafiq greeted him, Atherleigh thought. The Indian was normally difficult to read, but that day he seemed utterly opaque. It wasn't like the falconer to actually hide anything from him. Did he think he was being criticized? "It's just as well, as it happens. I have written to the Duke of Northumberland and I expect to hear back from him about his interest in the birds within the week."

"As you wish, My Lord," Rafiq said.

Atherleigh walked farther into the center of the mews and stood by the magnificent peregrine. Next to his stall was the one left empty by the loss of Chakor, the goshawk.

Rafiq's eyes shifted to the back of the structure from where he had emerged moments before. Just as Atherleigh was about to challenge him as to what he was looking at, a soft moan broke the stillness.

"What's that? Rafiq, is someone here?" Atherleigh didn't wait for the falconer's answer but marched past him into the area of the building that served as Rafiq's quarters. "My god, what's this?" he said and rushed to the side of Rafiq's narrow cot. None other than Miss Ambleton lay on her side, a compress against the back of her head, one leg sticking out from under a blanket. Although most of it was covered by her dress, he could see her rent stockings and the traces of blood from a network of scratches.

"Tell me what has happened here!" Atherleigh hadn't used that tone of voice since just before Nivelle, when he was in command of a battalion of soldiers, and he'd never used it on Rafiq.

"Please, My Lord, don't blame Rafiq. It's not his fault. It's mine." Miss Ambleton's voice was weak but calm.

"Rafiq, go and send a groom for the doctor!"

"No!" Miss Ambleton said and pushed herself upright, wincing. "I'm well. Just a bump on the head and a few scratches. I feel quite able to walk home again now." She made an attempt to stand, but her knees buckled and she fell against Atherleigh, who supported her and lowered her gently back onto the cot.

"So foolish, I'm sorry," she said. Her pale skin had turned a becoming shade of pink and she covered her eyes.

"I promise you I'm not a watering pot." The tears that flowed from beneath her hand made a liar of her, and she sniffed.

Malcolm fished a handkerchief out of his pocket, knelt down next to her and dabbed her cheeks with it. She resolutely turned away, but he took hold of her chin and lifted it. "Look at me, Miss Ambleton. You are not well. I will not allow you to walk three miles back to Amblemere."

She raised her expressive dark eyes to his. Those eyes. A world of sorrow and confusion seemed to lurk in their depths. "Please let me go. They'll be worried about me, I suppose."

"Not until I'm satisfied you can stand. And you will return in my carriage. I cannot drive you, so I shall send a groom with you." He turned to Rafiq. "I don't suppose you keep any brandy here? No, of course not. I recall that you don't imbibe."

"I have prepared a tisane, which will do just as well," Rafiq said, and once more filled a cup from the pot by the hearth.

He prepared to give it to Miss Ambleton, but Atherleigh took it from him and held it out to her. She grasped it with her small, delicate hand, which trembled slightly. Malcolm steadied it by wrapping his own fingers around hers, remembering how he had felt when he'd done the same thing to help her hold the reins of his horse. This time, though, she wore no gloves. He spotted them on a stool on top of her neatly folded brown cloak.

"You will tell me how you came to be injured, and how you ended up just here, Miss Ambleton. But not now. You have clearly had enough distress for one day." He looked up at Rafiq, who stood a discreet distance away, his hands clasped meekly before him. "Go and tell Garforth to put the horses to the landaulet. I shall escort Miss Ambleton to the drive as soon as she is ready."

"Very good, My Lord," Rafiq said with a bow and left them to do as he was bid.

Suddenly conscious of how close they were, of Miss Ambleton's soft hand beneath his, Malcolm said, "You'd best drink this or Rafiq will be offended." He was rewarded with a watery smile. He took his hand off hers and stood.

"My boots … " Miss Ambleton sat up and swung both her feet to the floor. Her stockinged feet.

Malcolm looked around to see if there were any ladies' boots lying on the floor nearby. "Where are they?"

She wouldn't meet his eyes. "Under the oak tree. In the back. I shall get them, if you will help me stand."

"Under the tree? Why?"

"I was, I mean, I couldn't think how else—I was curious, I needed to talk to Rafiq, and I couldn't see if he was here." She stumbled over her words, clearly uneasy.

"Am I to understand that you climbed up into a tree to gain a view over the fence into the weathering yard?"

She nodded and bit her lower lip. "I had to remove my boots. I left them out there. Rafiq must have carried me in. I think I lost consciousness for a while. As I said, I can go and fetch them."

Foolish girl! What was she about? "Nonsense. You stay here. Where exactly will I find these boots?"

"Under the big oak, the one nearest the fence," Miss Ambleton said, sighing in what he thought might be relief.

She really was done up. He should escort her home. But first, the boots. How in blazes did she get to that tree? She must have walked over from Amblemere. A three-mile walk through dense woods, and at this time of year a bitter cold one. Especially if she had no certainty of finding Rafiq there at the end of it. Why in blazes would she want to see his falconer?

It had been a long time since he'd left the weathering

ground through the gate to the spinney. It used to be a favorite way to escape to the comparative wildness of the woods in the summer. He knew which tree she meant. He'd climbed up into its branches many times as a boy. He found the boots with little trouble. She'd placed them neatly by one of the tree's big roots. When he looked up into the branches he saw by the evidence of a cascade of broken twigs how far she must have fallen. They told a clear story. Why would a lady of Miss Ambleton's quality—title or no title—be out climbing trees in the dead of winter?

When he brought the boots back she reached out for them, said "Thank you, I can manage," and put them by her feet. She leaned over to pull them on and tie the laces. "Oh …" she said, stopping before she had fully bent and closing her eyes.

She said she'd lost consciousness, so clearly she had a concussion, Atherleigh thought, if bending her head forward caused her pain or perhaps dizziness. "Let me," he said, and crouched down by her to lace up her boots before realizing that here, too, was something he could not do with only one hand.

Antonella laid her hand on his arm and said, "It's no matter. I'll move more slowly and it will be fine."

By then Rafiq had returned with the information that the landaulet was awaiting My Lady's pleasure.

Antonella and Malcolm turned to each other at the same time. A flash of communication passed between them. Malcolm had the momentary sensation that he had felt her pain, and she had felt his.

CHAPTER 21

*S*omehow Rafiq got the message that she did not want to say anything to Atherleigh about Zephyra. Fortunately, the baron appeared to be too concerned with her injury and getting her safely back to Amblemere to have expressed much curiosity about why she was there—although he knew she'd climbed the tree and fallen from it.

When she first realized that Atherleigh was in the mews she wanted the ground to open up and swallow her. What would he think of her? And how would she explain what had brought her there? Yet he had not appeared angry, only concerned. Far more than she expected he would be. And he had been so kind to go and fetch her boots and try to help her with them. He'd knelt down by her and their shoulders touched. It was nothing, but it felt oddly intimate, touching another person anywhere other than with a hand. Whatever the reason, it sent a jolt right through her. She tried to believe that it was simply the effect of the concussion, but she suspected she was fooling herself. It wouldn't do. And even if it would, even if for some strange reason he actually liked her, he would change his mind when he found out what she had done. How she wished she had simply told Rafiq about the goshawk from the start. Now Zephyra was in some kind of a decline. And it would be deucedly awkward to return her now, and in such a condition after having been in her care.

Despite her adamance, Atherleigh would not allow her to walk home. He dismissed her suggestion out of hand and commanded her to go in his carriage. His hard-edged voice had made Rafiq start. Was that how he was in the Peninsula? To be fair to him, she had to admit that she wasn't entirely sure she would have been able to make the challenging climb up the hill through the coombe. She had no broken bones, but every time she moved, something hurt.

So, Antonella meekly accepted the carriage ride. At first she was afraid she would be forced to endure Atherleigh's company. Even the distance of five miles by road would be enough time for him to ask her questions she did not want to answer. Plus, the thought of being so close to him in the enclosed space of a carriage felt dangerous in a way she could hardly understand.

But of course, she needn't have worried about that. Propriety dictated that he not ride in a closed carriage alone with her. Because of his missing hand, he couldn't drive her back himself in his open phaeton. He handed her up to the landaulet where she sat in state, a rug over her legs and a hot brick at her feet. Atherleigh's groom, Garforth, acted as coachman and sat on the box in front.

The horses went at a brisk trot. It wouldn't take long to get home, so she had to think quickly how she might avoid showing up in the courtyard in a carriage belonging to Atherleigh. How much better it would have been to be able to hasten back through the paths in the woods and sneak in by the kitchen door. If she had not fallen, she would have returned by early afternoon and no one would be the wiser.

There was only one solution. Antonella lowered a window and leaned her head out so she could call to the groom when they were almost at the entrance to the drive, "Garforth, would you be so good as to leave me at the gates, not drive in to the Court?"

He pulled the horses up and twisted around on the seat to stare at her. "I don't think the master would take kindly to me doin' that," he said.

"He won't know. I certainly won't tell him. Please! It's very important."

"I don't know, My Lady ..."

Ant didn't correct him. Perhaps she could use his misapprehension of her rank in her favor. "This is tiresome, Garforth. Please stop here and help me down," she said in her most top-lofty voice. If her head weren't still a little disordered she would have jumped down on her own.

"You mean to walk up to the house? It's a good 'alf mile," he said, a scowl on his grizzled face.

"Yes, it's quite all right. I shall go to the stables first. I must speak to our groom about my mare." He could not possibly guess how big a bouncer that was. "It's much quicker if I walk from here than go all the way to the house first."

Clearly Garforth had no idea of the exact location of the house and its outbuildings because he accepted this argument. He shrugged, secured the horses' reins, climbed down from the box, opened the carriage door, and let down the step so she could alight.

"Thank you, Garforth." She hoped her smile would make up for the fact that she hadn't so much as a coachwheel in her pocket to give him as a *douceur*.

Without looking back, head still swimming a little and knees unsteady, Antonella walked as briskly as she could down the drive to the path that led off it toward her shed. Wrapped in her cloak she held a jar of a preparation that

Rafiq had made for her, saying she should mix it with Zephyra's food. When she asked what she should do if the goshawk refused to eat, he said, *Turn away from her. She will think she is fooling you and taking something forbidden. Her disorder is likely to do with her mood.*

It did not surprise Antonella that Rafiq should speak of a goshawk's mood. Or that of any bird, really. They were sensitive creatures. The idea of a caged canary made her heart shrink. Their song, she fervently believed, was little more than a plea for release. As to Zephyra, she herself would not have wanted to remain forcibly immobilized inside a dingy shed for days. If only the hawk could understand why it was necessary.

By the time the shed came into view, the sun had dipped below the horizon and all was in shadow. Not enough, though, to hide the figure of Belinda pacing back and forth, wringing her hands. Antonella stepped on a twig and Belinda looked up and saw her.

"Oh Ant! I've been frantic with worry! Where have you been?" She raced forward and embraced her sister.

"Has Mama—Aunt Caroline said anything about my absence?"

Belinda's eyes clouded. "I don't think she noticed. She kept to her room in the morning and has been busy with Mrs. Cobbey since then. She's used to you going off by yourself."

It was clear to Antonella that Belinda aimed at an excuse for Lady Lewiston's lack of interest in her whereabouts. But it had ever been thus. Everything Belinda did had always been of greater importance to the dowager than Antonella's activities. That fact used to mystify her, but now that she knew the secret, it all made sense.

There was no time to waste fretting over that, though. "I'll tell you later what happened. Right now I have to help

Zephyra." When Belinda looked at her puzzled, she said, "The goshawk. She's off her food. Wait here for me, I don't think this will take long."

It was quite dark inside the infirmary. In broad daylight the narrow windows under the eaves let in little light. In half an hour it would be too dark to see anything. An oil lamp and a tinder box sat on a simple shelf, but she was afraid if she lit the lamp the bright glare would frighten Zephyra. No longer noticing her aching head, Antonella approached the goshawk. "Good afternoon My Lady Zephyra. I have something for you from Rafiq." She picked up the tin bowl with the scraps of meat in it, pulled the jar out and opened the lid so she could pour some of its contents into the bowl. It smelled disgusting. She held it out to the hawk.

Zephyra cocked her head this way and that, fixing Antonella with her orange gaze, then lowered her head to inspect the contents of the bowl. To Antonella's surprise, she quickly grasped a bit of it in her beak and swallowed it down, returning for more until the bowl was half empty, at which point she stopped. Her look seemed to say, *take it away, I've had my fill,* as if she was indeed a fine lady who had been offered a tempting sweetmeat.

Antonella sighed with relief. She had no illusion that whatever was wrong with Zephyra had been magically cured, but so long as the bird took nourishment, there would be time for recovery. She wondered if perhaps Zephyra recognized the smell and taste of something Rafiq used to give her and that it comforted her.

She joined a shivering Belinda outside. "You're mad to stand out here like this," Antonella said.

"You're right. I'm mad! But not in the sense you mean. I'm furious. With you. How dare you put me through such worry!" Her harsh words lost a little of their edge when she threaded her arm through Antonella's and squeezed. "We have a lot to talk about, but it's time to dress for dinner. Come to my room later?"

A desultory hour in the drawing room followed an uneventful meal. Everyone was relieved when Skilling brought in the tea tray. All three of them suppressed yawns until the dowager finally announced that she would retire for the night.

After she prepared for bed and donned her dressing gown, Ant went to Bee's room, as was her custom. Falk knew better than to linger there while the girls exchanged confidences, and soon nodded goodnight to them.

Settling herself on the bed with a pillow clutched in her arms, Belinda said, "Now tell me everything. No pretense."

As she unfolded the story of her day's adventures, Antonella watched her sister's expression move through worry, surprise, anger, amusement, and every emotion in between—just as it had done when they were children and Antonella would make up wild tales of pirates and brigands to while away the long winter nights.

When she finished Belinda cried out, "You should be seen by a doctor!"

"Oh pish!" Antonella said. "I didn't fall far, and my bump will soon go down."

"Did Falk notice when she brushed your hair?"

Antonella paused a moment before answering. "Falk hasn't brushed my hair since the day of Mama's announcement." In Belinda's company it was just easier to revert to the way they had always spoken of the dowager.

Belinda's eyes darkened dangerously.

Antonella held up her hand and said, "It's no use being angry. What does it matter after all? I should get used to being ignored. To not being treated with courtesy."

This did not erase the look from Belinda's eyes, but she

took a deep breath before speaking again. "I want to talk to you about Atherleigh. He's not what he seems. He isn't a kind man."

"What do you mean? You hardly know him!" Antonella bristled. What did Belinda know of it? She hadn't seen how he was with her, at the ball and earlier that day. "If he's a little abrasive is it any wonder, with his injury?"

Belinda's eyes opened wide. "I'm not speaking of anything at all to do with that. I just think ... I'm not sure what I think, only don't be deceived by his friendship with Mr. Gainesworth, who is quite the opposite. Gainesworth is not such a high stickler, perhaps because he has no title. But I believe, from what the duchess told me in town, that he's much wealthier."

Antonella could not imagine what Belinda was referring to. She smiled at Belinda's defense of Gainesworth, but how could she be so mistaken in Atherleigh? "What do you know about him that I don't? Has he been uncivil to you?"

Blushing, Belinda said, "No, not that. It was what he said after you fled from the ball. He and Gainesworth were talking."

"So you have judged a gentleman on one overheard conversation?"

"It was not overheard! He spoke in answer to a direct question, one that bears most intimately upon your situation. I refuse to say more."

She stubbornly pressed her lips together. When Antonella threatened to leave to return to her own room, Belinda said, "Stay! I have something else important to talk to you about."

Reluctantly, Antonella remained. She would hear Belinda out. She owed her that.

And so Belinda told her of her conversation with Gainesworth about trying to discover the facts of Antonella's birth. Why had she shared this with him? It was bad enough that Atherleigh knew as much as he did. Something else must be inspiring Belinda's zeal. Antonella had her suspicions about what that might be, but as she watched Bee talk and gesticulate her suspicions crystallized into certainty. Whenever Belinda mentioned Gainesworth's name, her expression subtly changed. She could hardly keep a smile from forming on her lips.

Belinda was in love with Mr. Gainesworth. Of course.

And that infatuation had led to indiscretion. "How could you? Surely my business is no concern of Gainesworth's. It was wrong of you to tell him so much! Really, Bee, I don't want you to pursue this further." Antonella stood and started walking toward the door.

"Don't go! And don't be cross with me. You must want to know?"

That was certainly the question. Did she? It surely wouldn't make a difference one way or the other. The damage was done. The genie was out of the bottle, Pandora's box was wide open. "No," Antonella said, "I don't think I do."

"Well *I* want to know. I think Mama is hiding something." Belinda threw the pillow at Ant.

Catching it deftly, Antonella said, "Why would she do that? I'm sure she is tired of hiding anything, after eighteen years of lying about me."

"But there are so many questions! Why not tell the truth from the beginning? Many families take on such relatives out of a sense of duty or actual kindness. And besides, Mama's way of revealing it felt strange. There had to be a reason she never said anything before, a reason that only mattered while Papa was alive."

Perhaps it was her fall, or the anxiety about Zephyra, but Antonella suddenly felt weak and tired. "Truly, I no longer care. My head aches and I long for bed. Besides, how do you propose to discover anything?"

Belinda took a deep breath. "With Gainesworth's help."

Now this was too much. No matter to what degree Belinda trusted Atherleigh's friend, Antonella did not. She paced around the room, her lips pressed in an angry line. "I think you haven't considered all this carefully. What if you discover something worse? What if in turning over stones all you find is ugly slugs?"

Belinda paled. "I hadn't thought ..."

Clearly she hadn't. "Can't you let it alone?" Antonella was ready to pull her hair out in frustration.

"I don't believe that even so, even if we discovered something shameful, you wouldn't want to know for certain."

Would she? And what might *worse* turn out to be? If Belinda didn't find out the truth, there was always the possibility that someone else would unearth the secret later—if there was one—and cause a scandal. "I suppose you're right. Not knowing, wondering, is the worst thing. But I'm still not happy about involving anyone else."

"I believe we can trust Gainesworth." The blush rose in Belinda's cheeks again, and she did not look Antonella in the eye.

"Oh, Bee! You do have a *tendre* for him, don't you?"

At this, Belinda's eyes snapped up and her color deepened. "No! I assure you! If you knew ..." She didn't finish her sentence.

"Now who's keeping a secret?" Antonella said and sat on the bed next to Belinda. She took both her hands and squeezed them. "What are you afraid of?"

To Antonella's surprise, tears leapt into Belinda's blue eyes and trickled down her cheeks. "It's just that I wanted so much for *you* to be settled first."

She didn't deserve a sister who loved her so well. For, no matter what their actual relationship, they would always be sisters to each other. She gathered Belinda into her arms and rocked her gently, murmuring, "You can start on this search tomorrow. With Gainesworth's help. So long as you don't continue to think badly of Atherleigh without further reason to do so. And so long as you don't expect me to take too much of a role in it."

Belinda nodded into Antonella's shoulder.

CHAPTER 22

*B*elinda's first task was to see if she could find anything related to the day of her birth, or the days surrounding it, that might shed some light on the circumstances of Antonella's arrival at the Court. The problem was that she had absolutely no idea where to start looking. Her mother had made it clear that Antonella came to the Court in great secrecy, so any documents might have been destroyed or at least well hidden. The latter possibility seemed unlikely. It was very difficult to keep anything secret in the country. The servants had connections among all the households as many of them came from the same families. Even the most seemingly invisible of them somehow managed to overhear things.

If only she could ask them! But none of their present staff had been at Amblemere Court when she and Antonella were "born." The housekeeper, butler, and cook at the time had all been quite elderly and were pensioned off when Belinda was just a little girl. She had no idea where they'd gone, and asking her mother would raise suspicion. The doctor and the midwife might well know, but the midwife had gone to live with her daughter in another part of the country, and the doctor had died.

There was even a new incumbent of the parish. The old vicar died ten years ago and the new one, Reverend Pendarves, was appointed soon after. The old curate had long since gone to a different parish in another part of the country as well. Belinda knew for a fact that she and Antonella were both baptized at the same time. It was one of their father's favorite stories, how Antonella had howled and complained, while Belinda simply smiled beatifically into the parson's face. Besides, she had seen the register, and Edward Ambleton, Marquess of Lewiston had written his name down as their father. Surely to lie about that would be a terrible crime, worse than lying about being someone's mother. Everything passed through the male line. Rank and money depended on knowing one's father. Even in the case of an heiress, once she married, the money became her husband's.

Could her late father would have gone to the lengths of falsifying a baptismal record? If so, why? Belinda couldn't imagine what he might have had to gain by it. He was a jovial, loving man and certainly no criminal. Not very practical, certainly. He'd lost a lot of money at the gaming tables and hadn't run the estate very well. When he died he left more debts than anything else. But Harry had worked hard to turn things around and even before he married the heiress, Olivia, she and Antonella were assured of a comfortable—if not affluent future.

Their dowries, although not magnificent, had been secured on their parents' marriage. The dowager brought a respectable fortune with her, and a large portion of it remained in trust to settle on any daughters. Belinda always assumed that meant that she and Antonella would each bring half of whatever that sum turned out to be to any marriage they contracted. But if Antonella was not her sister, then she would also lose any right to her share of Lady Lewiston's fortune.

It all depended on what really happened. If only they knew for certain!

The dowager mentioned a distant cousin. They had cousins on both sides of the family. The marquess was the oldest of three boys and four girls. One of the boys died as a child, but the other and all the sisters had married and produced children of their own. Her mother had one sister and no brothers. Aunt Amelia was the Countess of Rockland and the earl was still alive. Their six children ranged in age from nine years to twenty-three or thereabouts. None of those relatives could possibly have been Antonella's parents because they were still alive. As to more distant cousins—her Papa and Mama had never spoken of any.

Besides, the more Belinda thought about it, the stranger it all seemed. For Antonella to have been only a few days old when she arrived meant her mother had likely died in childbirth. Would her father not still have been living? She supposed he could have had some freak accident, or contracted a deadly disease. But again, why the secrecy?

While Belinda was going through all these possibilities alone, Antonella was off fussing over that huge hawk in her shed. Ant expressly wished not to take part in the search for evidence that might lead to an answer about her birth. It was enough that she permitted Belinda to do as she would, involve Gainesworth, and see what could be discovered. Stubborn, that's what she was.

Yet Belinda still couldn't really understand why Ant didn't want to know. It was as if she had given up, as if she simply decided to accept things as they apparently were. It wasn't like her. Antonella was a fighter. Her assurance that she would be just fine if she never married and instead became the spinster aunt simply didn't ring true. She was too passionate, too intense to fade into anyone's background. Belinda believed in her heart that Antonella was born to love someone, and love that person deeply. But only if that person returned her love in equal measure.

And only if that person didn't look down on her because of her change in rank—whatever the ultimate truth about her birth. Which meant *not* Lord Atherleigh.

Somewhere in the midst of all these musings Belinda decided the best place to start her search for information would be the old library in the Tudor wing. It was the one place in the mansion where an overlooked document might be found. Lady Lewiston rarely set foot in that room, and since their education had been deemed complete, she and Ant had also had less occasion to spend time there. It wasn't that Lady Lewiston had no interest in scholarship. She simply preferred the newer library in the main wing of the house with its fine selection of modern literature and poetry.

But for Belinda and Antonella, the old book room was something else altogether. The impressive collection of volumes, some now crumbling and worm-eaten, had been amassed over generations, and the crowded shelves held everything from religious tracts to histories to poetry and even some older novels. Lady Lewiston gave Miss Wilkins free rein to ensure that Belinda and Antonella had as thorough an education as possible. Unlike many mothers preparing their daughters for roles in society, Lady Lewiston never forbid them the study of any subject. They were always free to push their minds in unaccustomed or uncomfortable directions, so long as they remained anchored to the world of gentility—and so long as the usual ladylike accomplishments were not overlooked.

Of course, the books that Antonella loved most were the well-thumbed volumes of *The Art of Hunting with Birds,* one or other of which always lay open on the book stand. How odd, Belinda thought, that Ant had been fascinated by birds of prey long before she found herself harboring a wounded hawk.

Belinda well remembered the very day Antonella's ornithological obsession began. She had wandered off on her own one fine summer's day at the age of perhaps nine. When she didn't return in time for nuncheon, Miss Wilkins and Belinda spent hours looking for her, even traipsing through the coombe and down to the beach. Ant wasn't there or in any of her usual haunts. Just as they were ready to give up and sound the alarm for a proper search, Antonella came running out of the woods with glowing eyes and a tale of watching two men in the field belonging to their neighbor, Baron Atherleigh, flying trained hunting birds.

Of course Miss Wilkins used her student's passion as a way into lessons, even teaching her Latin so she could read the five volumes written by Frederick II Hohenstaufen. Belinda grimaced when she realized even *she* knew more about falcons and hawks than she ever really wanted to.

When she reached the library Belinda sneezed and wrapped her shawl more tightly around her. Dust everywhere, and no fire was ever lit in that room. Even though Harry insisted they needn't deprive themselves of basic comforts, the dowager still practiced economies that had become part of the pattern of her life. She instructed the maids to light fires only in the often-used rooms—the breakfast room and small dining room, the rose saloon, and the principal drawing room—and limited the number of candles the girls were allowed in their bedchambers. The formal rooms in the old wing—the state dining room and the great hall—remained closed off except when in use for parties. The other rooms simply suffered from benign neglect.

Before starting her search for she knew not what, Belinda

let her eyes rove over the shelves full of tooled spines and breathed in the scent of old leather and crumbling paper. It was one of those smells that, like that of the stables, could be either unpleasant or evocative, depending on one's mood or point of view. Today, she was inclined to revel in it and the memories it called to mind. She strolled over to the two globes near the mullioned windows and with a finger of each hand set them both gently spinning. These once handsome items now had fine cracks running over their surfaces and much of the ink on them had faded. In a similar state were the two comfortably shabby leather chairs on either side of the empty hearth.

Much as Belinda would have loved to find a favorite volume of poetry and while away an hour or two curled up in one of those chairs, the one place she thought might yield some useful information was the heavy oak desk in the alcove between two floor-to-ceiling bookshelves. Above it a portrait of the third marquess stared down in robes of state. She and Ant had entertained themselves imagining what the dour man must have been thinking at the time, what had happened to give him such an attitude of imperious disapproval. For all its antiquity it was an ugly painting, and so was never moved to the gallery in the newer wing.

The portrait glowered down at the desk beneath it, which Belinda had never seen her father use for anything on the rare occasions he entered the room. Important estate papers, deeds and maps and such, were in the old muniment room off the hall. The steward's office near the stables housed the account books. The dowager kept her own correspondence and papers in the escritoire in her private drawing room, so if the information Belinda sought was there, it would likely be impossible to get to. No one ever thought much about what might lie in this ancient piece of furniture.

The pitted and scratched slanted writing surface of the

desk was supported by two columns of cupboards whose doors hid small drawers and cubby holes. The few times she had idly wondered what could be behind the doors and opened them, Belinda had found nothing—or only a few scraps of old paper. Belinda really held out little hope that she would discover anything there—beyond mouse droppings and spider webs.

Neither of the doors was locked, although they both had keyholes and a locking mechanism. The one on the left covered two shallow drawers and one smaller compartment that was subdivided vertically into four even smaller ones. Belinda held a candle up close to look inside and saw nothing but emptiness and old dust. The cupboard door on the right hid an odd arrangement of small drawers of different sizes. She opened these one by one, pulling them out and peering into the cavities left behind them as well as she could.

So far nothing.

To see into the empty spaces left by the bottom-most drawers she had to crouch down on her knees and tip her head on the side. She was beginning to feel as if she had come on a sleeveless errand. Why would she ever expect to find anything important in such an out-of-the-way place? However, she'd started so she would finish, even if it meant dirtying her favorite dimity day dress.

When she got to the final small drawer, pulled it out—empty, of course—and held the candle so that the flickering light illuminated most of the cavity, she heaved a deep sigh. If there was nothing here, she couldn't think where she might look next.

She was about to straighten up and admit defeat when something about the back of the empty alcove looked odd to her. Instead of wood grain, it appeared as if the back of the space had been lined with leather. In fact, as she recalled, that one drawer hadn't closed as flush to the cabinet as the others. She reached in. The drawers were deep: her arm went in up to her elbow. That was one of the smaller drawers and, slim though she was, she couldn't get her arm in much past her elbow, which meant her fingertips just reached the back.

A little more exploration and her fingernail found a purchase under an edge of what was apparently leather. She dug at it with little success at first. Whatever it was had thoroughly stuck there, which might have been the only reason no one had found it and tossed it away, or removed it to a different location.

Not to be deterred, Belinda persevered. Bit by bit she loosened the object, until finally it came away and she was able to grasp it and pull it out. With an exclamation of triumph, Belinda held up a leather-bound pocket book, the kind of pocket book gentlemen carried to record sums spent, thoughts, appointments—any number of things. Belinda recalled her father having just such a little book always about him. Could this have been one of his? Had it fallen down behind and become lodged there, never making it either into the flames or into a collection of important documents?

She opened the palm-sized volume. In faded ink on the inside of the cover was a messy scrawl that included her father's name and the dates 1793–1796.

We were born in 1796.

Belinda trembled with excitement. She flipped through the pages quickly. What there was of sunlight had moved to the west side of the house and it was by now far too dim inside that room to make out the writing. She could see enough to know that the entries were written in pencil, as would be expected, and some of the words were smudged beyond recognition.

Fingers shaking, she tucked the book into her reticule, returned the drawers to their appropriate cubbies, closed the doors over them, and scurried out through the abandoned rooms. She wanted to have a close look at the treasure before she showed it to Antonella. Part of her worried that she might find something dreadful, and if she did, Antonella need never know.

"What were you doing down there, Belinda?"

The dowager's voice stopped her in her tracks just as she turned the corner to return to the newer part of the house. She stood ramrod straight immediately in front of Belinda, not a hair out of place, her head cocked on one side and a quizzical look in her eyes. What could she say about where she came from? "I was looking for a book," Belinda said in answer, "In the old library." It sounded unconvincing even to her own ears.

"I see that you seem not to have found any. Which is remarkable, given that a library contains many books." Her mother's tone was light and faintly amused and her eyes did not hold any hint of displeasure. But Belinda wasn't fooled. Lady Lewiston had a way of finding out everything that happened in the house, even things she and Ant put great effort into keeping secret.

Belinda smiled. "In truth, Antonella asked me to look something up for her in the falconry book. You know how fascinated she is with such things."

Her mother scrutinized her, slightly narrowing her penetrating eyes. "I see. Where is your sis—Antonella? Why couldn't she have done it herself?"

Belinda was oddly encouraged by her mother's slip. Clearly on some level she still thought of Ant as her daughter. "She went out for a walk."

"In this weather?"

"You know what she's like. I promised Wilkie that I would help her organize the pianoforte music before dinner, so I stayed inside," Belinda said, making up something she knew Miss Wilkins wouldn't contradict.

"Very well." The dowager smiled in a way that signaled she was going to change the subject. Belinda admired the way her mother could direct a conversation without any apparent effort and without showing the slightest alteration in her expression. "I wanted to show you this." She handed Belinda an invitation card.

She looked it over, the heat rising into her cheeks. "We're invited to a card party? At Atherleigh?"

"I've written to accept. We have no other engagements. I have suggested that Atherleigh invite Bartleson, who is staying with Sir William—with whom I believe the baron is on quite friendly terms—or at least, neighborly terms."

How could she dare make such a suggestion? If she was in any doubt of her mother's intentions before, that doubt had just now been completely erased. Still, a card party at Atherleigh could be turned to good account. Gainesworth would, naturally, be there. "Thank you, Mama," Belinda said, giving Lady Lewiston a genuine smile—even though it had nothing to do with Bartleson.

No doubt her mother would eventually guess that, too.

"I should also like a word with you, Belinda. Will you come to my drawing room?"

So there was more than the invitation itself. She might have guessed. And this could not be good. Her mother's expression was neither forbidding nor angry, but the only times Lady Lewiston summoned her daughters—individually or together —for private chats was to impart something important—often important in a bad way. She could not refuse however, and dutifully followed her mother up the stairs to her apartment.

Once the door closed behind them, the dowager gestured to the small settee—the one she and Antonella had sat on when that fateful news about Ant's place in the family had burst over them like a downpour. What news could possibly be forthcoming now? Were there more surprises about their family?

Lady Lewiston walked over to her escritoire and picked up a small pile of letters that she'd clearly opened and read. She did not hand them to Belinda, but waved them in her direction before setting them down again and taking her own seat on her customary armchair. "I have been making some inquiries about Mr. Gainesworth."

For a moment, a frisson of pleasure coursed through Belinda's body. If her mother was making inquiries about him, perhaps she saw him as a potential suitor. Although Belinda's first plan had been to match him with Antonella, she now realized not only that they wouldn't suit, but that her own feelings for him were far too real to ignore.

When Lady Lewiston spoke, however, her pleasure instantly turned to consternation.

"I have heard from several of my friends—including Lady Jersey and Mrs. Burrell—that Gainesworth has a reputation as a here-and-thereian. He is apparently considered dangerous by most mamas of the *ton*, and some go so far as to believe he is a hardened rake."

It couldn't be. Could it? Not that she really knew how to identify a rake. She hadn't even had one season yet. Gainesworth was charming and lively. Did that make him a rake? He was considerate and kind and had impeccable manners. Were those also characteristics of a rake? Besides all that, he was outstandingly handsome. No doubt a rake would have to be.

Added altogether, the qualities that so captivated her in Gainesworth were possibly the very definition of a rake. Her heart thumped into her stomach. "He has been nothing but polite and considerate to me." She mentally kicked herself for her defensive tone.

"As he would be. He is a gentleman of decent family—at least on his mother's side. He also has a handsome fortune at his disposal and can indulge his every whim for entertainment. That it was acquired through trade is unfortunate, but does not change its value. He has apparently raised hopes in the hearts of one or two ladies and not carried through on the expectations, leaving them broken-hearted and sullied in the eyes of the *ton.*."

Belinda knew such behavior to be reprehensible. But on whose authority was this information spread? Surely Gainesworth's kindness and attention to her was not meaningless. "Isn't every handsome, eligible gentleman deemed a rake if he doesn't become riveted within a year or two of his come-out?"

"Really, Belinda! Such language is not becoming to a lady!" Her mama let the remonstrance settle for a moment before continuing. "I am afraid I am unwilling to tell you anything more specific about Mr. Gainesworth. What I have heard is not for your ears. But I wanted you to know—before you allow yourself to entertain any foolish notions—that I will not sanction a match with him. That is, if indeed he were to seek permission to fix his interest, which is by no means likely."

Belinda's pulse raced and pounded in her ears. She felt like screaming. Was it not enough that her mother had destroyed Antonella's life? Did she have to pour cold water on her own tentative hopes?

And then, of course, she fully understood that her mama hadn't merely wanted to introduce her to the Earl of Bartleson. She had picked him out as her future husband. An old, paunchy, sweaty man who looked at her with disturbing lust in his eyes. He must be over thirty! "If you think telling me this will in any way make Lord Bartleson's suit attractive to me, you are greatly mistaken, Ma'am."

Lady Lewiston made no response to this. "I only expect what I have always expected of you: that you will behave in a way that will not bring shame to this family. You are young. There are many other prospects to suit you beyond Hector Gainesworth. He is, after all, the first personable young gentleman you have met. He is personable for a reason. It's one of the essential qualities of a man of the town." She held her hand out to Belinda and stood. "I've told you this today so that you have time to think about it before you next meet Gainesworth in company. Trust me. It's for your own good."

Belinda limply took her mother's hand but did not return her smile. If all this were indeed true, it would upset her plans very seriously. How could she discover whether Gainesworth's intentions—if he truly had any toward her—were honorable or not?

She must see him alone. It was the only way.

CHAPTER 23

*A*s soon as she came into the house after working with Zephyra, all but frozen through and her head still pounding from her fall two days before, Antonella was accosted by Belinda and dragged up to her bedroom.

"Bee, I really need to just sit down for a while, perhaps rest before dinner," Antonella said. What could possibly be so urgent?

"Rest? How can you! I've got something big and important to tell you. At least, I think it might be. And I need to talk to you about Mama."

How like Belinda to be so dramatic. "If it's the card party, I've already heard about it."

"Did Mama tell you?" She opened her eyes wide.

Why did Belinda seem surprised by that? "No, I stopped in the kitchens on the way in and Mrs. Mudge mentioned it. Although why she would think it important for me I have no idea." In fact, the cook was complaining that she'd prepared one of her special dishes for the next night and unless it was eaten then it would spoil, and it wouldn't keep until the night after.

"Well, the card party is important for reasons I shall tell you in a moment, but we have work to do before then. Look!"

Belinda opened her mesh reticule and took out a rather worn-looking notebook. A gentleman's pocket book, with a plain leather cover. "What is it?" Antonella asked.

After briefly recounting her explorations from the day before, Belinda said, "The trouble is, what's written in it makes little sense to me—what I can make out that is."

She riffled the pages and then held the book out to Antonella, who made no move to take it.

"Aren't you curious? Don't you want to know?" Belinda's face fell as she spoke.

Antonella relented just a little and took Belinda's other hand. "You want to tell me, I can see. But what could it serve?"

"It might give us a clue as to what really happened in December of 1796! Look—it's in Papa's hand, and it's dated 1794–1796." She opened the cover and pointed to the faded date. "We might have the true answer to why Mama has seen fit to tell us at this moment that you are not her daughter. At this moment, instead of long ago."

Antonella looked down at the floor and shook her head. "I have no doubt that she had a good reason. Think about it. I know this change makes you uncomfortable. I can understand that you might feel guilty, even. But it's not your fault. You must understand that!"

"I know it's not. Give me some credit for a little intelligence. That's not the point. The point is that you must know the truth. Don't you want to find out who your parents really are? I know Mama is still hiding something."

"Whether your mama shared the actual reason for not disclosing this to us earlier or made one up, what is the point of digging further? Especially of *your* digging further. You're the one who wants those answers, not me."

Belinda opened her mouth to speak but Antonella raised a hand to stop her. "I know you're sorry. I know you wanted us to be sisters together taking the *ton* by storm. But that was always *your* dream, not mine."

Belinda had a sweet and biddable disposition—most of the time. The look that came into her eyes at that moment, the compressed lips and defiant lift of her chin, signaled that this was not one of those times.

"You say that, but I know it's not true. I think you're afraid. Yes! I said it. Antonella Ambleton, who tramps through the woods alone not fearing wild animals or brigands, who feeds and cares for a vicious hawk, is afraid of taking her place in society."

"That's ridiculous and you know it!" Antonella's words came out sounding harsher than she meant. Belinda had touched a nerve. Without having any clear idea why, Antonella had always felt a bit of an outsider in their world. The things she was supposed to care about meant nothing to her. And what she did care about often earned her scolding and censure. But again, that was no fault of Belinda's. Gathering herself, she softened her voice and said, "It's unlikely that the book you found will reveal anything about us. I doubt very much Papa used such an item to write down matters that pertained to his children."

Judging by the mulish look that remained on Belinda's face, she was not to be discouraged. Antonella was smart enough to know that once her sister had a bee in her bonnet —another reason for her nickname—she pursued it until the bitter end. If only the bee in this case had to do with something other than this foolish matter.

Not to be silenced, Belinda said, "You say you don't care. But what do you intend to do with the rest of your life? You know we've been prepared for only one future, and that future depends upon finding a respectable husband capable of supporting us as befits our station."

"My station, as *Aunt Caroline* has made clear, is not the one I was raised to. So I must set my sights lower." Or, as she was beginning to hope, set them in a different direction. With the loss of her status came a certain freedom, ironic though that was. Although she'd always gone along with everything Lady Lewiston planned and was content to face a destiny that had been mapped out for her, that prospect had never given her much joy. All she had been able to see ahead was restriction. What husband would permit her as much freedom in the countryside as her mother's—or rather Aunt Caroline's—benign neglect afforded? She wished she could explain it to Belinda, but at this point, her sister was too focused on her one foolish aim to listen to anything else.

Belinda pulled Antonella down to sit on the settee by the fire and thrust the open book under her nose. "Who says you must set your sights lower? Who's to say you aren't from an even nobler branch of the family than ours—or a different family altogether? I have a feeling the answer is in here!"

Antonella gave an exasperated sigh. "Very well. I will peruse the book, but not for myself. I only do it because it means so much to you."

"It's important. You know it is. That's why, I think, you didn't answer my question. About what you'd do with your life other than marry well."

Did she dare answer that question in the way she wished? What she wanted to do was in fact so far outside the realm of Belinda's imaginings that Antonella feared she would do nothing but laugh in her face. So she said what she assumed Belinda would expect her to say. "I'm quite prepared to be the much-loved maiden aunt, if you'll have me. Or I could go and live with Harry and Olivia." She reached her arm around Belinda's shoulders and squeezed.

Belinda returned her embrace and said, "You think you'd want that. But I know otherwise."

Antonella let the retort die on her lips.

INDEED, BELINDA COULD HAVE NO IDEA EXACTLY WHAT WAS going on in Antonella's mind. She was far from resigned to her fate. She had not spent the day in the shed with Zephyra, but down at Atherleigh's mews as she had the day before, sitting at Rafiq's patient feet, absorbing everything the falconer had to tell her. Now that he knew about Chakor/Zephyra, he gave her answers that helped her gain a much better understanding of how to care for the wounded goshawk.

The most surprising thing of all was that he encouraged Antonella to unbind the wing.

"It has been enough time. If, as you say, the break was toward the outer extremity of the wing, likely one of the phalanges—or at worst the metacarpal—ten days is enough to give it the rest it needs in order to heal."

He told her this as she sat by him in his humble quarters, a cup of tea made with herbs sending tendrils of fragrant steam into her nostrils. "But what if it isn't yet healed?"

"Trust to Chakor. She will not exert herself beyond her capability. But you must give her the opportunity to spread her wings."

Yes, Antonella thought, the poor bird probably felt confined, especially in a strange place. Zephyra was accustomed to Atherleigh's capacious mews and to being sent into the air to hunt with freedom—yet tethered to the relationship between hawk and falconer. "I suppose that is why she has been off her feed. She has been sad not to be out and flying."

He did not say anything, but Antonella could tell by the way he closed his eyes and steepled his fingers that she had hit on it exactly.

"I have a perch outside my shed she can sit on with a tether. It's in a sheltered place that no one can see unless they come very close. But I don't know how to fly her. I'm afraid she would just soar away and never come back."

Rafiq nodded, held up his finger, and padded away to the room in the mews where the equipment was stored. She could hear him moving things and opening something—a wooden box or cupboard perhaps. A moment later he came back. In one hand was a fine leather cord of some length, coiled and tied together. In the other he held a pad made of leather with rabbit fur stitched to it. He held up the cord and said, "This is a leash. Chakor was trained with one and it will not seem strange to her." Then he held up the pad, which also had a cord attached to it, a shorter one. "This is a lure. You must tie some meat onto it when you use it at first."

Antonella's heart beat faster. He was telling her she should take Zephyra out on the glove! "Show me how!" she said, jumping to her feet.

"Softly, My Lady," Rafiq said, but in a way that did not hide his pleasure that Antonella was so enthusiastic about the ancient and noble art of falconry. "Attend me in the yard. I will join you presently."

Antonella, vibrating with anticipation, wrapped her cloak around her and left the warm, earthy atmosphere of the mews and went out into the icy weathering yard. A few moments later, Rafiq emerged with Altair, the tiercel, hooded and perched on his gloved left hand, holding the jesses securely between his fingers. He carried the lure in his other hand. Antonella knew not to approach and stood a few yards away.

"Altair would be angry to be on a leash now that he is an accomplished hunter. We trust each other. If I put the leash on his jesses I betray that trust. But the lure is still essential. For Altair, the lure is dry."

Rafiq quietly murmured, *ho ho ho* to the falcon, and Antonella the bird gathered himself, his head twitching slightly. Then in one smooth, graceful movement, Rafiq took hold of the top knot of the leather hood and plucked it off the bird's head. For a moment, falcon and falconer were both still. Somewhere in the distance, a seagull cried. Rafiq said "Hup! Hup!" and lifted his gloved hand, launching Altair into the air. The falcon soared away so high Antonella lost sight of him.

She held her breath. Rafiq stared up at the small, dark dot, then began swinging the lure and whistling. Like an arrow loosed from a heavenly bow, the falcon dove down so fast Antonella could hardly follow him with her eyes. Before she knew it, he snatched the lure in his talons and brought it to the ground. Rafiq whistled again and held out the glove. Between his fingers now was a scrap of meat, and with a single beat of his wings, Altair flew smoothly from the lure on the ground back onto Rafiq's fist.

"I've never... It's so..." Antonella gave up trying to say how she felt, what it was that watching Altair fulfill his role as a hunter—even with his only prey an inanimate lure—did to her insides. Magic. That was all.

Rafiq broke into her trance and said, "Chakor is a hawk, so she will not fly so high, but will fly farther. The leash will keep her close. When you are ready for her to leave the glove, you let go of the jesses but hold the leash. This will allow her to flap for a short distance. You drag the lure on the ground instead of swinging it. She will go to it. You reward her for returning to the glove."

It sounded so simple. But would she be able to do it herself? Zephyra was so much larger than Altair. "I see," she said, "Only I have no hood for her, and my glove is only something I borrowed from the gardener." Of course she could not do it. Antonella's spirits sank.

Rafiq hooded Altair again and tethered him to one of the block perches. Without a word, he went back into the mews. Antonella slowly moved toward the falcon, not getting close enough to upset him, but so that she could see his breast rise and fall with his breathing and the small feathers lift slightly in the winter wind.

A sound made her turn toward the mews to see Rafiq emerging, his hands full and extended toward her. "This was Chakor's hood. Here is a glove that should fit your hand. It was his lordship's when a boy. And I give you also the leash and the lure." He placed everything in Antonella's outstretched hands.

"Rafiq! Thank you. I shall bring them back, when—" She stopped. For days she had been trying to picture the moment when she would restore Zephyra to her rightful owner, whole and healthy. She still didn't know how she would manage it.

"Trust Chakor," Rafiq said with a bow, then turned and went back into the mews.

She had been dismissed. Antonella smiled. Here, in this small place, Rafiq gave the orders. She was a lowly apprentice.

It was time to go out the back gate and make her way through the woods to her modest shed, her reality, so far removed in all ways from the mews. Mews? Atherleigh's compound was more like a temple to falconry with Rafiq its high priest.

It had only been two days since her fall, but every day she was drawn inexorably back to that place. Rafiq welcomed her—or if he did not exactly welcome her, accepted her. Yet the falconer remained a mystery. Although deferential, he was never obsequious. In fact, she had the distinct impression that he held himself superior to her not just in knowledge, but in breeding. She wished she could ask him about his life in India, where he came from and why he chose to come to England. Somehow those questions—entirely appropriate in a staid drawing room—felt impertinent and invasive when the falconer was in his domain among the hunting birds.

And after all, did it matter? She had no idea where she came from either anymore. This thought gave her a strange feeling of kinship with Rafiq.

WHEN SHE RETURNED FROM THE MEWS, ANTONELLA KEPT TO her room. She wished she could simply remain there, but she had to join Belinda and the dowager for meals, much to her dismay. She was in no position to request a tray be sent up to her. It would have been considered the height of impertinence, putting their meager kitchen staff to such trouble. At dinner that night, the dowager had evinced little curiosity as to where Antonella had been all day, only inquiring as to her progress on the handkerchief she was embroidering. A handkerchief Antonella hadn't even thought about since the day nearly three weeks ago when her entire world turned upside down.

And after dinner, in the drawing room before Skilling brought in the tea tray, the dowager initiated only commonplaces. Belinda remained unusually silent as well. Time passed with excruciating slowness.

At last the ordeal ended. Lady Lewiston rose. "I shall retire. Antonella, I would like a brief word with you, alone." The dowager said it without even looking at Ant and left the room assuming she would follow.

Alone? She had never had a solitary conference with the dowager. Always Belinda had been with her. She exchanged a glance with Belinda before following in Aunt Caroline's wake. Belinda merely shrugged.

Antonella expected to be led once more to Lady Lewiston's private parlor, but she passed by the door to her apartments and continued down the hall to enter Ant's bedchamber. For a moment, Antonella panicked that the room would be disordered. The maids no longer made it a priority to make her bed and tidy her things. But one glance told her she needn't have worried. A few books littered the dressing table. A chair had been moved closer to the small hearth. Only a hairbrush and a hand mirror lay on top of the dresser.

"You are not very like Belinda. But I have always known that."

"To what do I owe this honor, My Lady?" Antonella couldn't help the slightly sarcastic edge in her voice. She half feared that news of her accident and return to the Court in Lord Atherleigh's carriage had somehow found its way to the dowager.

But she was wrong. Quite unexpectedly, Lady Lewiston launched into the conversation with, "I know you must hate me now, but I revealed the truth to you for your own good." At these words she took a seat on the edge of Antonella's bed and patted the space beside her.

So, Antonella thought, she didn't know about her fall and her visits to the mews. While that was a relief, she couldn't keep a sense of dread at bay as she waited to see what else Lady Lewiston had to say to her. After a long silence,

Antonella said, "I still find it very difficult to understand." She remained standing, knotting her fingers together, not bothering to explain what it was she found hard to understand.

The dowager sighed. "My feelings are of no importance in this, but I want you to believe that the marquess and I shared a profound affection for each other. It was an arranged match, and duty was always our first priority. Duty to him and to the title. If it had not been my duty, I might have refused to take you in when I did, and I would certainly not have allowed the marquess to treat you so much like his … well, his daughter. He had a peculiar regard for you."

This was torture. Why was she doing it? Couldn't she see it didn't help? "What use is that?" Antonella said, angry at the sting of tears behind her eyes.

"I freely admit that he was fonder of you than I was. I believe that only natural, since I had not birthed you as I had Belinda. I did try to do my share to uphold your fa—the marquess's facade concerning your parentage. I confess that at times I found it very difficult to do so."

I was right, Antonella thought. Not just now, but throughout her life this woman had preferred Belinda. Only now she understood that her preference didn't simply arise because Belinda was so much more the proper lady, the proper daughter of a marchioness. Her predilection went deeper than that. In some way, she could excuse the dowager for her feelings. Surely any mother would have felt the same. She didn't excuse her enough to make this conversation easy for her, however.

Lady Lewiston took a deep breath and continued speaking. "The marquess was an honorable man, but he was not faultless. He did not leave us in lavish financial circumstances. I had hoped to persuade your—Harry, the marquess —when Belinda and I went to London—to add to the funds available for both of your dowries. He was preoccupied with other concerns, and failed to see the urgency. He may in time do so.

"But I fear this lack means that there is no point at all in my taking you to London for a season in the spring. With neither birth nor fortune to recommend you, you have very little chance of making a good match. You had far better set your sights on someone of lower estate. An honest tradesman, or a clergyman perhaps." She'd started twisting her hands together. "What I mean is that you should not throw lures out to the likes of Mr. Gainesworth or Lord Atherleigh. I feel certain neither of them would countenance a match with you at present."

Ah, so this was Lady Lewiston's real reason for seeking her out. Quite unreasonably, her words stung. "I am not looking for a husband at all."

At that, the dowager turned the full force of her steely gaze on Antonella. "But you must. It is the only honorable option for a female brought up as you have been. You can do nothing useful. Your beauty is not extraordinary. Your education is extensive, but you will find few ways to employ it outside of a home and family. The world does not work that way. But you are intelligent and could make a good manager of a modest household."

Aunt Caroline's vision of her future made Antonella feel sick. No tradesman's or vicar's wife would be suffered to tramp alone through the woods looking for injured birds. And likely she'd be saddled with a quiver full of children and have to make and scrape for them. She shuddered. An image of Atherleigh came unbidden into her mind. He'd asked her to call him Malcolm at the masquerade ball, and he was well aware of her circumstances. *He* did not disdain her and consider her unworthy. He'd sent her home after her fall in his own carriage, after all.

Then an awful thought crossed her mind. Would an association with her diminish the baron in the eyes of the world?

"I've come to you today because I want you to think carefully about whether you should join us tomorrow evening at Atherleigh's card party. You have been invited. I will not force you to remain at home. It's your decision whether to accept. Excuses can easily be made, however."

After what had happened at the masquerade ball, it was so very tempting to simply say she would prefer to remain behind. Antonella had already considered inventing a headache to justify doing so. But the dowager's words awakened her stubborn, independent streak. Why shouldn't she go? Everyone now knew her true status. It was up to them to treat her as they would, to decide whether to consider her beneath them or to accept that nothing had materially changed about her. Besides, she risked suffering Belinda's wrath if she took this opportunity to beg off.

"Thank you, Aunt Caroline. But I believe to do so would be cowardly. As you have said, I need to become accustomed to my new situation in society. I expect learning how to behave with demure propriety, not putting myself forward or encouraging attention, would be a useful skill—as you put it—to develop."

The dowager stood and walked toward her, holding out her two hands. It would be pointedly rude to ignore the gesture. Whatever their relationship now, this woman had performed the role of mother to Antonella for eighteen years, ensuring she had the same education as Lady Belinda and giving her the same opportunities—until now. She put her hands in Lady Lewiston's.

The pressure of the dowager's grip surprised her. She looked up to see a frown creasing her forehead and tears standing in her eyes. "You're strong and smart. I don't think any of your education has been wasted on you. You will have a home here as long as you need it. The marquess would have wanted that." She gradually lessened the pressure on Antonella's hands and then let go of them.

Antonella couldn't help noticing that Lady Lewiston did not say that *she* wanted her to have a home at the Court as long as she needed it. But she supposed that would have been too much to expect. And she'd given her the truth with no bark on it, which was a kindness in its own way.

"I'll meet you and Lady Belinda in the hall at five o'clock tomorrow," Antonella said.

The dowager cast one last look back at Ant when she reached the door and nodded to her before opening it and walking through.

CHAPTER 24

*P*enrose brought the note to Gainesworth at breakfast on the morning of the card party. He read it through three times, not certain at first what he should do about it. Lady Belinda asked him to come and meet her at the Amblemere stables because she needed his help with something she had found.

The most extraordinary thing! I'm sure it means something, but I can't puzzle it out. Antonella won't help me. She's being ~~stubborn~~ cautious. I think she's a little afraid which is why I need your help. I'm doing this for her.

Surely Lady Belinda must be aware of the impropriety of inviting a gentleman to a clandestine meeting … No doubt she wouldn't have taken such a bold step if she understood that he was courting her. Or if she had any desire for him. And yet, surely she was not indifferent to him. Not when she looked at him as she did. Not when the hint of roses bloomed in her cheeks when he smiled at her. Perhaps she wasn't aware of it herself. She certainly had not thrown out any obvious lures. It seemed as if she was unaware of her own powers to attract. Belinda was not just pretty—there were always plenty of pretty girls decorating the *ton* ball-rooms during the season. She was different. She had a quality he found hard to describe. Warmth? Curiosity? Openness? Life with Lady Belinda would never be boring.

He sighed. And yet, there was the sister. He had a feeling that only by engaging in this quest for the truth of Miss Ambleton's birth would he be able to gain Lady Belinda's trust, and from there perhaps more. But how much more?

There it was again! The idea of sharing a life with her kept creeping into his mind. What was more, he found he had little desire to chase it away, which wasn't like him at all. It occurred to him to wonder how much of that willingness sprang from the fact that he wasn't absolutely certain how she felt about him, and thus she presented a challenge. He chuckled remembering how she sprung on him the notion that he should court Miss Ambleton.

If only Lady Belinda could see that it was Malcolm, not he, who would best suit the quirky, mercurial Antonella. But something Belinda had said made him think she didn't favor Atherleigh for her sister. He couldn't fathom why. No more decent a chap existed. Was it his injury? That didn't seem like something Lady Belinda would hold against him. Malcolm was a little thorny, of course. And he tended to be a bit Friday-faced these days. But would that be enough to put a lady off? Besides, the mention of Miss Ambleton's name had the power to shake Malcolm out of his doldrums, however briefly. Was Malcolm aware of that in himself? He did not know. In any case, Gainesworth could do nothing about that now. It was up to Atherleigh to sort out his feelings.

As for the matter of his own heart, he knew himself well enough to consider that meeting Lady Belinda alone would be dangerous. The temptation to declare himself might be too great, and could possibly achieve nothing more than scaring her off. Perhaps he should make his excuses and not meet her for the sake of her reputation and his sanity.

But no. He would do no such thing. Not meeting her to discuss something of importance to her sister's predicament would be a mistake. He had no doubt it would diminish him in her eyes. And if they were outdoors, in view of the grooms and stableboys, what harm could there be? Yes, he would go. It could be made to appear a chance meeting, after all. Perhaps he could say he was lost. He certainly didn't know the country around there very well. Or he could say he wanted the advice of their groom for something to do with his horse.

So it happened that Hector set out before noon on another bright, blisteringly cold day to meet Belinda as requested at the Amblemere stables, having claimed that he wanted to exercise his bay hunter without the distraction of another horse nearby. It was entirely believable, since the cold weather made even the most docile mount frisky. The ground was too icy for the horse's hooves to fling mud up and dirty his clothes so he could be sure of arriving in good trim. But that same hard earth was not kind to horses, and he would have to go easier than he would like and not jump any hedges. His spirited mount wouldn't get a good gallop. It would be a tricky ride.

Gainesworth was so occupied with keeping the bay in check that he missed the turning Belinda had told him about in her note. He found himself on a narrowing path that led in the right direction, he was certain, but the stables didn't come into view when he expected.

Instead all he could see over the slight rise was the roof of a small structure, a sort of shed, up ahead. He rode toward it, thinking it could mark the beginning of a cluster of outbuildings and he would be able to get his bearings.

Before he went much farther, though, a large bird—likely

a hawk, Hector thought—burst upward over the rise into his view and flew a short distance with a long tether dangling from one leg. Once he got over his surprise, Hector remembered Atherleigh training a hawk or falcon of some kind in that way once when he had visited him as a boy. The event was seared into his memory. Malcolm had told him then that there was no one else in the county who practiced the art of falconry. It was going out of fashion. So what had he seen there?

The the hawk flew up again.

Curious, he urged his horse slowly forward. As he drew closer, not just the hawk but its handler came into view. And although her back was to him, he knew right away that it was none other than Miss Ambleton. Her dark hair pulled back from her face and tied at the nape of her neck trailed in loose curls down her back, and although she faced away from him, he caught occasional glimpses of her distinctive profile, a nose that ended in a saucy lift at the end—not at all like Lady Belinda's perfectly straight nose with its finely cut nostrils. What in blazes was this young woman doing with a large hunting bird? Belinda had mentioned her sister's fascination with the creatures of the air, but not that she had taken to falconry herself. How could she do it? The Ambletons had no falconer, according to Atherleigh. And his friend had told him several times that he was planning to close his mews, that keeping the hunting birds in training when he could no longer fly them himself made no sense.

Miss Ambleton was so intent upon her work with the hawk that she did not turn to see him. He watched a little longer as she repeatedly released the bird to fly after some kind of lure and then whistled for its return to jump onto her glove. Bird and woman were completely engrossed, as if nothing outside of their repetitive ritual existed. Did Malcolm know about this? If he did, it only reinforced

Hector's sense that this small, elfin female would suit Atherleigh like a pair of well-fitting gloves, if only they could both be made to see it.

However, this was not why he had ventured out this morning. Surely the stables must be nearby. He turned the bay on the path that curved around the immediate area of the shed and urged him forward with a squeeze of his calves. Soon, the higher prospect he had reached at that point revealed a group of buildings scattered haphazardly some way below and to the east. Clearly stables and a livestock barn. Only when he was far enough away from Miss Antonella did Hector increase his speed. He didn't want to disturb her or for her to see him there—for her sake and for his.

Belinda paced impatiently up and down by the large barn that served as a stable for the Amblemere horses at one end and housed the pigs at the other. Partly she was trying to stay warm in the sharp cold that had persisted since the night of the masquerade ball. Partly she was trying to make sense of what she was about to do. She didn't want to admit to herself that her mother's words had disturbed her. She had taken Mr. Gainesworth very much as he appeared to her—a kind, attentive gentleman with a lively sense of humor and a caring disposition. That he had been intent on pleasing her had become clear at the ball. Why else would he have agreed to help her solve the mystery of Antonella's origins? How foolish she felt once he pointed out the absurdity of assuming she could choose something as important as a husband for her sister. Sometimes it was hard not to believe that Antonella felt exactly as she did, that if she found Gainesworth beguiling that her sister could not help but feel the same way.

Yet when Gainesworth spoke to Antonella she did not

blush and struggle to say pleasant nothings with a mouth as dry as dust—which is precisely what happened to her. Had she been the object of his regard from the very beginning of their acquaintance? Although she did not think so highly of herself that she would believe Gainesworth came into Cornwall only to see her, the possibility that her presence so near to Atherleigh Manor might have weighed in his decision gave her a secret little thrill.

Could it be that he really cared for her? Or was she naïve to think it possible? Could everything he'd done and said in these past few days not be seen as the behavior of a practiced rake?

It was all so confusing! If only well-bred ladies were free to ask gentlemen direct questions. If only people could actually *talk* to each other, say meaningful things instead of dancing around what really mattered. Such was not possible if one were to remain within the strictures of propriety, however. So instead she must gauge for herself what his intentions were, listen to what he said, observe his actions. She asked him to meet her mostly so they would have a chance to talk about the pocket book privately. But she also wanted to see him at close quarters and alone. At all their other meetings they had been surrounded by people. His behavior in such settings might be very different from how he would act towards her without an audience judging him.

As to what that difference would be, Belinda had made some wild conjectures. She imagined everything from finding herself confronted with icily formal behavior to having to fend off inappropriate advances. She was a little ashamed to admit to herself that the second possibility was vastly preferable to her than the first.

The chapel bell tolled the hour she had mentioned in her note and there was still no sign of him. She had a sinking feeling that he wouldn't come. It was brazen of her to suggest it. Verging on the hoydenish. Perhaps that would put him off. Would he think she was throwing herself at him? She shuddered at the thought. Mayhappen he wasn't at liberty that morning, or her note hadn't been delivered. He could easily be too occupied with preparations for the card party to get away. Or—and this thought sent a bitter lump into her stomach—perhaps he simply didn't want to come. That would be worse than anything.

But oh! She wanted to see him! She wanted to see him stride up with easy grace and smile in that way that could light up a room. She had used the flimsy excuse of the pocket book she found to justify her request to meet him. It was the truth, in a way. It was also a gamble. If her Mama ever found out—especially after having taken such trouble to paint him as a hardened rake—well, that didn't bear thinking of.

But she'd done it. No going back now. And no mistaking the fluttering in her stomach, her racing pulse.

When Gainesworth finally rode up on his spirited bay gelding, his laughing blue eyes fixed on hers, she hardly noticed his flowing greatcoat and the woolen muffler around his neck, or the fact that his cheeks were apple red from the cold. All she saw was the man who had captured her heart from the moment they met at the dress party. Or perhaps even before that, during their unspoken mutual appreciation of the ridiculous lady in her antiquated garb.

With a single elegant movement, Gainesworth lifted his right leg over the horse's neck and slid down from the saddle so that he faced Belinda. As soon as both his feet were firmly planted on the ground he folded into a graceful bow. *A practiced bow,* she thought. How many times had he greeted ladies in just that way? It was difficult to keep that objective thought in her mind, because when he unbent, his smile was all sunshine and she wished nothing more than that she could run into his arms.

He pulled the reins over the horse's head and led him snorting and steaming to her.

Belinda curtsied, suddenly overcome with shyness and confusion. Talking to him when she had marked him out as a match for her sister and when they were amid a crowd of people felt easy. Now, with every nerve alive to the possibility that he could either be the answer to her dreams or a nightmare of embarrassment and disappointment, words stuck in her throat.

"Lady Belinda, what is this information you've found?" He looked around a bit nervously.

Of course, they were in a rather compromising position, outside where anyone could see them. She had arranged it thus as part of her test. "You must think me a veritable jade, My Lord," she managed to say, unable to stop the rush of heat into her cheeks. "But I assure you I have a very good reason for asking you to meet me. I was afraid I would not have a private moment to give you this at your party." She reached into her reticule and handed him the pocket book.

He looped the reins over his arm and took it from her, opening it and perusing a few pages. "An appointment book, it would seem," he said, then looked up at her, narrowing his eyes.

"I found it stuck at the back of a drawer in a very old desk. It was my father's, the book I mean, from around the years Antonella and I were both born." It sounded suddenly foolish. Surely he would see her invitation to meet as the excuse it was. She shivered.

"You are frozen through! I'm late. I got a little lost. Can we go somewhere out of the wind?"

She was icy cold, but the look in his eyes had the power to melt her. No! She must keep her distance. She nodded toward the barn. "I told Ben, the groom, that you were coming to look at my mare, that I was thinking of selling her and getting a new one, that you knew how such things could be managed in town." She led him in through the slightly open door into the cavernous space and nodded to the groom. The old man, who had known Belinda since she was a little girl, cast her a suspicious glance. Please God don't let him go saying anything to mother! She gave him as disinterested a nod as she could manage and raised her voice. "As I said, Mr. Gainesworth, she's a sweet goer, but small, only fifteen hands."

Ben ambled forward and took the bay's reins from Gainesworth. "I'll walk 'im up and down fer ya, M'Lud. Too cold to stand still."

Gainesworth nodded agreement and followed Belinda to the loose box where her chestnut mare, Paloma, stood pulling at an armful of hay.

"I don't know how much you can really see with that heavy horse blanket on her," she said, again for Ben's benefit. She glanced up in the groom's direction and made sure he was walking away down the middle of the barn. The space was large, so they had a little time while his back was turned to speak of the pocket book. What a silly thing to have done! Why did she imagine it could work? He must think her foolish at the very least.

Gainesworth lowered his voice to just above a whisper. "From a quick look, as I said, it appears to be an appointment book. There are no names, only initials and times. Was the marquess a betting man?"

Belinda was both relieved and disappointed that Gainesworth took her at her word and immediately turned the conversation to the artifact she'd brought. And the question he asked—of course. It could easily have been a record of her father's wagers. Why didn't she think of that? She sighed. "Yes. All too much—She has a lovely head and jumps off her hocks," Belinda said more loudly, seeing Ben had turned and was walking the gelding back in their direction.

As soon as the groom turned again and led the horse halfway back down the barn, she whispered, "Could it only be that? What kind of bets might it be?'

Gainesworth turned several pages and paused to examine one or two entries. "I don't know. The dates don't match any of the Newmarket or York races. Still, I suppose it could be cards. But debts of honor must be paid immediately. And it's not all dates. Do you recognize any initials?"

"Not really, not more than could be mere coincidence. There is more of substance toward the end pages, some things that almost look like verses." Ben was on his way back again and Belinda said, "I don't know how much I would be willing to sell her for. I expect I must ask my brother, although she is mine to keep or dispose of as I wish." She patted Paloma's neck and silently sent her a reassuring thought that she would no more think of selling her than sending her to the knacker's yard.

"I would do much to have the privilege of possessing such a beautiful creature," Gainesworth said, not looking at the horse, but drilling his gaze into Belinda's eyes.

Oh God! she thought. That look could make her agree to anything. Perhaps her mother was right. A wave of something between panic and thrill washed over her. She opened her mouth to say something but all that came out was an embarrassed cough. When Ben turned away again, she cleared her throat and said, "If I gave this book into your keeping, do you think you might be able to decipher more of it? It may be nothing, but it's all I have now."

"Tell me," Gainesworth said, moving a step closer to Belinda—a step too close, she thought, and stepped back a little. He held up his hands, palms out in a gesture of surrender, as though she was an unbroken filly, and said, "what is it you hope to find in these pages?"

She bit her lower lip. "I don't know. Or rather, I fear I may know, but I can't say it."

He nodded, at last releasing her from his unflinching regard. "I understand. Do you want me to tell you what I decipher even if it's something that may be distasteful to you?"

Belinda took a long moment to think. She'd turned over the rock, as Antonella said. She must face whatever unpleasant creatures lurked beneath it. "Yes. It's for my sister. She needs to know the truth, whatever it is, even if she doesn't believe she does right now."

He took yet another step closer to her. This time, she stood her ground. When he spoke, it was barely above a whisper. "You genuinely love …" He paused infinitesimally, but it was enough for Belinda's breath to catch at the word before he continued. "… love Antonella, don't you. What if, in truth, she isn't your sister?"

By now that question began to feel irrelevant compared to the more pressing need to understand exactly what Gainesworth thought about her and whether she should believe anything he said.

"You must face that possibility," Gainesworth said, interpreting her silence as arising from indecision.

"It doesn't bear thinking about," Belinda said, berating herself for letting her mind wander so. "Of course I would continue to love her no matter what. But I have a feeling, I can't explain it. I know we have a closer connection than cousinship. We must!"

It was all Hector could do not to reach out and wrap his arms around Belinda when she looked at him with those big, melting eyes. How could he refuse to help her—although he very much feared that the little pocket book would bring to light some unsavory information. Why else would it be written all in code so that no one who found it could easily decipher what it contained?

"I shall endeavor to tease out the meaning of these entries," he said, reaching out a hand to tuck away a lock of her hair that had come out from under her woolen hat. Then louder he said, "Let me think about it, My Lady. Tattersall's might be your best option. I must return to Atherleigh now. I shall see you this evening, shall I not?"

After a tiny pause, she breathed, "Yes, My Lord."

He nodded to the groom, who brought the bay back to him. As he jumped up into the saddle and gathered the reins, his mind raced. What was that look in her eyes? Had he done something wrong? Against all his powerful desires to the contrary, he'd schooled himself to observe the proprieties during this unconventional meeting. Had she been disappointed that nothing of an amorous nature took place between them in that private setting? If she had been a different girl, if his intentions were merely to conduct a pleasant flirtation, he might have tried to steal a kiss. But kissing this particular girl would mean more than flirtation, and he did not want to do it in a horse's stall.

The honest truth was that each time he encountered the captivating Lady Belinda Ambleton, Hector was moving inexorably toward a declaration. The question was would she welcome it? He still didn't know for certain. Before that meeting, he would have been confident of a yes. But a certain guardedness had come into her demeanor that morning, almost as if she wanted to set him at a distance. It reminded him of an air from the opera—Mozart, he thought. *La ci darèm la mano*, if he recalled correctly.

Oh Lord! Did she consider him a Don Juan? Was that what accounted for her mixed responses?

She would be at the party later. He had no plans to return to London before the New Year, so there was yet time. He would do his best to unlock the secret buried in the scribbled lines in the pocket book, and only then ask for her hand— and prove that he was no thoughtless rake.

Before the year was out, he had every intention of becoming betrothed to Lady Belinda.

CHAPTER 25

*O*n the morning of the card party it suddenly occurred to Atherleigh to wonder if Miss Ambleton would actually attend. Gainesworth had written the invitations. Had he made it clear to Lady Lewiston that both the young ladies were invited? From what he'd seen of the way the dowager treated and spoke of Miss Ambleton she might well choose not to include her.

This thought sent his spirits sinking as he sought refuge in his book room from the feverish preparations for the evening's event. Atherleigh Manor hadn't seen so much activity for years. Housemaids whisked Holland covers off chairs in the disused saloons and polished all the wood in sight. The book room had already received a thorough dusting. Footmen unearthed leaves from a cupboard in the butler's pantry that made the dining table twice its normal length. Card tables were fetched down from the attics along with chairs and placed in the drawing room. Fresh decks of cards sat on each table, awaiting only someone to shuffle and deal.

Maids rolled up the carpet in the largest saloon so it

would be ready for impromptu dancing. Although not the full ensemble Lady Lewiston had hired for the masked ball, a trio of local musicians—two fiddles and a recorder—welcomed the unexpected work and would take their places before any of the guests arrived.

Once, he would have looked forward to an evening of spirited gaming and flirting. Now Atherleigh dreaded the party and how it would expose even more of his inability to lead a normal life. It would expose him as a less than welcoming host as well, he feared. He simply hadn't figured out how to manage many of the simplest things, even though, thanks to Gainesworth, he was beginning to think he one day would. At least if Miss Ambleton was there, one person besides Gainesworth would be sensitive to his situation already and wouldn't judge him.

Atherleigh pulled himself up. Could he honestly say that was the only reason he wanted Miss Ambleton to come? Because of her apparent greater awareness and understanding of his injury? Could there be another reason? Not the obvious one, he was certain. He wasn't interested in courtship. How could he be? And she hardly seemed the kind of lady who would normally attract him. Atherleigh's tastes ran to voluptuous beauties ripe for adventure. He'd had one or two such liaisons in Spain. Of course, he hadn't indulged in so much as a flirtation since his injury, and the women who used to make up to him would no doubt think twice about it now.

There was also the matter of Miss Ambleton's uncertain birth. None of that was her fault. But people loved to stir up scandal wherever they could. How foolish! He didn't know why he was even thinking about that. It wasn't as if he seriously considered trying to fix her interest. Or if he did, that anyone in his family was around to object.

But supposing he did consider it. Out here in the wilds of

Cornwall few of those scruples seemed to matter as much. If Miss Ambleton were to have a London season it would be a different matter. The most eligible gentlemen would avoid her, as would any looking to elevate their standing in society. A union with her would rather achieve the opposite. It was hardly fair for so lovely, intelligent, and innocent a lady to be considered tainted. For without knowing precisely who her parents were, conjecture would abound, and many would assume the very worst. And then what would her future be? Gently brought up girls were required to marry. The alternative of a life as a spinster aunt was cruel and unthinkable. It would be a terrible waste as well. As a man of means, he was free to choose a life as a bachelor and no one would judge him for it, especially in light of his maiming. Realistically, Malcolm foresaw a life alone, with perhaps a few sensual encounters with women whose trade it was to minister to men like him. He might perhaps find fulfillment in that—if the loss of so many pastimes didn't turn him into a mad curmudgeon.

Naturally such a life would never be an option for Miss Ambleton. She was no fainting damsel or insipid miss. Inside her slight frame, Malcolm suspected, lay a core of steely strength. It may have been that Lady Lewiston only recently revealed her true relationship to the family, but he guessed that if the dowager marchioness had known it these eighteen years, she had not lavished Miss Ambleton with the same affection or attention as she had on her own daughter.

What did he know of it! And why was he spending any time thinking about the girl? It was only that their three encounters had all been extraordinary in their way. His fall from his horse. His discovery of her hiding after her flight from the ballroom. And most recently, finding her lying injured in the mews. What in blazes had she been doing there, and how could she have been so foolish as to have climbed up high in the old oak tree? An ill-judged step if he ever heard of one. She wasn't unintelligent. She was young, of course. If she had an affinity for—or curiosity about—falconry, why had she not said as much to him on the occasions when he'd seen her? He hadn't asked her that when he sent her home in his carriage after her injury. She was still a bit muddled in her head and he was more concerned with her health than with discovering what had led her to that particular place at that particular time.

Was she feigning an interest in something he loved as a stratagem to lure him into offering for her? No, of course not! It wouldn't be like her.

He chuckled to himself. How did he know what would be like her? He knew little of her, but a kind of intimacy—not physical—drew them to each other every time they met. The connection was intangible and indescribable. A resonance of sympathy. Miss Ambleton had been wounded perhaps as deeply as he had. Neither his nor her wounds would ever be healed. They had both been changed by them for the rest of their lives.

A smile played on his lips as he pictured her in her drab, peasant-like clothes, then in her patched-together costume with its bird feathers. But when he thought of her lying dazed and abraded on the cot in the mews he did not smile. He remembered her dark, falcon's eyes looking up at him, uncertain, fearful. Despite those eyes she was no predator. If he had to liken her to any bird, it would be a wren—or a robin.

His musing came to an abrupt end when Gainesworth burst in through the library door. "I swear you haven't moved since I left! Your coffee cup is still half full."

Hector flopped down on one of the comfortable chairs and stretched his legs out in front of him.

"Did you have a good ride? Where did you go?" Atherleigh asked. Perhaps listening to Gainesworth's no doubt entertaining account of his morning's adventures would shake him out of his torpor.

"It was … interesting. I'm afraid I lied to you about why I was going out on this bone-chilling day." He stood and crossed to the sideboard where a decanter and glasses lay at the ready and poured himself a measure of Madeira. He raised his eyebrows at Atherleigh, who answered with a shake of his head. "As I said, I told you a lie. Well, a small untruth. Although Atticus definitely needed some exercise, that wasn't my primary motive in sallying forth."

He paused to sip his Madeira appreciatively and Atherleigh stood to poke at the fire, turning his back to Gainesworth. "So out with it, man!"

"I met Lady Belinda."

Atherleigh whirled around, the fireplace poker still in his hand. "Are you mad? Did you make a clandestine assignation with her? You'll walk right into parson's mousetrap that way!"

Hector laughed. "I didn't make the appointment. She did."

That seemed entirely out of character with the ingenuous, open Lady Belinda. "I didn't think she was the sort to be so brazen."

"It wasn't as shocking as all that. She's asked for my help with something to do with her sister and she found an item that might contain important information."

"Why couldn't she just tell you about it this evening?"

Hector paused to take another sip of his drink. "It's a secret. It's something she doesn't even want Miss Ambleton to know about yet. Or anyone, really. Although I gather Miss Ambleton knows of its existence."

How like Gainesworth to get entangled with some intrigue involving a lady. "Are you going to tell me what this is all about? One cannot mention a secret and then not reveal it." Malcolm strode to the sideboard, changing his mind and pouring himself a glass of Madeira.

"Wise," Gainesworth said. "You may need it."

Once they were both comfortably settled, Gainesworth explained Lady Belinda's quest to solve the mystery of Miss Antonella's birth, and that she'd found an old pocket book of her late father's that might well contain some clues.

"Do you think this is information Miss Ambleton would wish to have?" Atherleigh asked. Clearly the girl's nerves were already raw from Lady Lewiston's unexpected revelation. In Atherleigh's experience, long-buried secrets seldom existed to hide good news.

"That is in part why Lady Belinda is being so secretive about it. And besides, she couldn't—and I haven't yet tried to —decipher the contents of the book." He reached into his coat pocket to retrieve the book and held it out to Atherleigh, open to one of the scribbled pages so he could take it with one hand and see inside it.

Malcolm peered at it closely. "Wagers?" he said. "Or assignations. This could be very unsavory if you do manage to tease out its meaning."

Gainesworth grimaced. "I said as much to Lady Belinda. She wants to know no matter what and will judge whether, in the end, there would be any point in sharing it with Miss Ambleton."

Malcolm passed the book back to Gainesworth. "I still say you're playing with fire here."

After tucking the book back into his pocket and downing the rest of his Madeira, Hector said, "I discovered something else while I was out. Something that might be of greater interest to you because it concerns Miss Ambleton."

"Why should that be?" Malcolm tried for nonchalance, but he knew his good friend would detect the flush in his cheeks.

"Ah. I thought so," Hector said, a wicked grin on his face. "I took a wrong turn when I was on my way to meet Lady Belinda and ended up near a shed with a sort of yard outside it. Imagine my surprise when I saw a large bird—I believe some kind of hawk—fly up with a tether attached to its leg and bells jingling and then land out of sight a short way along."

Malcolm rested his elbows on his knees and leaned forward. "A hawk? Are you sure?"

"You know I haven't the knowledge to say exactly, but the bird was large. When I drew closer, I could see that it was Miss Ambleton casting out some kind of lure and then when the creature caught it, whistling for it to come and sit on the stout glove she wore on her left hand."

Malcolm's heart speeded up uncomfortably. "Did you ask her what she was doing?" What business did that slip of a girl have training a large hawk? This, of course, made some sense of her acquaintance with Rafiq. She hadn't said anything to him though. She knew he loved the sport, so why not tell him of her interest?

"Steady on! I didn't stay. I don't think she saw me. I was late already so I quietly went on my way, but I thought you'd like to know."

Did he want to know? And was he angry? Confused, more like. Malcolm didn't know what he thought.

"You can ask her tonight," Gainesworth said and got to his feet. "I think it's time to dress for dinner."

Antonella wasn't certain how she felt about going to Atherleigh Manor. Belinda pressured her to confess all concerning Zephyra to the baron while she had the chance, but still she hesitated. She wanted to take the goshawk back to Atherleigh's mews, but only when she was fully healed—and once she could flap her wings and fly with strength. Zephyra had already made so much progress in the two days since she had been exercising her. If she was doing it right, that is.

Why was it so important to her to prove herself in this way to Atherleigh? She could not deny that something drew her to him. He appeared forbidding, unfriendly. Yet he had taken the time to talk to her when she'd been so distressed at the masquerade ball. And then, his concern about her fall. Something had passed between them. She only had to think about those moments and her breath shallowed and her pulse quickened. But it was absurd! Surely it was just that they had the connection of falconry, a shared passion—although Atherleigh didn't know about hers, at least not completely. Atherleigh. Malcolm. He'd asked her to call him that. How could she, though?

It was time to dress for the evening's card party. She would see him again, amid a smaller gathering. Not so many places to hide. She would be exposed there. Best to do everything possible to fade into the background.

Antonella had gone to her wardrobe to select one of her nicer gowns—one of a sober enough color not to attract notice—when she heard a light scratch on her door. She'd accustomed herself to no longer having Fulk's help to dress, so she couldn't imagine who it could be. Aunt Caroline had said all she would say about the evening yesterday, so it was unlikely to be her. After throwing on her wrap Antonella opened the door.

"Might I come in?"

Miss Wilkins! The governess normally kept to herself these days, now that lessons were at an end and her duties ran instead to managing some of the household concerns—provisioning, cleaning, staff disputes. She always smiled at

Antonella when their paths crossed and sometimes engaged her in brief conversations, no doubt meant to cheer her up given recent events. But she had barely spoken to Antonella since the night of the masquerade, and never ventured to her room.

"Of course!" Antonella said with genuine pleasure, quickly recovering from her surprise. Miss Wilkins was one person she could be certain would not lecture her about her unsuitable pursuits or admonish her not to wear her drab and worn old clothing in order to tramp about in the woods.

As the governess entered, she brought a parcel out from behind her back. Something soft and flat, wrapped in cloth rather than in paper. "I hope you don't think me presumptuous, but I've brought you something I thought you'd like." She held the parcel out to Antonella.

"Believe me, Wilkie, I've sunk so far in everyone's estimation that nothing you did could be misconstrued as presumptuous!" The governess returned her mischievous smile with an expression of sunny warmth. Antonella wanted to embrace her, but the governess's hands were full at present with the unexpected gift. "What is it?"

"It's something I've been keeping for you, for the right time. I had to alter it a little, the fashions having been quite different at the time this was first made. It belonged to someone very dear to me. I could not use it—such a thing would be totally unsuitable for me, besides being too small."

While Miss Wilkins spoke, Antonella unwrapped the item. When it was fully free of its packing, she held it up and gasped. She had never seen anything like it. A shimmering white silk evening dress with silver embroidery of snowflakes at the hem, along the decolletage, and at the edges of the tiny puffed sleeves. "It's exquisite! But I can't wear this. It's too … elegant."

Miss Wilkins laughed. "On the contrary—it is elegant, but

you can and shall wear it. It's the perfect gown for a winter party. No lace, no ruffles. Not over-trimmed."

"Still, Aunt Caroline all but instructed me not to draw any attention this evening. I think she really doesn't even want me to be there." Antonella would be quite happy to evade the notice of most of the gentlemen herself. It would be just as well not to attract Atherleigh's notice. After all, whatever she thought or felt about him, he was a baron and she was no one.

But he had called her Nella.

Wearing this gown that Miss Wilkins held out to her would make it all but impossible for her not to be the focus of everyone's attention. That would necessarily include Atherleigh.

"Is it your true desire? To remain invisible? That isn't the Antonella I remember from the schoolroom. The Antonella who was brave to a fault, who wasn't afraid to have her own opinions and thoughts, whose sharp mind and incisive wit kept me and Belinda always on our toes. You have extraordinary gifts, dear girl. Gifts that should be appreciated by more than the birds you tend, or the hawk you're taking such great care of."

"You mustn't tell a soul!" Antonella froze. Had she made it clear enough to her?

"Please do not be uneasy. No one takes much notice of where I go, and it would never occur to Lady Lewiston to ask me anything about you or Belinda now that you are no longer under my direct care."

Antonella turned away, still holding the delicate gown, uncertain what to say or do. A gentle hand took hold of her elbow and drew her around again.

"Why don't you try it on? I'm not certain it will fit you, but the person it belonged to was close to your size."

Her attention brought back to the luxurious garment,

Antonella let her eyes wander over the fine fabric, the delicate embroidery, and the beautiful cut. Miss Wilkins was an adept seamstress, capable of mending the rents in Antonella's dresses so that they were hardly noticeable, and she could see no evidence of reconstruction anywhere. Whatever it had been before, now it was indeed in the very height of the current mode. Would it matter if she tried it on? Just to feel it against her skin? "Very well," she said, a hesitant smile lighting her face.

"You'll need your stays. The gown is cut quite low at the front."

Antonella put this garment on over her shift and Miss Wilkins laced her at the back. She never saw the sense of stays for the kind of clothing she normally wore. But she trusted the governess, who had never encouraged her to overdress.

A moment later, Miss Wilkins let the gown fall in soft folds over Antonella's head and drew the laces at the back of the bodice until it clung to her body. The silver embroidery decorated a three-quarter length gauzy overdress that flowed with every slight movement. The underdress was fashioned of a pure, unadorned white crepe. Satin would have been far too ostentatious, but the duller crepe saved the gown from being too dressy for a card party. The silk felt like a whisper against her legs. It was almost a shame to have to put on stockings, she thought with a smile.

"You look so lovely," Miss Wilkins said. "See?" She took hold of Antonella's shoulders and steered her toward the glass.

Antonella was struck dumb. Surely that lady, that enchanting princess with the black hair, pale skin, rosy lips, and dark eyes wearing a dress that danced in the flickering candlelight was a figment of her imagination. She ran her hands down the soft fabric and grinned. "I was right that night. I'm Cinderella. And you're my fairy godmother. But the clock has already struck twelve. I cannot wear this to the party—I have no slippers! And no time to do anything suitable with my hair."

What she didn't say was that she wondered if Atherleigh would ever be her prince. The prince in the tale had no wounds, no demons in his past. And he didn't care that Cinderella was a lowly maid.

"Ah. What fairy godmother worth her salt wouldn't provide you with slippers? Not glass, I'm afraid. And you'll have to wear your woolen stockings." Miss Wilkins reached into her large reticule and drew out a pair of white jean slippers. "No one will be looking at your feet, so I don't think it will matter."

Antonella donned her stockings and tied her garters, then put on the slippers and fastened their ribbons around her ankles. It seemed as if she could—as if she would—wear the gown after all. And why not? Just because her Aunt Caroline thought she should fade away as if she never existed didn't mean she must obey her. Perhaps this would be the last party she would ever attend. Perhaps this would be her only chance to make Atherleigh at least think well of her, so he wouldn't be utterly furious when he found out about Zephyra.

All that remained was to dress her hair. Miss Wilkins was quite capable of that, and somewhere she had a white ribbon to thread through her curls.

Minutes later the transformation was complete and Antonella picked up her fan, reticule, and gloves, then took a final look at herself in the mirror. She frowned.

"What is it?" Miss Wilkins asked.

"If Aunt Caroline sees me like this she may tell me to come back up here and change. I'm sure she has no idea of my making a spectacle of myself this evening.."

"Silly creature!" Miss Wilkins said and walked to the wardrobe where Antonella's much-more-ordinary clothes were stored. "You, I mean, not Her Ladyship. That's what long winter cloaks are for." She pulled out Antonella's dark blue merino cloak and swirled it around dramatically before draping it over Ant's shoulders.

Antonella looked up into Miss Wilkins's face, her eyes brimming. "Why are you so kind to me? I don't deserve it."

"Hush, my dear. Everyone deserves kindness. Now go and meet your mama—aunt Caroline, I mean—and Belinda. I think I hear the coach coming into the courtyard."

Before she could protest, Antonella rose up on her tiptoes and kissed Miss Wilkins on the cheek.

CHAPTER 26

"*I* can't believe I agreed to this." Atherleigh tweaked his neck cloth as he strode scowling down the stairs.

Gainesworth waited in the entrance hall where they would greet their guests, standing next to a rather over-dressed matron whose acquaintance he had only made the day before. "Allow me to introduce Mrs. Mottrow," he said. "She graciously agreed to act as hostess so we wouldn't scandalize the neighborhood."

The lady gave a broad smile that revealed a full set of white but rather crooked teeth. "How do you do, Lord Atherleigh. I'm a neighbor, although we have never met. My late husband was an attorney. I was a Trendale. You are probably familiar with the family."

Atherleigh bowed politely and looked a question at Gainesworth.

"I met Mrs. Mottrow in Boscastle yesterday. The vicar, Pendarves, introduced us. I had a small matter of business to attend to," Gainesworth said with a smile he hoped would disarm Atherleigh and silence any retort he might make. It had been a risk to take so much initiative without consulting Malcolm, but he had to put it all together quickly. The widow was as respectable as he could manage, although he suspected her presence wouldn't assuage the scruples of Lady Lewiston. There were enough other suitable neighbors coming, though. He hoped they would do.

He'd initially invited only fifteen people in addition to the Ambleton party. In consultation with the vicar at the masquerade ball he conceived the idea of pushing Malcolm past his stubborn reticence—and forwarding his own acquaintance with Lady Belinda—by means of this more intimate gathering. The jovial man was quite willing to enjoy another social event at such a quiet time of year. After all, his curate did most of the parish work.

Reverend Pendarves entered into the spirit of the plan when Hector put it that the sole purpose of the evening was to cheer up the wounded soldier for the holidays. The parson rubbed his beringed hands together and suggested most of the rest of the guests, giving Gainesworth unnecessary information about who they were and their various histories. He explained that those he named were all people who weren't entertaining their own house guests, or who had little opportunity for jollification at this time of year. That was how they ended up with a guest list that included Doctor Adams and his wife, Squire and Mrs. Henley with their two sons who were down from Rugby and Cambridge, and Mr. and Mrs. Curnow and their two hopeful daughters, who the vicar described as worthy and of good family, but in reduced circumstances.

And of course, the vicar and his wife would be there. Everything was working as planned, until Atherleigh got the note from Lady Lewiston asking if he would invite Sir

William Quilley and his houseguest, Lord Bartleson. He thought it quite presumptuous, but she begged forgiveness for being so bold, saying that Sir William was a recent widower and this would be his first Christmas without his wife.

How could he object? So off went another invitation.

That made the numbers twenty persons, which would have made up five whist tables except that Atherleigh refused to play. Hector had tried to persuade him that he could handle cards well enough with one hand, but he had no time to perfect the technique. Moreover, Malcolm simply wasn't willing to make the effort. *You cooked up this fiasco,* he said. *You can manage things.* That likely meant, Gainesworth thought, that the entire burden of being the host would fall to him and he would have difficulty finding a way to talk privately with Lady Belinda.

Hector didn't fool himself that all the young people would consent to sit at cards all evening, though. Some might choose more childish games—spillikins and such. And he counted on dancing to entertain them as well. All that considered, he hoped the number and makeup of the party would be convincing enough to make the event seem less like the convenient excuse to see Lady Belinda again that it actually was.

He had little time to worry. The guests began to arrive promptly at the appointed hour of four o'clock. Fortunately, although it was cold, not a flake of snow had fallen nor was it likely to, so even those farther away—like Sir William and his houseguest the oafish Bartleson—had little difficulty getting there.

There were no surprises at the beginning. The Curnow girls were sweet and well-mannered as well as moderately pretty—which would mean the Henley boys would easily have partners if and when the dancing began. All the guests were possessed of genteel manners and would not embarrass him. He breathed a silent sigh of relief.

The dowager and her daughters arrived a *ton*-ish fifteen minutes after the appointed time, and so their entrance caused a little stir. Lady Belinda's eyes sought Hector's almost immediately. But instead of the open, friendly smile he expected from her, she appeared troubled. He couldn't ask her why at that moment, but he was distracted anyway when Miss Ambleton removed her cloak and handed it to the footman. He almost didn't recognize the sprightly young girl who seemed more at home outdoors. She had undergone a transformation he wouldn't have thought possible based on his brief acquaintance with her, and it momentarily bereft him of speech.

He wasn't the only one who was surprised. When the dowager realized those standing in the hall had stopped talking and stared at someone behind her, she turned and gasped. Miss Ambleton did not flinch, but smiled at Lady Lewiston and waited patiently for her to lead them forward to greet their hosts. *Good for you, Miss Ambleton!* Belinda had said she was spirited and clever, but he hadn't seen that in her thus far. Although Belinda, in a blush pink evening dress trimmed with tiny flower buds and a delicate edge of lace, looked like spring itself, Miss Ambleton lit up the entire room in her flowing white gown with silver embroidery that twinkled in the candlelight. Her jet dark hair, rosy lips, and smoldering brown eyes were the only hints of color on her person.

Gainesworth didn't have to look at Atherleigh to know he was dazzled, because he'd inhaled sharply when Miss Ambleton swept off her cloak and draped it over the footman's waiting arm. *Yes*, he thought, and wondered how he might promote a better acquaintance between the two of them.

Lady Lewiston turned back to the hosts, having regained her composure. Her discomfiture—it would be too much to call it anger—only showed in the tightness at the corners of her smile.

"Good evening, My Lord, Mr. Gainesworth," she said with a nod of her stately head that encompassed them both. "So good of you to entertain the neighbors in this thoughtful way." She didn't wait for their answering remarks, but passed on to the drawing room like a ship sailing into port after a stormy passage.

Lady Belinda and Miss Ambleton walked up next arm-in-arm. Belinda's initial expression of unease had transformed into one of delight as she kept stealing quick glances at Miss Antonella and squeezing her hand.

Hector opened his mouth to greet them both, but Belinda interrupted him whispering, "Doesn't my sister look stunning! Such a good trick to play on Mama."

He was about to agree with her when Malcolm nudged him aside. "Miss Antonella, might I escort you into the drawing room?" He put out his arm and Miss Ambleton stepped slowly forward and laid her gloved hand lightly on his, her cheeks flushing as delicately pink as a winter's evening sunset.

Hector turned his attention to Belinda and murmured, "I had a few minutes to study the pocket book and have discovered something that might offer a clue concerning its meaning. I can't tell you everything now. We may not have an opportunity. May I speak to you tomorrow?"

She nodded. "Yes. At the same place?"

"No. I should like to call on you and have a word with your mother as well." Did he just say that? Apparently he did. And he meant it. But that troubled look came back into

Belinda's eyes. "What is it?" he asked, but she just shook her head.

They'd reached the drawing room. The vicar was busy making up the whist tables to start the play while Penrose circulated with a tray bearing glasses of wine.

"Lord Atherleigh says he won't play, which leaves a table of three. Anyone game for round-robin piquet?" Pendarves said.

As Hector predicted, the two young Henley boys had no desire to play whist either and called for a different game. Emily and Isabel Curnow joined the clamor, and Commerce was agreed upon among them. Belinda and Antonella were a little acquainted with the girls, who were sixteen and seventeen years old, and the young people tried to recruit them as well for Commerce instead of Whist. But Reverend Pendarves had already made up three tables and assigned partners—with the help of Gainesworth. Antonella partnered with Lord Bartleson as Belinda sat at the same table as Gainesworth. But he astutely offered to be Lady Lewiston's partner, pairing Belinda with Sir Richard Curnow. Hector thought this arrangement would possibly seem a little more haphazard than pointed, and he wanted to have an excuse to exchange pleasantries with the dowager and prove himself a decent fellow.

What in God's name! Atherleigh thought, fighting to keep back the questions that threatened to burst out if he didn't put a guard on his tongue. Did Miss Ambleton's choice of dress prove that she was in fact trying to maneuver him? He had no opportunity to ask her anything in the short stroll from the entrance hall to the drawing room. He didn't fully know why he had taken that step. He had only time to notice that her hand, though resting lightly atop his wrist, trembled ever so slightly, and an aura of evergreens and the outdoors hung about her, rather than the more ladylike scent of lavender or lilies that the use of perfume would have incurred.

If she was nervous, only that barely perceptible tremor in her hand revealed it. Once she lifted it from his arm and greeted the other guests, she simply shone. She had a smile for everyone and knew just what to say in response to pleasantries. She even quizzed Pendarves about his coming Christmas sermon, saying that she assumed the curate would be spared the job. She did it in such a light and humorous way that the vicar was not offended and even entered into the spirit, saying, "Boodle so enjoys sermonizing that I hate to deny him the pleasure. But he insisted ..."

All her vivacious brightness was not aimed at him, however. She avoided looking directly at him, turning her gaze away as soon as he came into the edge of her view. The one time she didn't do so, her bright eyes dimmed and a perplexed frown creased her forehead. Atherleigh thought it was likely in response to his own frown, an expression he lapsed into all too readily these days. As soon as she looked away from him her smile returned, and she happily joined her assigned table.

Once play began, Atherleigh pretended to have little interest in the card games and strolled around idly looking over the players' shoulders, spending as much time at the Commerce table as at any of the others. The ensemble at the other end of the large drawing room had begun to play quiet country tunes, and already several of the children—for they seemed so to him—were tapping their feet in time. It would not be long before they insisted upon dancing.

But none of that made any inroads on the thoughts that had started buzzing around in his mind ever since Miss Ambleton threw off her cloak and revealed her stunning evening dress. It wasn't just the dress, although it did show her figure to advantage and made her look much more womanly than she had at any of his other meetings with her. Her clothes were one small part of the entire effect. That evening she carried herself differently. She held her head higher, lifted her chin, and a defiant sparkle lit her eyes.

The deuce! She captivated him and angered him in equal measure. He had truly thought she wasn't like other young ladies, that she wasn't interested in throwing out lures to catch a husband. His suspicions that he had misjudged her had been awakened by what Hector told him earlier about seeing her exercising a large hawk. Gainesworth couldn't tell one bird from another, and all except the smallest hunting birds would have looked large to him—especially when compared to Antonella's slight figure. But it was doubtless a hawk, from his description of how she threw the lure. At that time, Atherleigh had suspected for just a moment—and then dismissed—Miss Ambleton's motives. But now… Arriving in a way that drew all eyes to her and dressing so that she outshone every other lady in the room—she showed herself to be all too like others of her kind. What else was she doing but acting the flirt to try to ensnare him? The subtle intimacy of their previous encounters must have been pretense. She wouldn't be making her come-out in the season this spring, so she took advantage of his proximity to lay her snare. If her behavior was anything to judge by, all she wanted was a wealthy, titled husband to wed and then make a May game of once the honeymoon was over.

Just like his mother.

Malcolm's memories of Lady Atherleigh were vague at best, but he had an impression of great beauty and dazzling charm. And then she was gone. Beyond that, he remembered his father shutting himself up in the library for what seemed like a very long time to him, until he took Malcolm out to the mews again and they continued their life as if nothing had happened. Damn it! He wanted to forget all about Antonella Ambleton. He wanted to tell her he'd taken her measure over these last few days and it wouldn't fadge. She would likely think it was because she was only a poor relation, no longer entitled to be called a lady, but so be it. The irony was that his tumultuous feelings had nothing to do with her fall from genteel grace. What did he care? He had every intention of retiring from society in any case, so the *ton* could go to the devil as far as he was concerned.

"If you're going to strut around like an evil giant looking over our hands and judging us, you might as well take a seat and play!" Gainesworth said, jolting him out of his endlessly circling thoughts.

Atherleigh forced a smile. "It's fortunate you're playing for chicken stakes, as far as I can observe." In fact, he hadn't noticed anyone's cards. At every moment he was aware of how animatedly Miss Ambleton played and how that lump of a partner of hers spent more time looking at her decolletage than his own hand.

This was madness. Why had he agreed to it? And why could he not stop thinking about Antonella? Her eyes flicked to his occasionally. Each time they contained a pensive little smile, as if she were trying to persuade him they had a connection no one else could perceive. How absurd! Yet despite all he'd learned and what he thought he now knew, he could not deny that something was still there, linking them together, drawing him toward her.

"Shall we take a turn around the room?" Mrs. Pendarves, the vicar's wife who was sitting out of the current piquet hand, took hold of his right elbow.

Of course he should have sat by her like a good host and engaged in conversation, so he could hardly say no now. "It would be my pleasure. I've been away some years. How long has your husband been the incumbent of the parish?" He hoped he could get her talking and simply nod politely every now and again, leaving him free to wear out the paths in his mind that led inexorably to Miss Ambleton.

But instead of following up on this comfortable line of questioning, Mrs. Pendarves said, "Miss Ambleton is beautiful, is she not? And not just in the common way."

He looked down at the elderly lady's gentle, smiling face, not certain how to answer.

"Come now, My Lord, I've been on this earth for a good many years more than you have. I have two married daughters and seven grandchildren. I know that look. But does *she*?" At this, she gave his arm a playful pat.

"Madam, I'm sure I don't know what you imagine. Miss Ambleton and I are in no way associated." His black evening neck cloth began to feel tight.

She raised one skeptical eyebrow at him. "Yet it seems to me that you would very much like to be. Such a shame that Antonella should lose her status in society just now, when she should be taking her first steps into her place there, finding a husband, a position to fill." She gave a deep sigh. "Now what will she do? She is ill fitted to engage in any gainful occupation. And anyway, for my money, far too unconventional and spirited to make a good governess or lady's companion. It seems a pity that she should face a future of being known as the quirky Aunt Ant—her nickname, you know. They call each other Ant and Bee."

Miss Ambleton had told him about her nickname that night at the ball. But he preferred Nella. It had more music to it, more grace, more light. What was he thinking? He didn't prefer anything about her, or he shouldn't anyway. "I'm very little acquainted with the family," he said, not able to conjure up anything more pertinent to say.

By this time, they'd wandered the room's perimeter and were back among the card players. A bright, tinkling laugh broke the relative silence. Atherleigh looked to see whose voice it was. But of course he knew already.

"We won again, Lord Bartleson! It seems we're unbeatable. See all these riches?" Antonella picked up the small pile of shillings and pennies and let them trickle out of her fingers and onto the table.

CHAPTER 27

*A*ntonella was quite relieved when the group at the Commerce table demanded the ensemble play a country dance and persuaded the young Dr. Adams and his wife to join them, thus disrupting the carefully arranged Whist tables.

She rose and wandered over to the lemonade table in the corner. This performance she had decided to put on was exhausting. Why had she done it? To defy her Aunt Caroline? Partly. To prove to Belinda that she did not need her to play matchmaker, that she was entirely capable of doing all that was required on her own? Perhaps. The truth was that Antonella wasn't entirely certain she wanted to make a match after all that had happened recently. She'd lost her identity once. She didn't want to marry and lose it again before she even got used to who she was now.

More to the point, none of those facts quite explained her actions that evening. Atherleigh. It was always Atherleigh who disturbed her. She should find a way to tell him about Zephyra and cut at least that one thread that bound her to him. But she could hardly look him in the eye, let alone converse with him. Something about him laid her insides bare, exposed everything she'd ever wanted to keep hidden. It was dangerous. He was dangerous. She had hoped her brittle, lively demeanor that evening would erect a barrier around her and set him at a safe distance. Yet how could she have thought such a thing? Even the three miles between Amblemere and Atherleigh was not enough for her to feel quite separate from him. As soon as she removed her cloak at the door, Antonella knew she had miscalculated. She hadn't even greeted Gainesworth when, instead of treating her with disinterested civility, Lord Atherleigh reacted with something closer to anger or vexation.

Ever since he led her into the drawing she'd been trying to shake off the feeling that no matter where she was, his eyes followed her. They didn't just look, they bored into her, fixing her with the predatory stare of a hawk. She forced herself to be charming and vivacious, and treated all the guests equally to her wit and attention. Yet every time she glanced in Atherleigh's direction she met his steady, frowning regard.

"Come, Miss Antonella, help us make up a full eight so we can dance a cotillion! We might as well practice here where it doesn't matter." Isabel Curnow took Antonella's hand and dragged her toward the end of the large room where the young ones were having a spirited argument about how to start out with the intricate dance. "I know Lord Atherleigh won't dance, but Sir William or Lord Bartleson might be willing."

No! Antonella thought.

"I'd be delighted to partner Miss Ambleton in the cotillion. Would you do me the honor?"

Antonella turned to see Lord Bartleson approaching her,

hand outstretched. It would be impolite to refuse him. "Of course My Lord," she said with as much of a smile as she could muster, and let him lead her to join the other six eager participants.

The dancing was lively and somewhat chaotic, with everyone not equally adept at the figures. Surprisingly to Antonella, Lord Bartleson was an accomplished dancer and did much to prevent the entire attempt dissolving into a melee. Whenever he crossed hands with her he smiled at her, but his eyes focused most disturbingly at her low decolletage. At one such moment he said to her, "We made quite good partners at the whist table, Miss Ambleton. Perhaps we should partner in other ways as well."

Antonella did not quite like the look that came into his eyes. He would hardly be suggesting any honorable alliance, since he well knew her situation and was a high stickler himself. She had the sickening feeling he might offer her a carte blanche or some other immoral arrangement, and began to wish she had worn one of her more sober dresses, something that didn't draw all eyes in her direction.

"I'm quite parched!" She said to Lord Bartleson at the end of the cotillion and spread her fan open to wave it emphatically in front of her face and cover her exposed bosom.

In the meantime, the young dancers began arguing over what dance should come next, when Atherleigh cut through them and said something to the violinist who was leading the ensemble. His stern, commanding presence silenced them all. "A waltz," he announced, and in two strides arrived at Antonella's side, bowed, and held out his hand to her in an assumption that she would take it. His expression never altered from bland disinterest. Only the intense glitter of his dark eyes hinted that something else was going on in his mind.

Antonella was tempted to refuse to stand up with him.

But she could hardly do so when everyone in the room had turned to look at the two of them. And she could never do so knowing that in dancing with her, in holding her in the position of a waltz, he would be asking her not only to see, but to touch the place at the end of his left arm where a hand used to be. It must have taken great courage—or great agitation—for him to put himself in that position. But why? And why was she so afraid of dancing with him? "With pleasure, My Lord," she said, wondering if she would regret it.

"I say, Atherleigh, I'd not led Miss Ambleton from the floor yet!" Bartleson came up to the two of them with a glass of ratafia in one hand, which he held out to Ant.

Atherleigh gave Bartleson a withering glance as he led Antonella to the very middle of the makeshift dance floor, bringing an angry flush to Bartleson's face. Antonella actually felt a little sorry for him. Her heart started to pound. Bartleson was annoyed, but Atherleigh was angry. Not just peeved. Somehow angry on a soul-deep level. She could see it in the way he held his imposing frame: erect, unyielding, a shield against all feeling.

If that weren't enough, Antonella caught Lady Lewiston's fulminating eye. So be it. That lady was not her mother, after all. Perhaps her attention would be distracted if Belinda would take the floor with Bartleson or Gainesworth. *Where is she?*

Antonella had no time to wonder. The music started. Atherleigh placed his right hand at her waist. She rested her left hand on his shoulder. When Ant realized he intended to dance with his injured left hand tucked behind his back, her indignation rose. If he sought to make a display of her in this way, she wouldn't let him get away with all his dignity intact. She held her right hand out expectantly as they began the steps and looked a challenge directly into his eyes.

He flared his nostrils and the muscles in his cheeks

worked. He was gritting his teeth, but he could not be so impolite as to ignore her gesture. He brought his arm around from the back and held his stump—now covered by a modified black silk stocking—so that she could place her fingers over it.

No doubt he expected her to shrink away. That only made Antonella grasp it more firmly and feel the raggedness of the bones beneath the bumpy layers of scarred skin.

They danced.

All this time she existed in her own intimate drama, unaware of anything happening around her. The music carried Antonella along, its rhythm reflected in the beat of her heart. She looked steadfastly up into Atherleigh's face, hardly blinking, taking in not just the shifting nuances of the light in his eyes, but the play of his muscles as he fought against something in himself, something she could only guess at.

When at last he spoke to her, his words sliced into the moment with the precision of a surgeon's blade. "What game are you playing, Miss Ambleton?"

The question was so unexpected, so outside the world she'd created in her head, that she had to suppress a gasp. "What do you mean?"

"You know what I mean," Atherleigh said.

"No," Antonella said. "I most assuredly don't know that, Sir." The enthusiastic dancers twirled around them and the movement temporarily inhibited further conversation, leaving Antonella feverishly trying to figure out what he could possibly be referring to. Had he found out about Zephyra? Did he feel he'd been misled about her rank? Why would that cause him to be so very furious?

When Atherleigh circled her and then caught her up again, his arm once more wrapped around her waist, she trembled. He pulled her closer to him and locked eyes with her, his dark and accusing, hers open and wary. "I am not to be ensnared, like a bird in a net," he said, his voice tight.

Oh my god! Antonella thought. He did know. How would she explain? "It's not—how did you know? I can explain. I meant no harm!" This was a disaster. All she wanted to do was run away, but this was no crowded ballroom where one person's absence would not be noted by anyone except those closest to them. She stiffened and lost her steps, tripping slightly, which only made his grip on her tighten uncomfortably. "You're hurting me," she whispered.

Immediately Atherleigh's hold slackened. "I advise you to think carefully about what you are doing. I am no moonling to be fooled. You think you know me, but you don't. I have set in motion the closing of my mews. By this time next week I will have sent all the hunting birds to a new home. I will never again call myself a falconer. Your efforts at flirting, at trying to make me believe you have any interest in my concerns, are futile."

This was becoming a nightmare. And why tell her of the mews? That was worse than anything. The way he said it, it was almost as if he were talking to himself rather than her. As if he had to convince himself that he had taken the right action.

Her throat closed and she fought to draw breath without sobbing. Antonella willed the music to stop so she could make her bow and walk away from him, collect herself and salvage what was left of her dignity. So much for telling him about Zephyra in a quiet moment—not that she truly had any intention of doing so, whatever Belinda advised.

When the ensemble played its final cadence, she curtsied and suffered herself to be led off the floor. Belinda. She must find Belinda.

Antonella scanned the drawing room and was about to go toward the retiring room to see if she could find Bee, but almost as soon as Atherleigh relinquished her, Lord Bartleson hurried to her side.

Out of the corner of her eye she saw Atherleigh scowl at the two of them and then turn away from her. Was he cutting her? "I am afraid I would rather not dance for the moment, My Lord," she said to Bartleson, too overset to notice the gleam in his eyes.

"Perhaps we may find somewhere out of the way to sit and become better acquainted," he said.

Without thinking, Antonella nodded. She had no idea precisely what he intended until she found herself being propelled out of the drawing room to the empty hall beyond and then engulfed in Bartleson's sweaty embrace.

IN THE GENERAL HUBBUB FOLLOWING THE BREAKUP OF THE card tables and the temporary lull in the dancing, Belinda at last caught Gainesworth's eye. She was relieved that Bartleson's oily attention had shifted away from her to Antonella— although she felt a bit sorry for her because of it. Especially when she spied Lady Lewiston quietly seething as she pasted a practiced smile on her face and exchanged polite commonplaces with the other older guests.

At a subtle signal from Belinda, Gainesworth nodded an excusing bow to the doctor and his wife, with whom he had been discussing the deploring hunting country around Cornwall. He took on the role of the good host after Atherleigh stalked off to claim Antonella for the waltz. And he truly had stalked. The baron's expression at that moment had made Belinda uneasy. She couldn't imagine what might have made him choose to dance despite his missing hand. It had been his excuse not to stand up with anyone at the masquerade ball. What was different about that night? She knew very little of Atherleigh, other than that as Gainesworth's friend he must have some good in him. After what she had heard him say at the ball, though, Belinda was keeping a keen watch for any further signs that he might disdain Antonella because of her murky breeding. It was curious, then, that not only did he ask her to dance, but insisted on a waltz. Did he, like Gainesworth, have rakish tendencies as well as a top-lofty disdain for those not as well-born as he was? It was all so confusing.

Belinda soon turned her mind to other thoughts, though, as Gainesworth came to her side and said, "I must speak with you. I cannot wait any longer," his low voice breathing directly into her ear. Despite her wish to act as though he had no effect on her, to protect her heart from someone who might merely be toying with her, she shivered.

The two of them quietly slipped out of the drawing room into the hall. Gainesworth led Belinda to a sheltered alcove that might once have housed a statue but was now merely a cavity large enough for two people to step inside. Although it did not completely hide them from view, it provided a measure of privacy at the same time as not being so secluded as to offend propriety should anyone chance to see them.

"What is it, Mr. Gainesworth?" Belinda whispered, every nerve in her body quivering with a combination of fear and hope. Would he try to seduce her? Or did he really only intend to give her information about the pocket book?

"I have a great deal I want to tell you. I can't say everything I would like to …" He grasped both her hands and pulled her toward him, but kept a little distance between them.

The heat emanating from his body and his light sandalwood scent enveloped Belinda in a way that both comforted and frightened her. Even their moments alone in the barn had not felt as intimate. Belinda's breathing shallowed, her pulse raced. "What have you found?" she asked. But the words felt inadequate to the situation. She wanted to know so much more than that. She wanted to know everything about him.

"I wish—" Gainesworth began, and then shook his head. "You must know—but not here, of course—I have discovered something."

He had drawn her the slightest bit closer, and now his breath swept her face when he spoke. She stood near enough to see every tiny expression in his kind eyes. No one she'd ever met had eyes like that. Surely they were not—could not be—the eyes of a hardened rake.

"At regular intervals in the pages a set of initials recurs, the letters P and W, normally about a week apart, as if to indicate a standing appointment of some kind. I don't want to imply something that may be very far from fact, but you should be prepared to learn that your late father might have been arranging assignations with someone other than your mother. These may have been quite innocent, perhaps even with a man of business. He would have to have had a reason to keep those meetings secret, however, if he resorted to using a kind of code for them." He spoke in a rush, his eyes darting around nervously.

Belinda took one of her hands out of his grasp and placed it on his arm in a gesture she hoped was reassuring. "Mr. Gainesworth, please don't worry that I will be shocked if you find that my father did not conduct his life in a wholly virtuous manner. I know, I believe, that gentlemen are wont to have their ... peccadilloes ... rather more commonly than one would think." She wanted to add that sadly, she expected to be subjected to the same sort of behavior no matter whom she married. It was the way of things, so her mother had told her. As to what the difference was between this so-called normal behavior and the supposed rakishness of someone like Gainesworth she had no clear idea.

Gainesworth let go of her other hand and took hold of her shoulders in a strong grip. "Do not distress yourself, Lady Belinda. No man in his right mind who was fortunate enough to win you would ever think of dishonoring you in such a way."

Had her thoughts been so easy for him to read? How she wanted to ask him if he had been accustomed to dishonoring other women, all the same! She simply couldn't credit what her mother had told her, seeing the genuine concern in his eyes, the way they probed into her soul and awakened sensations she could barely understand. He could never look at another girl like that. Could he?

Without realizing it, she drew closer to him and her lips parted to speak. He placed a gentle forefinger on them. "We shall talk tomorrow," he said, and after a pause, during which Belinda had the distinct impression he was bending toward her to kiss her, stepped away and released her shoulders.

At that moment, the drawing room door opened wide and Antonella hurried through, followed closely by Lord Bartleson. Gainesworth drew Belinda farther into their shadowed nook. Neither Antonella—whose high color and sparkling eyes betrayed her extreme agitation—nor Lord Bartleson noticed them there, and instantly Bartleson had engulfed Antonella in a very inappropriate embrace. Antonella struggled and pushed him away after a moment.

"Miss Antonella!" Bartleson said, his voice a bit slurred. He dragged a large handkerchief out of his pocket and mopped the perspiration on his forehead.

"I may no longer be Lady Antonella, Sir, but please do me the courtesy of calling me Miss Ambleton," was her quick and biting reply. "And keep your distance! You have had too much wine."

Belinda knew that voice. Ant was perilously close to erupting in fury. She must do something. She made a move to step forward, but Gainesworth stopped her.

Bartleson took hold of Antonella's arm and drew her toward him again as she tried to pull herself away. She was strong, but weighed barely more than a child, and could not withstand his superior strength. Before Belinda knew what was happening, he'd grabbed Antonella around the waist and had her in a tight hold.

"Let me go, Sir!" Ant said, pummeling him with her fists.

All he did was smile and look down at her bosom.

A moment later, the drawing room door opened again and out flew Atherleigh. In one swift movement, so fast Belinda wasn't entirely certain what happened, his right fist shot out and connected with Bartleson's chin, sending him sprawling to the floor. The blow did not knock the earl out, but he sat in some confusion for a moment before hoisting himself up on his feet and rubbing his chin, his face purple with fury. "How dare you interfere in a matter that does not concern you!" he said, at first clenching his fists and lifting them, then thinking better of it and dropping them again. No question that even with his two hands he was far outmatched by one-handed Atherleigh.

"How dare I?" Atherleigh spat out the words. "You owe this lady an apology. I will not have her dishonored in this manner in my house."

"An apology!" Bartleson sputtered. "She wanted it! You only have to look at her." He all but pointed at the deep decolletage of Antonella's evening dress. "Besides, she is no lady. She's barely better than a servant."

Atherleigh advanced toward Bartleson again. At that point Gainesworth set Belinda aside and rushed forward, grabbing his friend's elbows from behind. "Don't, Mal! He's not worth it."

Belinda dashed out of the alcove to Antonella, who had retreated to the top of the stairs as though she might run down them and out into the cold. Belinda wrapped her arms around her sister. "Hush, dear," she murmured.

The drawing room door had remained open, and a crowd consisting of all the other guests gathered just beyond it in stunned amazement to see what was going on.

"I demand satisfaction!" Bartleson said, dusting himself off and then marching up to Atherleigh, who showed no sign of discomfiture at that suggestion. "My seconds will call on you in the morning."

A gasp and scattered exclamations of dismay rippled through the other guests. The younger Miss Curnow began to cry. Reverend Pendarves said, "I say, this is no way to act during the Christmas season! Surely all may be peaceably resolved."

"Where is my daughter!" It was Lady Lewiston. The knot of guests parted to let her through.

Mama! Belinda thought, at first relieved, then horrified.

"What is the meaning of this? Belinda, Antonella, we shall return home. Kindly have our carriage brought round," she said to the butler, who had climbed the stairs in response to the commotion and looked wide-eyed back and forth between Atherleigh and Bartleson.

Atherleigh said nothing, but nodded to Penrose. Bartleson, having quickly adopted an air of wounded dignity, said, "Lady Lewiston, this fellow has insulted me. We must settle this matter as gentlemen."

Gainesworth placed himself between the two adversaries who still faced each other, Bartleson in a barely contained rage, Atherleigh glaring icily down at him. "My Lady Lewiston," Gainesworth said. "Lord Atherleigh simply defended the honor of your daughter."

"Belinda?" she said, shocked.

"No, I mean, not your daughter. I mean Miss Ambleton."

Belinda's heart sank. This was a complete disaster. Her mother would never entertain any suggestion of a betrothal from Gainesworth after he misspoke in that way. And the fact that the gentleman she had chosen as a suitor for her daughter had been assaulted in this house—however honorable the reason—would confirm every ill opinion the dowager had of the baron and Mr. Gainesworth.

Belinda said, "But Mama—"

Gainesworth held up his hand, stopping her from speaking. "It is time to bring this evening to an end. Penrose will have the carriages brought round."

Lady Lewiston, Belinda, and Antonella left with barely a word. Belinda sent a beseeching look at Gainesworth as she hurried by. She wasn't sure what she expected him to do, but surely a meeting between Atherleigh and Bartleson must be avoided.

After that, the squire and Mrs. Henley and their sons skirted the two men and hurried down the stairs, followed by Sir Richard and Lady Curnow and their daughters. Dr. Adams paused on his way past and said, "Do you require my services, Lord Bartleson?" casting an expert eye over his face, which had begun to develop an ugly bruise at his chin line.

"Damned impertinent," Bartleson muttered, and turned away from him.

Under protest, the vicar left. Sir William, who had brought Bartleson to the party, had fallen asleep in a chair in front of the fire and had not stirred at the commotion. Gainesworth nudged him awake.

After a stiff bow to Gainesworth and a final glare at Atherleigh, Bartleson snatched his evening cape and hat out of Penrose's hands and left the manor, trailing Sir William in his wake.

When they were finally alone in the hall, Gainesworth turned to Atherleigh and said, "You're not going to meet him, are you?"

"Watch me." With that, Atherleigh turned on his heel and left his friend standing in the middle of the hall as the footmen doused the candles.

CHAPTER 28

The dowager said nothing to the two girls all the way home in the carriage and they all went to their own rooms in nearly total silence—until just before they parted at the top of the stairs.

"Antonella, you are not to leave your chamber tomorrow," Lady Lewiston said in a clipped, icy voice. "I will have a breakfast tray sent up to you and will take the morning to decide what is to be done. Only then will I attend you and tell you my decision."

Antonella nodded submissively. There was no point in arguing with her, even if she hadn't been bred to accept parental decrees without question. Except Lady Lewiston was not her parent! Of course she knew that the dowager acted as her mother and had done so for the entire eighteen years of her life, and to quibble over titles was petty of her in the circumstances.

Sleep eluded Antonella that night, and not merely because she had been harshly scolded by her Aunt Caroline, treated as if she had done something wrong rather than been the victim of someone else's actions. It was entirely unfair! What, after all, had happened?

No, it was not only that. The events of the evening came to her in fragments: Atherleigh escorting her to the saloon; Bartleson staring at her bosom all through cards and then insisting on dancing with her in the cotillion; The waltz with Atherleigh.

The waltz. What a tumult of feelings just remembering it provoked! The sensation of his hand wrapped around her waist, pressing into the small of her back. The feel of his strong, solid shoulder under her own hand, and the strange sensation of covering the stump where his left hand had been with her right hand, feeling the absence and yet not, experiencing the illusion that his invisible fingers grasped hers. Most of all, looking up into his face and seeing the play of emotions as thoughts raced through his mind almost as quickly as they raced through hers. At one moment, his dark eyes were limpid with tenderness. The next, they hardened into flint, holding an unspoken accusation. What had she done? Why would he say those things to her?

Because that was what had truly stung. He judged her. Had he guessed, or did he know about Zephyra? Why else would he have referred to a bird in a net?

When she thought about it more carefully, really wracked her memory to piece together his exact words, it all began to coalesce into something quite different from what she had initially thought. The bird in the net was him. Atherleigh. He believed she was trying to entrap him. They had been together unchaperoned twice. She had worn a provocative, dazzling evening gown to his card party. Yet was that enough? Antonella couldn't help thinking there must have been something more. But what?

Most puzzling of all was why he had mentioned that he would be closing his mews. Yes, he had found her there after her accident and perhaps deduced that she had some interest in his hunting birds. Did he think she had engineered that meeting? That she had purposely fallen from a tree and given herself a concussion so that he would be forced to attend to her?

As she thought all these things through, her bewilderment and hurt turned to anger. Atherleigh assumed that her interest in hunting birds was a ruse, a trick to make him think she was somehow a suitable mate for him. How like a man! To assume that everything a lady did would be in service of finding a suitable husband. She didn't want any such thing! All she cared about was returning Zephyra to Rafiq's expert care—but only once she could be certain the goshawk was completely healed. Would she still do it only to have her taken far away to someone else's mews? How could she be certain a different falconer would care for her in the way Rafiq would?

Besides, she truly didn't want to marry. She didn't want to marry anyone, and certainly not the baron. If she would have to settle for someone who would see in her nothing more than an unpaid housekeeper and breeder of children, it would be far better to remain single.

Just as Antonella was about to lose her battle against sleep, she sat bolt upright in bed. "Oh God! The duel!" What in God's name had made Atherleigh provoke Bartleson in that way? Surely they wouldn't really meet over something so trivial. Bartleson, Antonella was worldly enough to know, did no more than many gentlemen would do when confronted with what they saw as a provocative young lady far beneath them in rank. Usually such behavior was limited to tavern wenches and parlor maids. But was she really any better than they? Of course, accosting her in that manner in Atherleigh's house was unwise. Bartleson was entirely in the wrong there, so how could he have any right to challenge Atherleigh?

Antonella had only the haziest notion of these matters of honor among gentlemen. They all seemed utterly absurd to her. No, Atherleigh would not be foolish enough to engage in a duel with Bartleson. Mr. Gainesworth would find a way to stop it, surely. She bit the side of her thumb until it bled. It mustn't be allowed to happen. She would talk to Miss Wilkins in the morning. The governess always seemed to have the answer to difficult problems.

MORNING CAME ALL TOO SOON, AND MOMENTS AFTER Antonella's breakfast tray had been taken away hardly touched, Lady Lewiston strode in, all business.

"Antonella—why are you dressed to go outside?"

She almost said, *I have to check on Zephyra and feed her,* but stopped herself in time. "I always walk at this time of day."

"Not today. And not until I see fit to release you from your room. You behaved abominably at the party last night. How dare you try to interfere with Belinda's betrothal to Lord Bartleson!" The dowager's eyes flashed fire and her lips were compressed in a thin, uncompromising line.

So that was what she thought had happened! How wrong could a person be? Lady Lewiston was not unintelligent, but clearly she was blinded by her ambition for Belinda. "I? I did no such thing! That … man—I will not call him a gentleman —accosted me in the most degrading manner!"

"I do not believe you. And your actions have provoked a quarrel. If one of the gentlemen dies the blood will be on your hands."

Dies? Surely even if they succeeded in meeting, they would never fight to the death! "No!"

The dowager's posture relaxed just a little. "I doubt it will come to that. But it is a very unpleasant situation in any case. You clearly cannot be trusted to behave in a way that befits your new station. So you will remain in this room—alone—to think about what you have done until I decide you may leave it."

"But Ma—Aunt Caroline! I swear I did nothing wrong!"

From the way the dowager's jaw worked, Antonella could see she was struggling with herself about what to say in answer to her statement. "Your wrongdoing started as soon as you chose to wear that dress last night. Where did you get it? I have never seen it before. It was entirely unsuitable for a girl in your position."

The last thing Antonella wanted was to get Miss Wilkins in trouble. But how would she explain it? "I-I made it, using leftover scraps from our gowns and things I found in the tower. Old dresses."

"You? You can hardly wield a needle! You most certainly did not do the fine embroidery on it."

"Belinda helped me." It was all she could think of to say that would preserve Miss Wilkins from the full force of the dowager's wrath. She knew that Belinda would go along with the lie.

"Where is it?" She looked around quickly then stepped over to the wardrobe and opened its double doors wide. Of course, the dazzling white gown lay atop all the drab day dresses like an angel's wing over barren earth. Lady Lewiston whisked it out and rolled it into a ball, not explaining what she would do with it. "I shall lock your door from the outside. Don't look for any intervention from Lady Belinda or Miss Wilkins. They are under strict instructions not to aid you to leave your room."

With that, she took her silken burden out of the door, slammed it behind her, and turned the key in the lock.

As soon as she heard the click, Antonella's mind went

into action. She couldn't stay in all day. What about Zephyra? She needed feeding. She needed exercising—or at least weathering. Could she leave without Aunt Caroline knowing? The servants wouldn't help her. They risked being turned off without a character if they defied Lady Lewiston. She wouldn't ask it of them. Belinda might. But she would never go near Zephyra.

Perhaps she would be willing to at least take a message to someone. To Rafiq! But how? What excuse could she have for sending something to the mews at Atherleigh Manor?

And then, there was everything going on around this ridiculous challenge. Surely Belinda could prevent it somehow. She could ask Gainesworth to intervene. Antonella believed him to be a genuinely kind person, and clearly very fond of Atherleigh. It didn't take much to see that the baron's re-entrance to society was largely a result of Mr. Gainesworth's caring influence.

She remembered something else about the night before. Gainesworth had leapt out from somewhere nearby—not the saloon—and held Atherleigh back from assaulting Bartleson a second time after the earl said those disgusting things about her. And Belinda had been with him. She was not in the retiring room. What was going on between them? Of course, Belinda's infatuation with the charming gentleman was obvious. That she could ever have thought he would make a good match for her, Antonella, was patently absurd.

But Lady Lewiston would never approve such a match. He was untitled. His fortune—although apparently substantial—came from trade. What is more, the dowager had her sights set on the Earl of Bartleson. The thought of Belinda marrying that unappealing man turned Antonella's stomach. She would never do it. The problem was, Antonella couldn't see any way that her sister would be permitted to marry Mr. Gainesworth instead.

She flopped into the comfortable, threadbare chair by the fire and gazed into the middle distance, unable to focus on any of the problems and enigmas that beset her.

Antonella was still in that same chair hours later, her mind no closer to untangling any of her knotty thoughts, when she heard a light scratching on her door. "Who's there?" she called. "I'd tell you to come in, but it's locked."

A whispered voice said, "Come closer, Ant! I need to talk to you."

∾

THE MORNING AFTER THE DISASTROUS CARD PARTY Gainesworth found Malcolm in the gallery on the first floor of the manor. He stood in his shirtsleeves, smallsword in hand, practicing thrusts and parries with controlled, precise, deadly movements.

"You're not seriously going through with this," Hector said.

"Why wouldn't I?"

"Because it's ridiculous! Bartleson's a slimy fool. He was on the go last night. Fighting him would be beneath you. I just met with Sir William and told him about your choice of smallswords for weapons and I thought he would faint dead away. I presume you have two of equal lengths? Although it hardly matters because I am determined that this meeting will not happen."

Malcolm gestured toward the open case resting on a credenza below one of the Atherleigh family portraits. A straight, elegant smallsword identical to the one he was using lay in it against a red velvet cloth.

"It won't be a fair fight," Gainesworth said.

"Why not? Because I'm missing a hand? I only need the other hand for balance. I see no handicap."

Gainesworth picked up the second sword and admired it. Its two-foot-long triangular blade had an almost mirror-like finish. The point was honed to be lethal, although it had no slicing edge, of course. The chased hilt added little weight to it, making it perfectly balanced. These swords were designed for efficient killing off the battlefield. "The reason the fight will not be fair is because you grossly outmatch Bartleson. He's an indolent, overfed dandy."

Ignoring him, Atherleigh said, "What did Sir William say?" and then executed a neat thrust followed by a parry sixte and a dégagement against his imaginary opponent's riposte, his expression never changing.

"He says it is for you to apologize, since you insulted Bartleson by flattening him rather effectively."

This brought a grim smile to Atherleigh's lips. "How easily he forgets his own insult to the lady."

"Come now, Mal! He acted like a cad, certainly. But a simple reprimand and tossing him out of the manor would have sufficed. You didn't have to plant him a facer. What made you fly into such a rage?"

Atherleigh didn't answer but relaxed from his taut fighting stance. "Is all arranged?"

Gainesworth huffed out a long sigh. "Sir William wasn't happy—either about the swords or the dueling ground. I doubt they even know how to get to the beach at low tide. Why did you choose it?"

"That should be obvious," Malcolm said.

"Well, it isn't. Enlighten me."

"Below the high tide line is not strictly considered English soil. Prosecuting us for dueling would be a tricky business."

This was not good. Was Malcolm considering a duel to the death? What could have made him so insanely furious? "Very well. If you insist on making a spectacle of yourself.

The meeting is set for half-past eight tomorrow morning, which—as you informed me—is when the tide will be ebbing, and at this time of year near enough dawn." The sand will be packed and flat, but likely sloping, Gainesworth thought. For a moment, he felt a little sorry for Bartleson. The earl had no idea what he'd got himself into.

"As you say," Atherleigh said, and turned back to face his imaginary opponent.

The duel cannot be allowed to take place, Hector thought. He must go to Sir William and try again to alert him to the danger facing Bartleson. This would be no gentlemanly fight to first blood. Atherleigh was accustomed to killing men, although only in the heat of battle. What can have happened last night to put him in such a rage?

Only one thing could account for Malcolm's extreme reaction to Bartleson's behavior. Although he didn't know the particulars, it was amply obvious to Gainesworth that his old friend was deep in love with Miss Ambleton. Only that reason made any sense. It was also obvious to Gainesworth that Malcolm likely hadn't admitted his feelings either to the lady or to himself. Perhaps therein lay the way to avert complete disaster.

He needed Miss Ambleton's cooperation in order to bring such a thing about, however. And the hours before the appointed meeting were limited. He had very little time to prevent his oldest friend from taking a step that could get him hanged, or at the very least, force him to flee to the continent.

And then he had a thought. What had incensed Malcolm the most was the way Bartleson referred to Miss Ambleton as little better than a servant, referring to her unknown parentage. Perhaps the secret to everything lay in the little pocket book Lady Belinda had found tucked in the back of a drawer in an ancient desk. He'd been withholding his suspicions about its contents from her, not wanting to expose what was clearly a deeply buried family secret. Doing so might be the lesser of two evils now, however. In the rushed departure the night before he hadn't had time to tell her what he had meant to. He had a feeling that what the notebook revealed would force Bartleson to apologize rather than fight, but he couldn't be certain without talking to Belinda.

Hector dashed off a note to Lady Belinda and gave it into the hands of a footman, whom he instructed not to deliver it to anyone other than the lady herself. Pray God she was at home to receive it.

CHAPTER 29

*B*elinda, breathless from running all the way from the Court, found Gainesworth pacing back and forth across the width of the stables, slapping the side of his leg with his riding crop and frowning. As soon as he caught sight of her, his frown disappeared and his eyes lit up with joy.

"Were you afraid I wouldn't come?" she said.

"I couldn't be sure you'd get my note. But you're here." Gainesworth lifted her gloved hands to his lips one at a time.

Belinda wished she could simply bask in Mr. Gainesworth's—Hector's—loving regard. No words had been spoken between them, but last night … if they hadn't been interrupted … she mustn't think about that now. She had a task to accomplish for Antonella. "Tell me, please. What have you discovered?"

He pulled the notebook out of his pocket. It showed signs that it had been thoroughly thumbed, with corners of pages notched down and some pages folded in half. Gainesworth had obviously spent time studying it closely and marked specific details. He leafed through the beginning pages until he came to one that had an odd sort of verse written on it that had been covered by many crossed lines.

"What is it?" Belinda asked.

"It took me a long time to figure it out, but it's an acrostic. I don't know exactly what it means, but take a look."

He held the book open. The words of the acrostic were hard to make out, but after a little while, Belinda gasped.

Peril walks with [indistinguishable], cl ake in court .

Words m serve as veils, not weapons.

I will not name what cannot be spoken.

Let lence, then, preserve what s betrays.

Know that I not forgotten.

I counted every gl , every se.

Neither time nor distance is the enemy—

Shame is, and suspicion, and all that watches.

EVEN WITH THE MISSING WORDS AND LETTERS, BELINDA COULD make out the initials that began each line. P W I L K I N S. "Miss Wilkins," she whispered.

"Who is that?" Gainesworth asked.

She looked up into his eyes, her own wide with horror and confusion. "Our governess. At least, I think it must be. Her last name is Wilkins. I'm not sure about her Christian name."

Gainesworth was silent for a long moment. "I can't be certain, but the date—it appears likely that the marquess was—"

"Yes." She cut him off. "I need to think about this."

"Don't you see what it means?" he said. "It means—or it could mean—that Miss Ambleton truly is your sister. Your half sister, at least. And if she's the daughter of a marquess, Bartleson would be forced to apologize for blackening her name in that way, even if she was born on the wrong side of the blanket. We could stop the duel."

Belinda's mind refused to grasp what she had read. Could it truly be? But surely Miss Wilkins wasn't old enough to be —good God, could she be Antonella's mother? She was so young when she came to them when they were both nine. Only twenty-two, she believed. So no, it wasn't possible. Was it? "I have to think. I need to tell Antonella and talk to Miss Wilkins." How would she do that, though?

"Don't take too long. I must go to Sir William and tell him, somehow wring an apology from Bartleson." He waited for Belinda to tuck the little book in her reticule and then grasped her hands again and pulled her closer.

She couldn't take her eyes from his. They looked down at her with such tenderness she could hardly breathe. "Mr. Gainesworth—"

He stopped her words by bringing his lips to hers, softly, sweetly. Belinda's entire body warmed and flooded with sensations she could never have imagined. A tremor passed through her torso and ended somewhere near her thighs. She returned the pressure of his lips, at first tentatively and then with more confidence as the kiss became stronger. He parted his lips and kissed first her upper lip and then her lower, wrapping his arms around her and nestling her against him. She leaned her whole body into his, wanting to melt into him, to become one single person with nothing separating them from each other ever again. So this was love, Belinda thought.

She pressed her hands against Gainesworth's chest and lightly pushed him away. "Mr. Gainesworth ..."

"Hector," he said and lightly stroked her cheek with one finger. "I must speak to your mother."

His words brought her back to earth as if she'd fallen from the tower of the Court. "My mother! Oh Mr. G—

Hector. I don't know what to think, what she must think. You cannot come today. Not until all of this business is resolved."

"But you will permit me? Belinda, I'm asking you. Will you be my wife?"

His eyes sparkled, and not just with the merry light she'd seen in them from the first moment they met. They brimmed with tears. "Yes," she said, and he kissed her again, this time leaving her in no doubt of his passionate feelings, deepening the kiss until she murmured with pleasure. When they broke apart, Belinda felt a little dizzy. "You must go. I have to see Miss Wilkins."

"I shall find a way to let you know what happens," Hector said.

When he let go of her and jumped back up on his horse, Belinda felt the full force of the icy wind whipping through the bare-branched trees, hugging herself as she watched him ride away.

"Evenin' M'Lady," said a voice behind her that Belinda recognized.

She wondered how long the groom had been there, and blushed to the roots of her hair. But he only looked at her with a knowing smile and nodded. Oh well, she thought. Everyone would know soon enough that she and Mr. Gainesworth were betrothed. And it was important that she shake herself out of her delirious haze.

This brought the rest of what they had been talking about back in a rush. The acrostic. A hidden affair. What had she started? Was it her fault? She had the pocket book in her possession again, but she wanted to hurl it off a cliff into the ocean.

Pandora's box indeed. Even though she thought she'd prepared herself for discovering infidelity on the part of her father, to have it now appear more of a certainty gave her a sick feeling in the pit of her stomach. And Miss Wilkins! What could she have to do with this? If the governess was twenty-two when they were nine, she would have been only thirteen years old at the time the notes were written in the pocket book.

No. Absolutely no. She would have been a child. It was impossible.

Still, P Wilkins? What did it mean?

Belinda walked back to the house in a daze. The evidence was very suggestive. However, what did it actually prove? What if the acrostic had nothing to do with Antonella? All it would prove would be that the marquess had been trysting with a lady around the time of his daughter's birth. As to why —she didn't want to think about that.

The only thing to do was to find Miss Wilkins and confront her about it, hope that she would say she had no idea what the acrostic referred to, and thus exonerate herself of any connection to the marquess. Wilkins was a common enough name. The initial could stand for Pauline, or Patricia, or Penelope.

The thought was not comforting. Belinda suddenly remembered the governess's first name: It was Persephone.

She wouldn't say anything to Ant yet. Not until she knew for certain whether Miss Wilkins had any role in those long-ago days.

She raced directly up to the schoolroom and Miss Wilkins' quarters when she returned, her heart racing. But the governess wasn't there. And her cloak and bonnet were gone, too. So she turned around and ran back down the stairs. She was about to rush out of the front door to go to Ant's bird shed when the morning room door opened and her mother stepped out.

"Where are you going in such an undignified hurry, Belinda?" she said in a tone that commanded attention.

"I-I'm just running an errand." How could she explain any of this to her mama? Even if it had nothing to do with Miss Wilkins, her late husband's infidelity was a very private matter. She clearly must have known about it and would not welcome its exposure after all the years she'd worked to keep its consequences hidden—if indeed what Gainesworth suspected was true.

"An errand? What possible errand could you be engaged on? I require your company in the morning room." She indicated the open door behind her and waited for Belinda to precede her inside.

"Yes, Mama," Belinda said, resigned to postponing her conversation with Miss Wilkins.

The dowager seated herself on the sofa and patted the space next to her for Belinda.

She could hardly ignore that direct appeal, and so she perched beside her mother.

"I have not had an opportunity to speak to you since last night. Suffice it to say that what happened at Atherleigh has put a different complexion on what I thought about the earl. I blame Antonella, but he behaved abominably nonetheless. I will not accept his suit for your hand."

Belinda was so relieved she wanted to cry and thank her mother. She opened her mouth to speak, but the dowager raised one elegant, beringed hand to silence her.

"That does not mean that I would countenance a match with Mr. Gainesworth. Yes, I see you with him. You are infatuated. He is not for you. His station is far beneath yours, and, as I said before, he is a rake."

"No, Mama! You don't know him! I swear—"

"I have not questioned you concerning your whereabouts just before that altercation at the card party."

The dowager fixed Belinda with a steely gaze that said *I know what you've been up to and you will not get away with it.*

But Belinda was not to be relegated to childhood by a look. "And what of my feelings? Do they not matter when it comes to finding a husband?"

"You are a mere child, and you don't understand what is at stake. Your infatuation will wear off, and if you marry him you will find yourself attached to someone who will not add to your consequence, or your children's consequence."

"But I love him!" Belinda felt the threat of tears and fought them, not wanting to make her mother consider her any more of a child than she already did.

"Love! That is not the proper foundation for a marriage."

Belinda opened her eyes wide at the dowager. "So you expect me to marry someone who does not love me and will find his pleasure elsewhere? Is that what you did?" She didn't really believe that was the case, despite the potential evidence of her father's straying from his marriage vows.

But Lady Lewiston went pale and her lips quivered. "We are not discussing my marriage. If I had made another choice, you would not be standing here."

Her reaction surprised Belinda. It added weight to what Gainesworth suspected. Until that moment, Belinda had half hoped the initials and the dates, the fragments of verse and the acrostic, were idle fancies, mere nothings on the part of her father. In barely more than a whisper, she said, "So that is why you hate Antonella."

The dowager sprang to her feet and walked to the window. "I do not hate Antonella. I simply have not a mother's feelings for her, since I did not bear her."

She did not bear her, but Antonella was no distant relation. She was the product of a true love affair. So true, that the marquess—unlike most men of his ilk—could not simply send the infant away to be raised by some childless couple, or consign her to an orphanage, only giving her financial support without ever acknowledging her. He brought her to this house, to have her under his roof, to benefit from his guidance and love, and yes, his rank. "I see," Belinda said. She would not question her mother any more. What would be the point? The question of Gainesworth was better left to another time as well. It would not serve her to press on that particular bruise.

Lady Lewiston turned around, once more the self-contained noblewoman. "Now, it is time for you to dress for dinner. I will not have our life disrupted simply because hot-headed gentlemen don't know how to behave with propriety and circumspection."

Belinda couldn't quite let everything go, however. "But what about the duel? What if someone is killed?"

"That will not happen. The gentlemen will face off like cockerels and delope so that their foolish honor will be satisfied. Nothing happened that would justify such a drastic step as a duel, and I'm certain that by this time, both Atherleigh and Bartleson have come to their senses and realize there is no point in fighting. Especially not over Antonella."

Until her last words, Belinda had begun to think her mother in the right of it, at least regarding the duel. The whole practice of men fighting to defend someone's honor was simply ridiculous.

But her mama was wrong about one thing. Her prejudice against an infant that had been foisted upon her by her faithless husband had blinded her to Antonella's true qualities. She *was* worth fighting for.

Yes. All at once Belinda understood that Atherleigh believed that, or he would not have punched Bartleson or accepted the challenge. He believed it even knowing of Antonella's undistinguished birth and not knowing that she truly was the daughter of a marquess.

She had misjudged him. Did Antonella know? Was she aware that the baron was in love with her?

Now it was more important than ever for the duel to be stopped. If Atherleigh were killed, Antonella's chance at happiness would be destroyed.

She gave her mama a perfunctory curtsy and left, going straight to Antonella's bedroom to tell her what Gainesworth found.

～

BELINDA SCRATCHED ON ANTONELLA'S BEDROOM DOOR praying she would hear her and come close. When light steps approached on the other side and her sister's voice said, "Bee! You have to help me get out of here!" she breathed a sigh of relief.

"I don't dare," she whispered in return.

"But I must go and feed Zephyra! You have to help!"

That blasted hawk! "Something much more important demands your attention Ant. You know that Atherleigh and Bartleson are going to fight a duel tomorrow morning."

"So it's really going to happen?" came the shaky response. "They mustn't. I'm not worth it. It's stupid."

"That may be, but Atherleigh is apparently determined, and I think I know why. But that is beside the point right now. The duel can't be stopped unless you allow me to share something that Mr. Gainesworth has discovered in his close examination of Papa's pocket book."

Silence. Belinda knew that Antonella shrank from probing into her history, likely fearing to discover something even worse than that she was the daughter of a distant relation. Was it worse, what Gainesworth had figured out? Or did it somehow make everything better? The important aspect of it all was that the information it revealed might apparently be able to stop this foolish duel.

"What has he discovered? How could it possibly help?"

"It's hard to explain. I've just come from meeting him—"

"You met him unchaperoned? Belinda! Mama will be furious."

"Sshh!" Belinda said. "It's not what you think. It was only about the pocket book." At least Ant couldn't see her face and know she was lying.

"Be careful, Bee. If anyone saw you ... Besides, how can anything that's in that old notebook possibly help?" Antonella said.

Of course, it might not. And then a likely hurtful truth would have been revealed for nothing. "You must trust me. I think it's important. You know I would never hurt you!"

Another pause on the other side of the door, although Antonella was leaning close enough that Belinda could hear her breathing. "Will the information be revealed to Lord Atherleigh?"

"Yes."

Another long pause. "Very well." The words were spoken so softly that Belinda could hardly hear them.

"Yes, dear sister! I'm sure it's the right thing to do. I hope to be able to bring good news to you later."

After another pause, a gasp. "What about Zephyra?" Antonella nearly shrieked.

"I shall send Wilkie to talk to you as soon as I find her. She would be better. She's not afraid."

"Quickly!" Antonella said.

Belinda scurried off to governess's room in the servants' wing. She desperately wanted to ask her directly about the acrostic in the pocket book, but after speaking with Antonella, she decided to wait. What if it had nothing to do with her? She would have insulted the woman who had been all goodness to both of them ever since she came into their lives.

And right now it was more important to ensure that

Antonella didn't fret about the hawk. Miss Wilkins had always shared Antonella's predilection and would likely be able to do whatever was necessary for the fierce bird. Something about the creature felt deeply interwoven with everything that had happened since the beginning of December. Belinda couldn't have said why she felt that, but the hawk seemed more and more like a secret link between Amblemere Court and Atherleigh Manor. She just couldn't figure out whether that was something good or something bad.

ANTONELLA WAS UNSURE SHE HAD TAKEN THE RIGHT STEP IN agreeing to Belinda's request to reveal Gainesworth's interpretation of whatever was in the pocket book to Atherleigh. Would it also be revealed to Bartleson? If it wasn't, how could it somehow stave off their duel? She didn't care if her reputation was somehow diminished in Bartleson's eyes—if it even could be. But what if Atherleigh thought ill of her after he discovered what Gainesworth had found?

This was one more source of unease for Antonella. She was already in a nervous panic about what the baron would think when she at last returned Zephyra to him and he discovered she'd been hiding the goshawk all this time. Whatever secret is buried in the pocket book might easily put the nail in the coffin of any possible future she could envision.

The future. Like it or not, she had allowed herself to hope that perhaps Lord Atherleigh felt some tenderness toward her, that he desired her. If his violent actions had been provoked by jealousy, by not wanting Bartleson to touch her, surely that's what it meant. And yet, she couldn't reconcile those actions of his with the bitterness in his voice when he accused her of trying to entrap him.

She had no more time to think because a key turned in

the lock of her door and Miss Wilkins entered bearing a tray of tea and biscuits. Antonella said, "How did you—"

"It's the housekeeper's key. I said I would bring you some tea so the kitchen maid could stay and help her with dinner." She placed the tray on the dressing table. "Lady Belinda said you wanted to see me."

"I need your help. I must feed Zephyra! And she really ought to be weathered as well. I couldn't take her out yesterday before dinner because of the card party. I thought I'd go early today and make up for it, but as you see—" She gestured around the room, her mouth screwed in a distasteful scowl.

"I would like to help you, but I don't see how I can. The bird doesn't know me. She'll be frightened, and I don't know how to approach her or do anything."

She was right. Zephyra might easily panic and hurt herself. What could she do? And then she thought: Rafiq. "Would you deliver a letter for me instead?" she asked.

"A letter to whom?"

"To Atherleigh's falconer. His name is Rafiq. He knows about Zephyra. See if he can come and help her!" She rushed over to the small desk under her window and took out a sheet of paper.

"Where is this Rafiq?" Miss Wilkins asked.

"In the mews, by the ruined chapel in the grounds of Atherleigh. I'll draw you a map of the route I take to get there." She took out another sheet and started sketching out the meandering way through the coombe and the spinney. "When you reach the fence, you'll have to call out to get Rafiq's attention. I'm afraid you must go right away. And if he agrees to come, you will have to lead him to the shed. Can you do that?"

"Are you sure about this, Antonella? Asking Lord Atherleigh's falconer to help you is a great presumption."

"But don't you see? Zephyra belongs to Atherleigh anyway, so he would be caring for the baron's hawk." The logic was a bit of a stretch, she realized. But in the end she was certain she could justify it to Atherleigh, if it came to that.

"All right. I can go immediately, but I must be quick." She held out her hand for the letter and the map.

Antonella folded both of them and grasped Miss Wilkins' hands, not letting her leave right away. "You should know something else."

The governess raised a questioning eyebrow.

"Belinda found something that might shed some light on my past. You've heard about the duel, I presume." Miss Wilkins nodded. "She thinks Mr. Gainesworth has figured something out that might force the two gentlemen to abandon the duel. I can't say more, because I don't know more."

"Has she …" Miss Wilkins looked off into the middle distance. "When you next see Belinda, tell her to come to me."

"Why?"

"I just think I should keep an eye on both of you, is all." She smiled her kind smile, the one that turned her gray eyes limpid and soft, almost loving.

"You're so good to us, Wilkie," Antonella said, and released her hands.

$\mathcal{M}$ alcolm carefully nested the smallswords in their case. He rang for his valet to help him roll down his right shirtsleeve and put on his coat. That accomplished, he dismissed Carter and strolled to one of the long gallery windows looking out over the formal gardens. The slanting late-afternoon sun, not strong enough to melt the icy dew, turned everything to sparkles of gold between the long shadows of the naked trees.

The transcendent peace of the world outside could not have been more different from his tumultuous feelings. What was he doing? Even knowing that Gainesworth was right that it was foolish to fight Bartleson, Malcolm could not shake his burning ire, his need to do something, to lash out. Miss Ambleton, no matter the facts concerning her birth, did not deserve such treatment. Even so, why had it driven him to the edge of madness?

After all, he too had accused her of something entirely unjustified last night. What had he said to her? He accused her of being a flirt. She is no such thing. Feminine strategems are foreign to her nature. She threw out no lures to him. She simply dazzled him. Knocked him off balance. Not just her appearance, but her essence. Joy, delight, and—yes—love emanated from her every movement, walking into the room, playing cards, dancing. She radiated uncomplicated happiness, until he spoiled it. No wonder she had looked at him with such hurt and confusion. Last night she had chosen to transcend the limits of her birth and be the extraordinary woman she was, and he couldn't see past his own self regard.

Something had changed today, though. Without her physically here, he could somehow see her more clearly. He could see that she was glorious. More glorious than any woman he'd ever known. She sparkled just as the magical world he gazed upon through the manor's windows did. She was there. Not physically there, but she belonged to that world as much as the ancient trees rooted in the spinney. A Cornish pixie sent to enchant him, she had appeared out of the woods that first time, seemingly from nowhere. She'd disturbed something deep inside him ever since the moment he touched her hands as she held Mercury's reins so he could remount.

If he'd never seen her again there would still be that distinct memory. A bone-deep recognition of something. But he did see her again, cowering in a corner of a closet and in his mews, after her fall, where they brushed together. That accidental touch sent a shock through him. Recognition. And when he held her in his arms for the waltz last night, it was as if his arms were designed for no other purpose than to hold her. She had taken hold of his stump without flinching. The entire episode unsettled him so much that he ended by insulting her. How could he ever tell her that he hadn't meant it, that he knew now he was mistaken? Tell her that he wasn't thinking straight because he could hardly breathe when he was so close to her.

And Bartleson. How dare the man—no gentleman by

Atherleigh's measure—dishonor her last night! Just thinking about it made his blood rise as it did before a battle. No one could have stopped him then. He wanted to demolish anything and anyone that threatened Antonella, to give her a life where she could spread her wings and become the extraordinary person she was meant to be. It mattered not in the least where she came from. In fact, it was all part of her magic. She came from nowhere. She was born for this moment. She was born for him.

Last night, young, innocent Miss Ambleton rose magnificently above the handicap of her uncertain parentage, above all the petty concerns of rank and breeding and dared to dazzle.

Yet for all his experience, he could not do the same. He had allowed his own handicap to limit him, to drag him down, to diminish him, as Gainesworth had said. But no more. Miss Ambleton, whether she knew it or not, showed him the way forward. He was supposed to be a courageous warrior. Yet this delicate young woman had shown more courage than he as she faced and embraced an uncertain future.

A future that, he now understood, must include him.

Malcolm hastened out of the gallery and down the stairs two at a time to the hall. "My greatcoat and hat," he barked at the footman standing by the front door.

A few moments later he was striding purposefully toward the mews. The hour was growing late, but the light hadn't yet fully gone, although dusky shadow had replaced those slanting golden rays. He must talk to Rafiq. Had the falconer started preparing the birds for their journey north, getting them used to the crates they would occupy? Was it too late to stop him?

Stillness reigned in the weathering yard, which did not surprise him at that hour. He opened the door into the mews and went in, moderating his pace so as not to startle the three birds left there, two of them hooded. The one unhooded—the sparrow hawk—gazed at him with alert interest. Three birds—not enough for so grand a mews. The space felt hollow. *I shall find another goshawk.* Chakor's absence created a palpable emptiness. Perhaps that was part of why he had made that hasty decision to close the mews rather than consider its place in his life as it now was.

"Rafiq?" he called. He walked further in, turning the corner toward the falconer's private quarters. But Rafiq wasn't there. Atherleigh scanned the space, not certain what he expected to see, and spotted two sheets of paper that had once been folded and were now tossed aside as if abandoned in a hurry. He picked one up. It was addressed to Rafiq.

You have to help me! I've been confined to my room and Zephyra needs food and exercise. Miss Wilkins will lead you to my humble shed. Perhaps you should reclaim her, as I do not know how long I may be forced to forgo the pleasure of being outdoors. I will abide by whatever you decide to do.

A. Ambleton

The other piece of paper was a crude map of a path through the spinney to the coombe, through that and up the hill on Lewiston land to a small shed not very far from the Amblemere stables.

Rafiq must have answered the summons. He had left his birds unguarded. Rafiq never went very far from the mews, unless they were out on a hunt. He always said that they needed human companionship all the time, to remind them who they worked for. Yet he left to help Miss Ambleton with a bird called Zephyra. What sort of bird was she?

And then Malcolm remembered Gainesworth telling him about Miss Ambleton exercising a large hawk. He'd witnessed her on his way to the stables. It fit.

A goshawk. It had to be.

Malcolm's first instinct was to follow the map himself and find Rafiq. But it was already early twilight. Finding the paths would be difficult in the daytime, let alone after dusk.

What was she playing at? The angry comment flew into his head again, this time not in the context of courtship. Had she stolen his goshawk? Lured the bird to her when it was out hunting, flying through the trees on Amblemere land?

A pixie. A sprite. A thief! He hurled his hat onto the ground, sank his fingers into a hank of his dark hair and pulled, closing his eyes. After a moment he snapped them open, snatched up the map, whirled around, and left the mews. Nervous call notes followed him out. He would find Miss Ambleton and question her about the goshawk.

"Atherleigh!"

The voice stopped him as he was about to open the door in the fence that gave onto the spinney. Gainesworth. What did he want?

Hector jogged down the hill to the weathering yard, let himself in, and approached Malcolm, panting. "Something important," he said, then held up a hand for Atherleigh to wait as he caught his breath.

"Out with it, Man!" Malcolm snapped.

"The duel must not take place. I have some evidence that Bartleson was in the wrong so he could not challenge you." Having got this long speech out, Gainesworth bent over and rested his hands on his knees.

"Of course he was in the wrong! He accosted Miss Ambleton." Just saying her name aloud made his stomach clench and his pulse speed up.

"More than that," Gainesworth said, now mostly recovered. "You had every right to defend her as a lady. She *is* the daughter of the late marquess. Just not of his marchioness."

So, Antonella had been born on the wrong side of the blanket. Yet Lady Lewiston had brought her up from infancy? "What proof do you have of this?" Even with proof, the excuse was slim. She was still illegitimate. It was splitting hairs.

"Remember the pocket book Lady Belinda found? I've managed to decipher some things. Initials. Dates. An acrostic with a name."

Atherleigh shook his head. "That might confirm an affair, but it doesn't prove the lady was Antonella's mother." If Gainesworth noticed his use of her first name, he showed no evidence of it.

"Yes, yes, it's a little bit of a fine distinction, but if Bartleson is a gentleman, he will bow out."

"That is the pertinent question. Is he a gentleman? I have my doubts."

"Then you must be the one to do the gentlemanly thing and cry off!" Hector's voice rose in frustration.

Why was Hector so insistent about this. "Do you think I can't win this duel? Is that why you're so concerned?"

Gainesworth sighed heavily. "You know it's not that. I fear you might win it too thoroughly and be forced to flee to the continent."

Malcolm tipped his head back and laughed, a cynical, mirthless laugh. "Don't be daft. Bartleson isn't worth the mud on my boots. I'll just frighten him and send him away."

Gainesworth paced off and turned in a circle, clutching his hands at the back of his head. "Damn it, Mal! You'll ruin everything if you go through with this ridiculous gesture."

Ah. Something to do with Lady Belinda, it seemed. "You want to marry her, don't you?" He assumed Gainesworth would understand that he didn't mean Miss Ambleton.

Hector's face transformed. His eyes lit up with ardor. He ran forward and grasped Malcolm's forearm. "You see, don't you? She has said yes. But she's underage, and her mama must consent. Lady Lewiston doesn't think much of me. I don't have a title, and my wealth comes from trade. But if I can successfully prevent an action that will cause scandal not just in Cornwall but throughout the *ton*, then I will be on firm footing when I ask for her permission."

Despite the recent revelation that Antonella likely had custody of the goshawk that belonged to him—and could only have somehow stolen it—Malcolm couldn't quite let go of the strong feelings that had worked on him in the gallery and sent him out to the mews. He had made an assumption that proved to be erroneous last night. Was this assumption equally wrong? If so, he really had Hector to thank for pushing him out of his dismals, for forcing him to wake up and grasp the life he still had. "I'll tell you what. If you can find some corroborating evidence that the marquess was, in fact, Miss Ambleton's father, I will present myself at Sir William's house and formally request that the plan for a duel be abandoned."

"But there's no time!" Hector said.

"You have until half-past eight tomorrow morning. I suggest we go in and dress for dinner." Atherleigh suddenly felt weary to his marrow. If he were to put up a good showing in a duel in the morning, he would need an early night. He had no confidence in Hector's ability to conjure up some additional evidence that would support his theory about Miss Ambleton, so he assumed he would be keeping his appointment on the strand.

As he trudged back up the slope to the Manor, Gainesworth keeping pace beside him and maintaining complete silence, Atherleigh tried to push the thought of Antonella and the goshawk out of his mind. He would deal with that tomorrow, after the duel.

"WILKIE!" BELINDA SAID, STOPPING THE GOVERNESS AS SHE removed her hat and cloak in the back corridor of the Court, having entered through the kitchens.

Miss Wilkins calmly hung her cloak on one of the hooks where the servants kept their warm clothing handy for stepping outside to the kitchen gardens or to feed the chickens. "Yes, Lady Belinda?"

"I need to talk to you. Somewhere private." Belinda glanced to either side at the kitchen maids and footmen who were preparing everything for the family dinner.

"The library," Miss Wilkins said, removed a candle from a wall sconce and started walking in that direction without waiting for Belinda to agree.

The pocket book weighed down Belinda's reticule like a burning coal. She was about to accuse her beloved governess of concealing an affair with her father. It was a terrible presumption—and a terrible risk. But she could see no other way of resolving this matter and ensuring that Antonella received the support and acknowledgement she deserved.

Once they were in the musty, paneled library in the old part of the house and Miss Wilkins had lit the three candles in the branch on the mantlepiece, Belinda took a deep breath. It was necessary. There was no getting around it. She walked over to the heavy old desk and laid her hand upon it. "Miss Wilkins, a few days ago I found something stuck in the back of this desk, something that must have fallen down behind one of the small drawers and been wedged there for some time." She paused struggling to stop the furious pounding of her heart. There would be no going back from this, no un-saying it. She reached into her reticule.

Miss Wilkins cocked her head on the side and wrinkled her brow. "What's that?"

The governess apparently didn't recognize the note book, which surprised Belinda. She half expected her to gasp and cover her mouth, to start weeping and uttering protestations. But she was as calm as she ever was. "This is one of my father's pocket books, dating from the years surrounding Antonella's and my births." Her fingers trembled as she opened the book to the acrostic. "Mr. Gainesworth has been helping me decipher the contents, since much of it appears to be in a sort of code such as gentlemen might use to record things they perhaps would not want someone to discover in its pages."

Belinda stepped slowly to Miss Wilkins, the book held out, open to the page with the acrostic.

Miss Wilkins took the book and read the pages, turning it around to decipher the various crossings, and then she handed it back to Belinda, dawning comprehension in her eyes.

"I am sorry to have to ask you this, but it's vital to my dear Antonella's future, and it might also prevent a duel taking place tomorrow morning—if I can confirm my suspicions. My question is, are you the P Wilkins the acrostic appears to identify?"

The governess closed her eyes and shook her head slowly. "I am not."

Belinda gasped. She was so certain! How could it be otherwise?

"I am not, but I know who is."

"Tell me, Wilkie!" Belinda demanded rushing forward and grasping her arm.

Miss Wilkins gently pried Belinda's fingers off and said, "I think Antonella deserves to be the first to know, don't you?"

Of course. After all, it was her life, her future, that hung in the balance. She was the one who had been insulted and who was the cause of a duel between two gentlemen of rank and fortune. "Very well. We shall go to Antonella now."

"There isn't time. You cannot be late for dinner, and

you've yet to change. After dinner, I shall visit Antonella and tell her. Alone. It will be up to her how, when, and with whom she shares this knowledge."

Belinda knew the governess well enough to understand that she would not waver from her decision.

It was going to be a very, very long dinner hour.

ANTONELLA STARED IN DISGUST AT THE COLD FOOD ON THE tray Molly, the housemaid, had delivered to her earlier. She tried to take a few bites, but everything tasted of sand in her mouth. How could she eat, when so much was going on around her? She had no way of knowing whether what Belinda had discovered would be enough to stop the stupid duel that would be fought tomorrow, or whether Rafiq had fed and exercised Zephyra, or what Lord Atherleigh was now thinking of her. This last, to Antonella's shame, had taken on life and death import—more so than the impending real fight. She began to think that she would die if she had lost his regard for good.

When the key turned in the lock on her door, she stood and walked away to stare unseeing out the window at the dark world beyond, assuming it would be Molly come to retrieve her untouched dinner. It was the last thing the girl would do before retiring for the night. She smiled. More than once she'd considered pushing the maid aside and bolting from her room. It would be easy enough. But then where would she go? And what did it matter? Especially now, when it was nearly midnight.

"Antonella."

She whirled around. It was Miss Wilkins. "What are you doing here?"

"I need to talk to you. You should sit."

The governess's eyes lacked their usual amused glimmer. This was something serious. "I-I'd rather stand."

Miss Wilkins nodded, then reached into her pocket and removed what appeared to be a much-thumbed and yellowed letter. "Belinda came to me with the pocket book she found, which contained some information that appeared to have something to do with me."

With Miss Wilkins? How could that be? "But …"

"Let me explain, without interruption please."

The governess began by telling Antonella about the acrostic and its apparently incriminating meaning. "But the poem did not refer to me," she said. "It referred to someone very dear to me."

At that, she held out the letter to Antonella, who approached her slowly, her eyes fixed on the paper. She took it from Miss Wilkins, her hand remarkably steady. She'd had so many troubling revelations in the past weeks. What was one more?

15 November, 1796

My dearest sister. I have been sent away in disgrace, as you know, but the child I shall soon bear is very precious to me. I don't know why, but I have a certain foreboding about the birth. Call me foolishly worried, but I must ask you to do something for me. I know you are still a child yourself, and should not be burdened with such a request. Papa will have nothing to do with me, though, so I could not appeal to him.

What I ask of you is this: As soon as I am confined, if all does not go well, write express to Lord L at Amblemere in Cornwall. Ask him to see that our child is cared for in whatever way he sees fit. I do not ask for riches or consequence, of course. The babe will forever be a bastard. I just ask that the infant be placed in a loving family somewhere and supported in some way.

I am sorry to ask this of you at your age, but I have nowhere else to turn. It is my hope that these actions will be unnecessary.

Nonetheless, my heart is now eased knowing that I have done my possible to see to my dear child's future well being, come what may.

Know that I love you, and please don't judge me or Lord L too harshly for the fact that our passions proved stronger than our judgment.

With fondness and kisses,

Phoenicia

Antonella stayed frozen in space and time for what felt like an eternity. "Is this true?" she finally whispered, raising her eyes to Miss Wilkins's, whose own brimmed with tears.

The governess nodded. "My sister was eight years older than I. Our father, a clergyman, was a younger son of a good family, as your Mama knows from when she hired me. At the time some months before this letter, when it was discovered that Phoenicia was unmarried and increasing, she refused to name the father. Unable to bear the stigma of having an unmarried daughter give birth in his house, our father banished her from our home. I wept for days. The last time I saw her was when she was on the seat of a dog cart being driven away before dawn one morning."

Antonella could feel all the pain of losing a beloved sister. She had felt that pain herself on the day Lady Lewiston told them that she was not her mother, and it seemed therefore that Belinda was not her sister, that she had lost her in some way. "So, the marquess was my papa after all. Belinda is my sister. And you are my aunt."

This made Miss Wilkins smile weakly. "Yes. When I saw the advertisement nine years later for a governess for you and Lady Belinda, I leapt at the chance. I thought then only that I might be able to discover the whereabouts of my sister's child, perhaps find a discreet moment to question Lord Lewiston.

"But the moment I set eyes on you, I knew you were she. I

see Phoenicia in you every day. Her dark hair, her lively eyes, her quick wit and intelligence."

"Yet you kept the secret."

"What would it have served to reveal anything then? The marquess had more than fulfilled what I had asked of him when I was just fourteen. I could see that he loved you enough to defy the rules and elevate you to the status of lady."

"Poor Mama," Antonella murmured. She included both Phoenicia Wilkins and Lady Lewiston in that simple utterance. The marchioness must have known that she was raising her own husband's love child. Considering that, Antonella's opinion of her altered. She might not have shown as much affection to her as she had to Belinda, and she might have ruined her chances to have a season and make a creditable match, but how could she be blamed for that?

"Does Aunt Caroline—the dowager—Lady Lewiston—I don't know what to call her! know about you?"

Miss Wilkins shook her head. "I don't much resemble my sister, so our family tie—yours and mine—is not obvious."

"But you are my aunt!" Antonella said again, her voice filled with wonder, her heart with understanding.

The governess nodded, and in an instant, both of them rushed to each other and embraced, Antonella releasing the sobs she'd pent up ever since the night before, Miss Wilkins shushing and soothing her, stroking her head and kissing her.

BELINDA KNOCKED FRANTICALLY ON THE DOOR OF Antonella's room. She put her ear to it and listened. Hard. Was Ant crying? She knocked again, more loudly, not caring if anyone heard her. This was too important to worry about Mama's discovering that she defied her by visiting Antonella.

Frustrated, Belinda tried the door. To her surprise, it opened. She stopped as soon as she crossed the threshold. Antonella and Miss Wilkins were embracing each other and weeping. She ran to them. "What's the matter? What's happening?"

Antonella lifted her face, streaked with tears but smiling. "Oh Belinda! Sister!"

She threw her arms around Belinda, who looked up at Miss Wilkins, a confused frown furrowing her forehead. "I thought you said it wasn't you?"

"It wasn't." Miss Wilkins took the crumpled letter out of Antonella's hands and handed it to Belinda. Antonella released her sister so she could read it.

After she had fully digested its contents, Belinda lifted her eyes to Miss Wilkins again. "You had a sister. P was for Phoenicia. But this is so timely!"

It was Antonella's and the governess's turn to be puzzled.

"I received this just now. It was written some hours ago, but I guess it took a while to get here in secret." She fished a note that had been folded into a piece that could fit in the palm of her hand out of her reticule and gave it to Antonella.

Ant unfolded it and she and Miss Wilkins studied it together.

"Atherleigh has asked for something that proves you are my half-sister before he will confront Bartleson and stop the duel," Belinda said, eyes shining, "And your letter is that!"

Antonella frowned. "Yes it is. But I don't know if we can share it with them. Aunt Caroline doesn't even know the whole."

"She knows the most important part. That you are Papa's daughter. She just doesn't know about Miss Wilkins, or that this letter exists." Belinda wanted to shake Antonella. Didn't she see that the means to both prevent the duel and elevate her in Atherleigh's eyes was in her hands?

ANTONELLA'S MIND SPUN IN EVERY DIRECTION. BELINDA WAS right. But how could she expose Lady Lewiston that way, after she'd raised her and cared for her for eighteen years? Yet men's lives could hang in the balance. Or at least, their honor, assuming neither of them intended to kill the other.

"Bee, this secret isn't just mine and Wilkie's. It's your mama's as well. We can't reveal it to anyone without her consent." She was adamant. Too many things had remained hidden for too long.

"But Ant! We have no time! The duel is at half-past eight tomorrow morning." She glanced at the small clock on the mantelpiece. "Nearly *this* morning! Don't you care about Lord Atherleigh? I was sure you did."

"Of course I care! What did you all think?" Antonella blurted out, hot tears once more springing to her eyes.

Miss Wilkins put her arm around her shoulders. "You are right, Antonella. This is too important to act hastily. The men will have to deal with their own folly."

Belinda covered her face with her hands and shook her head. "This is madness," she said, her voice muffled. She dropped her hands. "When will we tell Mama, then? She'll never be ready to hear it."

Antonella bit her lower lip until it hurt. This was going to be difficult, and there would be no good time to confront the dowager. "But *we're* ready now. Let's go to her. She seldom retires before midnight. We all need to be there. She may have questions."

She walked over to her chamber door and opened it wide, waiting for Belinda and Wilkie—her Aunt Persephone—to pass through it before pulling it closed behind her.

CHAPTER 31

*F*or a moment after the dowager read the letter—
standing in her brocade dressing gown in the
middle of her private parlor, her not-yet-graying hair bound
into a plait down her back—Antonella feared she would
attack Miss Wilkins.

Hard-eyed and rigid, the dowager vibrated with anger.
"You accepted this position knowing all this? How dare you!"
She had crumpled the letter in her fist and was about to
throw it into the fire dying in the grate when Belinda dashed
forward and took hold of her mother's wrist.

"Please, Ma'am," Belinda said. "This is all Antonella has of
her mother."

The dowager unclenched her hand and let the paper fall
to the floor. Antonella quickly snatched it up and smoothed
it out.

Lady Lewiston still glared at Miss Wilkins. "I suppose you
are going to tell this to all the world. You have it in your
power to besmirch my late husband's name and make me a
laughing stock in the *ton*. Your revenge would be complete
indeed."

"I have no such intention, My Lady," Miss Wilkins said. "I do not seek revenge. The marquess did the most honorable thing he could at the time. He took responsibility for my sister's child. I can accept the fact that admitting publicly to his affair would not have solved anything. Besides, don't you think I would have confronted you with this years ago if I had wanted to stir everything up?"

"Then why now?" The dowager spoke through clenched teeth, looking at each of them in turn, challenging, questioning.

Antonella cleared her throat. "It's because of the duel," she said. "At least, Mr. Gainesworth believes that knowing that I am in fact the daughter of a marquess will force Lord Bartleson to see that Lord Atherleigh was within his rights to defend me and that he would call off the duel."

The dowager's mouth opened in horror. "You mean you would tell all of them? Can you not see how humiliating that would be?"

Belinda laid a gentle hand on her mother's arm. "Neither Mr. Gainsworth nor Lord Atherleigh will tell a soul. The secret is yours and Antonella's."

"Why should I trust either of them?" Lady Lewiston fairly spat out the words.

Antonella and Belinda spoke at the same time.

Antonella said, "Because I love him."

Belinda said, "Because he loves me."

And they immediately turned toward each other, wonder and questions in each other's eyes. But there was no time for all that. Belinda went down on her knees before her mother. "Please, Mama! Help us stop this pointless duel. And allow me to marry Mr. Gainesworth."

The dowager gave a scornful little laugh. "So he offered for you without my permission!"

Belinda shook her head. "He was going to seek an interview with you today, but for tomorrow's duel. Which cannot go forward! Please, please Mama. Enough secrets and shame and hiding. Who knows what will happen later, but why should it all hinge on a mistaken idea?"

Belinda's comment hung in the air. No one spoke for a long moment. At last the dowager said, "Leave me. And do what you will. I want no part of it." Then she wheeled once more to face the governess. "Make no mistake, Persephone Wilkins, I can make your life miserable if I choose. A viper in the nest, waiting for her moment to spring this on me. You will never get another position as a governess."

"Mama!" both girls said in unison.

Miss Wilkins held up her hand to Ant and Bee. "Lady Lewiston has every right to be angry." She addressed the dowager directly. "I should not have taken this position knowing what I knew. But the temptation to be near my only sister's child was too strong. Please believe me, Ma'am, when I say I never meant you any harm. I have nothing but admiration for the fact that you took an infant you knew must have been your husband's by-blow into your house and brought her up alongside your beloved daughter. I honor you for your forbearance."

The dowager visibly shrank, as if she had been puffing herself up like a guard dog to look large and belligerent only to see the threat subside. "I want you all to leave me now. I meant what I said. You must do as you see fit."

She turned her back on them, and they passed quietly out of her room.

Not many hours later, Antonella, Belinda, and Miss Wilkins met in the courtyard, bundled up against the cold, breathing clouds of steam into the pre-dawn air.

"We must reach them before it is too late," Belinda said.

"We should all ride. It will be the quickest way down to the beach. The horses can manage it. I don't mind riding astride. What about you, Wilkie?"

"It's the only way I ever learned," she said with a chuckle.

Antonella froze. *No.* She could not ride. Especially not before dawn. In winter, the sun rose late. It was nearly half past seven, and the sky was only faintly fading to gray now. At the best of times, the idea of mounting a horse sent a shiver of terror through her body. In the dark, she thought she might die. But it was imperative that she get there before Belinda and Miss Wilkins. "You two go on. I shall come another way," she said. "Besides, I just need to check on Zephyra."

"Mr. Kahn said you'd done a very good job with the hawk, Antonella. I didn't have a chance to tell you yesterday," Miss Wilkins said.

"Mr. Kahn?" Antonella couldn't think who she meant.

"You call him Rafiq."

Of course, he had a surname. Most servants were known by their last names, yet the falconer had simply been Rafiq. "Ah," she said. "All the same, having not seen her all day yesterday I would like to just look in."

Belinda said, "Mind you don't linger. Miss Wilkins has the letter, but we need you there as well."

I must be there first! she thought. It was a gamble, but perhaps it would work. If she could find the path through the coombe in the near darkness, she would arrive before they would on the road, which took a circuitous route to the same place. It would be too dark for them to gallop, or even go much faster than a trot. A horse could easily lose its footing or the riders might not see a patch of ice. Antonella knew enough about riding to know that.

Besides, she knew every inch of the path through the woods and the rough terrain, over the rocks and down the cliff. But she also recognized that in the dark, the most familiar objects and landmarks took on strange aspects, the shadows giving them deceptive contours. For what she intended to do, however, arriving on foot was her only choice.

The three of them headed in the direction of the stables, Antonella splitting off to go to Zephyra's shed. "I'll see you there," she said and waved to them.

As Malcolm expected, Hector had not been able to produce any definitive evidence that the very suggestive notes in the little book proved anything. It could be that Miss Ambleton was indeed the daughter of the marquess, albeit illegitimate, but the information he had would not confirm it. So he met his friend an hour before the appointed time at the stables as originally planned. They would ride down to the beach where he had stipulated that the duel take place. Gainesworth brought the swords in their case strapped to the back of his saddle.

They rode in silence. It was odd to be setting out to fight a man who was not the enemy. Atherleigh was so young when he joined his regiment that he'd had only one season in London, and never had occasion to become involved in any affairs of honor—either as a principal or a second. And in the Peninsula, the idea of battling anyone but the French was patently absurd. Nonetheless, he was well acquainted with the conventions of a duel. Every gentleman grew up with those principles etched on his heart.

The going was rough—ruts had frozen in place and a brief melt had created treacherous ice that looked black in places. It took them more than half an hour to reach the beach. Thankfully the sea was calm so they would not risk having the waves wash frigid water up to their ankles as they fought.

He and Gainesworth tethered their horses to a wooden spar that had washed ashore from a long-ago wreck. There was no point in Gainesworth and Sir William meeting the day before to mark out the exact ground, since the sand shifted enough from day to day to make a last-minute decision preferable. Both parties would agree on it when they were present.

Malcolm dragged the toe of his boot through the sand just below the seaweed that marked the high tide line. At that hour, the water had ebbed only a few feet. It would have been better for the tide to be lower, but low tide was not until close to midday, which would be too risky for dueling.

The hard-packed sand was still wet. Atherleigh wore his most comfortable old top boots, the ones that had seen him through long tramps through the Pyrenees. His own sweat in the brutal heat had molded them to his feet, giving him superior control of his footing. That was necessary to avoid slipping on a slick stone, or losing his footing in loose sand.

Curiously, Malcolm hardly thought of his missing hand, since it had always been his practice to fence with that hand behind his back unless he needed to stretch it out for balance. Carter had pinned his shirtsleeve to cover the stump, and he looked down at it dispassionately. If only every other aspect of his life was so little affected by his missing left hand.

A few moments later, the crunch of loose stones announced Bartleson's appearance. He and Sir William did not ride, however. Four beefy servants carried them down the rocky path from the bluffs in sedan chairs. Stupid fellow! Now there were four more pairs of eyes to witness what was still an illegal meeting, even if its unusual location made it border on the unenforceable. He supposed they'd taken a carriage and left it at the top of the cliff, and there was a coachman who knew of it as well.

Sir William approached them, swathed in a heavy cloak over his fur-collared greatcoat. He bowed to Gainesworth. "I don't suppose I can persuade Lord Atherleigh to offer an apology to the earl," he said sotto voce, with a nervous glance at the stern, imposing figure of Atherleigh in his shirtsleeves. Standing in the gradually lightening winter dawn, Malcolm glowered darkly, etching a deep cleft between his eyebrows and drawing the corners of his mouth down in a fierce scowl. It was the look that many unfortunate French soldiers had seen.

Bartleson took his time climbing out of the chair. Sir William helped him remove his cloak and coat and led him to the dueling ground. A grim smile momentarily lit Atherleigh's face when he registered the barely disguised anxiety in the earl's jerky movements.

"My boots will be ruined!" Bartleson said, his lip curling in distaste. "I don't see why we had to do this in such a strange location."

"You'll be glad enough if any of your servants has a mind to lay information against you," Gainesworth said.

"They wouldn't dare!" Gainesworth flashed a quick look at the exhausted footmen, who perched on what boulders they could find to rest.

Pompous fop! Atherleigh thought, standing utterly still, emptying his mind of everything except the task at hand. They had agreed on a duel to first blood. He expected it all to be over in a matter of minutes. Minutes that—as he knew from experience—would feel like an eternity and the blink of an eye.

"Gentlemen, the hour is upon us. Please take your weapons and prepare," Gainesworth said, holding the sword case open.

"I prefer to use my own smallsword," Bartleson said, and nodded to Sir William, who retrieved it from the chair.

Gainesworth measured the blade against Atherleigh's and said, "Agreed."

Standing opposite the unprepossessing figure of Bartleson, Atherleigh found it a little difficult to summon up the fierce ire that had provoked him to flatten the earl the night before last. The fellow's face was pale and covered in sweat despite the icy wind that whipped off the sea and carried the scent of rotting fish with it. Hardly a worthy opponent, he thought, but Malcolm would not apologize. What the man had said to and about Antonella was unpardonable. Unpardonable and untrue, whether or not she was the daughter of a marquess. Yes, a few minutes would do it. He would aim for a hit on the upper arm. The sword arm, of course.

The two of them stood en garde. Hector, a few feet away from them further up the beach, called out, "*Allez!*" and the dance began.

Malcolm took his time, parrying Bartleson's initial thrusts, getting the measure of the man's skill and technique. His boot heel sank into the sand in places, but he soon became accustomed to the terrain and narrowed his focus to the blade and his hand, watching the tip of Bartleson's weapon tremble just slightly as he made his moves.

The earl was a better fencer than Malcolm expected him to be, but he was not in shape and would tire quickly. His nerves also made his decisions erratic. At that moment he lunged. Malcolm parried easily and avoided Bartleson's dégagement, following it up with a riposte that Bartleson parried.

Atherleigh was getting his rhythm, anticipating Bartleson's not unskilled but rather unimaginative moves. Time to bring this to a conclusion, Atherleigh thought, and quickened the pace of his swordplay.

He had Bartleson on the defensive. The earl was backing away, nearly to the edge of the dueling ground Gainesworth and Sir William had marked out.

But a peculiar thing happened at that moment. Bartleson raised his sword and put his left hand out palm up, stopping the engagement, and stared over Atherleigh's shoulder. His sudden reversal nearly caused Atherleigh to lose his balance as he held back a thrust that, because of his movement, would have struck Bartleson nearer his heart than the shoulder he was aiming for. "What is it Bartleson?" Atherleigh demanded.

Bartleson simply used his short sword to point.

Atherleigh turned.

Walking toward him from the opposite end of the beach was Antonella Ambleton. On her gloved fist she carried a hooded goshawk.

The duel was over. It could not continue in the presence of a lady. What the devil was she doing here!

Malcolm's heart pounded from the exercise, from the unexpected interruption, and from the sight of Miss Ambleton making her purposeful way forward, unhurried, her gaze never leaving his. At that moment, the winter sun rose above the bluffs surrounding the beach and bathed it in rosy light. It caught Antonella's extraordinary eyes and lit them as if the glow came from within her. The hawk on her glove must have felt the sudden warmth. She bated, but Antonella murmured to her and calmed her quickly.

By God, Malcolm thought, she can handle that goshawk. His goshawk, if he wasn't much mistaken. The bird wore jesses—he could hear the bells from where he stood—and an ornate deerskin hood. No one else for hundreds of miles had a trained hunting goshawk, or even kept a mews.

Antonella stopped a few yards away. Good, Malcom

thought. She didn't want to alarm the bird, who would sense the presence of others.

"Egad! What's that creature doing here?" Bartleson's voice split the air.

"Be quiet man!" Atherleigh roared. The goshawk bated again, and again Antonella soothed her.

THIS WAS THE MOMENT, ANTONELLA THOUGHT. SHE DARED NOT approach any closer. Even from that distance, Atherleigh's physical presence disturbed her. His sweat-drenched shirt-sleeves clung to his well-muscled arms and torso. His dark hair was tossed every which way by the unruly sea breeze, giving him an appearance of youth that made her heart ache with longing. But he would have nothing to do with her after that day, she was certain. She had done the unthinkable in a gentleman's eyes. She had caused the abandonment of an affair of honor.

"My Lords," she said, keeping her voice as steady as she could manage. "In a very short time, my sister and my aunt will join us here on the beach. They bring with them a letter that would render your disagreement null, and excuse you from continuing this duel."

She paused, the rapid beating of her heart making it difficult for her to draw breath. *Keep going,* she told herself, and lifted her chin a little higher. "I am asking your indulgence to call off this disagreement, to trust me that it is founded on nothing. I would not have the secret uncovered by my aunt and my sister shared with anyone who is not directly involved. Lady Lewiston, who has acted dutifully in the role of my mother ever since I was brought to her as an infant a few days old, does not deserve to have her life upended by scandal. I will not be the instrument of that outcome."

Bartleson stepped forward. Atherleigh put his sword arm

out as a barrier to his advancing any further toward Antonella.

"I say, who are you to dictate my actions?" the earl said. "I demand to know the scandal in the letter you speak of. Where is it?"

"First, I owe Lord Atherleigh an explanation." She turned to Zephyra, who now sat calm but alert on her gloved fist. With a quick, smooth movement, just as Rafiq had taught her, she grasped the ring on the crest of the hawk's hood and lifted it away, revealing the fierce orange eyes. Zephyra opened her beak and gave a loud cry, spreading her wings briefly. *I want to hunt!* she seemed to say.

"This is indeed your goshawk, My Lord. Chakor as Rafiq calls her, but I named her Zephyra. I came upon her trapped in a poacher's net at the beginning of December, one of her wing tips broken. I took her to my own modest bird sanctuary and did my best to heal her. She is fully recovered and can fly again, despite her still-bent wingtip. She is yours, and I return her to you, even though I know of your plan to send all your birds away and close your mews. I cannot keep her, sorely as I am tempted."

Dawning comprehension in Atherleigh's eyes transformed his expression from puzzlement to something much warmer. The corners of his mouth relaxed almost into a smile. It's over, Antonella thought. I have told him.

Flooded with relief, she did not turn at the sound of galloping hoofbeats behind her. They're here, she thought, and I have managed to say what had to be said. The pace of the horses slowed, their labored breathing and snorting the only sound on the beach for several moments. Bartleson's footmen, who until then had sat wide-eyed and silent on the rocks, raced forward as the two ladies dismounted. The footmen took the reins and led the horses away to munch on some frozen sea grass well above the tide mark.

Belinda reached Antonella first but stood on the side that was away from Zephyra. "Have you told them?" she said in a low voice.

"No. And neither will you."

Belinda opened her mouth in shock, looked at Miss Wilkins, but said nothing.

Bartleson pushed past Atherleigh's arm and walked toward Belinda. "Lady Belinda is my betrothed. I demand she reveal her secret to me!"

Gainesworth, until that point staring in wonder at the vision Antonella presented and rendered speechless by the appearance of his beloved Belinda, raced forward and took hold of Bartleson's arm.

"Unhand me, man! Unless you want to answer a challenge of your own," the earl said, making an unsuccessful attempt to shake him off.

"I mean no harm. I just think the ladies should be permitted to have their say." Gainesworth kept his voice gentle, but did not release Bartleson.

All through this drama, Antonella kept her eyes fixed on Atherleigh. The play of emotions on his face puzzled her. One moment he gave her a stern glare, the next, his expression melted to something approaching tenderness. And then, there was the amusement—delight even—when she explained about Zephyra.

Her thoughts were interrupted by the approach from behind her of two more horses on the beach. This was so unexpected that Antonella at last turned to face the other direction. Lady Lewiston! With Ben, the groom, following behind. She had not ridden astride, but wore an elegant brown riding habit trimmed with sable. She pulled up her horse and Ben jumped down to lift her from her mount so she could walk forward and join the others, the long skirt of her riding habit draped over her arm.

"What have you to say for yourself, Lord Bartleson?" she asked, not bothering to greet anyone.

"Lady Belinda, my betrothed, is keeping a secret that I demand to know."

She sniffed. "Lady Belinda is not your betrothed. And as far as I'm concerned, she may keep whatever secrets from you she chooses. However, I believe I know what she is hiding. I have come to tell her—and Antonella and Miss Wilkins, who is also closely involved in this, that I have decided I want them to reveal what happened eighteen years ago, contrary to what I told them last night."

"No Mama!" Antonella said, not noticing what she had called the dowager.

"I had some hours to think, and I believe it is right that the truth comes out."

"There is no need, not now." Antonella turned back around to face Atherleigh, desperate hope in her heart. "Is there, my Lord?"

He slowly shook his head. "I will not be party to revealing anything that could cause the lady I hope will soon be my mother-in-law—or indeed, any lady—to suffer scandal or regret."

What had he said? Antonella's stomach lurched and tears stung behind her eyes. Surely he couldn't be serious.

Before she had time to fully comprehend what was happening, Atherleigh dropped his sword to the ground, ran to her and engulfed her in a strong embrace. In her surprise, Antonella let go of Zephyra's jesses and the hawk flapped away, skimming the heads of the group clustered on the early morning beach, and soaring over the bluff toward Atherleigh.

CHAPTER 32

𝓘t took some time to get the assortment of people off the beach. The wind picked up and blew Lady Lewiston's plumed riding hat onto the rocks. Bartleson and Sir William had to wait impatiently for the footmen to finish chasing it until the four beleaguered men finally came and hoisted their burdens for the difficult climb back up. Sir William and Bartleson could have told them to go the long way and they would have had a gentler slope to climb, but the earl insisted they return as quickly as possible so that he could leave Sir William's estate and return to London, *where such foolishness was not allowed to prosper.*

Despite Antonella's and Atherleigh's protestations, the dowager had told all assembled the true story of Antonella's birth. Neither Atherleigh nor Gainesworth was completely surprised, knowing of the suggestive entries in the marquess's old pocket book. But Sir William and Bartleson exchanged shocked glances. No doubt the story would be all over the *ton* before the spring season, Belinda thought. Oh well, it couldn't be helped.

Lord Atherleigh remained at Antonella's side, his left arm

wrapped around her waist, her right hand resting on the stump hidden under his pinned shirtsleeve. Gainesworth had quickly taken both Belinda's hands when Bartleson, stung by the dowager's assertion that he would not be marrying her daughter, retreated to the background. Yet Lady Lewiston had not given her consent to either of the matches that sorted themselves out on the sand that day.

She did, however, look upon both of the couples with eyes that smiled, even if her lips did not. Perhaps more importantly, she looked as if a great burden had been lifted off her shoulders, Belinda thought, and could have sworn her mother grew an inch taller.

"I believe there has been enough excitement for one day, although that day has barely begun. Lord Atherleigh, Mr. Gainesworth," Lady Lewiston said. "I shall take my daughters and their governess home to rest."

She said *daughters!* Belinda's breast swelled with happiness. All was not yet settled, but she had hope. Surely her mother's benevolence would extend to her betrothal to Hector—and Antonella's to Atherleigh.

Before allowing Ben to throw her up into the saddle again, Lady Lewiston turned back to the gentlemen. "Tomorrow is Christmas Eve. I would be honored if you would join us for dinner at Amblemere Court. We keep early country hours and dine at five."

Without another word, she settled herself atop her docile mount and trotted off toward the gently sloping path that led back to Amblemere without having to cross the treacherous coombe. Miss Wilkins followed her immediately, but Belinda and Antonella stayed where they were.

"I shall have to go in a moment," Belinda murmured to Hector.

"Then I must bid you adieu—until tomorrow." He bent his head to hers and kissed her tenderly on the lips. She returned the pressure, marveling at how soft his felt. He parted his lips slightly and she did the same, allowing him to take first her lower lip and then her upper lip between his, teasing them with his tongue. She gasped and pushed herself away. "Did I frighten you?" Gainesworth said, frowning.

Belinda shook her head. "It's just all so ... new. I must go." Reluctantly she extricated herself from his embrace. He accompanied her to where Paloma stood waiting and cupped his hands to form a step. She put her left foot in them, jumped up into the saddle, and spread her cloak to hide the calves she exposed by riding astride. "Until tomorrow."

She turned and clucked Paloma to a trot and then a canter to catch up with her mother and Miss Wilkins.

"You did not ride," Atherleigh said, his arms still encircling Antonella's waist.

"No, My Lord. You know how frightened I am of horses."

"We shall have to change that," he said, planting a kiss on the top of her head, "starting with you not calling me My Lord any longer. I asked you what seems a long time ago to call me Malcolm, remember?"

She looked up at him, alarm in her eyes. "Is that necessary?"

"What, using my Christian name?"

She shook her head. "You know what I mean."

He took her chin between the thumb and first finger of his right hand and lifted it so she was gazing straight into his smoldering brown eyes. "As necessary as me learning to work with the hunting birds one-handed."

She smiled. "Then you aren't going to close the mews?"

"I sent the letter off this morning to tell Northumberland that I had changed my mind."

"Oh! But Zephyra!"

His brow creased in confusion.

"I mean Chakor. She has flown away! Will I ever see her again?" Foolish tears spilled over her lashes. She was exhausted and in a turmoil of feelings. After everything she'd been through with Zephyra, surely she couldn't simply have gone back to the wild? Perhaps she's angry at me, Antonella thought. I didn't care for her properly. I kept her away from Atherleigh too long.

Malcom turned toward the path up from the beach in the direction of the manor and pulled her hand through his arm. "Come with me," he said.

Antonella looked over her shoulder. "Mama will be worried."

"I don't think so. She will assume I will send you home in my carriage which is exactly what I shall do. But first, come with me."

He led her back via a route she didn't know, having never attempted to reach the shoreline directly from the manor. To her surprise, it led to the spinney. They passed through it to the back gate into the weathering yard of the mews.

"Rafiq!" Atherleigh called as soon as he closed the gate behind them.

A moment later, Rafiq came out of the mews building sideways on. He must have a bird on his glove, Antonella thought, wondering whether it would be the tiercel or perhaps the merlin.

But when he was fully through, Antonella gave a gasp of surprise. "Zephyra! I mean, Chakor," she amended, with a sheepish glance up at Atherleigh.

Rafiq had not hooded the goshawk—in fact, Antonella still had the hood in her pocket—and the bird fastened her keen, orange gaze first on Antonella, then on Atherleigh.

"You see, she was not lost," Malcom said. "I knew it when I saw what direction she flew from the beach. Although I've never hunted her, the beach was a favorite place of mine when I was younger, and my father's after I left for school and the army. She knew she was home."

Antonella turned in Malcolm's arms. "Just as I am home now," she said.

Rafiq quietly took Zephyra back inside the mews as Malcolm and Antonella found themselves melding their bodies together in the icy wind, surrounded by the ancient buildings, listening to the gentle chirrups of the raptors on their perches in the mews.

CHAPTER 33

On Sunday, December 25, 1814, Lady Lewiston, Miss Wilkins, Lady Belinda, and Antonella took their places in one of the front pews of St. Botolf's Parish Church to hear Reverend Pendarves' Christmas sermon.

The other was occupied by Lord Atherleigh—who had not graced the church with his presence yet that month—and Mr. Hector Gainesworth.

The service was nearly over when Reverend Pendarves looked up and smiled at those sitting in the front pews. "I publish the banns of marriage between Malcolm Tennant, Lord Atherleigh, of this parish and Miss Antonella Ambleton, also of this parish. If any of you know cause or just impediment why these two persons should not be joined together in holy matrimony, ye are to declare it. This is the first time of asking."

Silence reigned in the nave.

A moment later, he said, "I publish the banns of marriage between Hector Gainesworth of Cawley Parish in Somerset and Lady Belinda Ambleton, of this parish. If any of you know cause or just impediment why these two persons should not be joined together in holy matrimony, ye are to declare it. This is also the first time of asking."

Someone in the back of the church coughed, and a gentle chuckle made its way through the parishioners.

But of course, no one had anything to say against the matches. Including Lady Lewiston, who felt fortunate to have both the girls she had cared for over the past eighteen years settled in matches that promised at least a degree of happiness.

She had married her parents' choice, based on rank and fortune, and thought that would be the right course for her daughter, Lady Belinda. But how had her own marriage turned out? In many ways quite satisfactorily. She knew her husband was unfaithful to her and he gambled away nearly all their fortune, but his mistakes had resulted in Antonella, who she now recognized as a spirit with a true heart. And he had also given her Harry and Belinda.

She did not wish anything undone. She was not very old, after all. Only five and forty. She already had one grandson, and hoped for more. But perhaps she needn't hide herself away just yet. She had been a beauty. Disappointment etched lines in her face, but her hair was only just starting to gain some silver threads, and although she was stouter than she had been, her figure was still good.

No, she thought, life is by no means over. And Antonella and Belinda would be married before the end of January. Perhaps she would travel—to Paris, now that the war was over. She could do whatever she wanted.

Yes, life was altogether satisfactory.

The congregation stood and followed Reverend Pendarves out into the cold Christmas morning.

EPILOGUE

"*A*re you certain about this?" Antonella asked Malcolm as they made their way to the mews on a fine, early spring morning.

Lord Atherleigh squeezed Antonella's—Lady Atherleigh's—hand. "There's only one way to find out, isn't there?"

Antonella wished she felt as confident as Malcolm did, but everything had all happened so much faster than she thought it ever could and she'd hardly had time to become accustomed to the idea. The wheels were set in motion in London, during the time of Hector and Belinda's grand *ton* wedding at St. George's Hanover Square. One evening after dinner, Hector encouraged Malcolm to talk to the estate carpenter and a local farrier about making some accommodations so he could perform simple actions despite his missing left hand. He couldn't say exactly what those might be, but as Hector said, it was foolish not to try.

At first, Malcolm resisted the idea, but when it finally took hold, he went far beyond what Hector had envisioned. The two craftsmen entered into the project with enthusiasm, embracing the challenge with the zeal of true artisans. But did they really know what they were about? What if after all the preparation it was nothing but a crushing disappointment?

Antonella told herself to stop fretting. There wasn't time to do anything about it now anyway. Not with Belinda and Hector waiting for them in the same field near where Antonella had helped Malcolm remount his horse a few short months ago. Because of course, a disaster must have witnesses in order to be complete.

So much had changed since that fateful day. Could she have foreseen it? Not foreseen, but perhaps wished. Antonella could still conjure up the sound of Malcolm's frustrated curses and imagine his disheveled, muddied state. How magnificent he'd looked even then.

And now, she'd married him, moved into Atherleigh Manor, and stepped into the role of lady of the house. But all that seemed the smallest part of what had altered about her life. She was different, and yet still the same. No, not different exactly. Just that now, instead of having to hide her true self inside a mask of docility and suppress her feelings of shock and sorrow and confusion, a door had opened and she passed through it into a world where she could be herself in the fullest sense.

The irony was not lost on her. She, who was always aware that marriage meant loss of independence, loss of ownership, loss of self for a woman had married the one man who would not take anything away from her. She chuckled. She had no property to relinquish, and a dowry that would have been insultingly small to anyone who cared about such things. But Malcolm those matters meant nothing to Malcolm. That was because, she knew, he felt the same way as she did about their marriage. He could be fully himself with Antonella in a way he never thought possible.

And they were about to prove it.

Belinda and Hector had made the journey from London just for this day. They'd taken a break from their already hectic schedule of parties and balls. How quickly Belinda had adjusted to her role! Hector gave up his lodgings in Duke Street and they took up residence in Gainesworth House, a handsome mansion in Park Street that Hector used to rent out when he was single, preferring the freedom of lodgings to a mansion with a large staff and responsibilities. Belinda would have her season after all, even hosting her own ball, although as a newlywed rather than a come-out. She didn't mind, so she said, and Antonella believed her. Lady Belinda Gainesworth was born to be a society hostess, and from her letters Antonella knew her sister was precisely where she should be.

When Antonella wrote to tell them the outcome of the seeds Hector planted in Malcolm's mind a couple of months earlier, Hector had insisted they come to Atherleigh to support him, whether everything worked as it should or not.

And the day of reckoning was upon them.

The walk to the mews was not long. Antonella and Malcolm entered the weathering yard to see Rafiq standing in the middle of it, Zephyra perched hooded on his glove. Malcolm had insisted they keep Antonella's name for the goshawk. Because, he said, Zephyra belonged to her. She had earned that honor through the care she took in rescuing her from the poacher's net and nursing her back to health.

"She senses the hunt," Rafiq said, a rare smile lighting his face. "It is time, My Lord."

"Is the glove within?" Malcolm asked.

"As you requested, Sir."

"Shall I get it for you?" Antonella asked. "Will you need help with it?"

"No. I must do this on my own." He touched her cheek and smiled at her before entering the mews.

Antonella raised her eyes to Rafiq's. "Did you ever think this would happen?" she asked.

Rafiq nodded slowly. "God is great."

Yes, Antonella thought, knowing full well that Rafiq's God was not the same one she and Malcolm prayed to each Sunday in church, but that it didn't matter in the slightest.

After a minute or two, Malcolm came out of the mews. On his left arm he wore a modified glove that, instead of ending in the fingers of a hand, had a cleverly designed oval platform of leather-padded wood extending beyond his wrist, exactly the right size and shape for a hawk or a falcon to perch upon. On its side, a small brass ring provided a place for jesses or a leash to be attached—a necessity since he had no fingers to hold onto them. This left Malcom free to use his right hand for all the other operations necessary to hunt a hawk. Antonella had seen this object and helped Malcolm put it on when the craftsmen first brought it to the manor. He'd been practicing the operation by himself since then, and she was relieved to see that he'd managed to tighten the leather straps around his forearm and get the perch platform at just the right angle without any help. It was a start.

But they weren't merely going to give this a try in the safety of the weathering yard. "Shall we?" Malcolm said, putting his right arm out to Antonella and nodding to Rafiq.

The three of them and Zephyra walked to the stables, where Garforth had Mercury saddled and waiting, as well as Princess—the docile mare Malcolm had purchased for Antonella to help her overcome her fear of horses—and the cob for Rafiq to ride.

"I'm afraid I can't throw you up into the saddle wearing this thing," Malcolm said.

"Garforth will do just fine." Antonella smiled, put her foot into the groom's cupped hands, and settled herself in the saddle, spreading the long skirt of her habit over her legs. The horses would proceed at a walk, Malcolm had promised. Although in recent weeks she had been trotting and cantering in the ring near the stables, Antonella was still a little afraid of going at more than a walk across country.

She patted Princess's neck and watched her remarkable husband jump up and swing himself into the saddle unaided, using only his right hand, holding out the prosthetic falconry glove all the while. Once mounted he extended the glove toward Rafiq, who approached with Zephyra. The goshawk easily hopped from the falconer's glove to the baron's.

Malcolm led the way. Antonella gazed at his upright back, his noble bearing, and the magnificent bird she had cared for and nurtured hoping one day to bring her back to her rightful home. She had no idea that this home would also be hers, and she found her eyes misting over at the thought.

Before long they caught sight of Bee and Hector on their own mounts waiting for them in the middle of the open field edged with woods. Bee raised a hand and waved to her. Antonella nodded, signaling that they shouldn't make too much commotion. She, Malcolm, and Rafiq continued to the center of the field. She pulled Princess up a few yards away from Malcolm. He turned in the saddle to look at her.

His eyes were bright with tears. Antonella smiled and blinked back her own as he slowly, smoothly, took hold of the crest of Zephyra's hood with his right hand and lifted it off in one graceful movement. Zephyra was suddenly all focus, all intent. Her orange eyes sharpened and brightened. A quiver of anticipation ruffled her feathers. Malcolm raised his prosthetic glove up toward the sky and said, "Hut! Hut!" Zephyra spread her wings, with one powerful beat launching herself from the glove before heading at speed into the nearby trees, the tinkling of the bells on her jesses fading as she flew away.

Belinda gasped in wonder. Hector said, "Well done old man!" and Antonella held her breath, her eyes following the hawk until she was out of sight. *Would she come back?* Please, please let her come back.

No one said anything after that. They were so quiet Antonella could hear the distant ocean surf.

Just when it seemed impossible that Zephyra would return, she broke from the woods, her wings pounding the air as if in sheer joy of the movement. Rafiq whistled and clucked, and a moment later, Zephyra alit on Malcolm's glove, where Rafiq had placed a scrap of raw meat a moment before.

He did it. He could do it. He would be able to do it as long as he had the use of his body. All was right with the world. Now Antonella knew that Malcolm would be able to do anything else he set his mind on. One look at the glow in his eyes told her that he knew it too.

Hector and Belinda rode up to meet them and congratulate Malcolm, all curiosity about the special glove.

Antonella interrupted them and said, "We can talk about this indoors. Mrs. Cobbey has prepared a lovely nuncheon for us."

But before she could turn Princess in the direction of the manor, Belinda urged her horse forward to Antonella's side, shaking her head in wonder. "I would not have believed it if I hadn't seen it myself," she said.

"Isn't it thrilling! Zephyra in her element, doing what she was bred and trained to do. Can you understand why I have always loved these creatures?"

Belinda clucked. "Don't be a nodcock! I didn't mean the hawk. I meant you. Look at you—on a horse and not looking like a scared rabbit. How did Atherleigh persuade you to take that chance?"

Antonella looked up to see Hector and Malcolm riding

ahead, laughing and talking. She nodded in their direction. "I couldn't let him take the risk alone. He might have done it, but I would never have thought it fair. I'm still not very confident, but I suspect with practice I will become more so."

"I can't believe I ever thought the two of you unsuited," Belinda said.

"Or that you imagined Hector would ever want to court me!"

They laughed.

"Bee," Antonella said, suddenly serious, "the most important thing that has happened has nothing to do with either of them."

"Oh?" Belinda cocked her head on the side.

"The most important thing is that I found out you are my sister."

"I never stopped being your sister, even when we thought you were an orphan."

"Yes," Antonella said, "But there's comfort in knowing for certain that we are connected, that this kinship I have always felt was not in my imagination."

Belinda simply smiled at her for a moment, then said, "Shall we go and join the gentlemen? I'll race you!"

Antonella laughed. "Only if we don't go any faster than a trot."

The two sisters satisfied themselves with walking through the field, talking of small matters, making little plans, and hoping for the best in the future.

ALSO BY SUSANNE DUNLAP

I hope you enjoyed *The Falconer's Lost Baron.* This is the fourth book in my series of *Double-Dilemma Romances.* While all four books can be read as stand-alones, you'll meet characters in them that have been introduced before.

Other books in the series include:

Book 1: *The Dressmaker's Secret Earl*

When a baronet's runaway daughter stitches together a new life as a London modiste, she never expects to capture the heart of a wounded earl. But secrets from her past—and his own hidden scars —threaten to unravel their fragile happiness.

Book 2: *The Soprano's Daring Duke*

The Soprano's DARING DUKE

A DOUBLE-DILEMMA ROMANCE

SUSANNE DUNLAP

A gifted soprano and a princess with a dangerous secret step onto the glittering stage of Regency society. Caught between music, scandal, and unexpected passion, two women find that love—like opera—demands everything.

Book 3: *Miss Pauline's Perfect Present*

An unsigned letter, an impossible order, and a looming deadline force Pauline Dawkins to rely on the one man she thought she could never trust. Together, they discover the magic of Christmas love in this holiday novella.

Join my newsletter and receive a free prequel novella!

Get *Miss Winthrop's Vanishing Viscount* free when you sign up for my newsletter. Simply scan the QR code below!

A WORD ABOUT WHAT I WRITE

My stories are full of courtship, longing looks, and that delicious will-they/won't-they tension that makes Regency romance so much fun.

You'll always get:

- Swoon-worthy heroes and strong heroines
- Emotional intensity and sparkling chemistry
- A guaranteed happily-ever-after (because romance deserves it!)

What you won't find:

- On-the-page sex scenes
- Graphic content

Instead, intimacy happens "behind the fan"—suggested, tender, but not shown. Think of it as closed-door romance: all the passion, emotion, and heart-melting moments, without the explicit detail.

So if you're looking for a love story that's heartfelt, witty, and just a touch daring—while still keeping the focus on characters and courtship—you're in the right place.

AUTHOR'S NOTE

This story of family and courage was born of my own fascination with falconry. I was fortunate to work with hawks in a small way on two occasions and have been completely enchanted by these birds ever since.

Falconry was not practiced extensively in the Regency, as fox hunting and shooting became more fashionable country pursuits. Training, caring for, and hunting with the noble birds required a lot of dedication and time. And unlike horses, the birds had no other use on a country estate. There were still some holdouts, however, and I imagined Atherleigh as one such.

Although not very high quality, here are a few photos of one of my hawking days. I had the immense pleasure of going on a squirrel hunt with a pair of Harris Hawks—the only hawks that hunt in pairs, cooperating to snare their prey. They are not native to the UK, so there is no mention of them in this book.

To see some videos of that day, go to this YouTube link. In the videos at the end, you'll be able to hear the bells on the hawks' jesses as they fly.